ORIGINAL SYN

ORIGINAL SYN

BETH KANDER

OWL HOUSE BOOKS

Published in 2018 by Owl House Books
Cover Designed by Daniel Dauphin
Interior Design by Leslie M. Browning
ISBN 978-1-947003-99-6
First Edition Trade Paperback

Owl House Books is *an Imprint of Homebound Publications*
WWW.HOMEBOUNDPUBLICATIONS.COM

10 9 8 7 6 5 4 3 2 1

Owl House Books, like all imprints of Homebound Publications, is committed to ecological stewardship. We greatly value the natural environment and invest in environmental conservation. Our books are printed on paper with chain of custody certification from the Forest Stewardship Council, Sustainable Forestry Initiative, and the Program for the Endorsement of Forest Certification.

DEDICATION

You.

You're looking for your true self, while also looking out for others. You're curious. You want something better. You've experienced failure. You're always asking big questions... and that's why you will be part of the biggest and best answers.

It's also why this story is for you.

PROLOGUE
PROPHESIES

"[Computers] will not just be doing arithmetic very quickly or composing piano music but also driving cars, writing books, making ethical decisions, appreciating fancy paintings, making witty observations at cocktail parties... maybe we'll merge with them to become super-intelligent cyborgs."
—LEV GROSSMAN, "2045: *The Year Man Becomes Immortal,*" *Time magazine, February 2011*

"Standing here, I almost see
The girl I was, the crone I'll be,
The Blessing of age, passing of time
Teaching us all, profane and sublime,
We will never relent, we will never rely
Thus we will live.
And thus we will die..."
—*Song of the Original Resistance, circa 2030, author unknown*

"The outsider inside will end the beginning."
—*Prophecy from Heaven, 2063*

K ARMA IS TIRED OF BEING TOLD TO WAIT.
She knows she should listen to the war-scarred people telling her to wait—wait for the next update, wait for
more intelligence, wait until the time is right, *wait wait wait.*

But when is the time ever right?

*Sometimes it is not about the right timing. It is about being
in the right—today, tomorrow, right the hell now.*

As soon as she thinks this, she knows it in her bones to be true.
And so a decision is made.

Patience be damned.

Karma is done waiting.

CHAPTER 1: ERE

THE ATTACK IS COMING ANY SECOND. Ere's eyes dart from side to side, his sinewy limbs tightening as he assesses his own borders.

Left, right, behind, below, above—as soon as he thinks *above*, he hears a quick puff of breath as his attacker drops down toward him. Ere scrambles away, ungracefully but successfully avoiding getting clobbered.

"Curse of the world," he swears, heart hammering in his slim chest.

"Close call, runt," Cal says, idly brushing bark from his shoulder. "Lucky I warned you."

The cousins look nothing alike. Ere is small, lean, and pale, with a shock of straight sandy hair. Cal is tall and broad, with tight black curls, huge dark brown eyes, and wide, thick brows arched mockingly at Ere.

"You didn't *warn me*—"

"Like hell I didn't," Cal says, flicking bramble at Ere, flexing the taut, rounding muscles in his arm. The boys wear similar clothing—faded denim pants, tattered old cotton shirts; but on Ere, the outfit emphasizes his thin limbs. On Cal it celebrates his enviable physique. "Made enough noise for a dead man to hear me coming. Shouldn't have let me get that close to crushing you."

"Well, you missed," Ere retorts.

Cal's dark eyebrow lifts. "Did I?"

In a single-handed flip, he pins Ere flat against the earth.

"Curse of the—"

Cal's massive hand covers Ere's face. Ere struggles, then goes limp; Cal does not loosen his grip. So Ere opens his mouth, snaking his tongue at his cousin's salty hand.

"Ugh!" Cal snorts, rolling off of Ere, rubbing his hand across his shirt in disgust. "Is that your strategy if a Syn comes after you? *Lick them?*"

Ere shrugs. For all they know, licking might be a fine defense. They hate and fear the Syns without knowing much about them; very little information is required to fuel deep hatred among people who have never even met.

It only recently occurred to Ere that knowing so little about his enemy is probably foolish. Identifying liabilities like that is important; his mother taught him that.

His mother is always alert to impending threats. Ruth Fell's sixth sense has kept the entire tribe alive more than once. Until recently, Ere didn't understand how his mother could just *have a feeling* about something, react accordingly, and pretty much always be right.

His great-uncle Howard was the same way before he got old and forgetful. The tribe used to joke that while everyone erred on the side of caution, the Fells erred on the side of apocalypse.

"Yes," Howard replied, back when he knew himself, back when he was still strong, back when he stood tall and unapologetic, with fierce and focused eyes. "It's because I have firsthand experience with the world coming to an end."

Ere is new to listening to his gut. But the older he gets, the more his gnawing sense of iminent danger is just undeniably *there*, taking root and growing as persistently and uncomfortably as the hair in his armpits. Ere would rather be big and strong than paranoid. His prayers for more muscles and broader shoulders to accompany all the paranoia and pit hair have all gone unanswered. All the family brawn remains reserved for his cousin.

Ere and Cal are the best of friends and fiercest of rivals. Cal, barely three years older, dominates in every category. All the family's strongest stock was spent on him, leaving Ere scrawny and sidelined. More than anything, Ere resents the resulting disparity in respect. Cal is seen as an adult, Ere as a child. Ere wishes that he could at least claim that he was smarter than Cal, but he can't; Cal is smarter, stronger, nicer to the elders, and just generally a better human being.

"Have you seen my mother?" Ere asks, hating the whine he hears in his voice.

"She's with Uncle Howard," Cal says, tousling Ere's hair like he's a little kid. "And hey, runt. Don't be sore. I'm just trying to toughen you up."

Irritated, Ere seizes control of the conversation, steering it to a sober place by asking coldly: "How is Uncle Howard?"

Cal's laughter ceases as his expression darkens. "The same."

"So it's bad."

Cal nods. For three days the Original leader has been barely conscious. Hot to the touch, eyes closed, moaning, calling for his long-dead wife, Sophie; the great man has been reduced to a shell of himself. He recognizes no one save his niece Ruth (Ere's mother), and even his recognition of her is intermittent. When the fever abates, he knows her; as his temperature rises, his cognition drops.

Weary but fiercely loyal Ruth has not left his side, holding cool rags to his forehead, talking to him in hushed, soothing tones, caring for the man who has cared for them all.

"Well. Let's get the water."

With that, the young men head for the nearby well, where they will draw the water, boil it over an open fire, and drink it despite knowing it's tainted.

All water systems are infected, thanks to the Syns. Even when boiled, the water will continue damaging the Originals, at best lowering their immune system, at worst slowly poisoning them. But the other option is "don't drink water." So they boil the water, drink it, and hope for the best.

The Syns must still feel threatened by the Originals, Ere realizes; threatened enough to continue tampering with the water. But why? He rolls this thought around as he and Cal walk from the commune to the nearby well.

The Franklin Commune was once a school. A long, low, brick building, with hallways and many rooms. Some rooms were uninhabitable, but the brick bones of the building were sound. Electricity hadn't snapped through the building in years, but its old stoves could be safely stuffed with wood and left burning for hours, good for cooking and for warmth.

Best of all was the small internal quadrangle, surrounded by those solid brick walls, providing a safe place for the tribe to step outside and enjoy the sunshine while still protected. A yard, the elders called it. They spent hours tending to plants there, digging their fingers into the soil and coaxing new life from it. They planted a garden, anticipating vegetables they could cultivate rather than relying on wild berries and plants to be sought and gathered.

They arrived at Franklin almost a year ago, last summer, just as Ere turned seventeen. The tribe had traveled three punishing weeks. Uncle Howard developed a noticeable limp, which he tried to hide. When the plain, promising walls of the lumbering old brick building came into view the entire tribe rejoiced; at least for a time, they had a place they could all call home.

In addition to its sound structure, Franklin was remote. Surrounded by fields on all sides, with no neighboring factories or Syn power plants, the Syns had either never noticed it or written it off as too old to bother acquiring. This added to the dignity of the sprawling old place; like its new inhabitants, it was an under-estimated survivor. There were no holes in the roof, most windows were unbroken, and a few proud rusted metal letters still clung to the exterior:

B N M N FRANKLIN EL   T RY   C O L

This old house of learning seemed as if it had been waiting for them. There was even a well-stocked freebox that greeted them in the main entrance when they first arrived.

Freeboxes are one of the ways Originals help each other. In the post-Singularity world, it became arduous to make new shirts, shoes, underwear, soaps, all the once-common daily items. But most of those things lasted a long time, and once-upon-a-time, factories produced more than people really needed. *Overstock*, they called it in the old world. Years ago, Originals looted overstock centers, taking enough clothes and goods for themselves and then more, to leave behind in hidden boxes for other freedom fighters to find. In later years, as Original populations diminished, any still-usable clothes, toiletries, and other supplies left by those who passed on were tucked carefully into freeboxes for those who might still need them.

"Cal! Ere!"

A rending wail stops the boys in their tracks. Myrlie James is running through the field. She is moving impossibly fast for a woman her age, barreling toward the young men. Ere hasn't seen Myrlie move at that speed since—well, ever. Glancing at Cal, Ere knows they share the same thought. The breathless old woman calls out the news before reaching them, forcing herself to get the words out while she can still form them, confirming their worst fear.

"He's dead," she rasps. "Howard Fell is dead."

CHAPTER 2: SHADOWER

THREE MORE BODIES.

That's what Shadower has to focus on: the cold hard fact of three cold hard corpses. Not the danger of this work. Not the implications of the evidence. Dissecting and disseminating what this information really means will be the next step, but right now, only the facts matter. Ensuring that accurate information is collected and conveyed. That's it; that's all.

It's easy to get distracted, to start guessing ahead—and sometimes it's vital to make those leaps, to try to stay one step ahead of the situation—but not until they know what the facts of the situation are. But leaping to conclusions can lead to falling off cliffs.

Stay focused: Three more bodies.

These bodies were nothing but conjecture moments ago, a rumor whispered fast and low, blowing quietly and quickly through the narrow cracks and crevices of the clandestine network. Repeated over and over, growing in incredulity even as it grew in certainty.

More bodies, we hear it's three bodies, we think it's three bodies, it's three bodies.

Even Shadower was startled by this surge. Months ago, when they confirmed the first incident, it was startling: the unthinkable discovery of a discarded body of an apparently self-terminating Syn came out of nowhere.

Syns are supposed to live forever. That was the whole damn deal. The entire Synthetic movement was founded on the premise that with enough augmentation, upgrades, and all their enhancements—death could be not simply outrun but outdone. Eternal life was what they signed up for, what they schemed and fought and murdered for; self-termination was an abomination.

When the first body was confirmed, the clandestine network figured it was a fluke. With the second, they realized the fluke might have been more like a harbinger. And then with the third, and the fourth—

Stop. Focus: Three more bodies.

Shadower returns to the facts, reviewing them without speculation: The cadavers were Syns, each of whom had flat-lined on the Heaven monitors *for unknown/unapproved reasons*, immediately triggering a black-ops recovery of each body. Heaven's army moved fast. Too fast even for Shadower. Within moments of flat-lining, all three bodies were confiscated and incinerated, all physical remains erased and the electronic trail swept clean. Thanks to their own shared systems, Syn leaders knew that burning the bodies was not enough. To truly bury the evidence, they had to erase the electronic trail, too.

You can't just discard the shell. You have to dig out the creature within, and make sure everything burns. And they managed to burn it all, real and virtual, with rapid speed. Almost fast enough to make it seem that nothing had ever happened. Almost.

But not quickly enough to prevent rumors, which were carried by increasingly quick spies who sent word to Shadower. So now, thank whatever God remained in this cold mechanical world, Shadower can confirm the rumors. Shadower can do so using the strange, singular ability to eavesdrop on the silent communications carried on electronic waves.

Pressed against a wall, coated in sweat but not dripping a drop, Shadower slides into position, port hovering near a public outlet. Not plugged in, not alerting the system to any presence, Shadower begins extracting data. Siphoning intelligence without actually connecting and revealing any specific identity: A ghost in the machine.

No one else can do this.

Even Shadower is not quite certain how this particular skill emerged; it's truly a blessing and a curse. Like it or not, Shadower takes everything in. Everything: from ports, from people, from the wires in the walls. It's as if the entire world speaks at a louder volume for Shadower. It's useful for eavesdropping. It's also crazy-making.

Shadower is a magnet and the information is metal, always flying in and clattering against the magnet. The clanging is crazy-making, but Shadower has grown accustomed to it; has learned to filter, tune in and tune out as needed. If Shadower listens hard enough, even the most carefully hidden files call out, *here I am, here I am.*

Any quiet hum of information erased, any virtual-footsteps wiped away in a clever but not infallible cover-up, none of it is ever gone; it is only shifted over to another channel, and Shadower can tune in to every single station.

Yes. There it is.

Shadower presses closer, leaning into the quiet hum singing behind all of the larger, louder surrounding sounds, carefully following the faint but unmistakable path of lilting information still humming behind where hard data once lived. Facts cannot be erased, only smudged like a pencil eraser on an old sheet of paper.

A flash—a scene—a something—a someone—more than one—three—yes!

Shaking from the effort, tension running through steeled nerves and gritted teeth, Shadower siphons and saves one single image before Heaven's clean-up crew sucks everything else up, up, and away. Thankfully, the image secured is as damning as it is chilling: three bodies, too out of focus for their faces to be identifiable, but clearly dead, discarded Syn corpses—and beside them, a half-dozen live Syn soldiers.

Shadower imagines the cleanup crew, running programs to eliminate the electronic evidence, pouring chemicals over the dead bodies in preparation for incineration. Heartless, evil bastards, erasing their own neighbors to protect the all-powerful Syn leadership.

Bastards, all of them.

The confirmation of multiple suicides, willfully covered up by the Syn Council, will send shockwaves throughout the clandestine network. Rumors would became facts. Facts would inform action. Planning would continue.

Shadower doesn't give a shit about Syn terminations—well, unless the self-eliminating Syns could be reached and radicalized before they just went and killed themselves like useless little idiots; that might be nice. Shadower would be happy to give a suicidal Syn the option of doing something more productive, like helping the network burn the Syn world to the ground. Going out with a real bang, instead of just being erased.

Sad-sack Syns aren't the real concern here, though. Shadower's goal is not to prevent Syn suicides.

The real objective is to change the world before all Originals are extinct.

The dead Syns are only interesting because their cold corpses might just pave the way for an Original revolution. For a return to the way things were—the way they were always meant to be.

We'll have our revolution, God willing, Shadower thinks.

Assuming God hasn't also given up and offed Himself.

CHAPTER 3: EVER

I T'S NOT HYPERBOLE TO SAY THAT EVER HESS is the most beautiful girl in the world; it's verified fact. Her beauty has been confirmed via multiple assessments examining symmetry, proportions, dermal surface integrity, and every other objective measure of beauty.

As she likes to put it, pretty much everyone wants to bang her. (Old world vernacular is amazing; *bang* is such a satisfying expression.)

Ever's beauty is certified, and continually cultivated. She doesn't rest on the generous laurels of genetics and mechanical enhancements. She is a devout believer in daily doses of Vitamin D, and worships at the altar of excellent moisturizer. Her flawless skin is neither pale nor tawny, but a perfect glowing shade of health. Her eyes are large, brown, rimmed above and below with heavy black lashes. She is delicately bird-boned and just curvy enough. No knobbed knees or sharp elbows; she is rounded where softness is pleasing, toned where strength is desirable.

It's all by design. Ever was preserved at the moment of physical perfection, just past any trace of awkward adolescence but nowhere near the realm of graying, stiffening, wrinkling. She was suspended in that fleeting moment that passed her peers swiftly and irretrievably, while they were too busy lamenting their flaws to notice their beauty before it was gone.

In the old world, people somehow thought beauty was subjective. There were all these weird theories, like "different people peak at different times." Bizarre claims about how *some people crave thick thighs, others lust for lean legs, some really do prefer darker skin or lighter eyes or smallness or fullness or ski-jump noses or freckles—there's no one way to be beautiful!*

Ever's pretty sure that whoever came up with all that crap must have been ugly.

Committed as she is to the preservation of her looks, Ever is equally dedicated to the innovation of her "look." She likes to shake things up; her hair color is her favorite variable. She's a redhead this week. Changing the hue weekly has been a ritual ever since she first turned seventeen, a few decades ago. She's tried literally thousands of colors over the years. It's hard to distinguish Shining Cinnamon #347 from Shimmering Paprika #2,012, but each marginally-different color represents something scarce and thereby sacred: *the ability to change.*

She knows that her constant craving for altering her appearance stems from a strong rebellious streak, goaded on by a lifetime of living in a world where change and progress were celebrated while she herself was firmly locked in and told not to change a thing.

She is almost as self-aware as she is self-obsessed.

(But not quite.)

Ever strolls the deck of her family's boat, back straight, head high. A decade of dance lessons perfected her posture, and the voice of her strict, sleek ballet teacher still echoes in her mind, chiding her to be mindful of her movement.

"Remember, ballerinas," the instructor would intone in her thick Russian accent, hard and violent with her consonants as she raised her pencil-thin eyebrows and sucked in her already-flat stomach. "A dancer is always carrying herself well. A dancer remains a dancer wherever she goes, even just on the sidewalk, even in the dark. Every movement, it is a dance."

Recalling this reprimand, as Ever leans over the side of the boat she flattens her back, tightens her midsection, summons the old technique. Even the clothing she wears evokes her ballerina days—black, slimming as a leotard, the sleek fabric smoothing itself over her trim figure. She hopes the Russian dance teacher would be pleased with her look. No way of knowing: the woman has been dead for years.

Sometimes Ever thinks it would be preferable to be dead and well-remembered, which seems much easier than remaining alive and alluring.

"Ever!"

She closes her eyes, as if her lids might somehow block out the sound. There's no need to respond, as her mother knows exactly where she is, and could just as easily have sent a message rather than screeching like a harpy. Calling out for one's child is a leftover function, archaic and useless, like looking at one's wrist when someone asked what time it was; gestures often outlive the objects or tasks that inspire them.

Ever fights her mother's noise with silence. It's a tactical move. Predictably, to continue the cold war they both insist on prolonging, Ever's mother comes out to the deck to meet her stubborn child on their latest battlefield.

Marilyn Hess is striking, though not as perfectly-crafted as her daughter. Her hair hovers between blonde and brunette, chemically maintained but never varied, always pulled back in a low chignon. She displays just a hint of middle-age, given away by the soft impressions around her eyes and mouth that form when she frowns, little lines in her face drawing the blueprints for where wrinkles would eventually have appeared. Her high cheekbones and long arms give her the illusion of being taller than she actually is, but she's tall enough to tower over the petite Ever.

"You know it's time for dinner, and you know how I hate waiting on you."

Ever aims luminous eyes at her mother, feigning innocence. "I'm not as late as Daddy."

Marilyn's thin lips press together so tightly they nearly disappear, but she manages to shove a few terse words through them.

"We're not talking about your father. And don't call him Daddy. You're not a child."

"Then stop treating me like one, *Marilyn*."

Her mother stiffens further, something Ever wouldn't have guessed possible; a sudden jerking movement like that might just snap the stick up her ass. Ever almost laughs, picturing splinters throughout her mother's spine and synthetic system. Something flickers in the older woman's eyes before she drops the bomb Ever knew was coming but still hoped might not fall.

"Your father won't be joining us on this vacation.."

"Of course he won't," Ever's voice is ice, each cold word seeming to steam in the sweaty tropical air. "That might give the impression he cares about us."

"Ever—"

"No, really," Ever says, voice thick with sarcasm. "Work should come ahead of family. Let's console ourselves knowing that the work he's doing is so ground-breaking. The whole world waits with bated breath. Thank Heaven he hasn't vacationed in God knows how long."

God knows how long is, in fact, hyperbole. For Ever, and all Syns, there's virtually nothing she can't remember just as well as any god. A quick scan of her memory and she could summon perfect recall for every moment of the last time he had joined them: The Greece trip, a decade ago. That vacation, perennially fresh in her mental archives, was the last trip she enjoyed.

Greece was a land of pillars and layers, all of its structures vibrating with the stories of the rise and fall of civilizations. It was a land of philosophy and culture, cursed now to stand as a sad memorial, testifying to the fallibility of all cultures. All that high-and-mighty-history-buff stuff her father loved was kind of boring, but Greece itself wasn't; she loved every preserved pile of rocks, every rebuilt-temple, and all those stunning statues of alabaster nudes.

Oh, those statues! Pale stone men and women, proudly naked, blank eyes gazing into the distance. Ever loved the statues, shameless remnants of a time where hidden things were rarely so easily revealed and assessed. (She especially loved finding the statues whose genitalia had snapped off. So sad—perfect alabaster cheekbones, gorgeous torso, and then shockingly blunt trauma: a tragic little stump memorializing the missing dong. Being a statue had its drawbacks—hilarious, hilarious drawbacks.)

In Greece, they had one day explored the Acropolis, the next day Olympia, and then Crete, the site of a great battle in the Original War. Ever loved venturing into these uninhabited lands, far beyond the borders of the Incorporated Sectors. These old abandoned countries retained their pre-war names. Greece, Spain, France, Italy, so many other delicious monikers. They had also retained their pre-war uniqueness. Even without any Original residents left, the lands themselves clung to history. It was not like that in the Incorporated Sectors.

The Incorporated Sectors (formerly known as the United States) was devastated in the uprisings. The Originals targeted metropolitan centers, and many once-great cities fell. Syn strongholds like New York were heavily protected and survived the onslaught. Once the Original threat had been subdued, and all surviving Originals exiled from city centers, the Incorporated Sectors emerged where all the great American infrastructure had its firmest footholds. In the aftermath of the global war, the Incorporated Sectors became the sole global power in the post-Singularity world.

Throughout the once-united-nation, rural areas went entirely fallow. Anything damaged went unrepaired in areas outside of the Incorporated Sectors; power sources and all resources were diverted to the Syn centers. The abandoned expanses became the unofficial Diaspora lands of those barbaric Originals. There weren't any Originals in Greece, though. Only monuments to a people whose day had passed.

Costa Rica is nothing like Greece. Similarly devoid of Original inhabitants, where Greece was a land of architecture and artistic renderings of what once-was, Coast Rica was a lush land of opportunistic life—birds, snakes, shrieking monkeys, exotic plants. Ever had looked forward to seeing the natural beaches, the rainforests, the wildlife. She had been naïve enough to think maybe she would get to explore and experience something real, and instead her father wasn't coming and Ever was thereby not even going to be allowed to step foot off the damn boat.

If her father was there, he would take her off the boat. But he wasn't here, and the mere idea of adventure made the already pale Marilyn Hess go as white as a Grecian alabaster nude. Ever's mother is a woman who prefers to stay on boats and stay on-schedule. She's been even more of a stickler about that lately, insisting on dinner at six fifteen, every single day.

"You're still required at dinner, whether or not your father is here," her mother intones. "Angela prepared local seafood. It's incredibly fresh—she caught it this morning. You could fish with her tomorrow, if you want."

Ever forces a flat smile. "Fantastic. I'd been looking forward to seeing the local wildlife thriving in its natural habitat, but I guess we'll settle for killing and eating it instead."

"Ever," her mother sighs. If Ever had to guess, her mother ran out of patience with her about three decades ago, maybe four. "Access Heaven's VR rainforest program if you want to learn more about—"

"I don't want to learn *about*," Ever snaps. "I want to learn *from*. I don't want to *access*. I want to *experience*. I want to get off the damn boat. But oh shit, look! It's six-fourteen! I'd hate to throw us off schedule." She pushes past her mother, calling for their maid: "Angela? Angela! I'm coming down there. Did you keep the fish heads? I'd like to see them before you throw them away. I'm excited to finally get to see the beautiful Costa Rican wildlife I keep hearing about!"

Without awaiting a reply, Ever stomps her way down to the lower level, passing Angela en route. She hears Angela say to Marilyn, with something like sympathy: "Fifty years parenting a teenager. Never gets easier?"

"Worse than purgatory," Ever hears her mother say.

And for once, Ever agrees with her.

E RE LOVES FUNERALS. He doesn't love death, of course. Death is an enemy that invades too often, too quickly—or worse yet, arrives early and lingers, killing members of his tribe brutally and slowly. But in Ere's mind, funerals are to death as spring is to winter: one follows the other, completely usurping it. Where death is cold, funerals are warm. Ere loves the collective energy of so many people, so close to one another, forced to make room for one another. Hands brushing hands as the mourners pressed together to remember the individual now gone.

But the best thing about funerals is the other tribes that show up for them. Because other tribes arriving might mean, *maybe just maybe,* meeting a girl his own age.

A girl who might have a beautiful smile and soft skin. A girl who might somehow miraculously notice him before she noticed Cal. *A girl who might be so weary and dusty from her journey, she might need to take off all her clothes and bathe in the stream before—*

A rasping cough interrupts Ere's fantasy, slicing into the slim slab of hope and filleting it into fine strands of familiar fear. The cough is his mother's, and the sound makes his own throat tighten.

Ere looks around to see where she is and how she's holding up It's still early; after an unrelenting night of rain, a reluctant sunrise was finally yawning its way up, unfurling into a dull but expansive sky, heavy and low, the dull color of a dead tooth.

He can't see his mother; there are too many people between them. The crowd clusters, speaking in hushed tones, waiting. Going up on his tip-toes, Ere scans the scene and finally spots her. Ruth's hand covers her mouth, briefly; she drops it before anyone can see her suppress the brutal coughs. Ere notices, though.

Sensing his gaze, Ruth snaps her face toward her son and mouths: *Stop worrying.*

Ere nods, not completely relieved, but somewhat reassured. His mother is steel. She is Ruth Fell, unbreakable. She'll be all right.

As he knocks a bit of dirt from his leather-clad foot, Ere's thoughts drift back to the topic that has preoccupied him for the last several years now.

God, please, let there be girls. Or at least just one. No, two—two, God, if you're listening! There have to be at least two girls, or Cal will make sure I'm overlooked...

Ere knows this isn't what he should be worried about. He should be mourning the terrible loss of his great-uncle. But Howard was an old man and Ere is a young one, hungry to experience what the older generation took for granted. And seeing a girl might provide consolation at this difficult time. Was a little solace so wrong to hope for?

"There you are, runt."

Cal elbows him, a friendly gesture that nearly knocks Ere off his feet. Rather than being irritated, Ere actually appreciates the familiar feeling in this strange setting. When Ere shoves him back, Cal doesn't even wobble.

"See any girls yet?" Ere asks.

"Wouldn't you like to know," Cal snorts.

"So, no," Ere says, disappointed and relieved.

Cal does not reply, eying the new arrivals to his tribe's home with his standard distrust. Ere admires his cousin's vigilance. Cal has what Ere's mother proudly calls "a soldier's mentality." Ere just... doesn't.

"You'd tell me if you saw some girls, right?" Ere yanks a few dark wiry hairs from Cal's arm, a better tactic than his ineffective shove. "If there were two, you'd tell me, right?"

"Ow!" Cal says, swatting at Ere as if at a fly. "Why would I tell you? I could find ways to entertain two girls, all by myself."

Ere rolls his eyes. "Let's go over by my mother. The show's just about to get started."

"God in Heaven. Don't call it a show."

"Fine. The service."

"And we're not going to stand with your mother. She's doing the story-song, remember?"

"Oh. Right."

And then the funeral is underway. There is no formal call to worship, the service simply begins. A few elders start softly chanting an old prayer, and the sound moves through the crowd, each voice joining in as they hear the familiar words. When the first hymn ends, someone begins reciting a liturgy that all know by heart. Even the spoken prayers have a musicality to them; voices rise and blend, singing sentiments so strong and sincere the sound seems to radiate heat.

"Gone!" A woman moans, grief rising from her and pouring forth, a gush, a geyser.

Rather than interrupting the service, this seems to break it open, make it blossom into what it was always supposed to be. All of the other mourning hearts crack wider in response, as several other voices lift with hers, sobbing and soaring, together.

"Howard Fell is gone! He's gone!"

Swept up in the emotion surrounding him, all other thoughts leave his head and Ere hears himself join in; the aching loss stops tearing at his edges, and instead cuts right through him.

"Howard Fell!" Ere wails along with the others. "Howard Fell!"

The keening cries rise up like a wave, crests, and gently rolls out like one. The sound slips back into the sea, receding, the crowd fading into a hushed silence. This is a collective confirmation that they are ready for the song of Howard's life, which will be sung by his niece.

Peering between gaps of shoulders and elbows of the assembled crowd, Ere catches glimpses of his mother making her way to the front of the crowd. Formidable as she is, from far away and with so many people in between them, she seems so small.

Ruth Fell stands alone before the congregation. Closing her eyes, she hums, softly at first, and without lyrics; words will come when the music conjures them. All story-songs are wholly original: Originals sing them for one another, crafting them from memories, setting a life to melody. As is the tradition, before moving into the specifics of Howard's unique story, Ruth begins with a shared song of the Original resistance, paying homage to the entire community, their collective experience; then the same melody transitions seamlessly into the individual lyrics for the lost loved one:

Standing here, I almost see
The girl I was, the crone I'll be
Blessing of age, passing of time,
Teaching us all, profane and sublime

We will never relent, we will never rely
Thus we will live. And thus we will die.

Thus Howard Fell lived.
Thus Howard Fell died.
Howard Fell was born in 1962, in a city
Known then as Ann Arbor.
His father was Ernest Fell
His mother, Lila Golden Fell.
He had a brother—

Ere's ears burn at the mention of Howard's brother—his mother's father. His grandfather.

He leans in, craving some scrap, a line of the story-song to shed light on his enigmatic patriarch. Maybe his mother will share something in the song; a name, something? He was Howard's brother, after all. Surely, his mother will do more than acknowledge his existence; she'll have to say something about Howard's brother. But she doesn't; she sings of Howard, as the day and the crowd demand:

They had a house the family lived in alone,
and a house of worship they shared
and houses of learning that brought together
many different communities of people.

Howard Fell was a student of many teachers,
and a teacher of many students.
He was serious and silly, brilliant and bold
And everyone dreaded the jokes that he told.

At this, a few elders laughed affectionately, wistfully. Howard really had been terrible at telling jokes. And so very fond of telling them anyway.

He loved tame dogs, and the cinema,
The symphony, and meals from other lands

He married his wife Sophie.
And they had six children
Before things took that dreadful turn
Before their world began to burn...

Ere hears it—a catch in his mother's voice that no one else notices. He closes his eyes and aims his support and strength in her
direction. He hears her go on, voice solid, tone pure.

Howard survived Sophie
and all of their six children.
He survived the rebellions.
He survived, he survived,
and he helped others survive.
He stayed and he prayed.
He fought and he taught.
He knew and he grew.

And here the eulogy becomes its own song, departing from the
opening melody and abandoning any describable melodic pattern
or key, soaring past structure, rising and falling and so musical as
to lift the assembled into a higher sort of awareness, coming from
someplace or Someone more ancient and omniscient than Ere's
powerful mother—

He fought and he taught.
He knew and he grew.
He stayed! He prayed!
He knew the Original strength.
He chose the Original way.
He kept us intact and he kept us in touch.

His blood stayed warm when the world went cold.
He kept moving forward, unafraid to grow old.

He lived to a hundred! A hundred years! A gift!
His life is a prayer, and he a soothsayer,
and together we say—

And together they said: *Amen.*

Story-songs, rhythmic remembrances shaped by fresh mourn-ing, leave Ere breathless. They assault everyone with emotion, laying bare all the raw grief and love and fierce grit of their people. This story-song also triggers something else for Ere: a wild jealou-sy. He longs to know more about the fantastical details included in the lyrics, the world of tame dogs, cinemas and symphonies and exotic meals from other countries.

Before his mind began unraveling, Uncle Howard had de-scribed all of these things to him, in great detail. The aroma of curry, the bright colors of cultivated flower gardens, the feeling of silk. He found a way to convey what these things had been like. His memories were so strong, they were practically transmittable. He gave as much from his memory as he could, for as long as he could, to his sons, daughters, nieces, nephews, all of them.

Preserving joy, Howard told Ere and Cal, time and again, as he tantalized them with tales of a world now lost to them, *is as important as preserving or destroying anything else.*

The story-song concluded, Ere's mother comes to stand with Cal and Ere. Cal steps aside, and Ruth stands between them. She stands erect, taller than Ere but shorter than Cal. Her eyes are rimmed red, but remain dry as sun-stretched linen. She won't cry in front of anyone. But she trembles slightly, jaw tightening, and Ere knows she's suppressing another coughing spell.

The memorial concludes with words from an ancient psalm. Shared at one time by many communities of people, it remains the Original's prayer for the dead, always intoned in unison:

The Lord is my Shepherd, I shall not want.
He causes me to lie down in green pastures.
He leads me beside still waters.
He restores my Soul...

Ere knows the words so well, he says them without thinking, his mind traveling instead back into his earlier fantasies as he scans his surroundings, searching for girls. He is taking in the small signs of mourning—the bowed heads, the stooped shoulders, the watery faraway eyes—when the thought occurs to him: someday, he would have a funeral.

...through the valley of the Shadow of Death,
I shall fear no evil, for You are with me,
Your rod and your staff...

How has this thought never occurred to him before? In his own short life, Ere has already attended dozens of funerals. But somehow, before this one, funerals always seemed reserved for others. Something from a world that ended before his own life began. Going to a foreign country, or hearing the symphony, or falling in love—these things do not exist for Ere the way they existed for his ancestors. There is no more path leading to the sort of life his great-uncle led.

...and I shall dwell in the house of the Lord...

It strikes Ere that unlike curry or cinemas, death was not something he would miss out on. His death is inevitable. Plain as anything, he suddenly sees that although he won't get to walk the same paths as his ancestors, he'll still reach the same damn destination. He'll die. He'll die, and his funeral will have the world's most boring story-song—no; not even that. He won't have a funeral.

No one will be left to mourn for him, because in all likelihood, he is the youngest not only in his tribe, but also in the entire Original world. Unless Cal outlives him, Ere will be the last of his kind. Ere can see it stretching ominously ahead of him, the whole horrible future, like a story he's already been told.

...forever.

Beside him, unable to hold it back any longer, his mother begins coughing again.

T *IK, TIK. TIK TIK TIK.*
　　Ever taps the solid steel port of her left pointer finger impatiently on the bedside table. The table is dark wood, secured in place by several screws connecting it to the matching bed. Everything in this stupid boat-bedroom is dark wood, lightweight, and screwed into place. It's not at all nautical; the bolted-down-furniture and minimalist-décor makes the room seem more like a fancy jail cell. Ever increases the pace of her agitated tapping, maintaining the rhythm, hoping it will lull her into some sort of meditative state. Or at least irritate her mother.

Tik, tik. Tik tik tik. Tiktiktiktiktik.

Despite decades of its presence, the chunk of metal which replaced her original fingertip still feels foreign. It inhabits her flesh like an invader occupies a territory, claiming it as its own without belonging there. The temperature never matches the rest of her body—it's always much colder, regulated by the synthetic component cooling system. The only time her finger warms is during her nightly upload; the port connection creating a snug, hot little bed for the unnatural part of her hand. She shuts down during the overnight data transfer, as all Syns do, only noticing the lingering heat when she wakes up each morning. The warmth is fleeting, the cooling system swiftly returning her finger to cold, hard steel.

She's lucky to have a finger port—a third generation development. Technically, Ever is a late second-generation Syn, but her father ensured that the freshly-approved prototypes for the third and final Syn generation were secured for her: enhanced skin cell regeneration, faster mode shifting, and the coveted finger port.

Her parents both have first generation spinal ports, located at the base of their neck. That's why her mother's honeyed hair is always kept in that tight chignon knotted at her nape, revealing the sleek sides of her neck while hiding her port (she feels "too exposed" if someone catches a glimpse of her tech). Her father's port is always hidden, too, by his bulky lab jackets and stiff collars, but that's incidental. He's proud of his port. Her parents had no social reasons to be embarrassed by their spinal hardware. If anything, being first generation confirmed high social standing. However, it was considered uncouth to display old ports in mixed company.

Tik, tik. Tik tik tik.Tiktiktiktiktik...

Ever's mother hates it when Ever taps her port, but so far there's been no reaction today. So Ever drums a little harder, wanting the sound to be inescapable, wanting to punish her mother for this horrible wasted trip. Three days cruising around Costa Rica, staying on the boat and seeing only the sights viewable from the water, and now they were heading home. She taps so hard the metal finger begins leaving a dent in the wood, and then it occurs to her that her mother is probably napping, plugged in and shut down, unable to be assailed by her daughter's malicious finger-thumping.

Napping is Marilyn Hess' favorite activity; that's how boring she is. Ever pictures her slack-faced mother, dozing dreamlessly as she uploads her day's drab experiences and downloads the collective day's updates from Heaven.

Heaven replaced dreaming so long ago that for Syns, dreaming is only a murky original memory, a definition in the dictionary: *a succession of images, thoughts, or emotions passing through the mind during sleep; the sleeping state in which this occurs; an object seen in a dream; an involuntary vision occurring to a person when awake; a vision voluntarily indulged in while awake; daydream; reverie.*

The last few definitions, of course, are second nature for Ever. Voluntarily visioning herself elsewhere is basically how she gets through the day. But real dreaming, closing your eyes and drifting away to some unplanned, unpredictable, un-shared journey... *oh, Heaven and Hell, wouldn't that be incredible!*

She wishes she could dream again. She remembers dreaming, as a child—but only barely. She's haunted by one specific dream. Though foggy and remote, she clings to its organic delights, holds fast to its terror. In some ways it feels more real to her than almost anything else she's felt or experienced in the past several decades.

This is the original nightmare her five-year-old mind created:

> *Dark, swampy muck. Something primordial.*
> *Wet and threatening.*
> *A motion—a floating, silent log moving through the water—*
> *A dinosaur! No! Not a dinosaur! A dragon.*
> *No no no, wrong word, wrong word, what is it, big scary scaly—*
> *ALLIGATOR! An alligator!*
> *Alligators all around, coming at her*
> *Slowly but steadily, with glowing eyes*
> *Can't move can't move can't move,*
> *Cold water, so cold cold cold,*
> *Alligators approaching*

Unable to move away
From the evil eyes and dinosaur-skin
The hunger-snapping jaws,
coming coming coming for her…

The nightmare once terrified her, but now it comforts her. Recalling a time when stories could be privately manufactured by her own internal cinema gives her a sense of power. The idea of her own sleeping mind shaping something just for her is sweet and strange. And so night after night, she replays the one dream she remembers, sometimes watching it on a loop three or four times, before finally sticking her finger into her bedside outlet, closing her eyes, and slipping into the black pool of nothingness as she links with Heaven.

She can't bring herself to plug in the port tonight. She'll have to, eventually; a grounded connection is required once every forty-eight hours. Heaven provides a system recharge along with the data transfer. Connecting to Heaven is the law. It's vital for the trans-human ideal of data-sharing. And it's imperative for the Syn Council's commitment to citizen monitoring.

Heaven is invasive. But it's also so damn convenient. Resent it or not, Ever can't imagine giving it up. The shared images and ideas, bits of news, snippets of story, insights into everyone else in the world—it's addictive. Constant connectivity is not merely necessary for upgrades and maintenance, or even for sharing society-wide information; they need it for reasons that run deeper than regulation. There's a fear of missing something if you go too long without logging in; a sense of purpose to participating in the process.

Nevertheless, Ever delays her connection. After replaying the nightmare over and over, she's still awake and hungry for something more interesting than the rote routine, the shared system. Her appetite is for something hers alone, and she has been starving for too long.

Pulling on a pair of soft black shoes, she makes her way up to the deck of the boat.

The night air is pleasantly cool on her skin. Ever savors the silent starry world. The sleek vessel barely makes a ripple as it glides mildly through the darkened Gulf waters. They are still several hundred miles from home. Soon, the boat will dock for the night, re-fuel and service itself automatically, and then while its passengers slumber, the boat will continue homeward.

Ever's family lives on the small island just off the central mainland, the most populated borough in the heart of Sector 11. Previously called Manhattan, the center of the Syn world is now known, accurately if not creatively, as Central City. When Central City was restored to its vintage splendor, everyone wanted to live there, just as people had clamored to live there in the years before the Singularity and the uprisings. But Ever's family didn't contend with the regular real estate market. They lived in the center of it all, within the walls of the Synt itself.

The Synthetic Neuroscience Institute of Technology, more often called simply the Synt, is where Ever's father works, where Heaven's mainframe is housed, where the entire Syn world is headquartered. No other families have residences there, though there are people in the building twenty-four hours a day. The Hess' address trumpets their place in society. Her father runs the Synt, the central agency of the Syn world; his security clearance exceeds even the Syn Council members themselves. With the dissolution of old governments and the establishment of the Syn Council as the sole governing body, connections and power are of greater worth than the old wealth—though old wealth still has its place. And back when money mattered more than it did these days, Ever's mother was the fourteenth richest heiress of her generation. By any measure, the Hesses are the power family of the Syn world. The envy of all.

But Ever would rather be part of some other family.

She can see Dock 27 now, the lights twinkling from the shore. Looking at the soft glow, a lightbulb clicks on within her. The idea swells in her mind like a small revolution, the rebellious notion lifting like the raised fist of a resistance leader: *I can get off the boat.*

She begins testing the idea for weakness, building armor around it: She'll shift into private mode so she'll be a little harder to track. If she steels herself and does it right now, she won't be noticed before morning, which will give her hours away from this floating little prison barge.

Decision made, she crawls over the port side of the ship. She lowers herself slowly from the rail. The cold water sends a delicious tingle through her entire body for a moment, before her temperature regulation kicks in. But even with a normal temperature restored, the soft sensation of water lapping at her body assures her she's really doing this.

Keeping her head just above the surface, she kicks gently, swimming forward until, stretching her toes down, she finds that she can touch the bottom. She is not a particularly experienced swimmer, and is relieved to be able to half-step,-half kick; the water is shallow, and mucky-bottomed, which encourages her to hop along quickly to keep her feet from getting stuck. The water level drops from her chin, to her chest, to her navel.

And then something cold, scaly, and very much alive brushes heavily against her right leg.

Stifling a scream, Ever jerks to her left, nearly toppling over, but managing to right herself just in time to keep from splashing and falling underwater.

What in Heaven and Hell was that?

She cannot see anything, even as her eyes dart from side to side. For a moment, she holds perfectly still, not even breathing, willing whatever had moved against her to keep right on moving. She notes that her breathing is erratic, and commands an override to even it out, to halt the panic. Even as her synthetic system regulates her breath, her mind devises a thousand terrible things that could be in the water with her.

Snakes, sharks, fish with jagged teeth ... alligator alligator alligator!

Her nightmare flashes before her; Ever reels the memory in, forcing herself to focus on this very real terrifying moment. Suddenly her impulsive jump out of the boat feels idiotic. She considers turning around, climbing back into the boat, but she can't. She won't. She is already in the water. The shore is a hundred yards away. The unincorporated world awaits, at least for a few hours of blessed and dangerous exploration.

Don't you dare chicken out, Ever.

She snaps into motion again, moving more quickly toward the shore and hopefully away from whatever bumped into her, staying low to avoid being spotted by her mother, or Angela, or anyone who might peer over the side of the boat. The lapping waves guide her forward. The surface of the water is at her thighs now. Her knees. Ankles. The ship is well behind her, programmed to slow as it approaches land, while Ever picks up speed.

Striding through the last few yards of the water, wind whipping at her wet skin, she shifts from fear to elation. She walks more quickly through the shallows, then gives a sudden small cry as something slices through the bottom of her foot.

She stepped on something, not something alive, but something sharp, which cuts right through the flimsy sole of her soft black shoe. Ever feels a trickle of warm blood seeping from her foot, through her shoe, pooling and contrasting with the cold sea water. As the sea mixes itself into her foot, the salt lacing its way through the wound makes her wince, but sharper than the pain is the realization snapping into focus: *predators can smell blood.*

Though she is in barely four inches of water now, the idea of a water-predator coming after her in some sort of blood-frenzy triggers a primal motivation. Limping a little, she runs through the shallows, emerging quickly from the water. Once on dry land,

she summons all of her athletic training, real and archived, and
stretches out low to the ground, running as fast as her perfect legs
can carry her toward the tree line in the distance.

Her long black hair (Ebony #188) flies behind her, comingling
with the night sky. The pain in her foot is all but forgotten. She
runs forward, hell-bent on making it deep into the great unknown,
with no intention of stopping until she gets there.

L EAVES. GREEN. *Thick, heavy foliage. Heady, humid jungle air. He moves as quickly as the environment allows, stumbling frequently, getting caught and tangled, untangling himself by falling forward and just continuing to move forward.*

Breathing heavily, heart surging, sweating through his clothes, Ere tries to take a normal breath but can only gasp as he keeps half-running, half-falling forward. The fabric of his shirt clings to his chest and he wants to take it off, but his clothing is all that protects him·from the thousand little stings of barbed branches, underbrush, insects. He runs. Faster, faster, faster.

He becomes aware of a humming sound, realizes that this sound is what he is moving toward. He doesn't know what the hum means, or where it's coming from, he just knows that he has to get to wherever it is. Whatever it is. Whoever it is. As quickly as possible. Another sound cuts through the hum:

"Ere!"

He turns quickly, too quickly; a cruel root twists under his foot and his ankle snaps, sending him down to the earth as a sharp pain shoots up his leg. A blinding ray of sunshine cuts through the leaves, assaulting Ere. He senses danger, a Syn—a thousand Syns, a million Syns—
   "Ere!"
   Blinking and shielding his eyes with the back of his arm, he looks up, tries to see who is calling his name. How could a Syn know his name? Unless it wasn't—he sees her: a girl.
   She stands silhouetted, blocking out the harsh light but also shielding her features from Ere. All he can see is her hair—long, flowing, black. He wants to ask who she is, but feels he should already know her. He searches his mind for her name, or to recall the shape of her face, the color of her eyes. Even in shadow, without being able to see her face, he senses her urgency. She needs to tell him something. She needs him to do something. Something very important—

"Ere!" This time the voice is whispered and sharp, punctuated by strong hands gripping his shoulders. He is wrapped in a blanket, curled up in his corner of the main sleeping room in the Franklin Commune. His dream dissipates like a lifting fog as his mother shakes him awake.

"What is it?" He asks, forcing alertness in his voice. "What's wrong?"

Her voice is a loaded weapon: "Syns."

And with that, she's gone.

Whenever the Syns appeared, his mother disappeared. Ruth Fell would defend her people to the death, but only in an extreme emergency. Outside of an outright attack, she simply vanished, resurfacing only when the Syns departed. This was never explained to Ere; it was just the way things were.

Uncle Howard used to be the one who represented the tribe when a Syn approached. Interactions with the Syns had not been violent in quite some time, but they were never pleasant. Most often, when a Syn approached an Original tribe, it was to deliver an eviction notice, informing them that the tribe's camp was being developed for Syn territory expansion. But there is always the threat of something worse than a simple eviction notice. Ere's heart stutters at the thought.

"Ere." Cal stands in the doorway, fingers resting lightly on the knife at his side.

"Who's going to speak to the Syns?"

"Helena," Cal says.

"But she's so old—"

"Younger than Uncle Howard was."

"Yes, but…"

Cal gestures for his cousin to stop speaking. "I'm going to stand guard, while she talks."

"Should I get my knife—"

"You should never be without your knife." Cal snaps. "Get it. And stay in here. Don't come out unless I call you."

Embarrassed at how relieved he is at these instructions, Ere nods. He pulls his leather knife holster tight around his thigh. He curses himself, silently swearing that he will never again be caught without a weapon. He follows Cal as far as the window, then crouches, peering just above the sill, to watch Cal guard Helena Garrison.

Helena is already standing in the field in front of the Commune. Cal approaches her rapidly, but as he draws near, Helena raises a hand.

"Further back, boy," Helena calls out in a voice shaky with age but firm in its command. Ere can barely hear her. "Keep your distance. You can watch from right where you are."

Cal wants to argue, but Helena's seniority forbids him. He halts, keeping his fingers on his knife and his eyes on Helena.

Helena Garrison is one of the eldest of the Elders, somewhere around eighty-eight, though exact dates were hard for the

Originals to keep up with these days; a few months ago she referred to this year as her *piano year*, which made her contemporaries smile at a joke only they understood. Ere and Cal, who had never seen a piano, went blank at this reference, which wiped the smiles from the elders' faces.

Ere is amazed at how Helena holds her ground as the Syns exit their ship and stride toward her. One Syn is clearly the leader of the group. He looks as they all look, polished and svelte and cold. But there is something else about him. Ere squints, and realizes that this Syn looks somewhat like Louie Garrison, Helena's son, who passed away some years ago. From the subtle tilt of her head, Ere can tell that Helena is noticing this as well.

Louie, a wonderful storyteller, prankster, and great favorite in the tribe, died suddenly of a heart condition. That's what they thought, at least; one morning when out scouting for water, he simply crumpled to the ground and never got up. Now this Syn stands there with the same hairline, the same posture. The resemblance makes Ere's heart twist, and he can only imagine what it did to Helena. The Syns were sometimes able to do this: know something intimate about a tribe or tribesperson, and send someone who would unsettle them based on that knowledge.

Or maybe it's just coincidence.

The Louie-like-Syn appears thirty, which means nothing. Small but fit, a solid little package of a person, dressed all in gray, with a neatly trimmed mustache and close-cropped hair. Eyebrow arched, he swiftly closes the distance between himself and the wrinkled old woman.

"Greetings," he says, brightly. He speaks loudly, possibly assuming the old woman is hard of hearing; Ere is glad that at least it allows him to hear what's going on. As Helena draws near, the Syn's jaw drops. Whether he is genuinely shocked by her appearance, or simply mocking her to further catch her off guard, the Syn's next statement makes Ere's own jaw drop. "Heaven and Hell, you're a skeleton with skin."

"High praise from a robot," Helena says, unblinking.

"Ooh, good one," he chuckles, maybe admiring her moxie, maybe genuinely amused that she would fling that old insult his way. "How old are you, anyway, Original woman?"

"I'm sure your records can tell you that," Helena says.

The Syn grins waxily. "Helena Garrison, right? I'm Fredrick." He offers his name with a careless wave of his hand, as his eyes slide to the left and scans her records. He quotes from them aloud, looking not at her but at something only he can see: "Ah yes, here we are. *Garrison, Helena. Eighty-nine years of natural age. Born in Sector 17, formerly Ohio. Family history of high blood pressure, heart disease, and multiple types of cancer: breast, lung, pancreatic. Son, Louis Miles Garrison, died of assumed congestive heart failure, 2057. Husband, Robert Garrison, died in the resistance. Remaining relatives: none. Current health status: undocumented; no hospital visits since the Health Reallocation Act of 2045. Projected prognosis: Death within the year.*"

Helena remains stoic throughout this recitation. Frederick the Syn slides his eyes to the right again, then smiles that smile at Helena.

"That's you? Or did I look up the wrong Helena Garrison?"

"That's me."

"And you are leader of this tribe now?"

"I will speak for this tribe."

"Bet you can guess why I'm here," he says, almost playfully, a sick parody of Louie.

"I assume you're about to kick us out."

"You assume correctly."

"It makes no sense," says the old woman. "By your own standards, this area is worthless. Perhaps you're unaware, but there are few power sources here. None functioning. No reason for an evacuation. We are old. I'm dead within the year, as you said yourself. Let us live out our days here."

From his position behind the window, Ere is straining to catch the words, certain he is missing something here and there. But he is impressed with Helena's poise and clear, loud voice. He never before noticed her impeccable posture. He feels proud of her and almost expects the Syn to acquiesce to her request that the tribe be allowed to stay.

"Your information is incomplete, and thereby inaccurate," Fredrick says, matter-of-fact. "There is nothing of which we are 'unaware.' There are many power lines buried in the vicinity, and this building itself has several rooms which will be useful to us in resurrecting the utility of this sector. Nice try, though."

"We ask that you consider—"

"We consider everything before we decide anything," the Syn cuts Helena off, no longer even bothering to look at her. Instead, he shoots an almost flirtatious look over at Cal. "And you don't all have one foot in the grave, now, do you?" Helena opens her mouth to speak, but before even a syllable can escape, the Syn waves his hand again to silence her and keeps talking: "Your evacuation is effective immediately. Migration begins today. Head south, if you want the opportunity for a new camp. Everything north of here is marked for incorporation."

"South," Helena says slowly.

"South," confirms Fredrick, drawing the word out, giving it a ludicrous amount of syllables. "Oh, and while we aren't particularly interested in expediting your demise, if you decide not to leave, we'll go ahead and kill you. All right! That's all."

The Syn nods, message delivered, and turns on his heel. Helena stares after him, immediately flanked by a scowling Cal. There is nothing more to say. The days of resistance are long passed. The days of marching, not into battle but into retreat, are all that remain.

And just like that, another migration is underway.
Curse of the world.

The sheer mind-numbing boredom begins crushing Ere immediately. Each migration day might bring one isolated interesting incident (a rattlesnake, say) surrounded on both sides by an entire day and night of tedium.

But Ere's boredom pales as a complaint in comparison to the toll the trip takes on the elders. Crossing uneven terrain, sleeping in makeshift tents, exposed to the elements—nothing about the journey was kind to the aged. Covering twenty miles a day is taxing on the young, but brutal on the old.

They are bound for the swampland known as Sector 27, as far south as you could go before hitting the ocean. Sector 27 was largely neglected by the Syns, other than at its southernmost tip, a port area used by the Syns for business and travel; being such a hot and humid climate, the sector is not suited to serve as residential Syn territory.

Despite being free of resident Syns, Ere still isn't sure that this direction is best. The swampy sector is home to many large predatory animals, which saw population surges after the Singularity, following the gutting of Original communities there. And slow-moving elders could easily be prey.

Ere walks at the very back of the group, alongside Cal. Though the young men are the tribe's fastest, and could easily have ranged ahead, a better strategy was having them bring up the rear. From there, they could help any who stumbled, or sprint swiftly to the front to report if there was any danger at their heels, or respond if an alarm was sounded from ahead. The configuration is always Ruth in front, elders in the middle, Cal and Ere in the rear.

With Howard gone, the tribe numbers thirty-one. They almost never speak of their dwindling population aloud. It's considered bad luck (and is depressing as hell, Ere thinks). Their small census was taken only before beginning a journey, so that throughout the trek, the two young men at the back of the line could constantly count heads, silently tallying to ensure that all were present and accounted for throughout the journey and at the end of each day.

Ere can see his mother all the way at the head of the line, despite more than two dozen bodies between them, since the older tribes-people are all so bent and stooped. Even when he can't see her, he sees the glint of his mother's machete, held aloft and brought swiftly down, hacking away the terrain to clear the path for those in her wake. Ere sees the machete slash the air again, and then come up—and stay up.

Everyone stops, this visual cue of an alarm followed quickly by a verbal one as a sound passes quickly, from the front of the line to the back: *shh, see.*

Shh, see. Shh, see. A threat.

Holding still, Ere strains to see and hear, desperate to pinpoint the danger. His eyes find Cal, whose nostrils flare. Both boys keep their hands on their knives, poised and at the ready. Each knows the other's guilty secret: they are thrilled to have something happening, and while they don't want anyone to get hurt they sure as hell won't mind a little action.

Cal and Ere know that Ruth will swiftly identify the threat. Ruth Fell hasn't survived this long by overlooking anything. They watch as she holds stock still, listening. Ere strains his ears, darts his eyes, but beyond the damp hum of thick humidity and the looming greenery all around them, he perceives nothing. The absence of a telling sound, sight, or smell is alarming—but then, almost imperceptibly, Ruth Fell's head tilts up. Ere follows her gaze, and there it is, directly above this machete-wielding mother: a massive cat.

The cat is black, with huge paws housing sharp claws and moss-green eyes that seem to Ere to be trained not on his mother, but past her. He looks at where the big cat has fixed its stare: on the smaller, older, weaker prey standing behind Ruth.

Helena.

Ere hears Cal exhale, and knows his cousin has reached the same conclusion. Both of them are prepared to run to the front, to pull the cat off Helena if it pounces, to do their part—but before they can move, they are stopped by a mighty roar.

The sound comes not from the cat, but from Ere's mother.

It is not a scream; there is no shrillness to the sound, no fear, no alarm. It is a booming battle cry, a roar sending an unmistakable message to the giant cat. Ere hears the challenge as clearly as if his mother shouted the actual words.

We outnumber you. We are not prey. We are a pack. You are alone.

If you attack, we will defend. And we will destroy you.

Ruth's roar fills the swamp, reverberating through every member of the tribe, soaking into the heady trees. Everyone holds their ground, unflinching. Ere's ears ring with the sound of his mother's bloodcurdling cry, but he does not flinch. He stands still at the opposite side of the pack. He is ready to leap into action at any second to enforce the resounding howl's promised war, and he knows his cousin will be beside him.

The cat's green eyes flash from Helena to Ruth, then travel the length of the stiff-necked people. Ruth's cry goes on unbroken, aided by a primal power, her breath never running out. No cough cuts her short. Her howl is sustained and strong.

The massive feline flattens its ears, taking in the unrelenting sound. It hisses, shifts, then sits back on its haunches, almost seeming to nod: *fine, I'll wait for an easier meal, you stupid woman. Wasn't that hungry anyway.*

Ruth ends her yell, but does not stop staring at the giant cat. The big cat closes his eyes, yawns, feigning boredom, as if to indicate that such a fight was beneath him. Only then does Ruth lower her hand, and move forward again.

"Cal," whispers Ere a few hours later. "Does everyone seem tired to you?"

Cal, a few paces ahead of Ere, is carrying Helena Garrison, who stumbled not long before. Her knee twisted, and thus (under protest) she is allowing Cal to carry her. For the first half-mile, she kept assuring Cal she would soon be on her own two feet. Now she's sleeping, snoring lightly, secure in the strong arms of her tribe's gentle giant.

"Yes," grunts Cal. "Glad you and your big brain figured that one out for us. Someday, runt, you'll have to tell me how such a tiny body can lug around such a giant brain."

"Talk to my mother. Tell her we should make camp."

"Me? You're a little more... un-burdened at the moment." To prove his point, Cal shifts Helena in his arms, cradling the old woman like a drowsing baby.

"She won't listen to me. She'll think I'm being a baby."

"You are."

"I'm not. Everyone's exhausted. You're already carrying Helena. How many more can you carry before—"

"Fine. When Helena wakes up, I'll talk to Ruth."

Helena opens one eye, and aims it up at Cal. "Oh, put me down, you big brute, and go talk to Ruth. My ankle's feeling better. I can last another few steps if we're stopping soon."

Cal sighs and sets Helena gingerly on the ground, ever gentle with the fragile elders around him. She reaches up to pat his chest affectionately.

"Ere!" Cal turns and lifts a bushy eyebrow.

Ere looks at him questioningly. "What?"

"I'll ask, but you're coming with me."

"But what about the back of the line—"

"I'll scream if there's trouble! Scream twice if it's a snake!" Helena chirps cheerily, waving, as if a delightful encounter with a charming snake would be just dandy by her.

They reach Ere's mother in moments, quickly overtaking all the tired elders, who are moving at the approximate speed of a dying turtle.

"Aunt Ruth?"

Ruth Fell glances behind her, looking first up at her nephew and then down at her son. She does not stop walking nor slow her pace, but does also quickly scan the rest of the line behind her to make sure there was not a problem.

"Yes, Cal?"

"We should set up camp for the night."

"We have another hour of daylight, maybe more. We're far enough south that—"

"Forget daylight," says Cal. "The elders are tired. And I can't carry them all at once."

Ruth stops, holding her hand aloft, open-palmed, not clenched in alert. Cal halts, and raises his as well. One by one, hands raise from the front of the line to the end, signaling a stop but not danger. A collective sigh of relief passes softly through the line along with the outstretched hands.

"Fine," Ruth says. "But if Ere thinks he's tired now, he's going to be exhausted by the time he's done collecting the water for all of us tonight."

"What-!" Ere starts to protest, but his mother cuts him off.

"Don't send your cousin to make your requests for you," she chides him. "And make sure to collect plenty of water, son. I'm parched."

REACHING THE TREE LINE. Ever is disappointed. There are still signs of incorporation everywhere. Natural as they appeared from a distance, these trees all have small outlets in their bases, linking them to the harbor check point system. They are uniform in their appearance: same height, same coloring, same number of branches. They reflected the sort of uniformity prized by Syns and rarely found in nature.

Damnation.

So much for her big adventure. The night is almost over; soon the sun will rise, and her mother and Angela will wake up, notice she's gone, and send officers to haul her ass back to the boat. She should have gotten off in Costa Rica. Sector 27 was too close to home, and this place had clearly become too developed to be any fun.

On top of all that, her foot is throbbing. Wincing, she runs a quick self-scan. She's relieved when the scan confirms she's not losing enough blood to be in danger. The cut is small, but she shouldn't keep running on it. Adrenaline spent, even walking is now painful. She's on the verge of giving up, turning her own distress signal on, when something glints, catching her eye: a small fleet of sleek silver Chariots stationed near the synthetic trees.

She does an external scan; no cameras, no alarm system, no people. Gaining a second wind, Ever hobbles swiftly toward the unmonitored hovercrafts. Less than a mile behind her, several boats, including her family's vessel, are approaching the shore, self-docking, everything following the set order.

Of course.

No need for staff. The check point program is precise and runs automatically. The hovercrafts are access vehicles, on hand in case any need arose for manual technical support. If a Syn staffer was required to service a malfunctioning dock or misaligned ship-to-land-transport connection, he would need transportation. And access vehicles all use the same startup code, because theft is unlikely. Too easily traced, since both the object and the thief were registered technology, trackable and instantly identifiable. Property theft these days was a truly idiotic crime, and thus one rarely committed in Syn society.

Ever quickly weighs the risks of committing this truly idiotic crime. Would she get in trouble? Yes, but as a first-time offender, a minor offense would bring little punishment. Especially if she returned the Chariot when she was done with it. The Syn penal system was logical, measured: punishments always fit the crimes, and a petulant teenage girl taking a service vehicle for a joyride wasn't a very high-stakes offense. She might get a temporary alert added to her profile, which would be removed after three months with no re-offense. Besides, a court appearance might even get an interesting—perhaps even *interested*—reaction from her father.

Decision made, Ever hops onto one of the Chariots, and enters in the standard code, which is instantly accepted. The control pad illuminates. Ever Hess points the vehicle north, and speeds off toward uncharted territory.

A swamp! Heaven and Hell!

Covered in mud, swatting at mosquitoes, drenched in sweat, the cut on her foot throbbing dully—Ever is giddy. After an hour of breakneck speeding on the chariot, she's a hundred miles into the jungle, flying just above the muck and directly through the stinging flora, leaning this way and that to avoid the larger swaths of smacking overgrowth. She feels snakelike, fast and winding, old skin shed, like she slipped out of her sleek Syn self and slithered into a new, wilder jungle-identity.

Moving through the thick green world, Ever takes in every detail. In the cool and climate-controlled centers of Syn society, greenery is valued, but only in an ordered sort of way: cultivated rooftop gardens, museums of agriculture, city parks providing pockets of green. All manicured, all meticulously maintained. She knew the outlying areas would be less sculpted, but she hadn't expected them to be so utterly wild, verdant and heady.

A sharp stab from her foot reminds her of her injury, cutting into her exhilaration. She downloads information about plants suitable for natural remedies available in this environment, being careful not to download too much, not enough to be flagged; then she scans the greenery around her, and spots one of the recommended plants.

She slows her Chariot and tears free several leaves. Setting her vehicle on autopilot, she rips the large leaves into strips. She eases her leg upward, slipping her foot carefully from her shoe and letting it rest on the seat. With one deft hand she layers the strips of leaves to form a poultice, which staunches the flow of blood just as Heaven assured her it would. Then she crafts a raggedy bandage, wrapping the longer leaves all the way around, binding everything into place before easing her foot back into the shoe.

She's so pleased with herself that as she kicks the Chariot back into gear, she lets fly a loud burst of wild laughter, triggering the screech of some nearby bird. Startled by the sound, Ever looks up—just in time to get whacked by a low-hanging branch and knocked right off the Chariot. She slams to the ground as the Chariot continues on its way, zipping along and quickly disappearing from view.

"Heaven and Hell!" Ever swears, all smugness smacked out of her.

Running another quick scan, she confirms that she has no concussion or other injuries. She thinks for a moment about trying to catch up with the Chariot right away, but the fast-moving vehicle is already out of sight. Without a programmed destination, though, it will only stay on autopilot for so long before going into hibernation mode and awaiting further instruction. She can pursue it slowly and eventually catch up.

Distancing herself from the hover craft might actually be a good idea anyway. Those vehicles all have tracking devices, difficult to disable. Better to let it serve as a decoy until she's ready to ride again. For now, her foot feels better and she's happy to explore on-the-ground. She looks around as she walks; the land still looks wild, but on closer inspection this part of the jungle isn't quite as untouched as she initially thought. It just hadn't been touched lately.

Hadn't been touched by Syns, she realizes.

Aware now, she sees clues and fragments everywhere, subtle and quiet but certain. There are hewn structures. Signs, here and there. Tall tentative posts, rusted, jutting nakedly upward. There are even small wooden houses, crumbled and weather-beaten, half-hidden beneath tangled overgrowth. Some of the buildings collapsed long ago, others still thinking about it. Here and there she sees even more interesting details, like the decayed edges of a wooden frame (*a sandbox*, she identifies with a little help from

Heaven to jog her memory), or a scrap of random metal. Twisted within a cluster of weeds, her eyes widen at the sight of a small, half-disintegrated shoe.

Each remnant seems to scream a silent story, and she wishes she could hear those stories. She wants to know about the people who lived and worked and died here in this little Original town. She can almost feel the ghosts floating in this swampy now-dead hamlet.

Don't be stupid, Ever! There's no such thing as ghosts.

A small box catches her eye, tucked up against one of the ram-shackle old wooden buildings. It looks out of place, somehow. She walks over to the box, slipping a little on some moss along the way. Peeling back the rickety wooden box top and peering inside, she sees old fabrics. She gingerly pulls out a large rag, which it takes her a moment to identify as a shirt. She smells it; she can't identify the scent—musty, but not unappealing. Putting it back in the box, she wonders whose it was and why it was here. How long has this place been abandoned?

She begins a new search query, using her internal GPS to provide coordinates, and then eagerly looking up the history of this town. What had characterized this place? What industry, what traditions? She begins to open the first files on the place when she stops herself. If she accesses this detailed information, even in private mode, it might trigger an alert. She decides it's wiser to come up with her own best-guess as to what this town might have been. She looks around, noting the low houses near the water, the planks of weathered wood. She sees a low red-brick building, with faded yellow words painted on the exterior: GULF PINT & PATIO.

A fishing community?

A bead of sweat trickles down Ever's face, landing saltily on her lips. Licking it away, Ever is suddenly aware of how hot she is. It occurs to her that if she were to pass out and be unable to signal for help, she might be in real trouble. An emergency alert would be triggered, but she's so far from the docking area; reaching her would take a response crew a good bit of time. Her breathing is becoming a bit labored, and she's thirsty. Ever can't remember the last time she actually felt thirsty. In her world, such needs were always met before they were expressed.

The need is not yet desperate; she can always shift to override mode, tap in to her reserve energy, supplementing her organic needs with a synthetic-component compensation. But Ever wants to delay implementing this failsafe. Being hot, sweaty, thirsty— the novelty is wonderful. Trouble is intoxicating. She doesn't want to compensate synthetically, or sound an alarm, or be rescued. She wants to keep making her way on her own. Like an Original. She decides to focus in on what she actually needs, bare minimum, and find it for herself.

Excited to have a mission, Ever starts hunting for water. It's been a long time since she's had to locate something on her own. In a world so neatly ordered, archived, searchable, with nothing unmapped, a moment of uncertainty is the sort of thrill for which she has longed. She has no idea how the hell to find water, but that's the best part.

She pulls back branches, looks through breaks in the trees, tries to find clues. She sniffs the air, wondering if she could smell water. Does water have a smell? Perhaps if it were a waterfall or brook, she would hear it before anything else—

Shnikt.

She freezes.

Something else was in the swiftly-darkening woods with her. She holds her breath.

I should log in to Heaven. I'll use the network scanners to identify the precise location I'm in and cross-reference it with all native wildlife and—no. No, no. Then I'll be flagged.

Deciding again against using technology, Ever scans the area with her own eyes—and then, still stubbornly avoiding linking into the full Heaven database, she begins another internal scan, searching her own personal internal memory to help classify and identify the sound. She finally settles on a result that seemed appropriate to the context: *Snapped twig.*

With the sound identified, she should feel calmer, yet she remains on the edge of panic, with the larger question still looming: What snapped the damn twig?

As quickly as the rational result was returned by her search, something irrational from deep within her contributes its own overriding suspicion, squeezing out logic and screaming loudly in a voice powered by fear and pounding with illogical certainty. The pounding overtakes her mind, worse than the moment when something had brushed against her in the water. The fear now is strong enough to override all her other systems, as a murky memory surfaces and bares its teeth: *Alligator alligator alligator!*

Her breath catches in her throat. Her mouth curves into a reckless smile. *This is fear. This is real fear!*

She can hear her own heartbeat, taste her own panic. She draws in a sharp breath and is almost certain she can smell something serpentine. Thrilled, terrified, she looks around to find the source of the sound, be it alligator or snake or some other evil—

Her eyes lock with another pair of eyes—not evil, but warm. The eyes belong to a boy.

E RE IS ROOTED TO THE SPOT, unable to take his eyes off the incredible sight before him. His fingers remain locked, vice-like, around the handle of his water bucket. Alone, scouting for water while others set up camp, he hadn't paid attention, stepped on a dry twig—and now here he is, a speechless idiot statue, staring.

Staring at a girl.

An unbelievably beautiful girl.

Though flecked with mud, she's still somehow cleaner than anyone he's ever seen, radiating with a sort of glowing... glow, he thinks stupidly. She's wearing all black, blending in with the night; her hair, too, is black, but there's a radiant light to her skin, her eyes. He tries to remember a word, the word for something as ethereal as she. The word reveals itself: *an angel.*

Then the angel speaks.

"Who in Heaven and Hell are you?"

Her voice is not nearly as angelic as her appearance. It's sharp and oddly accented. He hesitates, and she looks at him, her eyes traveling from his face to his arms, his water bucket, back to his face. She speaks again, with less command and more curiosity.

"Can you speak?"

"Of course I can speak," Ere retorts.

"Then tell me your name."

"Ere."

"Air? That's a weird name. Like 'the air we breathe'?"

"No, Ere, as in—the way things were."

"Huh. I don't know if that's weirdly nostalgic or just stupid."

"I'll have to ask my mother whether she was being 'weirdly nostalgic' or just stupid when she chose it. What's your name?"

She does not hesitate. "Ever."

"*Ever?*" He repeats incredulously. And then, before he can stop himself, he snipes back: "Well, yes. *Ever.* That's definitely a less stupid name than Ere."

The girl bursts out laughing, then stops as abruptly as she started. She narrows her eyes.

"Are you… teasing me?"

It strikes him as odd that she would have trouble selecting that word. "Um, yes."

"What gives you the right to tease me?"

"The right…?"

"Do you know who my father is?"

"I don't even know who *you* are," Ere says, bemused.

Her eyes narrow further. "Where are you from?"

What's wrong with this girl?

Her questions made no sense. Where was anyone "from"? Who would ask such a question? He starts to respond, then realizes. That was too odd a query. A question no Original would ever ask another Original. Nomadic people don't compare many notes on "home sweet home." Ere cocks his head and listens closely—he has never been close enough to hear the sound before, but now— yes. There it is. A soft but unmistakable humming. Coming from the girl.

She can't be....

But even as he resists accepting the fact, he knows it to be true. The beautiful girl is not an Original. Despite the heat of the evening swamp, a cold sweat breaks out on Ere's forehead at this realization. He tries to quickly calculate why a Syn would be here, apparently alone, in the middle of the swamp. Unless she wasn't alone.

"I asked you where you are from," the Syn girl says, repeats, louder. "Identify yourself and your sector. You are required by law to do so, and you know it."

"I..." The boy's voice cracks and goes out on him. He wonders if he should run, or hold his ground and try to mislead her in some way. And then he sees it happen—the moment when his hesitation gives him away, and realization widens the uncanny girl's perfect eyes.

CHAPTER 9: SHADOWER

THE INCOMING MESSAGE WAKES SHADOWER
with a start. It's encrypted in an entirely new code.
But even before it is unlocked and deciphered, it has
Shadower's attention. Whatever the content might be, it was critical because of its sender.

It's from Karma.

Messages from Karma are rare, and always urgent. Shadower
does not know Karma's identity, just as—Shadower hopes—
Karma does not know Shadower's identity. But each has honed
the ability to message the other, sending missives encrypted in

such a way that only a handful of people would ever be able to decipher it. Shadower unlocks it in under two seconds:

Traveling to the old world. Must find the warrior.
Will send messages only when safe to do so.

Shadower has been expecting this message for some time, and is relieved and terrified to know that Karma's journey has begun. Shadower will have to be even more watchful.

Shadower does a quick scan for any flagged communal uploads, and notices a small alert regarding the unauthorized use of a Chariot, taken in the night from Sector 27. Curious, Shadower follows this rabbit down a hole, which proves a shallow one. No one else has yet accessed the dark and distant image from the nighttime security camera. The footage reveals the faraway but distinct profile of a very recognizable Syn, running ashore, taking a Chariot, zooming away.

Ever Hess?

What the hell is that girl doing out there?

CHAPTER 10: EVER

S HE SAYS IT ALOUD, CURIOUSLY—but as a statement, not a question.

"You're an Original."

She sees his Adam's apple bob as he swallows nervously, sees the sweat trickling down his face, can almost smell his fear. She practically starts clapping, she's so damn excited.

An Original boy. In the flesh. One who looks her age, which should be impossible. The water treatments and population regulations in place should mean that the youngest of the Originals would be forty-ish. This boy is much younger. From his beat-up jeans to his messy light-brown hair, he is trapped somewhere between boyhood and manhood—an intersection that feels at once familiar and foreign to Ever.

Ever has rarely interacted with Originals. A handful live in Central City, primarily working in menial jobs—waste collection, housekeeping, vintage electronics repair. They're easy to overlook, reporting to the Syns who supervised them but refraining from exchanges with any other Syns. Each year, there were fewer Originals in the Syn cities. When they died, no one replaced them.

No Originals worked for Ever's family. Even their maid, Angela, was a Syn. An older Syn, synched in her late forties, who enjoyed cooking and cleaning and was utterly boring. But a Syn, nonetheless. They had never employed any Originals in the Hess household. Her father would not hear of it. ("Why hire someone with a terminal disease?" That's what he called the human condition: *a terminal disease.*)

Ever has studied Originals; she knows about their history, their tendencies, their skewed sense of self-righteousness, their self-destructiveness. Originals are endangered, with extinction inevitable; an aging population that no one is interested in aiding. Due to population control measures implemented decades ago, the extinction process had been accelerated. This must be contributing to the boy's fear, she realizes; he is endangered and she is a threat.

"Wait," she hears herself say. "You're safe. I'm in a private setting—and I'll add another level of security. Hold on. Okay? Just—wait a minute." She briefly closes her eyes, then opens them again. "There, see? I'm offline, secure and encrypted. Full private mode. All right?"

The confusion in his eyes tells her that he has absolutely no idea what in Heaven and Hell she's talking about. He opens his mouth, looks for a moment as though he might ask her to explain—and then he turns and runs at breakneck speed towards the swamp, away from her.

"Wait!" Ever cries, indignant. "I said, *wait!*"

She's at his side in an instant, faster than she knew she could move, particularly with her foot, which rebukes her with another chiding stab of pain. She ignores it, more interested in the boy than in her stupid foot. The Original boy seems shaken by Ever's sudden proximity. His eyes, inches from her own, are two round dark spheres. She revels in his fear—*someone is scared of me*—but at the same time, she wants to comfort him.

How the hell do you do comfort someone?

Impulsively, she grabs his shoulder. He flinches and drops the thick wooden water bucket, which rolls away from him. She releases her grip, and he takes a step back, but doesn't run. Exhaling, Ever eases her approach, lightly touching a finger to his arm, consciously making sure not to use her port finger.

"You're hot," the boy says, looking with surprise at her warm, slender fingers.

"Yes," Ever agrees.

The boy swallows, steels himself, locks eyes with her. "Are you here with an eviction?"

"What? Oh!" She laughs. This poor Original has mistaken her for some sort of button-pushing incorporation official. "No, I'm… not involved with that."

He eases, a little. "Are you… is anyone else with you?"

"No, I just…" Ever allows herself a little smile, and tells the truth: "I ran away."

"Ran away?"

"That's right. And so like I said, I'm off the radar. I'm in private mode—right to privacy, you know? The Limited Autonomy Act? Never mind. Just… just don't worry. No one knows where I am, or that I'm talking to you now. So you don't have to be scared."

"I'm not scared," he snaps, and then adds, hesitantly: "But what's private mode? Limited auto…?"

"Oh." She searches for the simplest explanation. She never had to describe Syn structure to anyone. The knowledge of it is embedded in everyone she knows, as built-in as breathing or scratching an itch. *How do you explain breathing to someone without lungs?* "It's complicated."

The boy frowns. "I'm not stupid."

"I didn't say you were stupid—fine, okay," Ever says. "Limited Autonomy is a... protected right. Private mode, well, that's... I mean, it's ... you know. A basic function."

"Function."

"You... you do know how Syns... how we...?"

"I know how you work," he says defensively. And then, more slowly, more honestly: "I mean, I know you're... part machine." He stops speaking, as if worried that this statement might offend her. It doesn't. So he continues, encouraged, seeming almost proud of the small scraps of knowledge he has about her kind: "You don't get old and die like we Originals do. You have cures for your sicknesses. But you need to be near electricity. And heat can... damage you?"

"Yes," Ever admits, noticing again the thin film of perspiration covering her. She wipes her brow, trying to be delicate about it, hoping the boy doesn't notice how sweaty she is.

"You're sweating a lot," he says. So he did notice.

"Yeah, well, so are you." Her eyes flash irritation. Then she realizes that there is an almost-concerned quality to his question, and to his stare. "Oh. I mean—I'm fine."

"You were... born, right?"

"Of course I was *born*." What sort of idiotic question was that? Does he think she was built in some sort of factory?

"You were born an Original."

"Of course. Yes. Everyone was."

"But you made yourselves machines, and gave up being your Original selves—"

"We didn't give anything up. We *enhanced* our Original selves." She has never defended this before, but the way the boy is framing things pisses her off. She hates how much she sounds like her father, defending the Synthetic movement, but she can't seem to stop herself. "We used technology to fulfill our potential. Transhumanism was—is—all about expanding, not limiting. You Originals are the ones who clung to the dark ages, choosing inevitable death over the extended life. Your people are the ones who made the stupid decision to remain inferior."

His expression is cold, unreadable. "Inferior?"

"Yes, *inferior*," Ever replies with equal ice. She is the queen of frozen delivery, even as sweat pours down her back. "Inferior, *by choice*. Who wants to choose death over life?"

"Not everyone had a choice. Right?"

She pauses at this statement; he's not wrong. Not everyone was afforded the opportunity to upgrade. It cost a lot of money. But still. That wasn't the point. She gets back on track.

"Maybe, maybe not. But the Original resistance wasn't some noble campaign to extend the Syn option to everyone. The goal was to shut down the Syn initiative entirely—"

"If your world is so great and mine's so inferior, why'd you run away?"

"Because everything being perfect all the time is boring as shit," she says immediately.

This answer seems to soften him, a little. Something in his expression shifts. "Yeah?"

"Yeah."

"Well. Hope you enjoy your escape."

He sets his chin and stubbornly turns from her, exaggeratedly looking around, apparently looking for his wayward water bucket or something. Watching him, Ever feels irritation intermingled with pity, cushioned by something else. There's something riveting about him. His attitude, the stubbornness, his lean muscles.

The way he stood up to her. His eyes—big, brown, and focused, never sliding to the side and pulling information from elsewhere, something Syns constantly do. Everything about him is right out front, surfaced. She really wants to see his eyes again.

"Ere."

He looks back at her. She expects a retort from him, or a glare. But instead when their eyes meet, he seems just as confused and curious as she feels.

"What." He says it flatly, a statement, not a question. "What do you want."

You, she thinks. She wants him. She wants to touch him. She takes a step toward him, walking gingerly on her injured foot. She sees him note her uneven gait, wonder about it. She reaches out her hand. She doesn't just want to touch him, she *needs to* touch him. The thought wraps itself around her; something is set in motion, or maybe it was always in motion. *I've always been moving toward this boy*, she thinks wildly, feeling crazy and certain all at once.

"I want to keep talking to you," she says, slowly.

"Me? The inferior Original?"

"I didn't mean to insult you."

"Well," he says. "Good job hitting the target without even aiming."

He's clever, which adds to his appeal. She closes the gap between them, placing her hand on his narrow but sturdy chest. She feels him shudder at her touch. Her boldness shocks her as much as it shocks him. She feels like she's in a fairytale, but she's not the princess; she's the huntsman and the wicked queen and the hero and everything other than a damsel in distress. But still, if this is a fairytale, what sort of story would it be if she didn't kiss the handsome stranger she met in the woods?

"Let me make it up to you," she says.

She moves her lips onto his ear, gently biting it, and she instantly feels him tighten. She brings her hand from his chest up his neck, to his cheek, moving slowly across his nose and brow. His sweat dampens her finger, and without thinking she places her finger in her mouth and tastes it—warm, salty, real.

He swallows, hard. "What do you want."

"I want," she says simply.

The boy is right there with her now. He shifts his weight forward, just a little, and suddenly their bodies are touching. She can't quite tell, but she thinks he might be trembling ever so slightly. He is certainly waiting, wanting consent, terrified of doing the wrong thing. She nods, inviting, encouraging.

His mouth finds hers, and the spark of their first soft kiss makes them both open their eyes, staring in wonder for a moment before slowly lowering their lids and leaning in for a longer, softer second kiss.

D R. FELIX HESS CAN BE PATIENT WHEN HE needs to be. He knows the value of precision, and prides himself on being as fastidious as his close-clipped gray beard. The beard serves a practical purpose, deftly hiding the weak chin that he has always hated while giving him something to rub in times of stress. Like now.

He was less patient back in the days when his own biological clock was ticking away. The pressure was on, then; patience was less of a virtue and more of a vice. These days, there was almost never any legitimate need to rush. He could wait on the results of an experiment for months, years, decades if that's what it took. Rushing led to errors—a mistake he learned the hard way, years ago. So he is well-practiced in patience, to best accommodate actual progress.

But his patience is reserved solely for science. He has no patience for people. Which makes it very, very difficult to be married to Marilyn, and to have Ever for a daughter.

He closes his eyes and, for a second time, scans the message that Marilyn sent him:

Ever's gone. Stole a hovercraft, somewhere in Sector 27. Absence noted this morning during docking process. Tracking unsuccessful. Please advise.

Hess has a vast number of duties as Director of the Synthetic Neuroscience Institute of Technology. He oversees the staff, leads the research team, advises the Council, keeps the whole damn show running. Marilyn has one task. *One.*

Supervising Ever. That's it.

She has other people and other programs to cook for her, clean for her, plan the travel for her, wipe her ass. It should therefore be a reasonable assumption that she could handle her sole and single duty. But clearly, all the resources of Heaven were insufficient when it came to equipping Marilyn Hess with proper parenting skills.

"Jorge! Kennedy!"

"Sir?"

His assistants appear at his side as soon as they are summoned, almost as if conjured (which is why they both still work for him). He doesn't acknowledge their swift arrival. It's an expectation.

"My wife..." He hesitates, reluctant to even have to mention her. But the only thing worse than talking *about* her would be talking *to* her. If he has to look at Marilyn right now, he might run out of his last ounce of patience and simply stick a fork through her eye. Or his own. He needs to brief his employees and let them handle things so he can get back to work without fork-stabbing anyone. So he says: "I'm forwarding you a message from my wife."

"Should one of us go after Ever?" Kennedy asks, eyes darting toward Jorge, as the information lands in their files.

It's a dumb question; if and when one of the assistants is sent to fetch Ever, it will be Jorge.

Hess does need Ever returned unscathed to Central City, he hates to have his day disrupted unnecessarily. And unlike her mother, Ever is cunning. Resourceful. Probably not in immediate danger.

Hess turn to face the screen wall, a massive floor-to-ceiling display. He stares at it coolly, sniffs and blinks once as he projects his request to the machine he designed:

Locate Ever.

The walls hum softly. Everything in this building is part of the Heaven network, each piece of the structure part of an interconnected whole. The building, and the people within it, require no wiring whatsoever. Very little technology needed to be grounded after full integration kept constant energy in play. Other than the nightly plug-in, ensuring everyone was always running the same version and had all the proper updates installed (and all locations were monitored, and all data manged...), information and communication was all instantaneous and easy as blinking. Requests sent, results returned, all with incredible speed.

**Hess, Ever. Status: Private Mode. Location: Unknown.
Last Known Location: Sector 27 Port Harbor, traveling
North/101 MPH**

Dr. Hess shakes his head, though a small smile plays at his lips. *Clever girl.* Buying herself a little more playtime by going into private mode and zipping off on one of the chariots from an unmanned station. Private mode is overridden in extreme distress. Ever is thereby sending her father a message: she's fine.

"Do you need me to go get her?" Jorge asks.

Hess looks at bald, broad-shouldered Jorge, unquestionably the more indispensable of his assistants. The dispensability of his assistants is somewhat of a joke at the Synt. The joke is not, strictly speaking, funny: *Why do I have two assistants? I am a scientist, and a scientist knows the importance of a backup. If one of them were destroyed, I would still have a spare, ha ha ha.*

In addition to never earning a laugh at dinner parties, the joke is also inaccurate. The two assistants are not interchangeable; they serve very different functions. Jorge is strong, quiet, unquestioning, utterly reliable.

Jorge's sole "liability" is that he's not a true Syn. He's a Vost, a prototype tested prior to the Singularity, which makes him a second-class citizen. But Hess sees this as an asset: Jorge's inability to gain social standing outside of his service to the Director breeds a special kind of loyalty.

Kennedy is a quivering pile of cowardice. But he's bright. Meticulous, if not creative. Tedium suits him. Kennedy is also the nephew of one of the pillars of the Syn Council. Back when surnames mattered more, the one Kennedy was born into mattered quite a bit. While Jorge is a Nobody, Kennedy is inarguably a Somebody. His family was, anyway.

Family.

Hess forces his mind back to his own family. Ever is fine, and Marilyn is on edge, awaiting an update. So why not let the girl have some fun, especially if it extends Marilyn's misery a little? Serves her right, letting Ever slip away in the first place.

And although Ever doesn't know it yet, her father owes her a little leeway. Soon enough, her world will become smaller. Her role in a critical upcoming project is classified, known to few— certainly unknown to Ever. When everything is set in motion, excursions like this will be a distant memory. And so, knowing her physical safety is not a current concern and that her future freedoms will be even more limited than they already are, Hess decides to cut her a break.

"Go back to the lab. Both of you. I'll summon you if Ever needs retrieval, Jorge."

As swiftly as they arrived, Jorge and Kennedy exit, and thereby keep their jobs.

Felix Hess was born in Waltham, Massachusetts, in 1980. It was the heyday of the nation known as the United States of America. Technology's pace was moving along at a breathtaking rate, which would exponentially increase in the decades to follow. Back then, the future seemed bright; families felt secure in their homes and their futures, various now-disproven economic policies seemed to make sense, the Twin Towers still stood on an island called Manhattan.

People wore Day-Glo and denim, gave their children bad bowl cuts and shoved them into sailor suits, and everyone grinned more widely than seemed natural. They listened to bands that made up words and wore too much eyeliner. Everyone knew cigarettes were bad for you but you could still smoke them in restaurants, because dammit, this was the land of the free and the home of the brave, and God Bless America! Life was good.

The Hesses lived the American dream—albeit an academic and heavily subsidized version of it, with less Day-Glo and more Degas. Felix's parents, both professors, were focused on their own dreams, goals, aspirations and competitions. They ensured their son's every need was met; but rather than doing so with affection and attention, they did so by finance and proxy.

Felix's mother, Nirupa Agrawal Hess, was born in Calcutta. She came to the States as an undergrad and never left. She launched lauded departments of Asian Studies at not one but two of the dozens of universities that populated (over-populated, some locals might gripe) the Boston metro area. Nirupa's parents still lived in India, where they had plenty of money. They spent none of it on their impertinent daughter, who rebelled and made a series of bad decisions—foregoing medical school for a doctorate in Asian Studies, marrying that white boy Michael Hess, getting her green card and making a life for herself on the East Coast of that tasteless Western nation.

Felix never met his maternal grandparents. He was not even sure they knew he existed. As his mother assured him curtly, the one time he asked about them, her parents wouldn't like him. They had caste systems in India, she explained. Felix's father wasn't even Indian, let alone the right kind of Indian. Marrying him had sullied her, and Felix was basically a bastard.

Nirupa was only ever in touch with one cousin, Preeti, a quiet girl many years younger than she, and only about a decade older than Felix. Preeti came to study medicine in America, and briefly stayed with the Hesses while she got on her feet. Felix was fascinated to finally meet someone from his mother's family.

"She's the good girl," Nirupa said, introducing Preeti to Felix. "Your cousin Preeti here is pre-med, makes good grades, never talks back. She makes my aunt and uncle happy the way I one hundred percent did not make my parents happy. Bet she'll even marry a nice Indian boy."

Preeti had ducked her head and said nothing.

She soon moved in to campus housing, and rarely visited. When she took a residency on the West Coast, Felix never heard from her again, probably because his parents never reached out to her. That was the extent of his familial connections on the maternal side. Grandparents who hated him (if they knew about him), quiet doctor-cousin who disappeared, and that was it.

There were stronger family ties on the paternal side. Felix's father, Michael Hess, was a research scientist who worked at a massive hospital dedicated to finding a cure for blood cancers. The product of two fiery immigrants, an Irish-Catholic mother and an

Eastern-European Jewish father, Dr. Michael Hess subscribed to no religion save science. But that was not true of his own parents; each factored God into their life equations, albeit unequally.

Catherine O'Brien Hess went to St. Richard's Catholic Church, dragging her children Michael and Rebekah along with her until they were old enough to refuse.

Morton Hess did not attend synagogue. But he played poker weekly with a group of his B'nai B'rith brothers and never ate one bite of pork, not once in his entire life. Morty Hess wouldn't let his children eat pork, either, but that's where his outward displays of religion started and stopped.

They were an odd match, Catherine and Morty. But they had enough in common to understand one another (immigrant families, an up-by-our-bootstraps attitude, the feeling of being an outsider, the fierce desire to be an insider) even if they rarely agreed with one another (she was certain he'd burn in hell, and he thought her crazy Catholic beliefs made her a lunatic). Somehow, their rickety little marriage worked, right up until Morty made an early exit.

Catherine was made a widow at fifty-two when her husband was stopped short by an aneurysm, right in the middle of an argument. He was bellowing about corruption in the government when his face blanched, he gave a small laugh, and dropped dead.

He had been brash but warm-hearted, and his death left Catherine lonely. She missed their nightly fights, and their tender, silent morning breakfasts, making amends without words as they munched on toast and stirred cheap powdered creamer into the bad instant coffee they both swore by ("who can taste the difference, anyway, and such a bargain!").

Before meeting Morty, Catherine's life was not flashy. She left Ireland at fourteen, and none of her brothers or sisters ever joined her in the States. She wanted to be close with her children, but never managed it; Michael was so serious, and even surlier than his father, while Rebecca was a wild redheaded girl who dropped out of high school and ran off at sixteen with a much older man. Although that relationship must have gone down in flames, Rebecca never came home. She died of cervical cancer in 1975; a friend of hers called Catherine with the news. It hit Catherine hard. She wept and prayed for her wayward daughter's soul, awash in regret. She always thought they would have the chance to make up, and the fact that they hadn't weighed more heavily on her than any mortal sin.

When Felix was born, he represented Catherine's last chance at family. So she offered to move in with her son and daughter-in-law to help raise her only grandchild. In the end, much to the relief of Nirupa and Michael (despite Nirupa's initial resistance to the idea of her mother-in-law moving in), Catherine did not help them raise Felix—rather, she went ahead and raised him for them, entirely on her own.

To Felix, Catherine was always Nana.

Nana was his grandmother, his nanny, his surrogate mother. He knew everything about her, as if she were an extension of himself. Her smell, a delightful mix of sweet whiskey, talcum powder, and clean linen; her laugh, low and intermittent, like the steady creaking of an old rocking chair; the soft, comforting feel of her pale papery hands.

She called him Fee, which no one else would ever be allowed to call him. It was the only nickname he ever had; to the rest of the world, he was Felix, until he finished his education, at which time he was Dr. Hess. But to Nana, he was Fee.

"Little Fee, Little Fee," Nana would coo. "You'll set the world free."

She doted, made up songs and stories for him, gave him her undivided attention. Since being fiery and firm with her own children hadn't yielded good results, the pendulum swung the other way with Felix. He was fed a steady diet of adoration, praise,

lullabies and encouragement. He was never spanked, rarely scolded; the apple of his grandmother's eye.

She shared Bible stories with the boy, which was kept hidden
from his adamantly atheist parents. Somehow even as a tiny child
Felix knew Nana's God-stories were secrets. He never repeated to
his parents anything that she told him, but he did cling to every
word. Nana told him stories of Noah and Abraham, of Moses, of
the blessed virgin Mary and her precious little baby Jesus. ("Your
grandfather, he wasn't altogether sold on those last two, but he'd
back me up on Moses, sure'n you're born," she assured little Fee.)
She told him about sacrifice, and God, and heaven. They said
prayers together at bedtime, between lullabies, behind closed
doors where his parents would not see. They even sang spirituals
and hymns.

This little light of mine. I'm gonna let it shine.

Jesus loves me this I know, for the Bible tells me so.

Joshua fought the battle of Jericho, Jericho, Jericho-ooo-ooo-ooo,
Joshua fought the battle of Jericho and the walls came tumbling down!

This last one was Felix's favorite, since he and Nana would
both fall comically to the floor, laughing, just like those Jericho
walls.

They spent the days outside all summer, and when the New
England winds turned crisp, leaves converting from gentle green
to brilliant reds and golds and finally to dried-out brown tum-
bling-down, they moved the songs and stories inside. There they
baked cakes and cookies and breads. Autumn was a warm, heady
kitchen, scented with molasses and raisins. Winter was for co-
coa and stories while it snowed outside. And then, soon enough,
spring returned.

When Felix was five, his family rented a cottage on Cape Cod,
a seaside town filled with stone-and-thatched homes, cluttered
little restaurants offering mouth-watering fresh lobster rolls, clam
chowder, and fried morsels of small sea creatures just-snatched

from the water. The beaches were rocky, and everywhere carried the smell of salt and sound of seagulls.

The whole family went to the Cape—Felix, his parents, his Nana. But once there, his parents set about networking with a vengeance. Nirupa and Michael had no taste for relaxation. What they did have was a large collection of colleagues who frequented the Cape. Some, like his parents, rented or time-shared miniature mansions. Others owned their vast seaside homes, and these were the ones whom his parents aspired to someday be: Wealthy, stylish, East Coast intellectuals with humongous homes for every season.

His parents had a party to attend every evening at a different New England castle. They stayed out late and slept in later. They might join Fee and Nana for lunch, but even if they made an appearance to share fried oysters and shoestring potatoes, they would then disappear into their bedroom, arguing an academic point raised the night before, scenting the indoor air with perfume and shoe polish as they prepared for the night ahead, already anticipating the impending benders of boozy envy and the status-hungry hangovers that would devour them again the next morning.

Felix didn't care. His parents could have their horrible, greedy vacation. The one he was on with Nana was far better than parties and fancy clothes and nonsense words like ten-your, whatever that meant.

Nana and Fee rose early, walking the beachfront before anyone else was there, gathering shells and stepping carefully around dead jellyfish washed up by the tide. After their morning walk they'd come home to eat a large breakfast of Nana's homemade Irish soda bread slathered with strawberry jam. Since they were near the water, Nana felt compelled to teach her grandson all the shanty songs of her youth, Irish song-stories of boats crashing into rock and young maidens scanning o'er the seas for their likely-dead sailor-loves.

The tales of young husbands lost at sea and young wives who threw themselves from lighthouses, staunching the pain of their broken hearts by dashing their bodies against stone, were a bit dark for one so young. But Felix had no happy Disney-edited fairy tales to compare these stories to, and thereby assumed that most stories ended in death. It didn't upset him a bit.

Lots of time was spent on the beach. Nana would lay out on a fluffy towel, cheering equally loudly when Fee built rounded piles of wet sand and declared them castles—and when he knocked them down, bringing enthusiastic destruction to his own creations. After lunch, they wandered into the charming little village if the day was nice, or curled up with books in the cottage if the skies were unfriendly. Each day brought its own adventures; one day, they watched a wedding party lining up for the ceremony in one of their Cape neighbors' beautiful backyards.

"Look at that pretty bride," Catherine pointed at a woman in a billowing white dress. "And that handsome groom! Oh, I love weddings. They're a gift, sure'n you're born. Someday I'll dance at your wedding, if the Lord lets me. Oh, look there, Fee! Someone's wavin' at us!"

Sure enough, the groom had lifted an arm in greeting. Felix and his grandmother waved back, arms high and fingers wide, enjoying their almost-attendance of the celebration.

At night, unless it was pouring rain, they walked to the pier, looking for seals and dolphins, watching the setting sun. On the next to last day of that magical summer in Cape Cod, Felix was splashing in the waves, pretending to scan the waters for a dead sailor, when he heard his grandmother yelling from the shore.

"Michael!" She was screaming. "Michael, you come back here this minute!"

Felix looked around for his father, Michael. It took him a few moments to realize that though she was calling his father's name, his grandmother was directing her cries at him. Felix, in the sea. He came in from the water, confused as he approached her. For reasons he could not explain or understand, the little boy felt almost afraid. He asked, scared: "Nana, what's wrong?"

"Sure'n you know better than that, Michael! What were you thinking? You can't swim."

"I'm not Michael, Nana. I'm Fee. And I'm a good swimmer—"

"Don't go giving me that lip, boy!" She said, and smacked him hard, right across his small face.

Felix's eyes filled with tears, but he held in his wail. Placing his hand on his cheek, pressing against the welling red where her open palm had landed, he kept his eyes on her as he slowly backed away. He repeated, firmly, in his quiet little-boy voice: "I'm Fee. I'm Fee."

He knew if he just kept saying it, she would understand. And so he just kept saying it, keeping his distance so she couldn't hit him, repeating over and over and over: *I'm Fee I'm Fee I'm Fee I'm Fee*, until at last something flickered in her eyes. Recognition.

"Oh God, oh my sweet little Fee. I'm so sorry, oh bless you, oh my wee little man. Did I hurt you? Oh, Jesus, Joseph and Mary..."

She sank to her knees in the sand, beckoning him to return to her. He hesitated for a moment, cheek still singing, but then went to her. She hugged him tightly. He stood stoic, troubled, wanting her to be who she had always been, but knowing something was different now. At age five, he instinctively knew. Things had changed, and they would never be the same. Nana was broken. Like his He-Man toy with the snapped off leg. He glued it back on, but it was never the same. The damage was done.

They did not tell his parents about the incident on the beach. It was another of their secrets, but this one wretched. The details of her lapse at the beach could be kept quiet, but the bigger, scarier truth about Nana was not a secret that would keep for long.

Their final day in Cape Cod dawned salty and perfect. Felix was afraid Nan would be different again, but she was herself that day. Little Felix savored and imprinted every moment of that sun-soaked morning. The walk, the shanty-singing biscuit-breakfast, the swim, the village, the last sunset on the pier, all the way through to the bedtime wrapped in homemade lullabies: "Little Fee, Little Fee... you'll set the world free. Always part of me, always mine you'll always be. But Fee, Little Fee: you'll need more, ye see. You'll be the one to set the world free."

The next morning, the Hess family returned home to Waltham. A few weeks later, Felix started kindergarten. His grandmother began forgetting things more frequently, almost as if his absence exacerbated her condition. She started leaving the oven on after she baked biscuits, forgetting to pack lunch for Felix, mixing up words. She began talking in her sleep, repeating names and dates and places. Felix would stand outside her door, hearing her repeat the names in her sleep, knowing she had to stop. She had to, or his parents would get rid of her. They had no patience for difficult or inconvenient things.

He crept into her room one night, listening as she repeated: "Cork to Ellis to here to there, but where but where but where, Cork to Ellis to here to there, but where but where but where..." Then she began whispering, over and over: "Rebecca... Rebecca... Rebecca..."

He put his small hand over her mouth, trying to stem the tide, to stop the words. She talked around his hand, like he wasn't even there. He thought about putting a second hand over her mouth, but feared suffocating her.

A few short weeks later, she forgot to put up the garage door before backing out, leaving a tremendous dent in the garage door, the Volvo, and her family's trust.

Nana was sent to what his parents called simply "a home." Felix hated them calling it that; home was home, period. Felix saw Nana only on Sundays, when Michael would grudgingly go visit. Nirupa never joined them—she always had an excuse, papers to grade or a committee meeting. She never cared for her mother-in-law, and dementia added no appeal.

Felix hated the nursing home, its antiseptic smell, the old unkempt strangers sitting in wheelchairs in the lobby, some yelling, some crying, some staring. But he never missed the chance to see his beloved Nana. She was still the only real parent he had ever known, his light in the darkness. But she faded more and more as time went on. When she first moved to the nursing home, she always knew who he was when he visited. By the time he was nine, she never did.

He realized they had reached the inevitable part of the story. He was the Irish lass, looking out over the craggy rocks for his lost love; Nana was the dead sailor, lost in the depths of the indifferent sea.

His Nana had disappeared, and into the shell of her body a sad stranger had taken up residence. Like some sort of human hermit crab. He hated this invader, the not-Nana residing in her old body. This stranger. This *interloper*.

One dreary March day, the sort where rain threatens but never delivers on its promise and the entire day stretches out into one long and ultimately forgettable gray moment, Felix went to visit his grandmother. He needed to determine for himself once and for all if anything of her remained.

He rode his bicycle the five miles to the nursing home, alone, knowing his parents wouldn't miss him. He propped his bicycle up against the Victorian-style railing of the nursing home. It was just a façade. The outside looked old-fashioned in a nice way, but the inside was all bedpans and despair. It was the waiting room for death.

Felix did not check in at the front desk. The kindly buxom black nurse behind the desk probably assumed that he was meeting up with some adult family member who had already signed in or would do so shortly. She acknowledged his entrance only with a friendly nod, and Felix did not see even that. He walked directly into Catherine O'Brien Hess' room.

She was sitting in a chair, gazing out the window. Someone had dressed her, costuming her like a generic grandmother. The clothing did not look like her own. Felix noted with disdain the bright yellow crocheted shawl draped across her thin shoulders. It had garish blue flowers, badly patched here and there to cover rips in the crochet. Nana would never wear that.

But he was not there to assess her wardrobe. He was there to see if she was still there. He needed to determine this for himself, reach a conclusion based on fact. Just as he had been learning in his science class: come up with a hypothesis, then design experiments and measures to put the hypothesis to the test, and either disprove it or determine that it might, in fact, be true.

That's what Felix found most frustrating about hypotheses: easy to disprove, impossible to prove. Which was infuriating, but also intoxicating. Felix's hypothesis was that although she may have left her body behind, his Nana was gone. Her intrinsic Nana-ness was no more. If this was the case, he'd make his peace with it and move on. He would no longer need to join his father to visit the vacant-eyed woman in Nana's old body.

Felix had devised a three-part experiment to test his hypothesis: first, a physical assessment; second, a cognitive test, to see if she had any intellectual capacity; and finally, an interactive emotional evaluation.

She was failing the physical assessment based on appearance alone, but the assessment wasn't simply about appearance. He stepped directly into her line of sight, standing between her and the window. He'd gone to the natural science museum last year, and was unsettled by the dead glass eyes of the animals on display. She looked very much like one of his least favorite feral corpses, one that still frequented his nightmares—a taxidermied silver-faced raccoon, clinging to a strip of bark.

Felix steeled himself and gathered some skin from the fold of his grandmother's arm. Feeling a flicker of guilt, he pinched her. Hard.

She did not cry out. She did not move.

So he moved on to the cognitive test. He pulled a notebook from his backpack, and asked her question after question. *What day is it today? Where are you? What is your name? Where were you born?* He noted her response, the same to each question: Nothing. Silence.

She had failed his first two tests. But the third and final was the most critical. He took her face in his hands, turning her cloudy eyes toward his own. When he spoke, his voice cracked.

"Nana," he said. "It's me. Fee. I love you. I love you very much. You are the only person who has ever loved me, and I need to know if you still do. If you love me, tell me. Tell me. And if you do, I will come see you every day. I promise. But if you don't… if you're not there… I will never come see you again."

For a moment, there was no response. And then her eyes shifted. Focused. The clouds cleared, and she met and held his gaze for one single, perfect second.

"Oh, God," she said. "Fee."

"Yes," he breathed, feeling weak.

"We didn't have enough time, Fee. You need more time… we need more time…"

His heart soared and sank and battered around his chest like a bird. But then her eyes closed. And when they opened again, they were the dead raccoon eyes. And before he could say or do anything, she opened her mouth, looked somewhere past him—and screamed.

She screamed as if she were being murdered, a bloodcurdling cry that filled the room and sent Felix scrambling away from her. He grabbed his backpack, leaving the notebook behind, and bolted from the room. Her scream followed him down the hallway, past the nurses sleepily making their way to the sound of the room to see which invalid was yelling and why.

His father was mildly surprised the following Sunday when he asked Felix if he was ready to go for their weekly visit and received a negative response. But he did not ask his son why. He simply shrugged "Suit yourself," and went without him.

Much to his own heartbreak, Felix's very first hypothesis, put to the test at the tender age of twelve, had proven more true than most. This secured his belief in science and unseated his belief in God. Prayer wrought nothing. Science at least gave him an answer.

His parents did not move in to fill the void in his life left by Nana; they merely widened the chasm, placing more people and more distance between themselves and their son. Nana was replaced by nannies. For the brief remainder of his youth, Felix was dumped on a long parade of foreign au pairs, empty-nesters turned nannies, broke students studying under his parents, or sullen neighbor kids. Felix hated them all, and they all hated him. None lasted more than three months, and that was only because the Hess parents paid handsomely.

When he reached high school, Felix was deemed old enough to care for himself. This was his preference, but it also meant that there was no one to greet him when he came home from school, or to remind him to eat something other than potato chips, or to take the call that he answered from the nursing home, informing him that Catherine O'Brien Hess had passed away in her sleep.

By this time, Felix was sixteen. Since he had lost her long before then, he expected to feel nothing when he found out that his grandmother had stopped breathing. Much to his surprise, when he got the news, his eyes went hot and wet, and he tasted sea-salt in his mouth.

The funeral was a colorless blur. The only moment of the service when Felix felt anything at all was when he saw his father check his watch. Furious, Felix felt a strong urge to reach over and snap his father's arm in two.

Felix finished high school early. Feeling little connection to his parents and having less than zero desire to become a student in their tight-knit East Coast academic circles, he applied only to schools on the West Coast: Cal-Tech, Stanford. When he got in to Stanford on a full academic scholarship, Felix informed his parents that they could feel free to turn his bedroom into a study, because he never intended to return home. He never did.

Palo Alto, California was a shiny new world for Felix, and he did not particularly like it. After his childhood in New England, California was abrasive. Too much sunshine, too many shallow sorority girls and overconfident frat guys, too many wide highways and absurd palm trees and weirdly cheerful people in sunglasses. (The Bay Area was bad enough; Los Angeles would have killed him.)

Hess wanted to get his undergraduate degree checked off the list as quickly as possible. Summer school was an obvious move. He also petitioned the registrar's office to allow him to take more than the maximum allowable course-load. When his request was rejected by both the registrar and the dean of students, he scheduled an appointment with the university president. The president was so impressed with the bright, diligent young student's initiative that he did something unprecedented: gave him a waiver, allowing him to enroll in as many courses as he wished, every semester, so long as he only took on what he knew he could complete.

Though good-looking, with sharp striking features and darklashed eyes, Felix had no social aptitude. Which was fine, since he also had zero social interest. He didn't want to date. He didn't have a girlfriend. Instead, he had a rival.

Her name was Claudia.

Claudia Lee was young; she finished high school at fifteen, spent two years studying in a private biogenetic lab in Beijing, and was still only seventeen when she enrolled at Stanford. At five feet tall, she was easy to overlook in a crowd. But the girl was impossible to miss in the classroom. Her hand was perpetually aloft, her papers often distributed as examples. In class rankings, she was always either first or second—directly below or directly above Felix.

"You're Felix Hess," Claudia said, finding him as he strode across the quad, en route from organic chemistry to bio lab. She fell in step with him and cracked open a Red Bull.

"I am," he said, not slowing his pace.

"I'm Claudia Lee. Sometimes you're at the top of the Dean's List, and sometimes it's me. Just thought you should know—I like being on top."

The innuendo flew right past him. "Don't we all."

She smirked, assuming a returned flirtation that wasn't actually there. "Well. I'm graduating first in our class. Just so you know. But if you're interested in a consolation prize—"

"Good luck with that," Hess said, and took advantage of his longer legs to outpace her, not hearing anything after *first in our class.*

He couldn't stay ahead of her for long, though. A few minutes after he reached his lab, the same chirping voice trilled in his ear: "Aw, are you in this section? Looks like I'm your T.A.. Want a cookie?"

He locked eyes with Claudia Lee, who held a tray of fresh baked goods (her first-day-of-class tradition: give treats to the students before making them crumble like cookies).

"But you're an undergrad," Hess protested.

"I know," she grinned, marveling at herself.

Felix went straight to the registrar to switch lab sections.

But this too was insufficient in ridding himself of Claudia. She was in his phys-chem class the next day. But at least she wasn't teaching it. When she saw him, she dropped her book bag in the seat beside him.

"Future overlords should stick together," she said. "So. What's your end game?"

"What?"

"How are you going to save, end, or take over the world?"

He almost didn't want to tell her; he felt certain if he did, she might want to take it from him; or worse, share it with him.

But his ego got the better of him, and on the off chance he might be mentioning something she didn't know much about, he said: "Cyborganics."

"Figures," she said, neither surprised nor impressed. "I'm AI, all the way."

Hess barely managed to not roll his eyes. Artificial intelligence was an interesting thought experiment, but ultimately pointless. He didn't believe robots would overthrow their inventors or anything stupid like that, he just didn't think the best use of technology was something separated from man. Reinventing wheels didn't interest him; building upon what already existed was a smarter tactic.

"Why AI?" He asked, only half-interested in her reply.

"I like playing God," she said.

"It's a good game," he allowed. He could respect her motive if not her method.

"You want to have a drink sometime? Not to brag, but I'm kind of into wine and I just got this killer bottle of—"

"I don't really drink," Hess said, which was more or less true. He certainly didn't "get drinks" with people.

"Suit yourself," she shrugged. "But you're missing out. No wine? No baked goods? You might be able to prolong life, buddy, but you're sure not gonna enjoy it."

Claudia and Felix did not become friends. But they did become lab partners, occasional study-buddies, and constant competitors. Against his better judgment, Felix found himself beginning to warm to her. Maybe sharing research with her down the road wouldn't be so bad. She was bright, she was a workhorse, and he had to admit her baking was phenomenal. But then one night while studying for their p-chem final, Claudia pulled the rug out from under him.

"I'm transferring," she told him. "Going somewhere that'll let me focus on AI. Get my hands dirty with real experiments, not bullcrap to prove how well we know the boring basics."

"Transferring where?" Hess asked.

"Well, that's the catch," she said. "The school I want to go to isn't technically open yet. But that means I could get in on the ground floor when—"

"Don't transfer," he said abruptly. "This is Stanford."

"Stanford is way behind on the AI front—"

"AI, Jesus," he grimaced. "AI's like having kids—showing off what you can make. Some new shiny little thing. Shouldn't you tap into your own potential?"

He tapped her forehead, surprising both of them, but she didn't flinch. She stared at him.

"Go on."

"Artificial intelligence, robots, aliens... that's all fantasy-bull-shit. It's not going to be something outside of us or beyond us that takes us to the next level," he said, getting excited as he articulated what he had long believed. "If we want to rise up, we can't be lifted by something else. It can't be something wholly external. It has to be us."

By *us*, Felix Hess really meant *me*, but Claudia Lee missed the subtext and took his hand.

"Us, huh?" She took a sticky note from her binder and pressed it to his forehead.

"What? No," Hess said, dropping her small hand and gathering his things. "If we're done studying, I have an article to read."

"Right," she said, grabbing the sticky note from his forehead and crumpling it before he could see what she had scrawled upon it. "Yeah, me too."

After that semester, he saw less and less of Claudia Lee. They both planned to graduate early, which left little time for interaction anyway. Hess completed his undergraduate studies in two and a half years, thanks to summer coursework. He triple-majored in computer science, organic chemistry, and biochemistry, and tossed in a minor in philosophy, figuring that counted as "having a little fun in college," something everyone kept assuring him he should do.

As the number one student in his class, he was offered the role of valedictorian. He turned it down, since that was not the sort of thing that interested him—although years later, he would regret turning down the platform to address his peers. Not that he would have known back then how to speak to them in any sort of inspiring or memorable way. And not that most of the idiots at Stanford would have even been capable of really listening.

Claudia Lee gave the commencement address. Felix wasn't even there to hear it. Having gotten what he needed from Stanford, Felix returned to Massachusetts.

It wasn't a sentimental homecoming; having family there was the biggest strike against the Boston area. But he had full funding at the Massachusetts Institute of Technology, and more than that, he had an obsession. There was a scientist who taught part-time at MIT but spent most of his time doing fully-funded research in cyborganics. And Hess needed to meet him.

Cyborganics was still over the heads of most, and against the morals of many. The man championing the efforts was a polarizing figure, a maverick pioneering the new Wild West of medicine, technology, humanity. They called him, among other things, the Cyborganics Cowboy.

Felix's own obsession with cyborganics metastasized as he plowed his way through Stanford. The technology had so much potential. It could fix faulty human wiring, eradicating everything from learning disabilities to autoimmune disorders and all manner of disease. Most intriguing to Felix were the implications for addressing memory loss, and perhaps the entire aging process. It raised as many moral questions as potential benefits, but Felix didn't care. Let others sort out the ethics; he was done with his philosophy minor.

He knew he had to have the Cyborganics Cowboy as a mentor, and his best shot was to impress him in the classrooms at MIT. That was the reason Felix returned to Massachusetts: to become the protégé of the man the media couldn't stop nicknaming: "Cyborganics Cowboy." "Robot Prophet." "The Synthetic Moses."

The Synthetic Moses reminded him of something his Nana had once said, about how his grandfather would agree with her about Moses. In due time, Hess became the Joshua to his mentor's Moses.

One Tuesday morning shortly after he began his first semester at MIT, men with angry souls flew airplanes into buildings. This sent the world into a panic, and everyone around him into a political fervor. One of these airplanes took off from Logan Airport, just a handful of miles from campus. Police were suddenly everywhere. Flags appeared on every porch. Students marched in rallies. A world away, a war began—or continued, depending on who you asked.

But Felix had only one thought in regards to the tragic events of September 11, 2001, and everything that followed: *The pace continues to accelerate.*

Stubbornness served Felix well. It was stubbornness that landed him the fellowship with his mentor, the front-row seat to the Singularity, the director's position at the Synt. He sees that same stubbornness in his daughter, which both pleases and irks him. He knows that she is too smart, too independent, and too beautiful for her own good. At a very young age, now forever maintained, his daughter had become the sort of woman who should come with a warning label.

She's too damn much like me, he thinks, rubbing his short bristly beard. *But better she turn out to be too much like me than too much like her idiot mother.*

Enjoy the joy ride, Ever. It'll all be over soon.

CHAPTER 12: EVER

KISSING. LOTS OF KISSING. The sort of kissing that enthralls those engaged in the activity and appalls anyone unfortunate enough to witness it. Luckily no one is around to be disgusted by Ere and Ever's tangling tongues as they explore a world of new sensations.

"Curse of the world," Ere gasps between kisses.

"Is that a good thing or a bad thing?" Ever asks, laughing.

"Yes," he says, and they allow the kisses to overtake the conversation again. But after another few fevered moments, the boy whispers: "I've never…"

"Never what?" Ever whispers back, moving her hand down his torso, her palm resting against his firm stomach. "Had sex?"

"Curse of the—no!" Ere sputters, reddening. "Kissed. I've never… kissed anyone."

At the shock of this information, Ever laughs harder. Ere immediately pulls away from her, hot-faced. Realizing her blunder, Ever hurries to reassure him.

"I'm not laughing at you! I'm not!" She covers his face with kisses, runs her hands down his arms, reassuring him. "I've just never met anyone even less experienced than I am."

Somehow, this clarification fails to mollify Ere.

"Yeah, well," he mutters, turning his face from her. "Not a lot of opportunity for this sort of thing in my life."

"Mine either," says Ever.

"Yeah, right," he says, doubt and insecurity scrawled across his face.

"It's true," she says, and it is.

Ever was still two months shy of her eighteenth birthday when she became a Syn. Underage synchs were formally made illegal weeks later, a direct result of her father's actions in pushing her procedure through so quickly. When it became clear that there might be an indefinite freeze on synchs until the uprisings were handled, Hess decided that his entire family needed to be set, prior to any hiatus. Records indicate he also petitioned the Council about some "long-term benefits" related to her synch, but kept whatever those long-term benefits might be tightly under wraps.

Ever's father was also always maniacally protective of her body. Before and after synching, she was kept under lock and key. Always a dependent. Never an adult. And certainly never allowed to interact, alone, with members of the opposite sex. Which didn't mean she had never interacted, alone, with members of the opposite sex. It just meant it wasn't allowed, and if ever Ever's father got hold of her private mode memories, she'd have some explaining to do. Still, she was a virgin. Technically. (As she put it once in a memoir she started writing: "If a massive disease swept through the land and killed all of the non-virgins, I'd get really, really sick… but I'd pull through.")

She's never understood her father's fanaticism about her purity. She knows that historically, sex was hazardous. There used to be horrible diseases and unintended pregnancies; but these risks were eliminated for Syns. Avoiding overt promiscuity was a matter of propriety, but sex wasn't taboo—not even premarital sex, because while marriage was still practiced, it wasn't a go-to choice for everyone. '*Til death do us part* became an intimidating prospect once death was staved off indefinitely.

A small subset of Syns even underwent a hormone-modification treatment to regulate libido, decreasing desire and eliminating that distraction so they could focus on self-actualization. Ever was surprised her father had never suggested she adhere to a lust-suppressing regimen, but then again he deemed most elective treatments or unnecessary supplements unwise. He wanted his daughter's organic components maintained, not modified.

Ever has no idea how the hell she could possibly explain any of this to Ere.

Ere's eyes travel her body meaningfully before lifting again to meet hers. "I'm sure someone like you has had plenty of … opportunities."

"I haven't," Ever says. "My father's protective. And I don't meet many … eligible men."

"You're… you look my age," said Ere. "I thought Syns were older."

"They are. Except for me. But you're young, too. I thought all Originals were older…?"

"They are, except for me," Ere says quickly, willing Cal out of existence. (Technically, Cal is older… only three years older, but still.) "They're mostly really old."

"Well, that sounds like destiny. The youngest Original. The youngest Syn," she says, giving just enough of a shrug that the sleeve of her garment slips slightly down her shoulder. "You should probably kiss me again."

"I… should…uh…" He seems suddenly unable to cobble together a sentence, poor thing, but he does manage to kiss her.

He's clumsy, fumbling. He bites her bottom lip accidentally, and drools a little. She's into it. The increasing heat makes her feel alive, connected. Her thirst is forgotten as she hungers only for Ere, leaning in as his hands roam across her body, finding every curve, tracing his fingers down her torso, and she feels so warm, so warm… and then too warm. And then the pain in her foot asserts itself again.

Heaven and Hell.

She taps Ere gently on the chest, then sits on the ground and exhales sharply. She peels off her shoe and makeshift leaf-bandage, exposing an oozing wound. He drops to the ground beside her, face painted with concern.

"Injured in my escape," she says, wincing slightly. "Cut my foot, on a rock or shell or something. When I was in the water."

"Well, the water might've helped you clean it out, but might've also swept germs in. Have you put anything on it since you got out of the water?"

"Just these leaves."

"Wait here."

The Original boy lopes off, before she can tell him not to worry. When she returns home, she'll receive medical treatment and be as good as new. Still, the throbbing's unpleasant. She hasn't experienced this much pain. Not since her synch. Any discomfort was immediately treated. Syn palliative care, for troubles from moderate to severe, was quick and effective.

"Here, let's see."

The boy is back, already, several plants in his hand. She does not recognize them; they are not the same leaves she procured based on Heaven's recommendations. Without the archives at her immediate disposal, she will just have to trust the boy. With a practiced hand, he tears one end off of a long, spindly plant, and squeezes out a gelatinous liquid. "This will attack bacteria, stave off potential infection. Helps the burn, too."

He gently rubs the juice of the plant on to her wound, unfazed by the ugly cut. The application stings, but only mildly. He gently re-packs her foot. These leaves wrap more easily around her foot than the ones she had found. Once the wrapping is in place, he picks up the last of the plants—a strong, deep-green vine—and uses it to bind and secure the plant bandage.

"I'm—a bit warm—" She hates having to say this, seeing the conflicting emotions cross the boy's face as he remembers that she is a Syn, overheating because she's part-machine.

"Do you... would water help?" He's off again, and soon returns with water in his wooden bucket. She forgot he had that bucket. She knows this should make her realize something, but she's having trouble connecting dots. She's so hot... she takes the bucket from him.

"Wait!" Ere cries. "It hasn't been purified or tested or—"

"It won't hurt me," she says, and slurps at the water, closing her eyes in ecstasy at the coolness of it. He watches, wordlessly, and she knows he'll stay as long as she wants him to—which is even more delicious than the water. Something still tickles at the back of her mind; she'll remember it in a minute, just as soon as she cools down a little.

CHAPTER 13: RUTH

SOMETHING'S WRONG.

Ruth knows it in her gut. It's not that Ere has been gone for too terribly long. He hasn't; not considering his exhaustion from all of their traveling of late, or the fact that he wasn't as good a water-finder as Cal. It's just a gut feeling, and Ruth trusts her gut a hell of a lot more than any other part of her body.

"Cal!"

She does not call loudly. There is no need alarm the elders, and it does not take much volume to get Cal's attention. He has the ears of a hunter, alert to any small sound, always ready.

He is behind her immediately, silent, but she doesn't flinch at his approach.

"I need you to find Ere."

Cal nods, no questions asked. "I'll go now."

"He'll be easy to track," Ruth says. "The boy steps on every twig in his path." Then she adds, as an afterthought: "And if he hasn't found water yet, find some, all right?"

Cal grins, and Ruth allows a small smile in return as they both acknowledge Ere's deficiencies. Then without further comment, Cal turns and sets off after his cousin. Ruth's mind calms, knowing Cal will swiftly locate Ere and ensure his safety.

"Everything all right?"

Helena Garrison approaches Ruth, her gaze on Cal's swiftly disappearing back.

"Everything's fine," Ruth says smoothly. "I just sent Cal to go help Ere. We'll need plenty of water brought back."

"Ah," Helena replies. "He should've taken a bucket, then."

Ruth smiles, reminded she's not the only strong, sharp-witted woman in the tribe. And then, falling into a task they have shared for so long they never need name it, the women set about scouring the immediate area for edible plants, berries, and perhaps even any still-stocked freeboxes or old storage centers or cellars where they might find more food. Ruth's stomach rumbles loudly.

Her gut has a lot to say today.

CHAPTER 14: ERE

E RE AND EVER SIT, SIDE BY SIDE, not sure what
to say or do next. For all its intensity, sudden attraction
is also confusing and stilted. Neither is fluent in the language. And so the boy and the girl just sit in the grass, under the
trees. The steady hum of bird and bug provides a soundtrack for
their awkwardness; tension seeps from their pores in thick beads
of sweat.

Ere tries to think of something to say. Something that will
make him sound appealing, smart, funny. Something magical,
basically. He comes up short, lamely lobbing a question her way.

"Tell me how you ran away?"

She stretches, arching her back prettily: "We were on a cruise.
Costa Rica. But it was just awful. Just my mother and me and
our maid. I couldn't leave the boat, couldn't go explore anything.

107

So damn scheduled. I wanted some excitement. Something like…
you."

Encouraged, he leans over, placing his mouth on hers. She
eagerly returns his kiss; encouraged, he moves in closer. Seated
beside her on the ground, the angle is awkward, but the boy is
willing to work with what he's given. He leans in to her warm
body, shifting his weight—and knocking her arm from beneath
her, causing her to fall back. He lands on her as they fall the short
distance from sitting to lying on the forest floor.

"Oh—I'm so sorry—are you all right? I'm sorry—"

He quickly props himself up, his eyes searching hers, apolo-
getic and terrified. But she laughs, grabs his shirt, pulls him all
the way on top of her. He can barely breathe, he is sweating pro-
fusely, and he feels absolutely certain that no one in the history of
the entire world has ever been as fortunate as he, Ere Fell, in this
very moment. Ever grabs his arm, releasing his supporting hand,
causing him to buckle, his full weight now pressing her into the
ground. She runs her fingers through his hair, down his neck and
the length of his spine, finally landing on the small of his back,
grabbing him and pulling him against her—

Suddenly, her hand moves with lightning speed from his back
to his chest, pushing him away and off of her. He rolls to the side,
landing heavily on the earth, on his back. Ever crouches above
him, her hand still on his chest but her eyes elsewhere. He manages to form a single word:

"What—"

But before he can finish the question, her hand moves again,
from his chest to his mouth, silencing him. Her eyes dart to the
left, then up. Giving him a look that clearly says *keep quiet*, she
stands up, soundlessly, and cocks her head. Listening.

Then he hears it, too: a soft electric hum, somewhere in the
distance.

"Chariot. Nearby." Her voice is hushed, focused. "I'm still in private mode—they must have tracked the vehicle I took. I should have thought—dammit. Tree."

"Tree?"

"Climb a tree. Hide. Now."

Ere launches himself toward a tall, solid oak several yards away. He shimmies up the trunk, and no sooner does he reach a high, thick branch than the approaching hovercraft zooms up to Ever. Ere, hidden by leaves and branches, strains to hear the conversation below him.

A man steps off the hovercraft, removing his helmet.

"Lance Briggs. Transportation Deputy, Sector 27. I'm here to retrieve the Chariot you stole, and get you back to your family."

"Well, you caught me, Deputy," says Ever. "So what happens now? Specifically?"

"My supervisor isn't pleased at your theft of his property. But he respects your father, and will write off the minor infraction if the Chariot is undamaged." The Deputy pauses, receives another transmission, blinks. "And your father requests that you exit private mode."

"Fine. I'll shift my settings. After I… relieve myself."

"In the woods? Are you sure you wouldn't rather… wait until we reached the port?"

"I'm afraid the need is too urgent for that."

"Understood." A curt nod. "After you relieve yourself, we will return to the station. I've been given strict instructions to escort you, ensuring the safe return of yourself and the vehicle."

Ever points into the distance: "The Chariot I took is close, right? Go grab it and give me a little privacy. I won't run off, I know I can be located, and anyway I'm overheating. Okay?"

The deputy hesitates, then nods. He puts his helmet back on, climbs back up on his vehicle and glides off to retrieve the other Chariot. Ever walks swiftly to Ere's tree.

"Ere!"

"Don't worry, I'm not looking!" He whispers and turns his face away.

"What do you mean you're not—Heaven and Hell. I don't really have to piss, dummy."

"Oh," he says, his face flushing idiot red.

"Listen. Your tribe should stay here. There's clean water. It's far enough away from a station to be safe, and I've been on private mode this whole time so no one will know you're here. And if you stay here … I'll be able to find you."

He grins, a smile stupider than his blush. "So I'll see you again."

"If you're lucky."

"If *you're* lucky—" He starts to tease back, but she shuts him down.

"Be. Quiet. *And stay up there* until you can't hear or see the Chariots!"

He opens his mouth to say something more, but the look she gives him shuts him up. He leans back against the trunk of his tree, leaves hiding him once more. She disappears from view. He hears the hovercrafts start, listens as the electric hum goes from near to far to nonexistent.

He drops to the ground from a low branch. He lands lightly, but feels his knees nearly buckle under him. His entire being vibrates, already feeling a void. He will not feel right until he sees her again. His damp hair clings to his neck, and he can feel each strand. He can feel *everything*. His body is alive and alert and making requests like never before. He is drenched in sweat and longing, shirt plastered to his chest, body on fire. Ere now has a mission in life, one that will propel every step forward from this moment.

Get back to Ever.

CHAPTER 15: MARILYN

MARILYN HESS SIPS HER BITTER COFFEE. Angela put two creamers in the coffee before serving it, as always. But this morning, it tastes awful; it tastes like punishment. Marilyn takes one more sip, then puts it aside, disgusted. After another moment, though, she pulls the mug back to her and takes another bitter sip. She doesn't know what else to do; old habits are all she has left.

She received a curt message from her husband's assistant five minutes ago, informing her that Ever had been found. So, her daughter would be home soon. But her husband would likely avoid coming home for the next several days. When Felix was mad at Marilyn, he preferred not to see her. He'd mumbled something vaguely threatening about forks once or twice before disappearing for days on end. Marilyn was able to make out enough to know she should probably be grateful that he stayed away when enraged.

Scanning her archives, Marilyn tries to locate the most recent instance of Felix tossing an approving, thankful, or even moderately-affectionate word her way. Finding nothing in two minutes of scanning (which covered more than two decades' worth of daily details), she gives up and takes another terse sip of the coffee she now officially despises.

"Mrs. Hess?" Angela is standing in the doorway, drying her hands on her apron. "I got the message about Ever coming back. Shall I fix something for dinner she'll like? Greek, maybe? I have some grape leaves. Maybe some dolmas would be nice. She loves my dolmas. If it's something she likes, maybe she'll eat."

Marilyn takes another slow, punitive sip as she considers Angela's words. Then she sets down the cursed cup, knowing Angela will clear it away for her. She stands up, smoothing the invisible wrinkles from her dark, form-fitting dress, and shakes her head, as if making a regrettable but necessary decision.

"I've been craving salad nicoise. Make that for tonight."

"Salad nicoise?"

"Salad nicoise," Marilyn says firmly.

Both women know Ever despises salad nicoise. Selecting it for dinner is an easy way to rile the girl, to make Marilyn's anger evident, right on the plate. Ever will refuse to eat, giving Marilyn an excuse to chastise her, and the endless cold war will continue.

"If that's what you want," Angela says carefully.

"It is," Marilyn snaps. "And this coffee is terrible."

She sweeps past Angela, determined not to feel guilty. Angela says nothing. After years of knowing the Hesses, first as a friend and later as an employee, Angela is well-versed in Hess family warfare. She is familiar with each warrior's favorite weapon, from passive aggression to withheld affection to the occasional outburst of real emotion. But she herself is not a soldier in this family's war. She is a bystander who knows better than to choose a side. Marilyn wonders what side Angela would take, if anyone ever asked her opinion on a dispute.

Once upon a time, Angela had been her best and only friend. Years ago, over a much better cup of coffee (back then, Marilyn was the one who fixed the coffee), a sobbing Marilyn had begged Angela to come with them when the Hesses moved from Massachusetts and into the walls of the Synt. Later, sobbing again, she begged Angela to synch, to stay with her.

At first, Angela refused. She was a few years older than Marilyn, and not as obsessed with youth and beauty. She had a son who despised the transhumanism movement. But Marilyn pleaded, pathetic, unrelenting: *Please leave this life. This world is ending. I'll be so lonely. Come with me.*

And as she knew she would, Marilyn got her way.

Marilyn thought bringing a friend with her would make this new life easier. Bring some stability. And in a sense, it had. At Marilyn's request, back when she still had some small sway with him, Felix landed the capable math-minded Angela a solid mid-level administrative role at the Synt. For years, Angela spent her days working at the Synt. Every Sunday evening, Marilyn would have her over for coffee, and Angela would tell her about the work she was doing, the languages she was learning—French, Spanish, Mandarin, Hindi. They occasionally even discussed the uprisings, so far away from their own well-defended ivory tower.

After awhile, Marilyn grew jealous. Angela was contributing to this new society, while Marilyn sat at home. And so for a third time, a sobbing Marilyn begged: *Felix won't let me work and I'm so lonely. Live with us. Take care of us. Help me with Ever.*

Again, Marilyn got her way. She was delighted at the prospect of an ally at home. But things didn't work out as planned.

Hiring Angela to keep house altered the dynamic of their friend-
ship. Making coffee went from being Marilyn's pleasure to being
Angela's job. Neither can remember when Angela began referring
to her as "Mrs. Hess;" when they went from friends to The Boss
and The Help. But at some point, it happened. Marilyn gave orders. Angela followed them. Like tonight: Marilyn declared the
Battle of Salad Nicoise, and Angela would have to prepare the
battlefield.

"Start boiling the eggs," Marilyn says, and Angela returns
wordlessly to the kitchen.

CHAPTER 16: ERE

ERE WALKS BACK TOWARD THE TRIBE IN A blissful haze. He's been away too long. His mother will be worried, and they'll all be waiting on the water—which, fortunately, he'd located when Ever needed the cooling water. He's lugging not one, but two full-to-the-brim buckets—the one he brought on his expedition, and another he found by the stream. Those buckets, along with his knowledge of where to refill him, will keep him from being in too much trouble.

But all of those thoughts are lounging lazily in the back of his mind. Up front, he is eagerly replaying every moment spent with Ever, and imagining new and more naked scenarios featuring the two of them. His distracted brain takes too long to register a strange, subtle sound—a rustling leaf in the windless night. Before he has time to notice a thing, the buckets are jerked from his arms and he is shoved to the ground.

"Where in Heaven and Hell have you been?"

"Hell, Cal," says Ere, rubbing his shoulder and glaring. "Why'd you knock me down?"

"Because you let me," Cal says. Holding the brimming buckets without spilling a drop, he fixes his stern gaze on his younger cousin. "Where were you?"

"I found a water source," says Ere, gesturing to the buckets. Then, unable to stop himself, he lifts an eyebrow and adds simply: "And."

Cal's own brow lifts. "And?"

"And..."

"Boys!"

Ruth appears out of nowhere, on the warpath, her sharp voice and angry mouth making them both flinch. They are so near the camp, she must have heard Cal ambush him. Ere hopes she didn't hear him telling Cal there was something more than water he'd found in the woods.

"Mother! I found water," Ere says quickly, hoping to head her off at the pass. "A good source! And we'll be safe here for awhile, no one's coming here. We can move the tribe closer to the water source, even. It's for the best—the traveling has been so hard on everyone..."

Ruth's eyes narrow as she looks into her son's eager face. "And just where exactly did you come by such specific information, Ere?"

Ere realizes, too late, that he should have used his walk to come up with a story to explain himself. He couldn't tell his mother, or anyone, about the Syn girl. But he'd concocted no cover. He'd been too busy replaying the heated moments with the very girl he needed to lie about. So now he was stuck, staring blankly at his mother's increasingly suspicious face.

"An old man," says Cal smoothly.

"What?" Ruth turns to Cal, still wary.

"Ere was just telling me that he crossed paths with an elderly man out in the woods," says Cal. "A remnant, you said?"

Feeling like an idiot for the umpteenth time that day, Ere exhales and nods, shooting a grateful look to his cousin. "Yes. I met an old man. A remnant. Last of his tribe. He'd passed through this territory before. So he knew. About the borders and waters and everything."

"Really. And what was his name?" Ere's mother asks.

Ere throws a wild glance at his cousin, but this time Cal stands impassive. The next lies have to come from Ere himself.

"Deputy," Ere blurts.

"Deputy?" Ruth's expression is hard, skeptical. "And he—"Deputy"—turned down your invitation to join us?"

Double damnation. Obviously, if Ere encountered an old Original wandering alone, custom and common courtesy meant he'd need to invite him to join their own tribe. Ere was quickly proving to be a real idiot at deception.

"Yes, of course. I mean, of course I asked him to join us. I offered. But he didn't want to, because he was just—passing through. He thought there might be another tribe out there who would know some of his former tribesmen," Ere is fumbling now, giving too much ludicrous information. He tries to find a stopping point. "He also had some sort of... infection."

"Infection?" His mother's eyes shift from skeptical to concerned. "What infection? Why didn't you bring him back with you, Ere? Helena could try to help ease his pain—"

"Deputy's infection wasn't anything that could be helped. It was more like...like..." Ere rushes on, his stopping point clearly not a stopping point. His mother is a skilled interrogator, and Ere a novice liar. Not good. "Like... a general sickness. He... he told me that he had already seen a healer. When he came across another tribe. Last week. Healer told him that what he just has an... old person disease. Probably. But just in case he's contagious, he kept his distance. Said he'd rather die alone than infect others. That's all I know, he wasn't very talkative."

"Not talkative? Really? He seemed to share plenty with you."

The more lies he stacks one on top of the other, the more the tower wobbles. If he weren't already drenched in sweat from the heat, the perspiration squeezed out of him by his dishonesty would give him away. So this time Ere just nods, afraid that if he opens his mouth again, nothing will come out—or worse, he'll let loose another uncontrolled, rambling lie, the one that will bring the whole great tower of untruth crashing to the ground.

Ruth is unsatisfied, but coughs again, and when the coughing subsides, so too does the interrogation. "Very well, then. Where did the second bucket come from? Deputy?"

"No. Found it by the water." Finally, an opportunity to tell the truth.

Ruth turns on her heel. Ere doesn't even have time to feel relief before Cal's large hand claps down on his bruised shoulder, making him wince.

"You're welcome, cousin. But you owe me the real story once we've relocated. *And*"—he hits this word particularly hard, hoisting the buckets again—"it better be good."

CHAPTER 17: KENNEDY

KENNEDY'S ON EDGE. The already volatile boss-man taking it up a notch is downright panic-inducing. For three nights in a row, Kennedy has had nightmares featuring pants-wetting.

The Ever mess is making Hess more irritable than usual. He's been riding Kennedy's ass, barking at Jorge, coming up with more tasks than usual for his assistants to complete. Kennedy hasn't made it home before ten any night this week. This doesn't seem to bother Jorge. But unlike his tragically boring colleague, Kennedy has a life. He likes the sort of things that living, breathing human beings tend to like—dating, day trips, decadent meals at nice restaurants.

Kennedy wishes his co-worker would at least feign a little interest in anything other than work. Or that he had any other co-workers, so he could at least bitch about his boss and about dry, dismal Jorge. He longed for the old proverbial water cooler, buddy-buddy co-workers congregating to shoot the shit. But the water cooler had gone the way of the dodo bird long ago, and talking about Hess is out of the question. The man values loyalty and discretion. If he heard that Kennedy was disparaging him, the consequences would be severe.

Still. If ever there was a week to bad-mouth the boss man, this was it. On top of his short temper and the ever-lengthening to-do list, this morning Hess had presented them with yet another unexpected task: assessing the health and mental status of every Vost.

Which, of course, included Jorge.

Unsurprisingly, the damned robot hadn't even blinked at this additional assignment. He simply nodded assent when Hess gave them their marching orders. No comment, no nothing. When Hess left the room, Jorge turned from Kennedy without a word.

Out of courtesy, Jorge's Vost status is rarely mentioned. Everyone knows, of course. The Vost code on the back of his hand is clearly visible: 5/333. He has older technology. His rights and legal standing are not the same as full Synthetic citizens. But Jorge is also Hess' personal assistant, his muscle, his longest-term employee. So, Vost or no, Jorge has little reason to flinch.

Still, if Kennedy were a Vost, he'd be less indifferent about these system-wide tests. Depending on the outcome of the assessment, there could be ramifications for Vosts. If there were malfunctions detected, serious action might be taken. You'd think that might make Jorge sweat, at least a little.

The Vost program was key to ushering in the Singularity. The final Syn template came about only after a long and arduous testing period. After the spectacular and very public failure of the first synch, many precautions were put in place to ensure no larger-scale catastrophes on the path to the Singularity. Of these, the most important step taken was the interim program, dubbed VOST—the Volunteer Synthetic Test program.

Young, healthy volunteers were sought to participate in experimental trials, testing each element of the synch process. Fusing man and machine presented numerous riddles to solve. Monkeys went first, but human testing was a vital part of the process. Language synthesis, cognitive testing, there was a lot for which there was no substitute. Volunteers were needed, and since the risks were high, rich people weren't interested in being the guinea pigs. So the early volunteers were lower-income folks, drawn to the program by significant financial incentives.

Like the first computers or solar cars, synching wasn't cheap. If you were broke, you weren't going to live forever—unless you rolled the dice and volunteered to be an early experiment in the whole "synthetic" thing. Kennedy had seen some of the cheaply-produced flyers promoting the program, plastered in poor neighborhoods throughout New York:

> Do you want to live forever? Hey, who doesn't?! Sign up for the Volunteer Synthetic Test program, and at no cost to you, you can experience the wonder of cyborganics. Make history. Be a part of the future. Compensation provided to volunteers and/ or their designated beneficiaries.

> *Young, healthy, physically fit volunteers only. Safety not guaranteed. Side effects unknown. All volunteers must pass a rigorous series of tests before being accepted into the program.

Thousands of volunteers signed up. Hundreds were selected. The Vost Program proved invaluable in refining and re-tooling the synching process. There were few fatalities (and even fewer *reported* fatalities), although there were many "identified deficiencies"—the designation given when a Vost experienced one or more unfavorable side effects.

Blindness and debilitating migraines were the most common side effects for the first Vosts. No one wants to live forever if they're blind and in intense pain, so after a few years of testing, re-calibrating, and data-gathering, those volunteers were humanely terminated. This did not count as "fatalities." Just program termination, clean, simple, quiet.

The blindness and migraines, although corrected, still echo through the communal coding: Syns reflexively blink when processing information, and are prone to headaches, but are not plagued with sight deficiencies or crippling migraines. The sacrifice of the Vosts spared the Syns anything more troublesome than a minor tic.

In second generation Vosts, paralysis on the left side of the body was the most common side effect. This generation, too, served its purpose and then met its end. Third generation Vosts, such as Jorge, mercifully emerged as fully functional Syns. So they weren't terminated. But they also weren't given full Syn status. They were categorized as Vosts, second-class citizens with little means, who bore their testing ID numbers on the back of their hands, forever marking them as less-than.

Vosts were allowed to live in Syn cities, and to hold some jobs, and to rent apartments. But they were not allowed to own property, or serve on the Syn Council, or oversee Synthetic citizens. Their primary value is that they still serve as canaries in the coal mine. A glitch in an individual Vost might never appear in the Syn population—but the emergence of any glitch revealed its potential impact, and pre-emptive patches were subsequently designed to ward off similar glitches. Once tested on Vosts, perfected patches were automatically installed in Syns, but were encrypted to prevent Vosts from downloading the final versions. Over-immunizing the Vosts was unwise; how, then, would the next glitch be detected?

In the early days, Kennedy was part of multiple Vost assessments. He spent hours examining samples under microscopes and in data reports. He knew the case studies he reviewed were real people. So were the terminations he signed off on when a cancerous glitch was confirmed. Maybe he had condemned to death the guy who took out his trash. Or the woman who sold him his morning coffee. It made him shudder when he let himself reflect on what they had done, and what they still did—how the Vosts were treated, to this day. But when the topic of Vosts came up, Jorge never showed emotion. Not ever.

Maybe that's his own personal glitch: Lack of a damned soul.

Kennedy glances over at Jorge as they wait for the Vost registry list to finish generating. He wonders what Jorge is thinking. Surely this process must be uncomfortable for him. He had to participate in the study himself, and test his peers, and process the results. It was a strange position to be in—unique and lonely, not to mention invasive and humiliating.

Kennedy tries for the millionth time to engage Jorge: "How long you think Hess'll be in this mood?"

Jorge shrugs, keeping his eyes on the screen.

Kennedy tries again: "What d'you think? About the—this latest Vost testing?"

Jorge gives the obvious answer, curt and dismissive: "I think it'll be best for everyone if there are no glitches."

Well, obviously.

If any Vost exhibited a glitch, it would be Jorge and Kennedy's responsibility to report them. Someone from Technology Maintenance would be sent to retrieve them. And then they would be disconnected from the system ("pulling the plug," the more callous TM guys called it) so they could be assessed; all components would be disassembled so the problem could be identified. Organic and synthetic elements would all be tested.

That was always the term. "Tested." Or "evaluated." Never "dissected."

And if the glitch proved unfixable, or was for any reason deemed dangerous, the Vost would be "handled." Never "destroyed," never "killed."

Kennedy considers Jorge's position and his stomach lurches. He doesn't particularly care for the guy, but he doesn't wish him ill. The idea of having to put down a man he's worked alongside for years unsettles Kennedy. After all, if Jorge's test results indicated anything too serious, he could be on the chopping block. That's how it is for Vosts, no matter who their boss might be.

"Yeah," Kennedy mutters. "That'd be best."

"CAN I ASK YOU SOMETHING?" Ere asks his mother as they walk toward the old fishing village, Ere leading the way, the entire tribe shuffling along behind them.

"*May I*," she says reflexively, hacking down underbrush with her machete, still walking.

Ere will never understand why his mother is unrelenting about instilling good grammar and vocabulary in her son and nephew. As if sentence structure is as important as tracking skills or knowing how to source and purify water. Apparently, as a child, she had won something called a spelling bee. Words mattered to her—absurd as adherence to syntax might seem coming from a woman who screamed at wild cats.

"*May I* ask you something?"

"Of course."

"Syns..." Ere says, hoping his inquiry sounds casual. "They have to stay cool, right?"

"Yes," she says, brusque. "Their machinery generates heat internally, and external heat makes it hard for them to stay cool enough. Without climate control, they overheat pretty rapidly. So when they're all burning in hell, it's really going to be miserable for them. Why do you ask?"

"Oh, just... because. It's so hot here. Maybe we'll be safe here for a long time. They'd hate a place as sweltering as this, right?"

Ruth swings the machete again. "They have cooling devices. They'll incorporate this sector eventually. It's always just a matter of time."

"How did it get like this?" He licks his lips, knowing he's not asking this right. "I mean—how things are now. How did it get this way? Originals, Syns, this whole... thing?"

"Damnation," she sighs. "You know the history, Ere."

He recites what he knows, stupid and hollow: "Sixty years ago, everyone was Original. But then the Singularity happened. And things changed really quickly. And there was a war, between the people who became Syns and the people who didn't. The rebellions, the Original resistance against Syn tyranny, all that. But how did it happen?"

His mother exhales sharply, then speaks quickly, walking faster as she talks.

"The transhuman movement ripped people apart, forcing the question whether or not joining people and machines was ethical. Then the experiments started working. The Singularity happened. The debate was no longer hypothetical. There were real Syns, real divisions, and real choices, all happening fast. *Impossibly* fast."

"But why did people want to be Syns?"

"Because they thought living forever was a good idea."

"Who's 'they'? I mean, before 'they' were Syns. Rich people?"

"Mostly rich and powerful people, yes," Ruth says, wiping sweat from her brow, big knife glinting. "After they synched, and stopped aging, they became richer and more powerful. Syns inherited their Original relatives' wealth when family members died. Privilege kept consolidating. Laws were passed limiting who might qualify to undergo the procedure."

"So it wasn't an option for everyone, after the laws were passed?"

"It was never an option for everyone, Ere. Early on, it was a 'capped' program. Do you know what that means? Strict rules about how many people could become Synthetic citizens. They wanted to keep their numbers small. The gap between Syn and Original became huge. Resources were hoarded by Syns, who were planning for very long lives. There were uprisings. At first the battles were ideological—not merely fighting for resources, but also for reasons."

Ere knows the reason. "To preserve the Original way."

"To preserve the Original *ways*," his mother corrects. "People forget that. There were so many variations in what it meant to be a *human being*. Before the Syns, things weren't perfect. There were wars among the various human tribes, territorial and ideological disagreements, different belief systems; subtle distinctions, in retrospect. With the rise of the Syns, the old differences fell away and soon we were simply fighting for the most universal, basic components of the human experience. Birth, death, pain, love, life as we knew it—the Singularity took our understanding of the human experience and threw it into the sea. Drowned it. We rebelled, and the Syns fought back—until they realized they didn't really have to."

"Because we're all going to die someday anyway."

"Because we're all going to die someday anyway," his mother confirms grimly. "So for the most part, they decided to just wait us out. They just built up their world. The Synt. Their central cloud, which they called Heaven, mostly to piss off the religious among the rebels."

"So the Syns stopped fighting..."

"They stopped fighting, walled up their cities, and just started waiting. We have an expiration date. They can afford to be patient."

"Oh," Ere says, not knowing what else to say.

"Yes, 'oh.'" Ruth pauses, reflecting. "It was a simple calculation, in the end. As long as they protected Heaven and kept their core structures safe from rebel attacks, all they had to do was wait us out. Although they did decide to make sure we didn't keep repopulating."

"The water." Ere pictures Ever gulping the unpurified water, unafraid.

"The water, yes, with chemicals to cripple our fertility and lower our immune systems. The hospitals, reserved only for Syn repairs, so diseases easily prevented, treated, and cured, became swift death sentences for Originals. Travel was limited, and international travel banned for Originals. Within a generation, everything was different."

Here she pauses, and Ere is again afraid that she will clam up and say no more. It's incredible that his generally taciturn mother had shared this much. When she speaks again, it is almost to herself, or to someone unseen in the distance.

"Everything was different," she repeats. "All Originals lived in poverty, and all Syns had wealth as vast as their lifespan. Syns eradicated schools, because they share all knowledge through Heaven. They could instantly access any information they needed, and forgot the value of teaching, learning, wrestling with ideas. They took away everything ... they thought they had everything, but they couldn't see ..."

She trails off, and for a moment, her mouth wavers ever so slightly, as if the information she has just shared is the saddest she has ever known. It is an admission of emotion rarely seen in her stoic face. Ere waits a seeming eternity, walking in silence beside his contemplative mother. Finally, he can't help but whisper:

"What couldn't they see?"

Ruth's eyes re-focus, and she swings her machete fiercely. "Anything beyond their own selfish desires."

"You were only five when the Singularity happened."

"Yes. Just a little girl."

"It was a long time ago."

"It was not that long ago, Ere." She coughs, suppressing it as quickly as she can; when she speaks again, her voice is soft and weak, weary as an elder's. "You'll be surprised to see how quickly the world can change."

N O MORE BODIES. Not yet. Still, with the announce-
ment of the Vost testing earlier in the week, it had been a
tense few days. Vost testing always tightened Shadower's
stomach, since the tests meant the sickening possibility that there
might be another slaughter of innocent Vosts. In addition to the
heartless terminations, the patches developed after collecting and
dissecting malfunctioning Vosts ate up a lot of bandwidth and
re-wrote a lot of code, which meant slowdowns and setbacks for

the clandestine network. Even Shadower caught a lot of static post-patch.

In a massive patch deployment, virtual roads were torn up and re-laid; the hidden pathways utilized by the clandestine network were reduced to rubble. So if there were Vost glitches detected, patch deployment would mean huge setbacks for the clandestine network. But mercifully, the Vost test has just completed—and there were no glitches.

No one was seized, tested on, and terminated. The network remained intact, at least for the time being. And so, with this danger behind them, Shadower's unseen comrades can return their full focus to the ongoing mission. Monitoring for bodies, planning for the next step, tracking, analyzing, and responding to all other matters that arise along the way. Like the brief but mysterious disappearance of Ever Hess.

Although Felix Hess undoubtedly wanted the incident kept quiet, enough individuals had been involved and shared reports with Heaven that the news had broken.

Broken, but not cracked open enough to reveal much at all. The most intriguing thing to Shadower about the incident is how undocumented it was: Ever stayed in private mode for the duration of her escapade, and thus far Shadower has been unable to find one single scrap of information about what the Hessling had actually done down in Sector 27.

The Synt Director's daughter was home now, brought in by Deputy Lance Briggs. But she had been gone for hours—the better part of an entire day—and for most of that time, her activities were off the grid. She had uploaded nothing of interest to Heaven, and in the gap where her time in the woods should have been shared, there was merely a long stretch of protected private-mode time. So whatever memories the girl has of her adventure are hers and hers alone.

Shadower can find what had been erased, but finding what had never been there in the first place... that was harder. (Not impossible. But harder.)

People assumed this whole bizarre incident was a childish escapade, poor little rich girl trying to shake things up. She probably just stayed in private mode to avoid being tracked, most reasoned. Bought herself some extra time. No reason to think she was up to anything interesting. But Shadower knows all too well to never take anomalies like this one lightly. Instances like this were just like finding a malfunction in a Vost. A harbinger of things to come.

A glitch in the system.

CHAPTER 20: EVER

HAVING SELECTED SOLAR INSPIRATION #849 for this week's hair color, Ever is trying to decide if blondes really do have more fun. She lays in bed, fingering a fresh strand of her chemically-cultivated sunshine, curling it around her finger, unwinding it, then curling it again, contemplating her next move. She arches her completely-healed foot; a faint scar remains as a reminder of her injury.

She could easily have the scar removed, but she never will. She loves it.

Being on the bottom of her foot, the small imperfection is unnoticeable, so there's no pressure from her parents to have it removed. Just in case, when the bandages were off, she kept the flat of her foot pressed to the bed or the ground, just to be sure it never caught their eye.

So far, it hasn't. *She* hasn't. To her surprise, she's been ignored by everyone since she was hauled back home. No questions asked, no mention of how long she was in private mode. Her father didn't even bother coming home for the first several days she was back. Not until this morning, when she found him sitting at the table for breakfast, coolly slicing a grapefruit.

Her mother, too, ignored her—other than the passive aggressive punishments she made Angela and others dole out. Marilyn ordered meals Ever hated and invited over guests Ever despised. Still, things could be a lot worse. Unable to believe she was getting off so easily, Ever braced herself for a second and more serious round of reprimands from her father. But it never came, and after several days, she stopped awaiting it. Things are just back to normal, which is a relief and a disaster. Ever spends her days in her room, avoiding her mother, coloring her hair, and plotting out how and when she will find and kiss and be teased by that Original boy again.

Ever. That's definitely a less stupid name than Ere.

She smiles. This moment—the teasing—is her favorite recollection of all. Eyes still closed, she starts a new search, scanning for her earliest record of that delicious feeling of being teased. And buried amidst some of her earliest organic memories, she finds it.

Springtime, 2011.

Ever's earliest Organic memories are fuzzy, captured only in her organic brain and not imprinted in her synthetic memory. They're harder to categorize and cross-reference, trickier to verify—and yet, somehow, so much easier to believe.

At five, she was a smaller-than-average girl, energetic and fearless. She wanted to touch and experience and explore everything, from goats at petting zoos to spicy foods and waterslides. And even way back then, before the Singularity, before everything, along with her curiosity and fearlessness there was already one other constant in place: her absent parents.

Ever's father was rarely around. He had to work all the time, on Very Important Projects. Her mother was there, but perennially distracted and nervous, always looking like she might crumble into dust and be blown away by a moderately aggressive puff of wind. She was prone to gazing off into space and losing track of things. "Things" included her daughter.

Luckily for Ever, the parental void in her life was filled by the ebullient family that lived next door. These neighbors were her world—a large family, with seven children, and this is where Ever spent her time. They were the ones who taught her about love, and teamwork, and best of all, teasing.

The seven children all had names that started with the same letter, an overt way of making it even more plain that they were united, a team, a family. Concentrate as she might, Ever can't remember their names, or even which letter they'd all started with... *was it A? No, maybe J?* She wishes she could remember. There were four boys and three girls, she knows that much. One of the girls was Ever's age, and all seven of them claimed her as their eighth sibling.

"We were short a girl, anyway," the oldest boy had once winked.

"And she's a short girl, so it's perfect!" Cracked the oldest girl, and they all laughed.

Ever loved being part of the giant pile of kids, rolling around with the family's two big yellow dogs, or tangled together on the couch watching movies, or splashing together in the kiddie pool. The kids are clearer in her mind than the adults; Ever can't conjure the parents' faces, only their laughter. She remembers a warm feeling, a deep and palpable affection. The mother and father teased each other, and teased their kids, and the kids even teased the parents back, all with humor and respect softening the jabs and jokes.

Ever was among the youngest of the kids; the next-to-youngest girl in the big family was the one who was her age, Melody.

Melody! The word surfaces from the organic memory like a little song. *Yes! That had been the young girl's name. They must have all had "M" names.*

Remembering this warms her. Yes. Their names all began with "M," and they all called her "Ev." She loved the nickname. When she was very little, her parents called her Clever Ever when she correctly inserted a round peg into a round hole on one of her toys. She used to do everything she could to make them proud, to get them to call her Clever Ever. But by the time she was three, they were done being impressed by her. They dropped the encouraging nickname, only calling her Ever, if they spoke to her at all.

She was four the first time she wandered into the neighbor's yard. One of the M-kids asked her what her name was. She said with perfect diction and sounding for all the world like a miniature adult: "My name is Ever Catherine Hess."

The kids had laughed, not unkindly.

"Uh, we're just gonna call you Ev," said one of the M-boys. Then with a grin, he picked her up, put her on his shoulders, and dashed across the yard calling out. "Freeze tag! Ev and me are IT! You have five seconds to run! One... two... three... four... FIVE!"

The nickname stuck. The kids all called her Ev. And that alone was enough to make Ever never want to leave their yard again.

One hot summer day, Ever, Melody, and the youngest M-boy were splashing around in the family's bright-blue kiddie pool. The older kids were at a party at a neighbor's house—a party they kept calling a Real Pool Party, since those neighbors had a big in-ground pool with a deep end and diving board and everything. The littlest kids had to stay at home in the baby pool. But it was better than nothing. The parents were keeping half an eye on the kids, but had for once forgotten to slather sunscreen on the littlest bodies. After hours outside, they were all burned something fierce. They felt fine while they were in the pool, but when they went inside for lunch, their skin got hot and tight. They lay down on the couch, sun-exhausted, and fell asleep.

When Ever woke up to go to the bathroom. After flushing the toilet, she washed her hands and looked up, into the mirror. Which was when she saw, written on her forehead in green Magic Marker, two small words screaming out from her red skin: *Ooooh! Burn!*

It was something the kids always said after a particularly good zing: "*Ooooh, burrrrn!*"

Ever gasped. Then she turned even redder under her sunburn, livid. She flung open the bathroom door, and there, waiting in the hallway, sat all five of the oldest kids. As soon as they saw her furious little face, they all began to howl with laughter.

Startled awake by the sound, Melody and her little brother came stumbling into the hall to see what all the fuss was about. Each of their small sunburned foreheads bore the same Magic Markered message: *Ooooh! Burn!*

Seeing them, Ever clapped her hand over her mouth. Her anger dissolved into giggles, and soon she was howling along with the older kids. Melody and the little boy stared at Ever. It took them a moment before they pointed questioningly at their own marked-up foreheads. This comical gesture only made everyone scream with even more uncontrollable glee.

"Family burn," said one of the older boys, grinning.

I'm part of the family, Ever thought happily. *I'm part of the burn.*

She stayed at the neighbors' house almost every single night. The first few nights she slept there, the neighbor-parents would call Ever's mother to make sure it was all right. After several consecutive instances of Ever's mother either assuring them that it was fine, or not even bothering to answer the phone, they stopped calling to check.

Ever slept curled up beside Melody. She dreamt, back then. Some dreams were good and some were bad, but when she had a bad dream, waking up and having another small, snuggly body next to her own was reassuring.

At the M-family's home, Ever had a place in the world. And then, one night, her lovely little life was suddenly snatched from her. Ever was deep in slumber alongside Melody, probably dreaming something warm and wonderful, when she was woken by the shrill shriek of her mother's voice.

"Ever! EVER!"

Melody sat up first, pulling the covers up to her neck nervously, whispering: "Is that your mom? Are you in trouble?"

Ever shook her head, still half-asleep. She didn't know. She couldn't think of anything she'd done that would have angered her mother. The bedroom door opened and her mother burst through it, followed closely by the neighbor-parents. Her mother was wearing a long trench coat, but beneath it, Ever could see the paisley-silk of her mother's favorite pajamas.

"Ever," said her mother. "We have to go. Put your shoes on right now."

"But I'm in my PJs—"

"NOW." Her mother threw back the comforter and grabbed Ever forcefully, dragging her from the bed. Ever's heel hit Melody's head as she was bodily removed. Melody whimpered.

"Is everything all right?" The neighbor-father asked, still uncertain why Mrs. Hess had shown up at their door in such a panic that night. Never before had she summoned Ever home, or shown any interest in her daughter's whereabouts.

Ever's mother ignored him, moving quickly, shoving Ever's feet into shoes, taking her by the hand and pushing past the other grown-ups, through the door, down the hall, out into the shadowy night. But the night didn't stay in shadow for long. As soon as they stepped outside, they were surrounded by bright, flashing lights, cutting through the moonless dark. Cameras, video cameras, microphones, a cacophony of voices, people shouting, screaming questions:

"Mrs. Hess—Mrs. Hess—"

"Just a few questions about your husband—"

"Mrs. Hess, is it true that your husband—"

"Is this your daughter? Is this *his* daughter?"

Ever's mother held one hand up to shield her own face; her other hand shoved Ever's head so her face pointed down. Her mother steered her by her scalp, navigating her past the screaming paparazzi. Ever's heart was beating, and her throat felt thick with fear.

"Mother, what's going on—"

"Your father," was all her mother said. "Your father."

There was a car waiting for them at the curb, a black car with black windows. Ever's mother opened the car door, shoved her daughter inside, and slammed the door behind them. Ever never saw the M neighbors again. She never got to say goodbye. Never even got to apologize for kicking poor Melody in the head.

Ever sits bolt upright, a solution presenting itself to her from the midst of this memory.

She knows how to get back to her Original boy.

T*HIS CAN'T BE HAPPENING.*

Hess is going to have to run the algorithm again. The Prophet is pissing him off.

There are countless programs designed to maximize the use, efficacy, and security of the Syns' mainframe. One of the most critical programs is a predictive algorithm. The algorithm is connected to the core of Heaven; the core's organic components are what makes it unique. This particular algorithm was designed to assess existing information and render projections regarding possible outcomes—specifically, predictions regarding potential threats to Syn society.

They call it the Prophet.

Like all algorithms, The Prophet is a pure method of analysis, expressed as a finite list of well-defined instructions for calculating the likelihood of an incident. As Hess once described it to his daughter, when she was a little girl—The Prophet reviews all the available relevant data in its universe, and predicts what storms, literal and metaphorical, might be rolling in.

The Prophet's unique organic component is what makes it both incredibly powerful and infuriatingly enigmatic. Purely computer-generated outcomes were clean and linear—less poetic, more discernible. The Prophet's irreplaceable organic component makes it singularly brilliant. But the brain that powers the program twists its outcomes, making each prophecy a puzzle; adding a literal mind-of-its-own to anything brings a collection of complications.

Over the course of the past several decades, The Prophet has accurately predicted catastrophic events—from natural disasters to Original attack strategies—enabling Syn society to adequately prepare for and thereby mitigate the impact of said events. Though it was often obscure or wrapped in some sort of riddle, The Prophet never yielded *false* information.

But now, for the past several months, The Prophet has returned the same mystifying prediction, over and over. Felix Hess has kept the unwaveringly insistent, indecipherable missive classified—until he can figure out what the hell it means, he doesn't want to share it with anyone. Not the Council, not anyone. And so far the vague sentence continues to elude him: *The outsider inside will end the beginning.*

Hess has analyzed this prophecy in every conceivable way, and come up with nothing. Since The Prophet keeps repeating itself, throwing these same words onscreen every time Hess runs it through the motions again, he knows it's potentially critical information. But maybe it's a damn tease. Maybe somehow the algorithm is taunting him. Hess knows that's a stupid theory, but nothing's impossible. That damn thing is inscrutable, and the way it keeps stubbornly spitting out the same prophecy, Hess doesn't know what to think. He has become irrationally angry at the prophecy itself—a poker-faced prediction, defying definition.

Despite not knowing its true meaning, he's taken several steps inspired by the prophecy. Most recently he assigned Kennedy and Jorge to conduct an unscheduled scan of the Vost population. He'd hoped that might yield something of interest—*could a Vost be someone who was "inside," though also an "outsider"?*—but no luck. No glitches. No nothing.

A message flashes before his eyes.

Father: Can we meet? I have a request.

He sighs. Ever is not allowed in Heaven's core chamber—no one is, save Hess himself—so meeting with her will mean returning to his office. He hasn't spoken with her regarding her little joyride. He doesn't particularly want to speak with her about it, and certainly not at this moment. She was safely home, intact, and her post-incident update had not included anything of note. She spent a few hours in private mode, but that made sense. She ran away. It would have been foolish not to do so in private mode. Hess has too many other important matters demanding his attention. Parenting his petulant daughter is not high on his priority list.

He swipes his finger across the Heaven core's security pad, then enters a code, then looks into the retinal scanner to enter the series of blinks required after the initial ocular confirmation. Biometric security has come a long way, but Hess still layers component upon component to ensure the highest level of defense. He exits before responding to his daughter:

My office. Two minutes.

Hess hypothesizes that Marilyn is making Ever's life miserable post-excursion. No matter how many times he has refused to referee their spats, Ever still tries to draw him in. His wife gave up long ago. It's the only trait of Marilyn's he wishes Ever would embody: resignation.

When he reaches his office, Ever is already there. She raises an eyebrow at him. He raises his own in return, reflexively. No one else would dare enter his office without his invitation.

Dr. Felix Hess' office is something of a wonder. A vintage little alcove, completely at aesthetic odds with the rest of the Synt. The architecture of the Synt, like every building in Central City, is clean and minimalist. It was engineered for maximum technology and efficiency, and the style supports the tech: high ceilings, wide cooled halls, glass walls with embedded display screens, interactive technology woven into the very structure. But Hess' office hearkens back to a much earlier era. At Hess' insistence, the room was designed and furnished to exactly match the office of his mentor back at the Massachusetts Institute of Technology.

The room exudes an extinct, old-world academic feel. Hess commissioned a massive, impractical mahogany desk, surrounded by mismatched bookshelves of oak, cherry, and pine, recovered from Original wreckage and meticulously restored to their former glory. Books line the shelves—genuine antiques, priceless copies of canonic works and first-edition prints of seminal science texts. A black swivel chair is behind the desk, and in the far corner sits an overstuffed brown leather armchair, with big brass buttons decorating the chair's back in three proud, vaguely-military lines.

"I'd like to request your permission to return to Sector 27," Ever says without preamble.

"Oh?" Hess says. He admires her brash refusal to beat around the bush, and is mildly relieved that she made no mention of her mother. "You want my permission this time?"

"I assume the easiest way to prevent any sort of trial, or charges, or … ill will, might be if I make amends. Directly."

Avoid penalties? Her transgression was not even a true crime, and with a clean slate otherwise, to say nothing of his own influence, she wasn't facing any actual consequences. There must be some reason she wants to return to the sector.

"Charges and a trial seem unlikely, given the resolution of the situation."

"Unlikely, but not *unheard* of. I mean, given the circumstances and all. I did commit larceny, even if really I only *borrowed* the vehicle. It was safely turned over to them in a matter of hours. But the point is, wouldn't it be better if I personally delivered an apology gift?"

"Ever, why do you really want to go to Sector 27?" He asks, impatient.

"Because I'm bored," she says, rolling her eyes. "Mother is constantly breathing down my neck. You're always at work. I just want to go *somewhere*, okay? It's completely safe passage between here and Sector 27. A straight shot down the coast. I can—"

"All right."

"All right?" She can't conceal her surprise.

But he has already stopped listening. He gleaned the information he needed, and ran his own calculation. There's no logical reason to be concerned about Ever going to Sector 27, and in fact, it might work out well for him—if she was safely occupied elsewhere, she couldn't bother him with domestic drama. And, of course, unbeknownst to Ever, the clock was ticking on her ability to go off on any sort of jaunt. Soon, even leaving the Synt itself would be off the table.

All things considered, having her out of the picture for a few days would be good for all of them. So long as she was safe, it might be best to continue allowing her a wide berth before reigning her in, indefinitely. If he tried to control her now, she might just run off again. Better to give the permission and stay on top of the situation.

He also knows Ever was telling the truth about being bored, and a bored Ever often leads to trouble. His only concern is for her actual physical safety. It's imperative that nothing harm Ever. But her statement about the low-risk nature of this expedition was correct. The entire area between the Synt and Sector 27 was secure. So he nods once more, confirming.

At this second nod, Ever scrambles from the chair and hurries out of the office without so much as a thank you. Probably doesn't want to give him the chance to change his mind. On that front, she need not have worried. Once the question of what-Ever-wanted had been answered, she was no longer on his mind. Even before the door shuts behind her, he is already back to thinking about the prophecy.

The outsider inside will end the beginning.

As with all things, it's only a matter of time before he unravels this knotty little sentence. He'll decipher the prophecy, identify the threat, and eliminate it. By any means necessary.

E VER WASTES NO TIME LEAVING. Her plan was in place before she approached her father with her reasonably well-constructed cover. In order to maintain the appearance of embarking on the alleged goodwill trip, she registered an itinerary that would align with expectations, and shared it in her evening upload. She even had one of the Synt's many junior-level staffers, a skinny bird-like man called Nichols, help her make the arrangements to secure a light rail reservation. She was set to depart at ten the next night. She made sure everything was documented, and that Nichols kept a record of it all in his log, as well.

Unbeknownst to anyone, prior to having Nichols secure her arrangements for a nighttime departure, she had already procured herself a ticket for the morning train.

She knew that reservation could easily be discovered, but only if someone went looking for it. She'd give them no reason to do so. She would just quietly board the morning train, with her apology gift in tow, and then log her arrival at the later time—buying herself at least eight or ten unmonitored hours to spend with the Original boy.

She wasn't sure exactly how to contact Ere, since Originals couldn't receive Syn messages. The electro-telepathic messaging program was a synthetic function, not an Original ability. She wasn't sure if Originals had any old tech she could somehow tap into; were there still phones out in the territories? She doubted it. Hopefully, arriving this much ahead of schedule would give her the time to find him.

The top-of-the line Chariot she was bringing along with her would help make that more doable. This, of course, was what she had told her father she thought would make the perfect apology gift for her to bring the Sector 27 council.

And indeed it would. After she was done using it to get back to Ere.

"HURRY ALONG, BOYS, I'LL DIE 'FORE WE'RE done if you keep dawdling."

Howard Fell's death made Jonah Marks the oldest living man in the tribe. He looks it, too: his short, tightly-curled hair, once raven, is now white; his brown skin is wrinkled and dotted with dark skin tags. But he still walks erect, holding his head high, staring at everything with such intensity that it's easy to forget he's completely blind.

Jonah's is Cal's great-uncle, on his father's side; though not related by marriage or blood to Ere, both boys call him uncle. Uncle Jonah is too old, too blind, and too frail to be helping Cal and Ere gather water. But he insists on doing so nonetheless, stubbornly working alongside the boys to fill the buckets and haul them back to their new camp in the old fishing village.

The village is a good fit: the tribe hollowed out several half-rotted cabins, clearing away the dead wood and rebuilding the sunken siding to create cozy, relatively-secure shelters that were well-shaded and even managed to catch a breeze now and again through the empty window sills. An old garden's graveyard yielded now-wild but still-plump tomatoes and other vegetables; the tribe also set up snares to catch the small game that filled the surrounding woods. It was almost as good as Franklin had been, so long as you overlooked the humidity, Helena declared.

Life quickly shaped itself into new routines. Each morning and each evening, Cal, Ere, and Jonah made their way from the cabins to the nearest mouth of the stream, carting several vessels for carrying water. Ere carried a medium-sized water drum long transported by the tribe; Jonah, a smaller drum. Cal had found an old rain barrel, still sound and sturdy, and carried this to and from the water source. When it was full, Cal grunted and turned red carrying it back to the cabins, but never complained and rarely spilled a drop.

"I'll know if you spill," teases Jonah, using his jokes to hide his own struggles with the smallest of the water vessels. Jonah will not admit to any difficulty, and the boys respectfully avoid commenting. They just joke back.

"He just spilled!" Ere cries out in mock alarm. "The whole barrel!"

"Then there'll be no water for you. Elders drink first," Jonah retorts, and they all chuckle.

They deliver their initial water load, wipe their brows, scoop up the buckets, and head back to the stream for more. As they bring it, bucket by bucket, the water is boiled. When they have enough, the whole camp will gather, ladles in hand, to drink and cook, maybe even to tell stories or sing. However brief this respite might be, it is sweetly, reverently savored.

Ere is glad for the tribe's ease, but walks around constantly anxious himself. He wonders how Ever might contact him, and when. When he should be focusing on another task, his mind wanders to her instead. Like now, as he continues filling his already-overflowing water bucket.

"Hey, Ere! What 'Ever' is distracting you?" Cal booms wickedly.

Ere gives his cousin a look. Late into the night, on the fateful day when he met her, after all the other members of the tribe were fast asleep, Ere told Cal everything about Ever. Almost everything, including her promise to return to him, and probably too many specifics about her mouth, her eyes, her breasts. He omitted only one small detail—the fact that she was a Syn.

Ere had no choice. He couldn't tell Cal about the whole Syn thing, but he also couldn't lie about Ever's existence. There were no secrets between the boys, and no concept of discretion when it came to these things, because "these things" *did not happen*. Only a handful of times, as children, had these boys even glimpsed girls their age. The only naked female bodies either boy had ever seen were accidental glances at bathing elders—not exactly ideal fantasy fodder.

Both Ere and Cal believe that someday they'll cross paths with another, larger tribe—a tribe with girls their age. But in the meantime, Ere's enviable experience of kissing a girl would be shared over and over again. Ere is aware that in addition to featuring in his own fantasies, Ever warms Cal's blood on a regular basis, too. He does not begrudge his cousin this shared imagined-Ever; the real one, however, he intends to keep all to himself.

Keeping her Syn status secret isn't hard. When Cal asked what she was doing alone in the woods, Ere said she was part of a community but ventured out on her own. (Technically true.) She might be able to make her way back here again (he honestly hoped so). Maybe her community would connect with theirs (he honestly hoped not). Cal, having no reason to believe that the girl kissing his cousin might be something other than human, came to the logical conclusion that she was indeed their long-desired unicorn: a young, beautiful, single and alluring Original girl. But the more questions Cal asks, the harder it is for Ere to cling to honesty.

"Do you think she has a sister?"

"I don't know," Ere says. *Truth.*

"Still. She's perfect."

"Yes, she's perfect," Ere says. *Half-truth.*

"And if she returns, you'll introduce me? And we'll ask her about her sister?"

"Of course." *Lie.*

It's been a week since the encounter. With each passing day, it's more difficult for Ere to believe it really happened. But she's so vivid and vibrant in his dreams, he knows he could never have fabricated such a fully realized person, with so many precise little details. It must have happened. And it had to happen again. She would come back. She promised.

The sky is darkening swiftly as the three men, one old, two young, haul up the water buckets and begin making their way back to camp for the last time. Cal and Ere both keep a watchful eye on Uncle Jonah.

"Don't look so hard at me, boys," Jonah grunts, shifting his water vessel. "I can hear you staring. If you're waiting for me to fall, you'll be waiting awhile. Ere's more likely to trip."

Ere opens his mouth to retort when a small sudden movement catches his eye. He instantly tenses, eyes darting to Cal. The look is unnecessary. Cal has already unsheathed his blade.

There it is again—a flash of something pewter, moving behind a nearby tree. Ere reaches for his own knife. Another flash of the silver, and a shadow casting a shape that almost looks female. *Could it possibly be—?* Ere's breath quickens. He wonders how he can get his cousin and the old man to leave, tries to figure out a way to keep them from finding out—

"Come out, girl," Jonah commands.

Ere is so surprised at Jonah's words that he spins around to face the old man. And thus, staring bug-eyed at Jonah, Ere is the last one to witness Ever emerging from behind the tree.

Cal is gaping. When Ere finally sees her, he recognizes her immediately, although her hair is different. Before, it was black as night, but now it is shining silver—not gray with age, but live and crackling with a metallic sheen. Cal notices the hair discrepancy, and gives Ere a quick look that clearly says *God be praised—a sister!*

Hating to disappoint his cousin, he shakes his head, and mouths: *That's Ever.*

"Who are you, girl?" The blind old man asks.

Ever's eyes meet Ere's, and he shakes his head. She blinks once, understanding. If she talks, her accent or an odd turn of phrase might give her away. As it is, in daylight, even her clothing could give her away to Cal, if he was paying attention to her outfit rather than fantasizing about the body beneath it. Her fabric is dark, sleek, clean, not faded and patched like the tattered old-world clothes worn by the Originals. And if she steps closer, they might hear her soft electronic humming.

"Speak up, girl!" Jonah barks.

"She's a mute!" Ere blurts out.

"What?" Jonah says, confused.

"A mute. She's mute." Ere stares desperately at Cal, begging him to go along with this. Cal is better at bullshit than Ere, and Ere has to hope his cousin will help him out yet again. "She's... I mean, I heard that she's a mute. I heard about her from the old man in the woods, that day when I was out scouting for water. His name was Deputy..."

Cal's admiring gaze at Ever becomes an incredulous stare at his dumbass cousin.

Jonah turns his vacant eyes toward Ere, suspicious.

"I thought your mother told us he was the only one in his tribe?"

"He is. He was. I mean—he said there was a girl in the woods, who couldn't speak. He didn't really know her, he had just... seen her... in the woods..." Ere trails off, lamely, and then asks for backup. "Remember, Cal, when I told you..."

Cal chimes in, clearly reluctant to throw his credibility behind Ere's clunky lie. Ere also knows Cal has no inkling as to why Ere is lying about the girl to begin with—but he goes along with it, to keep her from disappearing.

"Oh... right. Yeah. You mentioned the mute. Girl."

Shooting his cousin a grateful look, Ere mouths to Ever: *Come back in a little while.*

She pouts, and for a moment he fears she has not been able to read his lips. But then she takes off running. She makes plenty of noise as she runs, purposefully stepping on twigs, slapping her hand against leaves, so the blind old man can hear her departure.

"Girl! Wait! Where is she going?" Jonah asks. "Stop her! The woods could be dangerous, for a young girl on her own—"

"She's tough," said Ere. "I mean, that's what the old man said."

"And her tribe's probably looking for her," Cal adds quickly. "She's probably running back to them. Maybe only a day or two behind them. I'm sure she'll be fine."

"You two seem awfully cavalier. Especially considering how pretty she was."

"How do you know how pretty she was?" Ere says, incredulous.

"Don't need eyes to see that," grunts Jonah. "Anyone who could get the two of you to shut up like that when she shows up, then start tripping all over your words like fawning little hound pups when she takes her leave, must be a damn goddess."

Ere knows he doesn't have much time to get back to her. He, Jonah, and Cal deliver the water, then Ere whispers desperately to Cal: "Don't let Jonah tell anyone."

"How am I supposed to do that?" Cal growls.

"Figure it out. Please. And cover for me. I'll be back."

Cal looks pained, but nods. "There better be a sister."

Ere takes off at a run, thwacked by branches and tripping over bramble. He calculates as much as he can about the situation. He knows Cal will do what he can, but eventually Jonah will say something to someone. When his mother finds out, Ere's in for it; she'll know he lied, will sense something is off about the whole thing. She'll hunt him down.

But he pushes that thought aside. Even his mother wouldn't want to come after him once it got dark; it was too dangerous for her to leave the elders unprotected. He'll figure out how to deal with the consequences in the morning, for now he just has to get to the girl.

AN URGENT, STINGING MESSAGE JOLTS Shadower from a slumber-like state. Unlocking the encryption, Shadower expects it's finally an alert about another Syn termination, or better still, an intercepted termination and possible ally—but instead, the surprising missive reads:

Ever Hess is back in Sector 27.
No additional information at this time.

Processing and then deleting these words, Shadower is still not sure what to make of them. Ever's solo journey into the swamp was odd the first time. But it is absolutely suspicious the second time, especially since there was no family boat from which she easily hopped. All of the other Hesses are safely ensconced in the Synt. Ever is alone.

What in Heaven and Hell is that girl up to?

Ever Hess is now a person of interest. She was always on the radar, as Felix Hess' daughter, but seemed so painfully un-interesting that the network neglected to monitor her. Until she turned up on that security video.

And now, missing again. Back in the swamp, alone, exact location undetermined due to a shift into private mode—essentially off the grid, for the second time in as many weeks. There has to be something more going on here. Something that means the network should pay a little more attention to little Ever Hess.

What are you looking for, little girl?

Or what have you already found?

Shadower considers sending a message to Karma, if not the whole network—but there is nothing to share, really; not yet. There will be, if Shadower waits long enough.

Fortunately, Shadower is good at waiting.

E RE SNEAKS UP ON HER QUIETLY. She's standing in a small clearing, alone but alert. Her silver hair sparkles. He's only a few feet away—and then his stupid foot slips on a slick moss patch, he grabs a branch to catch himself, and the sound makes Ever's head snap toward him.

It triggers more than her head; she swivels and aims a small shining silver gun at him.

"Is that a gun?" Ere says, entering the clearing, staring at her.

"Heaven and hell," Ever exhales, and tucks the gun back in her pocket. "Don't startle me like that. I could have shot you."

"Which is why maybe you shouldn't have a gun," he counters.

She glares, and for a moment they just stand there, at an impasse, once again unsure how to interact. This isn't how it was supposed to go; it was supposed to be all kissing and fireworks and starry eyes, wasn't it? Ere tries to push it back in that direction.

"Your hair's different," he says, like an idiot. Like she doesn't know her hair has gone from black to practically white? Why didn't he say "your hair's beautiful" or something slick? *Stupid, stupid, stupid.* He tries to recover quickly: "I want to show you something."

Every night since their first encounter, Ere has been hard at work. The day after that fateful meeting, he found a lone shack, set apart from the other closely-clustered cabins. It is more than a mile away from the heart of the little cabin village, situated near the wider expanse of water that opened toward the sea. An overnight fishing post, or something, he guessed. The past few days, he snuck out to the modest little shack whenever he could slip away. He spent hours clearing out cobwebs, making sure there were no burrowing animals in the walls, sprucing it up in anticipation of Ever's promised return. He decided that rather than refer to it as a shack, now that it was cleaned up and cozy he needed a nicer word for it. From somewhere in the recesses of his mind, a more charming word revealed itself: *cottage.*

"Where are we going?" Ever asks.

"You'll see."

"Shall we walk, or ride? I came in on a Chariot, it's just over there..."

For a moment, the idea of whipping through the jungle on a Syn vehicle is thrilling. Ere knows this may be his only opportunity to experience such a joyride, and opens his mouth to say he's all for it. But as quickly as Ever makes the offer, she rescinds it.

"Actually, never mind—it has a tracking device," Ever says.

"Oh."

After a few paces, Ever asks: "Is it safe for us to talk?"

Ere looks at her quizzically. "Are you worried about predators hearing us?"

"Oh, shit! I forgot about the... predators," Ever says, looking equal parts amused and terrified. "Ha, right. Being eaten by animals would be bad."

"Yes, being eaten by animals always ruins my day," Ere quips, proud of his ability to crack a quick joke. His confidence is growing. She came back. She must like him. "Every. Time! So, ha, what did you mean, is it safe for us to talk?"

"What I meant was... can your information—your memories and stuff—can it be accessed later?"

"Uh. Accessed how?"

"Accessed by everyone else, like..." Ever shakes her head, trying to figure out how to ask whatever she's asking. "I'm just worried about someone finding out, about you getting in trouble, or... I know you Originals don't have a collective memory storage system or anything, but could you be, I don't know... interrogated?"

"I mean, I'm pretty terrible at lying," Ere admits. "But there's no one who would *interrogate* me. Well, my mother will—but she won't torture me to get a confession or anything. I don't think she will. I hope not. Anyhow, the point is—we're fine. Okay?"

She looks doubtful. "I'm sure no Original ever accidentally leaked information in the whole history of history."

"Not that I know of," Ere agrees cheerfully, deciding to meet her evident sarcasm with blithe ease. "But I'm a pretty shitty historian."

This earns him a small, nervous laugh from her, which is good enough for him. They continue walking, Ere leading the way and delicately holding aside any hanging branches or grasping thorn bushes, ensuring the path ahead was always cleared for Ever.

"You're weird," she says, when he bows as he pulls back a low tree limb and gestures for her to pass.

"Yeah," he agrees amiably. "Anyway. When you asked, earlier, about it being safe to talk... did you want to talk about something?"

Ever raises an eyebrow. "I don't know. Apparently I'd be risk-ing animal attacks, and having a conversation with someone who won't even remember our chat well enough to be an interrogation risk later, so."

"Eh, don't worry about the animals," Ere says, with an un-earned amount of swagger. "I'll keep you safe. I'm very strong, and I have my trusty knife. And you have that cute little gun."

"It's quite powerful, despite its small—oh, you're teasing again, aren't you?"

"So it would seem."

"Huh. I always heard that you Originals were all religious nuts with no sense of humor."

"Really? Who told you that?"

"My father."

"Oh." He pauses. "I guess I shouldn't call your father a xeno-phobic shit-for-brains."

"Nah, I'm fine with that," she shrugs.

"So, we're all religious nuts with no sense of humor," Ere mus-es, swatting at a mosquito, pushing another large branch out of the girl's way. "And all Syns are cold, calculating robots?"

"We're not robots," she snaps automatically, then takes a mo-ment and considers more carefully. As she answers, she shoves aside an overgrown bush, clearing the path for the boy and lifting her eyebrows at him "Cold, maybe not everyone. Some more than others. My family isn't doing anything to warm up that reputa-tion. Calculating, well—yes. We can't really help that. Analysis is pretty automatic."

"Then, in your expert estimation, based on the calculations that you just can't help, would you have to agree that I am the smartest, funniest, strongest and most attractive Original man you have ever met?"

She chuckles, a low and lilting sound. "You're the only Original boy I've ever met." She pauses, then: "I guess, more accurately… you're not the only Original boy—it's just been a very long time."

"How long?"

"Long."

"And were you as harsh to that boy?"

"Those boys."

"Boys?" He wonders how many she's remembering now, and if she ever walked down a moonlit path with any of them. He wonders if they were tall and muscular. He hopes they all had terrible breath, then wonders if he chewed enough mint leaves earlier.

"Yes, boys. And no, I wasn't harsh. I was a little girl then."

This stops Ere. "You were a little girl… when?"

She looks at him, and seems to be choosing her words carefully. "A long time ago."

"How long?"

"A lady never tells."

"You don't look older than I am."

"I am. And I'm not."

"What's it like?" He is genuinely curious. He looks at her, this girl who is his age but not his age. He needs to know about her, how she got this way. Knowing that the question might cost him, he also knows he cannot ask it.

"What's what like?"

"All of it," he says. He brings his hand to her cheek to soften the hard inquiry. "Tell me from the beginning, how it started, for you. How did you become a Syn?"

CHAPTER 26: EVER

WHEN I WAS BORN, MY FATHER WAS ALREADY one of the Singularity Scientists, working tirelessly to reach that event horizon. They were the pioneers of transhumanism. When the technology allowed, they would fuse with machines and become the first man-computer hybrids, synthetic human beings.

My father was focused entirely on work. Not on family. My arrival on the scene was an accident. "A surprise," others said, since normal people try to be polite about that sort of thing. I still don't even really know how that happened. I've never seen my father touch my mother, so my conception seems pretty impossible. Immaculate. They should start a religion named after me. Everists. Ha. God, that actually sounds like a thing.

My mother didn't tell my father that she was pregnant until she was in her second trimester. I think she was afraid that my father would want her to terminate the pregnancy. To get rid of me. Quite the opposite: to everyone's shock, my father was apparently excited when he finally got the news. I don't know why.

The pace of my father's work was accelerating. That's a phrase he uses a lot, "the pace is accelerating." The more he said it, the more true it became. The pace kept accelerating, and when something didn't go as planned, they learned from it, course-corrected, and then kept moving, always faster and faster.

When they attempted the first synch (it wasn't called "synching" at first—it was called "fusion") something went wrong. Whatever it was, it was bad. So bad they kept it completely confidential. The archives are still sealed. I don't know the details. The origins of the Singularity are classified. What we do know is that the early-attempt failed, so then there was volunteer testing and process recalibration and all these safety precautions put in place. There were more fatalities; "no meaningful change ever occurs without a cost."

I was still a baby when my father informed my mother that he himself would be undergoing the new fusion process—synching. He would be the first in the post-volunteer-testing, full-scale launch. The real Singularity.

My mother was hysterical. She was afraid it would kill him, or worse. She didn't want to have a fatherless child. She threatened to kill herself if he went through with it, but my father knew her threats were all empty. He did what he was always going to do.

In my very, very earliest memories, my father was already a Syn. I never knew him as anything else.

At first only his research team and wife knew. He wanted to be sure that there were no side effects, no glitches. That he was the first perfect specimen. Everything was kept secret for as long as possible. He wore lots of turtlenecks to hide his neck port—any pictures you see of him back in the day, he was wearing a dark black turtleneck, even in July. There were rumblings, of course, but beyond his inner circle, it was all just rumor and gossip. Very few people actually believed that it could have happened already: the fusion of man and machine.

My mother had five years to observe him, post-synch. To see him healthy, unharmed. She began to accept the idea that synching might be safe. She also had time to see her own hairline begin to gray while her husband's remained pristine. I was ignorant of all of this, of course. Until I was about five years old, my childhood was fairly normal. All I knew was that my father worked a lot and my mother cried a lot and I was alone a lot. A pretty standard Original family picture, if you read any books at all.

And then, on the fifth anniversary of his procedure, my father held a press conference. Live, on television. He made an official statement, addressing the rumors, confirming the biggest of them. He showed the world his port. He sent commands to his computer without touching it. He provided an X-ray, showing all of the technology embedded in his body.

All hell broke loose.

The media descended on my family's home. People sent everything from fruit baskets to death threats. My mother panicked. My father had not told her about the press conference ahead of time. I was spending the night at my best friend's house the night he did it, and as soon as the news hit and the reporters showed up, my mother snatched me up in the middle of the night and brought me to my father's laboratory. That's where I lived for the next twelve years, under lock and key and constant surveillance.

The Syn population grew quickly. Who wouldn't want to be smarter, faster, to stave off death? Even my gun-shy mother underwent the procedure, convinced by all those years observing my father and her profound fear of being left behind. I became the first child of Syn parents. I, too, was destined for synchronicity. My parents had decided that seventeen was the ideal age for my own procedure. I would be physically mature, but still legally a child. Their will would prevail. I had no choice in the matter.

But there were those who did not see things the way my family did. There were those who rejected the gift, who rejected the whole concept of rewriting humanity's story. For most of my pre-synched life, rebellions were already raging. My father and his contemporaries began calling those who opposed the Singularity "Originals."

A lot of the Originals were poor, and thereby unable to access the Syn option even if it was what they wanted. Others, I guess, opposed it on some sort of ethical level. They banded together, all these bitter and angry masses. They climbed up on their proverbial soapboxes, railing against the "unnatural" cyborganics movement. Their fiery words became literal bombs. It was war.

I was a target, especially prior to my procedure. I was still entirely vulnerable, before synching. Death is final for an Original; Syns, once synched, can be revived and reprogrammed in many different ways. Not always, of course, but in many instances, when a Syn's heart is stopped or breathing ceases... if the organic components are not left untended for too long, the entire system can be revived. Death is still a real threat, but not nearly as much of a given.

Everyone knew Dr. Felix Hess had a daughter, who would probably be converted as soon as possible, but hadn't been yet because no one wants a perpetual child. (I think if they could go back, my parents would realize no one wants a perpetual teenager, either, and maybe waited until I was in my twenties or something—but that's another story.) So the clock was ticking for those who wanted to seize me—"the Hess child should be kidnapped as soon as possible."

My parents shielded me from all of this as much as possible, of course, but news trickled in. One time, I saw a news segment, a mob of angry Originals trying to penetrate the Synt and getting shot down by our guards. Two of the screaming young rebel men looked very much like my old next-door neighbors. The camera caught the moment that a bullet struck one of them; he crumpled to the ground, and his broth-er—I think it was his brother; no, I know it was his brother—caught him in his arms, and sobbed.

I watched it, and I sobbed, too. I knew they were trying to come for me. And part of me wanted to be taken. But I was just a kid then, and terrified, and it felt safest to be where I was: within the walls of the Synt, in my parents' new world, watching from inside my heavily guarded new home. With each passing year, though, I wished more and more that someone had managed to steal me away. I felt like a prisoner. Might as well have been a prisoner of war.

Soon after I turned seventeen, I woke up one morning to find this port in my finger. Third generation technology, my father told me with pride. I didn't have an old clunky port at the base of my neck like his, no, I had this sleek little access point at my fingertip.

I had gone to bed the night before still an Original. I didn't know it would be my last night of dreaming. I woke up and my Original life was over. Just like that. And there was my father, calm and unapol-ogetic, explaining how my port worked and telling me about the new procedures I would need to follow, how I would access Heaven, what to expect now that I had been converted.

They hadn't even woken me up for the procedure.

When Ever opens her eyes, she is surprised to find that she is crying. And so is the Original boy, his tears flowing freely as he gently cradles her face in his hands.

H

ESS RARELY TAKES MEETINGS. Meetings are for people who have nothing important to do, and he's never in the position of having nothing important to do.

On the rare occasion that he is forced into a meeting, Hess' eye is always on the clock. Not that he needs to literally glance at a clock, since internal time-coding was patented and uploaded to every Syn decades ago, but he insists on doing so to make his impatience clear. His vintage office houses an old grandfather clock, a handy prop, enabling him to avoid eye contact with whoever he's meeting with and instead stare at the clock's face the whole damn time.

Anyone who ever met with Hess never wanted to suffer through that hell again. So Hess rarely had to take meetings. But tonight, Hess has a meeting. He couldn't avoid it without causing a political kerfuffle. The chair of the Syn Council, Lorraine Murray, was insisting that Hess meet with her husband Joshua.

Lorraine rarely asks for favors, and when she does, she gets them. Given the indulgence Lorraine has shown Hess over the years, even he could not turn down a request from her. *Request* is a misnomer; Lorraine doesn't make requests, she makes demands.

"You'll be meeting with my husband," she told Hess flatly.

Hess has met Joshua Murray several times over the decades, at fundraisers in the early days and Synt socials more recently. Joshua was a journalist before the Singularity, and worked now with the Department of Information Dissemination. That was all Hess knew offhand. It would take him less than a second to pull up a full history on the man before the meeting. But *taking* the meeting was time-waste enough. *Preparing* for it was laughable.

There's a knock at the door. Hess' office is the only room at the Synt with an old-world wooden door, as opposed to the sleek, brushed-steel automatic drop-doors at the entrance to all other rooms in the building. There is no electronic element to this door, no quiet coded entry. Visitors must knock, be invited in, turn a knob, push the door, walk through it, decide whether they should pull the door shut behind them or leave it open. All of these little steps, seemingly menial choices, reveal something about the person entering the room.

A second, louder knock.

"Come in," Hess barks.

The knob twists, and Joshua Murray steps into the room. He pulls the door shut behind him, gently but certainly, the quiet click of the catching lock echoing unnaturally, caught between a tick and tock of the grandfather clock. Joshua stands in front of the door, respectfully waiting to be invited to sit. Hess lets him stand there longer than is polite before finally saying:

"Heaven and Hell. Sit down. I'm a very busy man, Mr. Murray."

Joshua Murray closes the distance between door and desk quickly. He is tall and solid, though he moves lightly on his long legs, carrying himself with the litheness of a much smaller man. He eases himself into the chair opposite Hess. The chair for Hess' guest is a significantly smaller, lower seat than Hess' own. This subconsciously makes most people feel weaker, even submissive.

Joshua Murray is tall enough that he can still look Hess in the eye when they both sit. He does not seem submissive, but even without the chair designed to underline the point, both men know who wields the power in this room and in the world beyond it. Felix is lord; anyone in the lesser chair, supplicant.

The supplicant clears his throat.

"Thank you for seeing me, Dr. Hess."

"Lorraine insisted," Hess cuts in, fixing his gaze on the grandfather clock, as if lecturing the inanimate object. "Look. Small talk is bullshit. I don't believe in it. So cut to the chase."

"Very well." Joshua Murray clears his throat again. If Hess were a courteous host, he would offer him some water. He doesn't. "It's about my daughter."

The mention of a daughter is mildly interesting. Hess was not aware that Lorraine Murray was a mother. It feels like something he should have known. Filing this information away, he keeps his eyes on the clock.

"Your daughter."

"Yes. My daughter." Joshua Murray's voice wavers, cracks. "Her name is Shayna, and she's an Original."

Interesting indeed, and surely something Hess should have known about before. There had to be a story here. Lorraine Murray, with an Original daughter. How had that come to be? Lorraine had obviously used her significant power, second only to Hess' own, to keep this intelligence buried.

"I was unaware that you and Lorraine had Original offspring."

Joshua, clearly expecting this question, answers evenly: "We don't. I do."

Hess smiles wanly, updating the file to amend the intelligence: Lorraine didn't have a kid, the schmuck she married did. That made more sense. Lorraine was the self-made billionaire whose vast wealth funded the Syn enterprise. Joshua Murray was a writer, a pauper. Yet he must've been fool enough to step out on Lorraine, and she must have found out and refused to secure a spot in the synch program for her unfaithful husband's bastard daughter. The story was so cliché that Hess lost interest as soon as he pieced it together.

"I can't see how your illegitimate Original descendent is any concern of mine."

"She's not illegitimate," Joshua snaps. "I was married once, before Lorraine and I got together. My first wife and I were quite young, and we—never mind, not important. But our daughter was neither a mistake, nor illegitimate. We shared custody after her mother and I divorced. I remarried. Lorraine. And then, in the Singularity, when the opportunity presented itself for us to… Lorraine generously offered to secure early synching spots not only for the two of us, but also for my daughter and my ex-wife. But my ex—Estelle—she was ill. Sick enough that at her final check-up prior to the procedure, she was told she didn't qualify—"

"Mr. Murray, I told you, I'm a very busy man. If you can't get to the point—"

"Hear me out," said Joshua. "Please. For Lorraine, even if you don't give a damn about me. Just listen. Since her mother was kicked out of the program, my daughter chose to remain Original. She knew if she didn't, she might not see her mom again. Given the choice of Syn society for eternity, or a few more years with her mother, she chose her mother. She cared for her. Parkinson's. That's what Estelle had. Parkinson's. She died a few years after the Singularity. I had very little contact with them, when Estelle was sick, after Lorraine and I synched… with the uprisings, the security measures… I did get word, when Estelle died. But I haven't heard from Shayna in years. But I found her, recently. She has Parkinson's, too. As you know, there's no treatment available to Originals, and—"

"Murray," Hess says, out of patience and ready to be out the door. "Cut. To. The. Chase."

"I want my daughter to be synched."

For several long, well-marked seconds, the unhurried and unrelenting ticking of the old grandfather clock is the only sound in the room, tick after tock, tock after tick, measuring out the length of time between the request Murray has made and the response he awaits. Hess knows why Murray stopped talking as soon as he made his request. An old journalist trick: *Ask a question or make a statement and then wait. Don't feed the line. Don't apologize or take the offer off the table, just wait. Make the other guy speak first.*

Hess has dealt with many reporters. None as stupid as this guy, though. An Original daughter. With Parkinson's disease. She must be well into her sixties now, if not seventy. Heaven and Hell, a dinosaur with a debilitating condition to boot? Even if synching were still actively available, this woman would never make the cut.

"There's no way—" Hess begins, and unthinkably, the man interrupts him.

"We can pay," Joshua says, desperate, his well-rehearsed calm falling away.

"Mr. Murray. There have been no new synch procedures approved in nearly twenty years. It's not a question of money. It's a simple question of the law. And the law does not allow for the creation of new Syns."

Joshua Murray knew this; everyone knew this. Synching was halted years ago. It was a logical decision: the world's resources were finite. Once synched, an individual would live indefinitely—and thus need not be replaced, whether by procreation or the synching of additional individuals. Maximum capacity was maximum capacity, period. And as Originals aged they became poorer synch candidates, anyway. Eventually synching would be obsolete; in a hundred years, everyone remaining in the world would already be synthetic.

Joshua Murray's daughter was a perfect example. Old and sick, probably not strong enough to survive the synch procedure itself. And if she did, she would be stuck in her aged condition. There were age-preventative measures all Syns took (periodic organ replacement, skin regeneration regimens, all the standard system upgrades), but there was no such thing as age-*reversal*. Even if she survived the procedure, she'd still be elderly, wrinkled, fragile-boned. Possibly already mentally declined. Who would want to live forever like that?

She would be of no benefit to Syn society, and Syn technology would be of limited benefit to her. The very thought was preposterous. This man's request was illogical, based purely on emotion. Guilt, probably.

Guilt. The most useless of all emotions.

"Please," the man whispers. "I'm begging you. She's my daughter. You have a daughter, Dr. Hess. What would you do, if you were me?"

Finally looking away from the face of the clock, Hess takes in the details of the man's face. Faint wrinkles, gray hair at his temples, small signs of aging that arrived before he synched at forty-three. The man probably barely qualified for synching himself, health-wise. He looked like someone prone to a weak heart. Such pathetic eyes—were those tears?

"I would never have allowed my daughter to opt out of her future. The fact that you didn't ensure your daughter's future is not my problem. Give my regards to Lorraine."

The taller man is wild-eyed now. "Treatment, at least. If she has to remain Original, at least grant a treatment exception. Let her go to a hospital. We can treat Parkinson's. We can make her last few years comfortable."

"We can treat early-onset Parkinson's in a successfully synched Syn," snaps Hess, his own calm gone. "*Those* are the patients we can help. Synthetic Citizens. We do not treat Originals. We cannot reverse advanced Parkinson's in an old worn-out husk. There are no exceptions, Mr. Murray. Exceptions are cracks in the dam that eventually flood the world."

"But my *child*—"

Those are the last words Joshua Murray manages to get out before Jorge bodily removes him from the office. Hess had sent a security request thirty whole seconds ago. He will have to reprimand Jorge for the delay.

E RE DOESN'T KNOW WHAT TO SAY TO EVER'S story. He's always believed that things were simpler than that. Originals were good, Syns were bad, and that was that. He assumed all Syns had lives of ease. Perfect and eternal lives; evil, sure, but comfortable. Hearing her tale of a stolen childhood, stolen choices, such loneliness... it was disorienting.

When they both stop crying, he pulls her to her feet. They walk in silence. All he knows to do is to take her to the cottage, and hope by the time they get there he can think of something to say. When the cottage comes into view, Ever gives him a questioning smile; he nods, and she walks a few paces ahead of him, opens the door, and they go inside.

Ere's efforts have paid off; the cottage is even cozier than he recalled from his last visit. Maybe it's Ever's presence that warms the little space. Her eyes travel the room; he watches as she takes in the sparse pieces of furniture he righted and restored, including a table and a single chair. On the table, there is a bouquet of wildflowers, tied together with knotted grass and crammed into a cracked but still lovely blue-and-white porcelain vase.

"How beautiful," says Ever, and she sounds like she means it. Ere's heart flutters, relieved and revived. Ever picks up the flowers, and smells them, which is when her eyes alight on the other piece of furniture in the room. Tucked into the corner, there is a small, unassuming bed.

"I wanted it to be nice," Ere says shyly.

He looks around the dim room again, and his confidence momentarily wavers. Relative to all the lovely things she must have back in Central City, this place must seem a hovel. He sees all the flaws now—the cracks in the vase, the dirt in the corners, the water-stained walls. How could he have ever thought this was charming? Ere wonders if this whole cottage project was a stupid mistake. Better to be have just stayed out in the woods if—

"It is nice," she says, and her voice is as warm as the humid night. "It's one of the nicest places I've ever seen. Thank you."

"You're welcome," he says, exhaling sharply, his faith in himself and in God and in this wonderful little cottage all instantly restored. He pulls the door shut behind them, plunging the one-room shack into darkness.

"Sorry, sorry, wait—just wait, I left a candle in here somewhere—"

"It's all right, I've got this," says Ever, and she illuminates the room.

Ere isn't even sure what he's seeing. Ever is shining with a soft light, not emanating from any specific point but from her whole being. Her skin glows, creating an environment of radiance and long shadows like nothing Ere has ever seen.

"How are you doing that?"

She shrugs her luminescent shoulders. "It's just another basic function. Night-lighting. I shouldn't keep the light on too long, or I'll overheat. But for short periods of time, it's quite useful. Good for thunderstorms. Brief power outages. Or just for finding my way to the bathroom in the middle of the night."

He realizes she's trying to be funny, but seeing her lit up like this lays another solid brick in the wall dividing them. The action is so unnatural, so inescapably Syn. As close as he felt to her after she shared the story of her stolen childhood, he feels distant again, staring at her from the other side of an insurmountable wall. Guilt floods Ere as he thinks of his mother, his great uncle, everything his people fought against. They sacrificed so much, and here he is, in a hideaway with the enemy. Her inhuman illumination highlights this reality, and his stomach turns. For a moment, he fears he might actually get sick.

"Ere? What's wrong?

"I asked my—" Ere realizes he doesn't want to say *my mother*. "I... I've been trying to learn more, recently. About Syns. How do you—they—Syns, how do Syns justify the Original persecution? Messing with our water, making us live outside the cities, all of it?"

Her luminous face darkens somewhat. "Heaven and Hell. I didn't make the rules, but they're in place for a reason. They're protective regulations."

"Protective of who? Syns?"

"Who else?" Ever says, and then her eyes widen. Apparently hearing her own words aloud, she realizes how they must sound to someone who isn't a Syn. "Oh."

"Yeah, 'oh,'" Ere says.

"We were only protecting our way of life. Your people were bombing our cities—"

"Your way of life is unnatural—"

"It's not! Even before the Singularity, people relied on machines to keep them alive. Breathing machines. Feeding machines.

Mechanical parts for hearts and hips and limbs. This was the next logical step. Merging with machines, before we were half-dead. Transhumanism was just evolution, Ere. It was inevitable."

"My Uncle Howard always used to tell us nothing's inevitable. There are no guaranteed outcomes, no foregone conclusions. We always have a choice. We might not always like the choices we have, but we always have a choice."

"Death is inevitable for you. You'll die someday! Where's the choice there?"

"Actually, that's the choice your people introduced," Ere realizes the truth of his words as he says them. "A new choice, of real life, with its inevitable but unpredictable end, or synthetic life-everlasting. Death is inevitable only because of our choice. Thanks to you, something we used to think of as inevitable ... isn't."

"Ere. I didn't come back here for us to debate the old war."

"Why did you come back here, Ever?"

She lunges for him, kissing him on the mouth, hard. He is surprised, how his body reacts one way while his mind reacts another. But after a moment, his mind overrides his body, and he shoves her away, not roughly but firmly.

"No. We can't—we just can't. You should go."

Her face falls, and her light goes out, plunging the small room again into darkness. Ere is glad for the darkness, so the girl cannot see his own disappointment. But he can't do this, can't be with her. How could he have ever thought he could? His attraction is treason. He turns away. No matter how much he wants her, she is not worth the risk, nor the sacrifice.

But she's vulnerable. Her life isn't fair. She's not just some Syn. She's a good person.

He pushes these thoughts from his mind, certain they are coming not from his head but from his heart, or some region even further south. As his eyes adjust, he can make out the shadow and shape of her. She's crying.

Curse of the world.

He wants to comfort her. Everything in his body cries out for her. But Ere is also angrier than he has ever been. The world she comes from, everything she believes in, smacks of superiority, oppression, even evil. He can't accept it. He can't get past it. He opens his mouth to tell her this: "Ever, I don't think—"

Before he can finish the thought, she finds him again, kisses him again. Then she whispers something surprising, something that unexpectedly reveals a window for Ere to give her another chance.

"Maybe you're right."

He hesitates, hope and hormones opening his heart to her words. Holding her loosely in his arms now, he does not shove her away nor draw her in. He simply waits, tense and unsure what to expect or desire. She seizes upon this opening.

"Maybe the more I learn about you, the more I'll understand about the... about your people. I've never had any real freedom. No choice or say in anything. Not as a small child, not when I turned seventeen, and not since then. Not now, not ever. I figured my whole life was inevitable. But maybe that's wrong. Maybe you're right. Because all I know right now is how much I want to be with you."

This time, he kisses her.

The subtle shift from hatred to passion is age-old. But Ere is young, and the short distance from lashing out to full-on lust takes him by surprise. He has never experienced anything like it, and it propels him forward toward the unexpected. What he had sworn not to do only moments ago now seemed to be exactly what he must do.

Nothing is inevitable, he thinks, wrapping himself around the Syn girl.

CHAPTER 29: KENNEDY

KENNEDY'S FIRST ASSIGNMENT OF THE morning is to confirm that Ever Hess has safely arrived in Sector 27. *Why* his boss' daughter was going south again isn't something Kennedy gives two shits about. He's never had any interest in Ever. The girl was hot, but off-limits, probably crazy, plus came with the insurmountable boner-killer of having Dr. Felix Hess as her father. Kennedy decided years ago that his quality of life would be vastly improved by steering clear of her.

He checks Ever's log. She had checked in right on schedule, dropping a pin to confirm her location in Sector 27. Kennedy is tempted to go ahead and confirm her arrival based on that alone, but Hess made very clear that he wanted Kennedy to "check and double check," so Kennedy also calls up the light rail boarding records.

Hess, Ever: Passenger not scanned.

Heaven and Hell. Here we go again.

Thinking fast, Kennedy instantly calls up all of the light rail transportation records for the past two days. No one could board the light rail without being scanned. Even Originals who travel by light rail have to carry microchipped cards for scanning. If she'd gotten on to any other light rail, she would have to show up somewhere in the system—

There she is.

For some reason, Ever had boarded an *earlier* light rail, without filing an update to her planned itinerary. Strange, but then again—at the end of the day, what did that matter? All Hess had asked of Kennedy was to make sure she was safely in Sector 27. And she was. She hadn't boarded a rail bound elsewhere or anything. Just departed a little early for her destination.

His shoulders relax a little. Hess had told Kennedy not to bother him unless there was an issue. An early arrival wasn't an issue, and definitely not the sort of detail Hess would care about. Kennedy is confident that until and unless there was an actual problem, Hess would never give one rat's ass about which train his daughter wound up taking for her trip.

Kennedy reviews Ever's itinerary once more. She should be meeting with sector leadership over breakfast, in about an hour. So just to check all the boxes, Kennedy decides he'll make sure Ever is exactly where she should be—the itinerary notes a room reserved, so she could sleep for a few hours between arrival and the breakfast meeting. Easy peasy, and then Kennedy can get on with his day.

Locate Hess, Ever.

The results should have been returned instantaneously, but five seconds later it's still running. With each passing moment, Kennedy's shoulders hunch up a little further. After nearly a minute, the screen in front of Kennedy finally displays the results:

Hess, Ever.
Status: Private Mode
Location: Unknown
Last Known Location: Sector 27, Light Rail Station

Damnation.
The fact that she had arrived in Sector 27 was good, but the fact that her current location was unknown was bad. Bad, bad, bad. Kennedy decides to give it five minutes, hoping against hope that he had somehow managed to catch her in private mode due to a bathroom visit. Maybe it was just bizarre timing. But five minutes later, the results are the same.

And three minutes after that.

And one minute after that.

Kennedy starts to panic. This might be an actual problem. This might mean he had to deliver bad news to Hess, who has a tendency to pulverize the messenger.

Think think think.
In a burst of glory, something occurs to Kennedy. Jorge had said that Lance Briggs was the one who found Ever last time. Jorge and Kennedy both knew Briggs; he was at the Synt for a few years before being stationed way out in 27. Real rule-follower, kind of old-fashioned. But a good guy. Maybe he could help.

Kennedy sends a brief, urgent message asking Briggs if Hess had checked in with him.

Briggs replies instantly.

Negative. But she is not due until later today.
Regards, Lance Briggs

Allowing himself a quick eye-roll at Briggs' overly-formal response, Kennedy resumes panicking. The idea of going to Hess with this news dries his mouth and moistens his armpits. Kennedy was a nervous child, raised by aggressive parents. He sucks at confrontation.

I just can't do it…

And so Kennedy decides that he won't. Not yet. After all, Ever has not yet missed her appointment. And she arrived right *where* she was supposed to arrive, even if not right *when* she was supposed to arrive. Lance Briggs isn't worried, so why should Kennedy be? No need to let Hess know that there *might* be a problem.

Just as Kennedy is settling into this decision, Jorge walks in. He acknowledges Kennedy with a curt nod. He's sipping coffee, beginning his own morning tasks, totally anxiety-free. So little gets under Jorge's skin. Realizing his possible salvation, Kennedy's face lights up.

"Jorge! You see Dr. Hess yet?"

"Not yet. I was about to find him, close out the Vost post-evaluation paperwork."

"Would you mind letting him know something else? I mean, if you're already going to be speaking with him?"

"What." There is no inquiry in Jorge's question. His voice is flat, awaiting an answer but not inviting it.

Friggin' robot. But if he'll help me out…

Kennedy begins babbling: "Well—I—he asked me to follow up on Ever, make sure she got into twenty-seven okay, and she did, but not when she was supposed to, and now she's in private mode and off the grid, and I checked in with Briggs but he doesn't know anything about this change in plans or whatever, and I figure if someone needs to go after her it's going to be you, anyway, and if

you're already about to go see him we don't both need to bother
him—"

"Send me the info," Jorge says, taking another sip of coffee. "I'll
review it with Hess."

Relief floods Kennedy, and he nods eagerly to the screen still
up in front of him. "Here, it's all still right up here, if you want to
pull the info—Jorge, I really appreciate—"

But having already scanned in the information, Jorge is out
the door.

CHAPTER 30: JOSHUA

JOSHUA MURRAY SITS ON A BENCH IN ONE of the neatly manicured parks adjacent to the campus of the Synt. He's been there all night, ever since Hess dismissed him. Eyes downcast, he has taken up residence on this bench, maybe permanently. He sprawls, long legs stretched out in front of him, and does something he has not done in decades: he makes a heartfelt attempt at prayer.

It is the same prayer, over and over, a simple heartfelt entreaty: *Please, God. If you exist. If you ever existed. If we didn't drive you away. If our hubris didn't force you to finally give up on us and our egos. We were originally created in Your image, and then we rejected Your design. But if you're all-merciful, if you forgive us our sins… please, God. I need an answer.*

His prayer may or may not have been noticed by God, but it was certainly ignored by his fellow man. He didn't get so much as a second glance from any of the professional Syns on their way to the Synt for their workday. He wonders why they hurry. Why a morning commute still matters. They had all the time in the world. What the hell was the point of rushing to your workday, when thousands of endless days stretched ahead of you? It only made sense to hurry when there was a ticking clock, a countdown. Numbered days, with time certain to run out.

God, I miss the clock.

It was a week ago that Joshua had managed a miraculous meeting with his long-lost daughter at the central light rail station. It was hard to arrange the reunion, difficult for him to locate her, to reach the tribe she was traveling with—the people who were not her original family, but had become her Original family. He was her family. Her father. She should have been with him. But she had been noble, choosing her mother, Estelle, the sweet first-wife Joshua should have been loyal to, instead of stepping out with the intoxicating but dangerous Lorraine.

He had not been entirely honest with Hess, telling him that he and Estelle had separated before Lorraine came along. He felt repulsed enough, having to go begging to that cold, despicable man. So he omitted the details of his first family's disintegration. And why not? Hess wouldn't have cared, anyway. So Joshua told him a simpler story, of young love hitting its expiration date, an amicable split but a daughter still shared.

It wasn't exactly like that. Joshua and Estelle had married too young, yes, but Estelle never stopped loving him. It was Joshua who had grown bored, and wondered what other lips and legs and lives might taste like. It was Joshua who had strayed, and when Estelle told him she was willing to forgive him, it was Joshua who had spurned her mercy and filed for divorce. Those were his decisions. His mistakes. He had to live with that—and as a Syn, he was sentenced to live with it all for a long, long time.

He could never make up for the indiscretions of his youth, and could no longer apologize to Estelle. But Shayna was still alive. Still willing to speak to him. Still someone he could save. His daughter.

He knew she would be an old lady, and in ill health, but his face still twisted in shock and grief when he saw the bent and weary woman his baby girl had become. Her face registered just as much surprise, seeing her father exactly as she remembered him from her childhood. Still tall and strong, and now so much younger than she. She stared up at him, wordless and wide-eyed, as oblivious commuters streamed past them.

"Shayna," he whispered, thick with emotion. Even with the new layers of wrinkles and age spots, he could see his baby girl beneath. Those eyes. "Still so beautiful."

They wept, embraced, began talking. Shayna talked, mostly, and Joshua listened, because she had so much more to say. So much richer a life. She told him about the years spent caring for her mother, living underground during the uprisings. They were not activists, they were not soldiers. They were bystanders, caught in the crossfire. A sick woman and her daughter, trapped in the turmoil of an old world waging war against a new one.

Estelle died after a slow and painful decline, losing mobility, developing terrible shaking in her limbs, becoming dependent on Shayna for everything. Bathing, eating, toileting. Shayna told her father, as her own hands trembled at her side, that she did not want that for herself. She knew she was facing the same downward spiral she watched her mother experience, and she would have no one to care for her. There were no young people in her tribe, no medication for Originals, no therapies or treatments or anything to slow symptoms or relieve pain and suffering.

That was all she saw in front of her, she said to him, her voice shaking even more than her hands. Pain and suffering.

He promised her that he would take care of her. He would find a way. He would get her synched, or get permission to get her the best of modern care in a Syn hospital. One way or another, he would save her from suffering. He reminded her that his wife Lorraine was very well-connected in the Syn world. She had the ear of the director of the Synt. He would claim every favor. He would save her.

Now, favors had been begged and strings had been pulled, all to no avail. There was no salvation. There would be no synch, no treatment. Nothing, absolutely nothing he could do to save his daughter from the suffering he had promised to ward off.

Please, God. I need an answer.

"May I sit here?"

Joshua looks up, squinting against the sunrise. A woman is standing near the bench, her face in shadow, backlit by the morning light. Holding up his hand to shield his eyes, he nods. The woman sits beside him, heavily, and that's when he takes in the details of her: wiry, pale-gray hair. Wrinkled skin. Eyeglasses, which were sometimes worn by Syns for fashion—but these plain-framed glasses were clearly an old prescription to correct an Original vision problem.

She turns her thick glasses toward him. He sees that the old frames are rusted, the glass splintering in thousands of little spider-web cracks.

"I'm sorry to bother you, sir. I'll move on momentarily. My knees… I won't sit long. Just needed to rest my legs."

"It's no bother," Joshua Murray says. He stares openly at the woman. If he had to guess, she looked to be in her sixties, maybe seventies. Shayna's age.

"Thank you," she says. She stretches her legs, so much shorter than his, and leans back on the bench. She has that faint gentle smell of the well-kept elderly, powder and parchment, soothing scents of tobacco pipes and sweet peppermints. Or maybe he's just imagining it.

"What's your name?" He asks softly.

The Original woman looks at him, surprised.

"Faye," she says.

"I'm Joshua," he says. "It's nice to meet you, Faye." He swallows, and then asks: "Can I ask you something? It's personal, and if you don't want to answer me, I'll understand."

She cocks her head at this inquiry, which makes her appear younger. He noticed this with Shayna, too—the magical way an old and wrinkled face could shift and change, and then right there, just beneath the exhaustion and wrinkles, the child they once were shines through. This excavation, this amazing personal archaeology, takes Joshua's breath away. It's a comforting confirmation, knowing that beneath the layers of age and experience, one's truest and purest self might still hopefully, quietly linger.

"All right...?" She looks at him, expectant, awaiting the question.

He chooses these words carefully, knowing they are still in all likelihood too open-ended, but also that this big and broad question is the very one he needs answered.

"What do you fear most?"

And then he waits, putting his journalistic training to use. He has to let her talk, and whatever her reply, he has to accept it. If she responds with something like death or illness, he will weep, because he cannot save her from these things, and worse, he cannot save his Shayna from these things. But maybe there is something else, something he can still save her from, if only he can determine what that might be.

"Being alone," she says simply, taking off her ruined old glasses and absently rubbing them as she blinks weak-eyed at the blurred world that abandoned her. "There's this awful feeling, that in the end, there won't be anyone there. Fear I can't shake. Follows me like a shadow. Yes, sir. Being alone, in the end. That's what I fear most."

"I hope you won't be alone," he whispers, a tear slipping down his cheek.

"Well."

She puts her glasses back on. She is kind enough not to tell him what he knows to be true; she is already alone, and probably has been for years.

"I mean it," Joshua Murray says, and he does. "If there's anything I can do for you—"

"There's not," she says, shaking her head. But then she looks at him, and from behind her broken glasses, her eyes are sympathetic. Faye puts a hand on his shoulder, and squeezes it. "But thank you. For wanting to do something."

With that, she slowly gets to her feet, her knees cracking as she stands. She adjusts the sad old pair of glasses once more, looks down at Joshua, and smiles. Joshua wonders if she is an angel. She shuffles away slowly, likely to a job scrubbing dishes, folding laundry, keeping house for a Syn family who will replace her with a Vost when she dies. She turns back once, and catches Joshua looking at her. She raises her hand in a small wave.

A lump forms in Joshua's throat as he returns her wave. He is not sure that his prayer has been answered, but he is not sure that it hasn't. Whether it's what God would want or not, Joshua now knows what he can do.

He stands and walks quickly away from the Synt, his feet marching to the steady rhythm of an old clock, wound up and ticking once more.

CHAPTER 31: ERE

THE BIRDS ARE NOT YET SINGING WHEN ERE opens his eyes. It takes a moment to orient himself to the dark room, the unfamiliar old-world bed, the strange rhythmic breathing coming from his left.

Ever.

He looks at her closely, memorizing every inch as she slumbers. Then he remembers the night before, and his cheeks flush. The argument. Original debating Syn, Syn deriding Original, a battle their parents and grandparents had fought before them. And then, somehow, there had at last been a return to kissing, in a dark cabin, alone.

And then came fumbling. Hesitation.

Oh, damnation.

And just as he begins to wish she might never wake up (not that he wished her dead, but if maybe she could just be in deep, deep sleep like an old fairy tale princess or something), Ever's large, heavily-lashed lids twitch and lift, eyes slowly opening, focusing first on the room. Then she turns her head and focuses her gaze squarely on him. Seeing him, she smiles.

"Good almost-morning."

"Good almost-morning," he says, voice cracking like a small boy's, face still burning.

"What's wrong?"

"Ever, last night... I'm sorry. I'm sorry that I was so awkward... that we didn't..."

She takes his hand in hers and presses his fingers to her lips. "I'm glad."

"You're glad?"

"We had... a lot to talk out, apparently," she says softly. "And as far as... as far as anything more between us, it's ... it's something I would want to be special, Ere. We just met, and I already feel so strongly about you—"

"I feel strongly about you too," he says quickly.

"I want to find a way," she says. "For us to be together. Not for a night. For more than a night. Do you want that?"

He nods. He wants that. He also wouldn't mind something more, now, because what if a big cat or poisonous snake killed his stupid virgin self stone-cold dead that very day? But he'll be patient. Because he does want her. On her terms. Even with the Syn complications. He does not know how to say this to her, but he hopes she can tell from his expression just how deep his feelings run, an unfamiliar river coursing through him, carrying him forever toward her.

She smiles, closes her eyes, and resumes the even breathing that tells Ere she is dozing. With the bright sunlight pouring in through the window and ceiling cracks, Ere can see Ever's lovely body quite clearly. Wearing only soft, transparent undergarments, every delicious detail of her is on display. Ere leans back a little, trying to see her entire body at once—and then, he rolls over a little too far and falls out of the small bed, landing hard on the dirt floor.

At the solid thump of Ere's body smacking the floor, Ever sits up. She looks around, then looks down, and sees Ere sprawled on the floor. He looks up at her from his crumpled position, and smiles a sheepish smile.

"Oh, hey, Ev."

"What did you call me?"

"Ev?" He says, afraid she'll tell him not to call her that. Instead, she grins. He starts to untangle himself, easing into a seated position. He pats the ground, like he's inviting her to join him. "Yeah, so it's surprisingly nice down here—"

She throws back her head and laughs, and Ere laughs too. They crack up, getting louder and louder, the sound filling the cabin, spilling outside, and giving them away.

The cabin door flies open, flooding the room with the suddenly harsh, fully-deployed sunlight. Two silhouettes block the door frame, halting the laughter and hiding the first rays of light that had just started streaming in. The two figures stand like angry statues, one large and stoic, the other small, strong, and fuming. The smaller figure growls, low and menacing.

"Get. Up."

J ORGE ZIPS THROUGH THE JUNGLE ON HIS Chariot, a thousand thoughts crowding his mind and none of them showing on his face.

When he delivered the Ever update to Hess, sparing his cowardly colleague Kennedy from taking on that task, Hess turned several interesting colors. Jorge stood patiently, waiting for the colors to fade and the command to come. After the reddening, the purpling, the return to a pallid hue, Hess said only: "Get her."

Jorge took the very next light rail to District 27. When he arrived in the Southern sector, there was a Chariot waiting for him at the station, courtesy of Deputy Lance Briggs.

"All charged up and ready to roll," Briggs said. "Here's a helmet."

"No need," Jorge replied, waving away Briggs' offer of a helmet. He didn't see a need for the precaution. He was full of solid Syn engineering, and if he somehow sustained an injury it could easily be treated. Besides, he was already sweating, and a hot helmet sounded miserable.

"You're sure?" Briggs. Always following the rules.

"I'm sure," Jorge had said. "Thanks."

Jorge mounted the Chariot and sped away. He's not a betting man (not anymore), but if he were, smart money would be on Ever retracing her steps. She must be trying to get back to something—or someone—from her first little jaunt. Despite her pretense of apology, Jorge is certain now that was the reason she had returned to the area. He doesn't know what the girl is up to, but he knows it must be something her father wouldn't like. Which won't go well for the girl.

Jorge fears few people and few things in this life, but Hess is on the short list of things that unsettle him. The only one who risks his wrath on a consistent basis is his daughter. As Jorge sees it, she underestimates her father—almost as much as her father underestimates her.

Bring her back, Hess commanded Jorge, low and dangerous. *In one piece. Is that clear?*

A low-hanging branch connects with Jorge's cheek. He swerves, rights the Chariot, and swears under his breath. Should've worn the damned helmet. He quickly shifts to private mode and erases the embarrassing memory from the public record as he zooms forward. Gritting his teeth against the swiftly-dulling pain in his throbbing face, Jorge hunches down even lower, sliding his shoulders back, extending his torso until he is almost flat against the vehicle. He increases his speed and sails toward the heart of the jungle.

He doesn't want any more problems, either.

CHAPTER 33: ERE

"I SAID *GET UP.*" Ruth Fell snarls, louder this time.

Ere scrambles onto the bed, trying to conceal Ever's body from his family's furious eyes.

He looks to his cousin for any possible help, but the back-lighting obscures Cal's face. Ere can't really see his mother, either, but her rage is palpable. Before the boy can so much as open his mouth, Ruth leaps forward, descending upon her son like an avenging angel.

"Get up, Ere," she says for the third time, cold and commanding. Her hand is poised above his head, ready to grab and drag him out if he does not obey orders. She snarls at Ever. "And you. Who are you?"

Ever reaches down to retrieve her over-garment, and in what seems to be one effortless move, slips her sleek black outfit over her head and stands fully clothed, facing Ruth Fell without fear. Ever's hand is in her pocket, and Ere suddenly remembers the small silver gun.

"You must be Ere's mother."

"I am."

"Mother, if you'll just—" Ere pleads, but Ruth reaches out, grabs her son, and shoves him behind her. Shame flames through Ere's entire body. He's a small child, scolded by his mother, embarrassed in front of the girl and in front of his cousin, and all of this is unbearable. He tries to lunge forward, to get around his mother, back to Ever, but as soon as he even thinks about moving, Cal's heavy hand presses down on his shoulder. Hard. Ere's not going anywhere.

For her part, Ever is still nonplussed. She meets Ruth's gaze directly.

"Your son speaks very highly of you. His family. His people."

Ruth fires her words at Ever like bullets. "Really? He's said nothing about you—"

And then Ruth dissolves into a fit of coughing. She staggers backwards with the intensity of it, half-kneeling, almost falling to the floor. Ere slips from Cal's grasp and places a hand on his mother's back, steadying her.

"Are you all right?"

"No." She chokes out the word and jerks away, shoving him roughly back to Cal, who grabs him more firmly this time. Ere winces; Cal is not being gentle.

Ever looks at Ruth, blinks, and then says: "Terminal lung cancer."

Ruth wipes her mouth, glaring at Ever but saying nothing.

Cal and Ere both gape at Ruth. This diagnosis, simply and clearly given by the Syn girl, is a new and shattering revelation for both of the young men—and an additional glaring realization for Cal.

"She's a Syn?" Cal's grip on Ere's shoulder becomes brutal. The incredulity in his voice outweighs any anger. He looks down at his cousin, shocked and appalled.

"Cal, I—I—" Ere stammers, lost.

"Runt. Shit-for-brains. Curse of the world! She's a Syn?"

"Yes," says Ever evenly. "My name is Ever Hess. My father is the director of the Synthetic Institute. So yes, I am a Syn. In fact, I'm about as Syn as they come. But I promise—"

"No," whispers Ere's mother, soft and ragged but still powerful enough to silence Ever and both young men. "It can't be..."

Ever continues, somewhat more hesitantly, looking at Ruth: "I can assure you, as I assured Ere, I've maintained a private mode setting. I'm not going to reveal your location or bring any harm to you."

Ruth seems not to have heard a single word—nothing since Ever told them her name. She simply stares at Ever, her face drawn and ashen, her eyes round. And then she says again, with such conviction and horror that the words chill the room.

"It can't be."

Ere looks from his mother to Ever, uncomprehending. Cal keeps one hand on Ere, the other on his knife, unsure how to interpret his normally unshakeable aunt's frozen terror.

"You're more than 'Ere's mother,'" Ever says slowly, realizing. "What's your name?"

At this question, his mother pauses. Makes a decision, weighing variables unknown to Ere. Despite her grating breath and evident shock, Ere watches his mother draw herself up from her knees, until she is standing perfectly erect, her strict posture at its finest, making her seem so much taller than she ever was. She proudly raises head, and addresses Ever coldly and plainly.

"My name is Ruth Fell."

Hearing this, Ever gasps.

"Ruth Fell," Ever repeats, incredulous. "No way. You can't be that Ruth. That Ruth is a ghost." She shakes her head, slides her eyes, speaks as if she's reading the words: "Fell off the grid after the last uprisings. No confirmed sightings in years. Presumed dead."

Ruth strangles back a cough. "Not... dead... yet."

Just then, a small red light illuminates on the top of Ever's hand, near her wrist, straight back from her finger port. A quiet but persistent beeping commences, accompanied by the pulsing light. Ever looks up, and Ere detects panic in her eyes. But when she speaks, her voice is eerily calm.

"My locator has been activated. They'll be here to get me soon. If you're here when they arrive, they may assume you kidnapped me. It won't look good for you. Particularly not for you, Ruth Fell. I recommend that you run."

Cal, Ruth, and Ere all stand rooted to the spot. Too much has happened at once. They can't process it. All three are paralyzed, the young men confused, the old woman still shocked by something that has clearly shaken her to the core.

The beeping in Ever's hand grows louder. She looks up, cocking her head, listening, and then her face shows the panic plainly. She locks eyes with Ere and then with incredible speed she closes the distance between them and presses her small metallic gun into his hand. He looks at her, questioning.

"Take the gun," she says, then turns to Cal and Ruth. This time when she addresses them, she yells the word, not a suggestion, but a command.

"RUN!"

C AL TEARS THROUGH THE WOODS AT
breakneck speed, Ere flung across his shoulder like a
sack of potatoes, his aunt trying to keep up with him as
best she can. Cal is squeezing Ere tighter than is necessary, hoping
that it hurts the little bastard. His furious thoughts propel his
feet, carrying him forward with angry force.

Serves him right, lying traitor runt, rat bastard little piece of shit—!

Periodically, Ere claws at him, struggling, trying to free himself. This only urges Cal to run harder, faster, to grip his cousin
more roughly. But behind him, Ruth is slowing. She begins to
cough, trying to suppress it, to press on and keep pace, but Cal
can hear her falling behind.

"Aunt Ruth? Ruth!"

"I'm fine," she wheezes. "Keep... going."

Cal keeps going, but slows his stride, unwilling to lose Ruth. He has never worried about outpacing her before, not ever. He should have known his aunt was dying. The fact that a damn Syn gave that cold, clinical information out of nowhere is tearing Cal apart. He channels his heartbreak into rage. He should have asked his cousin more questions about the bizarre run-in with a girl in the woods. The lying little prick took advantage of his trust. How could he have guessed that his cousin was cavorting not with a girl, but with a Synthetic whore? Cal swears to himself that he will never be the last to know anything, ever again.

For his entire life, ever since his mother died when he could barely walk, Cal has only counted three people as his true family, his reliable rocks: Great-Uncle Howard, Aunt Ruth, Ere. These three people—one dead, one dying, one a liar—are all abandoning him at once. He suddenly wants to stop running. He wants to scream and ask questions and break something, possibly Ere's head. But they are still only a short distance from the cottage, where the Syn whore's robot hand is glowing red and beeping and summoning the enemy.

Behind him, his aunt has slowed to walk. Another relentless coughing fit overtakes her, and this time it brings her all the way down. Cal spins around in time to see her lurch, stumble, her once-sure foot sliding from beneath her, sending her sprawling to the ground. She lands hard.

"Ruth!" Cal screams. He heaves Ere off his shoulder, tosses him to the ground, and gives him a look that would freeze an ocean. "If you run away from us now, you are dead to me. When I start running, your ass is going to be running right. Behind. Me." Then Cal lifts Ruth, and puts her on his shoulder, where Ere had been.

"No," she coughs.

"I'll carry you now," he says.

"Cal—" Ruth protests.

"It's my turn to carry you."

"Mother," Ere says in a thin voice, approaching tentatively. "Are you okay?"

The coughing flares again, and when she is able to stop, she looks not at her son but at her nephew, and wheezes: "We have to get to the tribe. We have to warn them…"

Cal's feet are moving again, running toward their camp. His aunt is even lighter than her skinny son. Her muscles are gone, her skin clings to bone. How had Cal missed this? *Terminal lung cancer*. Curse of the world. She weighs nothing at all. Without looking behind him or slowing his pace, he yells out at his cousin, somewhere behind him.

"You better start running, you little bastard!"

He hears twigs snapping behind him, assuring him that the boy is doing as he was told. Cal knows he can't think about what will come, but only about what is happening right now. He has to run to his tribe, stand guard, move them if necessary. Hide them. Save them. Evacuate the cabins and take to the woods. The first priority is surviving the current threat.

And only then, once he has protected them all, will he decide what to do about his stupid runt cousin, who lied to him and endangered the tribe, all for the love of a Syn whore. A Syn whore whose perfect body fills Cal's mind, even now, even as he flees from her.

Heaven. And. Hell.

A S SOON AS THE ORIGINALS FLEE, Ever sprints in the opposite direction, toward her Chariot. She forms a plan as she runs: if she can reach the Chariot quickly enough, she can speed her way back toward the incorporated area of Sector 27, not only leading the search party away from the Fell tribe but also arriving where she was supposed to be before she's found elsewhere.

She'll go straight to the central office, immediately hand over her Chariot, her apology gift to the leadership of Sector 27. She'll invent some silly story about wanting to test the sleek, beautiful vehicle before handing it over.

Just giving it a spin. Didn't think anyone would miss me, ha ha ha...

The beeping from her hand is unrelenting. She wishes she could stop it. Another thought occurs to her, as a flash of heat dampens her neck: if she passes out, her system override will kick in, triggering a distress signal, even louder and more unrelenting than the current beep. And passing out is imminent. She's panting heavily, finding it difficult to maintain this pace. She's too hot. She's been ignoring her temperature for way too long.

The shocking encounter with Ruth Fell (*sonofabitch*, had that really happened?) elevated her pulse, the streaming morning sunlight heated the room, and now, running through the damn jungle, she's pushed it too far. Her clothes are soaked with sweat, and she feels dizzy. She has never been so dangerously and recklessly overheated. A system alert buzzes, *generalized fever*. Her human and machine systems have both been compromised. She needs to cool down, and soon. But not before she protects the Originals.

I've got to get them off the trail... lead them away... have to get to the Chariot...

She can see the Chariot now—only a hundred yards away. She's going to make it. And then she'll get on the Chariot, and floor it to the incorporated area and... and then she'll—

The Chariot swims before her eyes. She feels a system-wide jolt as her override mode kicks in, shifting her out of private mode, fully activating her tracking device, stopping her in her tracks. She collapses on to the damp grassy ground. The cool green of the grass is the last thing she registers before the world clicks off and goes dark.

CHAPTER 36: ERE

UPON REACHING THE CAMPSITE, CAL GOES as fast as he can from cabin to cabin, informing each elder of their newly perilous situation. Those who are nimble enough spring into action, helping to get the word out, grabbing their few belongings. The moves are practiced. They know what to do, and will keep doing it until they met their end.

As Cal raises the alert, Ere stays at his mother's side, supporting her. She rests her weight on him but still refuses to meet his eyes, keeping her gaze fixed instead on the activity around their soon-to-be-abandoned campsite. Her breathing is still labored.

215

"Mother, what Ever—what she said, about you being sick... terminally ill...?" He swallows hard, not sure he wants to confirm the diagnosis, but he has to know. "Are you?"

"Not... now," rasps Ruth, brushing him away like a leaf.

But at this, Ere rebels; clinging stubbornly to the branch, a leaf unwilling to fall. He knows he's in the wrong, they're in danger, he's to blame for all of this—but he's also angry, and worried, and scared, and he pushes back against his mother's gust of ragged air.

"Now is not the time to talk? Then *when*? *When* is the time to talk? When we're migrating? When we're running from Syns? When we're hiding? When you're treating me like a helpless child? When the cancer kills you?"

In the distance, Cal calls from the last cabin, whistles and waves to signal that everyone had been alerted, soon they'll be ready to move. Ere raises an arm automatically, acknowledging. Cal ducks into the cabin he and Ere had shared, gathering the knives, the cooking pot, their small collection of books and other scant treasures.

"Yes."

His mother says the word so softly, it is almost carried off by the wind before it could be heard. She is the leaf, not him, and she has almost separated from the branch. So quiet. But Ere heard her. He just wants to pretend he didn't.

"Yes...?"

"Yes, I'm dying," says his mother. She looks at Ere, and he notices that the whites of her eyes are tinged yellow, and that the dark circles below her eyes are dramatic and pronounced. How long has she been like this? For the past week, yes, his thoughts were dominated by the Syn girl. And before that there was the migration, and before that the funeral, but still...

"Did you get it from Uncle Howard?"

"No, Ere," she says, somewhat more gently. "Cancer isn't contagious. Cancer, it's just... it's just something that attacks you silently. You don't realize the knife has been slipped into your back until you shift one night, in your sleep, and jostle it. Then you feel the stab, and it's too late to do anything about it. That's cancer."

Cancer. Cancer. Cancer.

The sound of the word, its shape and thickness and slithering sound makes Ere feel sick. He heard the word before, when Helena's husband took ill and the ugly word was whispered throughout the tribe. *Cancer. Silent killer. A death sentence for Originals.*

And there had been the other whispers, indicting and angry: *The Syns have a cure.*

But there was no access for Originals to hospitals, to treatment, to cures. When cancer attacks, Originals die. Helena's husband died. Ere's mother has cancer, and she'll die, too.

Unless he could bring the cure to her.

"The Syns have a cure," he says quickly. "Right? I heard the elders say it before. The Syns have cures. For all kinds of sickness. I can talk to Ever. We will get you into one of their hospitals, and we'll get you the cure—"

"Ere, stop." She coughs again. The sound tears through him, ripping an irreparable hole. "Just stop."

"But do they? Have a cure?"

"Syns have a cure for almost every known disease. But the cures are for Syns and Syns alone. They view any treatment of an Original's ailment as a waste of resources. Expensive medicines would never be thrown away on any Original, least of all me."

He tries to remember everything that Ever had said about his mother.

You can't be that Ruth Fell. That Ruth is a ghost…

"Why did Ever… know you?"

"Ere…" She shakes her head to stop his words. Then she coughs several long moments, but when she ceases coughing, her voice is stronger and clearer than it has been in quite some time.

"When Uncle Howard died, it was a risk for me to give the eulogy, because people came from all over. Confirming that I was alive, even just confirming it to other Originals—that put all of us at risk."

"But why…"

She cuts him off again. "Uncle Howard could negotiate with Syns because even though he was a resistance leader, he was non-violent. As far as they know, he was just an old teacher who gave some incendiary speeches, hosted a few meetings. When the up-risings ended, his crimes were of less consequence; futile, tooth-less. Mine were not."

Cal and the small band of elders are approaching them, ready to vacate. Ruth raises a hand, weakly, gesturing for them to come her way. She will still find a way to lead them. She will find a way, at least for today, to still be the Ruth Fell they expect her to be.

Ere's heart twists; he's so proud of her, so scared for her, and so riveted by her. He needs her to finish what she was telling him, about her crimes, about why the Syns want to punish her.

"Why wasn't Uncle Howard wanted for whatever he did, but you—"

"Uncle Howard never assassinated anyone." The words of her confession rattle like a snake, and when she looks back at him, her yellowed eyes are unapologetic. "I did."

THE SYNTHETIC NEUROSCIENCE INSTITUTE of Technology has no peer agency. In addition to serving as the foremost groundbreaking research institute of the post-Singularity world, it also serves as headquarters for the governing body of Syn society, the Syn Council. It is the White House, the United Nations, the CIA, MIT, all housed in a compound ten times more impenetrable than Fort Knox.

Serving as the Council's home base is its most important non-scientific function, and one of the reasons for the high security throughout the building. After the formal dissolution of the last remaining national governments, the Syn Council emerged, a small handful of individuals who oversee everything from law and order to research and development. Their power is consolidated, extreme, unrivaled.

There are eleven of them on the Council, four women, seven men, all of whom were rich and powerful prior to the Singularity—and all of whom served on the advisory board of the Synt back in the old days, before their titles and entire physical selves got an upgrade. Dr. Felix Hess holds a permanent position as Council ex-officio. Officially a non-voting twelfth member of the group, Hess' opinion holds more sway than anyone's vote.

The Synthetic Neuroscience Institute of Technology began as a modest research outfit in Cambridge, Massachusetts, on February 15, 1995. Before its formal incorporation, the team there jokingly called it The Kurzweil Institute. The nickname was in honor of Raymond Kurzweil's appearance on a television game show, wherein he gave the world a preview of the evolution to come. The game show aired exactly thirty years earlier, on February 15, 1965, when Kurzweil was only seventeen. The name of the show was *I've Got a Secret*.

The premise of *I've Got a Secret* was simple. Each episode featured "special guests," each of whom had a fascinating secret that competing panelists had to guess. Panelists were given clues and allowed to ask questions of the guests. When Kurzweil was a guest, following a brief introduction from the show's host he sat in at a piano and played a short composition. The footage is preserved in the Synt archives; viewers often note how the young man seemed so small beside the gregarious game show host, and smaller still at the massive piano. The true secret contained within Raymond Kurzweil's small frame was that this tiny teenage prodigy would be posthumously hailed as the first prophet of the Singularity.

The grainy, black-and-white footage of Raymond Kurzweil's game show appearance is shockingly banal. The undercurrent of power is missed by the camera. It could be any other episode of *I've Got a Secret*, any other "special guest" going through the motions, following the rules of the game. When he plays the piano, Kurzweil's pale, slender fingers glide effortlessly across the ivory keys. The melody he plays is brief, forgettable.

What was it? What was his secret?

The panelists that day included a comedic actor, Henry Morgan, a performer with a forgettable face sporting a jaunty bow tie; and a beauty queen—Bess Myerson, a regular on the show, and a former Miss America, the only Jewish woman ever to hold the title. Bess' hair was so coiffed, proud and stiff, you could almost smell the aerosol across the airwaves. Her heavily kohl-lined lids stayed focused on the young Kurzweil as he played his simple tune.

After his piano-playing, the panelists asked Kurzweil questions. They knew the rules of the game, and made their moves: sizing him up, trying to determine what mysteries and magic might be running beneath the surface of the mild young man. It was Henry who finally guessed correctly: The music was composed by a computer—a computer of Kurzweil's creation.

"I designed and built an electronic computer," he confirmed as an uncomprehending studio audience applauded. "The computer wrote the melody I just played."

This was absolutely paradigm shifting. Not only that Kurzweil had created the machine, but all the more so that *the machine had created the music*. Creation, maybe even creativity, could be manufactured by something that was, itself, manufactured? It was unheard of. It should have brought the world to its knees, right then and there. It took decades to actually do so.

That day, it was an innocent novelty, its implications present but not accounted for by anyone save Kurzweil himself. Kurzweil showed off the composer—the computer he built. A large machine, big as a bureau, connected to a typewriter; its exposed wires looked like an open brain on an operating table. The audience and panelists were not nearly as impressed as they should have been. And then, the round was over. The show moved on. The panelists were ready for the next contestant—one Mrs. Loney, hailing from Rough and Ready, California (her secret was that she taught President Lyndon B. Johnson in first grade).

For his troubles, for his tremendously under-heralded secret, young Ray Kurzweil got $200 that day. He was just a run-of-the-mill game show guest. A computer whiz, yes, perhaps even a savant. But few in the audience-at-home saw him for the prophet he truly was. After his fifteen minutes of game show fame, the general public saw little of him. But he never stopped working with artificial intelligence and trans-humanism.

He was obsessed with futurism. He was driven by questions: was intelligence, creativity, self-expression merely reserved for humans? Could these things be simulated by machines? More importantly, could these things be *experienced* by machines? Most importantly, *when would it happen?*

Kurzweil believed in the inevitable transition from organic human life to artificially enhanced existence. It was Kurzweil who asserted that a technological-evolutionary leap known as The Singularity was an achievable goal for humanity. More than that: it was a worthwhile, inevitable, *unavoidable and ultimate* goal. It was not a mythical fountain of youth, but a scientifically sound hypothesis. A logical approach to the pursuit of eternal life.

In 1990, he wrote "The Age of Intelligent Machines." Nine years later, he revised and re-published it as "The Age of Spiritual Machines." In 2005, he again revisited the text, emerging with the presciently-titled "The Singularity Is Near: When Humans

Transcend Biology." His writing provided a glimpse of what was to come; humans augmenting their minds and bodies with technology. He correctly identified the three primary elements of the techno-evolutionary jump: advancements in the studies of genetics, nanotechnology, and robotics. The Singularity, claimed Kurzweil, was our next step. Period. The functionality of the human brain was technologically quantifiable, and its components could be built, re-constructed, melded with robotic enhancements. He credited his own Baby Boomer generation, their numbers and their longevity, for the exponential growth of technology. They were the ones to allow tech to intersect and surpass the processes of the human brain.

The rapidly accelerating science pointed to what man would at last be able to do: rebuild himself in a new and better image. Recreate without traditional reproduction. Extend life. Rather than being created, man would be Creator. As Kurzweil famously stated at the conclusion of his film *The Transcendent Man*: "You might ask, does God exist? Well, I would say... not yet."

The team at the institute that would become the Synt all loved Kurzweil. They read all his books. Even reached out to him, asked him to join their team (he must have turned them down, but there are no records of a response). But by then he was in the early stages his own next-enterprise—Singularity University. It was a benefit corporation, not a traditional school, where the world's greatest scientific minds strived to solve humanity's grand challenges.

"Humanity's grand challenges?" Hess had echoed dubiously when he first heard about SU. He was still young but already unconcerned about coming off as impertinent, even to a man he once idolized. (As soon as Kurzweil started emphasizing artificial intelligence above elevated humanity, Hess had taken the man off his short list of heroes.) "And what might those be?"

It turned out that food, water, energy, security, global health, education, environment and space exploration were the "grand challenges" Singularity University aimed to solve, through artificial intelligence and robotics, biotechnology, computers and digital fabrication. Hess scoffed: "So the problems all basically due to over-population will be solved by bringing robots into the mix? Introducing a new population rather than upgrading the one we've already got?"

When the institute filed for incorporation, they selected a formal name—no namesakes. They became the Synthetic Neuroscience Institute of Technology. At some point people began calling it the Synt. Hess hated the nickname, but his mentor liked it, and everyone used it, and eventually even Hess gave in. It was more efficient, anyway, and he couldn't win every fight. Just most of them, he reassured himself.

As the Synt's profile began to rise, as associate director, Hess briefly became a regular on the conference speakers circuit. He hated going to conferences, despised sitting through sessions, abhorred pressing the flesh and all of the muckety-muck. But he did relish the opportunity to promote his own theories, and even more so, the chance to tear down those of his rivals.

"Artificial intelligence is a joke," he'd say when asked, practically grinning whenever he was tossed that bone, usually by some overeager grad student. "Ask any economist—they'll tell you that giving more jobs to robots will take jobs from the working class, reduce purchasing power, and cripple the economy. Ask any conspiracy theorist—they'll ask you if you're ready to welcome your robot overlords." The crowd laughed. He had them eating out of the palm of his hand. "But in all seriousness. Why invest billions of dollars, hours of research, into something artificial? I'm interested in something real. Human potential—augmented by technology. Machines working within us, not apart from us."

"Are you saying that because you're already part-machine?"

The cheeky question came from the back. Hess strained to see the inquirer. Even when standing, she was barely taller than the people seated in front of her. It was his old Stanford foe.

"Still championing AI, Miss Lee?"

"It's *Doctor* Lee," Claudia called up to him. "And yeah, I'm still all about the science that doesn't require human test subjects."

That really started the room buzzing, wondering—*was Hess' group really experimenting on human subjects? Was he working with a team of madmen? Was he a madman? Hess' hermit-like mentor always sent Hess in his stead. Was the Cyborganics Cowboy already a cyborg?*

More hands went up. The undercurrent running through the room went from friendly to suspicious. Hess knew he might lose them if he wasn't careful. And so he chuckled, a measured and derisive little series of huffs (he carefully kept the laughter soft, and not loud enough to be potentially taken as nervous or maniacal).

"Pardon me, *Doctor* Lee. Thanks for bringing a little bit of fiction to our science today. And thank you, all, for coming, and for all the excellent questions. I have a plane to catch, so I'm afraid that'll be all the questions for now. Enjoy the conference."

There was polite laughter, healthy applause. They would remember the big ideas of his speech more than Claudia's attempted derailment. As the next sessions began beckoning, the human sea before Hess parted, receded, and disappeared—leaving only one woman washed ashore, standing with arms crossed amidst all the empty folding chairs.

"Hell of a speech, Felix."

"I didn't see your name on the presenters list, Claudia."

"I'm not here to present. I'm here to recruit."

Hess folded his notes, tucked them into his pocket, and took his time stepping out from behind the podium. He stopped at the edge of the raised platform on which the podium was positioned, and did not step down. He relished the additional two feet in height this gave him over the already-vertically-challenged Lee.

"Don't tell me: You want me to come work with you."

Claudia's mouth twitched. "Well, I don't. But my boss does. So here I am."

"And who's your boss?"

"Can't say."

"Is he a robot?" Felix asked, careful not to smirk until after he had delivered the line with a face as straight as an arrow.

"Why do you assume it's a he?"

"Sorry. Is she a robot?"

"I don't remember you having such a sense of humor."

"I always had a good sense of humor."

"I didn't say it was good. And how can a guy obsessed with cyborgs be so high-and-mighty about robotics? We're working in the same world, Felix. The same people who think I'm a lunatic think you're a lunatic. Of course, you actually *are* a lunatic."

He regarded her, respecting her audacity and intellect—qualities he had already decided were lacking in his recently-acquired wife, Marilyn. But Marilyn was far prettier than Claudia, and also obscenely rich, and not nearly as self-important or hung up on artificial intelligence.

"So what exactly are you doing these days, *Doctor* Lee?"

"Still playing with robots," she said with a Mona Lisa smile.

"What's the offer, Claudia?"

His old classmate stepped forward and handed him a sealed envelope. "You have twenty-four hours to accept or decline."

"You're not going to stay here while I read it?"

She shook her head. "I heard you have a plane to catch. Where you headed?"

"New York. Location scouting," he added, wanting inexplicably for her to know that his project, his team, his institute was growing and would need a presence in the center of the world. But Claudia Lee was unimpressed.

"Read the offer before you sign a lease," was all she said. And then she left.

Hess tucked the envelope into his jacket pocket, alongside his notes. It burned a hole there, but he prided himself on his willpower. He didn't open it until he was at the airport, made it through security, got a coffee, and found a seat to await his boarding call.

The letter was brief—an invitation to create his own position on a "groundbreaking team of future-focused scientists committed to extending and enhancing the human experience." It listed several of the already-recruited scientists, Claudia Lee among them. It included a financial offer. The offer was seven figures. Annually.

The letter was signed "Lorraine Murray, Founder, Future Focused Science Institute of the Americas." Beneath the name of her organization were two phone numbers, office and mobile, and a hand-written note in painstakingly perfect cursive:

> Dr. Hess: From everything I hear, I need you on my team. I anxiously await your reply, and hope you will take seriously this offer. Call me anytime to discuss your future with the Future Focused Science Institute of the Americas.—LM

Terrible name, was Hess' first thought. The Future Focused Science Institute of the Americas? What the hell did that even mean? (Not that "the Synt" was much better. But at least it was succinct.)

Poorly played, Claudia, was his second thought.

"Welcome to flight 5775, service to New York's John F. Kennedy Airport. At this time, we'd like to invite any passengers needing assistance—wheelchairs, small children—to begin boarding the aircraft. Next, our first class passengers will be welcomed aboard," chirped a bright, sunshine-y airline professional.

Hess pulled his smartphone from his pocket. He ran a quick search as he stood in line, not meeting the bright eyes of the airline attendant who scanned his boarding pass. When he was seated in his first class window seat, he called his mentor.

"It's me. I'm about to go see the property. And I think I may have found our angel investor for the institute.... Yes, this one seems to have the interest and the capacity. I think you should reach out and call Lorraine Murray. M-U-R-R-A-Y. She's in Los Angeles. All right, I have to go—we're about to take off."

His plane took off five seconds later. And almost as quickly, so did everything else. Hess is still gleefully grateful to Claudia Lee for being the inadvertent guarantor that the Synt never had a true peer institution. How could they, when his team poached her investors? They then set about looting and recruiting the scientists, too—all but stubborn Claudia, who refused to acknowledge that the stupidly-named Future Focused Institute was officially a thing of the past.

With the consolidation of money and talent, unwittingly facilitated by Claudia, the Synt outpaced everyone else in the race to the next evolutionary leap. In a world with a pace ever-accelerating, this institution would always be moving the fastest, without exception, without hesitation, and without apology.

"NOT YET," MUTTERS DR. FELIX HESS, reviewing the latest mule research data. "Not yet."

He repeats the words like a mantra, a reminder that while answers still elude him, they will ultimately be found. Such is the promise of *yet;* literally everything that exists was once a *not-yet.*

Hess is exhausted, though he knows the fatigue is more psychological than physical. He checked all of his systems; everything is in perfect working order. No malfunctions, no parts in need of replacement. But even with its enhancements, his body still houses the mind of a man. Human heads were still prone to stress, to worry, to the occasional headache.

Right now, the headache is being triggered by the upcoming upgrade evaluation. Liver, heart, lungs, eyes, kidneys—none of these were designed to last for eternity. Stem cell organ cloning is vital to Syn survival. They honed and perfected processes for growing organs, harvested and kept on hand for the regularly scheduled organic-upgrades for Syns. Skin and hair treatments to keep every aesthetic element as polished and updated as the neurological elements were also developed.

Electronics need updates. Organic elements need upgrades. This was a long game they were playing, and every curveball had to be anticipated and caught. Or smacked out of the ballpark, or whatever the right metaphor would be. (Hess never was much of a sports guy.)

To that end, Hess' team has two primary mandates: *maintain and sustain.*

The first mandate, *maintain,* includes overseeing all organ growth, synthetic updates, scheduled general maintenance, testing and assessments. For example, every five years on a rotating schedule to accommodate the entire population, Syns come in for an extensive physical, to examine every element of their functionality, health, mental competence, everything. This is when organs are tested and scheduled for replacement, skin is resurfaced, mental acuity is confirmed, and on and on. Dr. Hess and his team take information gleaned from representative samples during each round of tests and use it to develop the next system-wide updates.

Staving off any ill effects of aging is what first compelled Hess to focus in on this science. Death never frightened him much. But aging—failing strength, failing health, and more than anything, failing mental capacities—those are his nightmares. Forever haunted by the ghost of his grandmother, dementia is the devil he is hell bent on destroying.

No matter how much progress he spearheads or problems he solves, Hess can't erase the power Catherine O'Brien Hess still has over him. It seems a poetic injustice that the woman whose own memory was robbed looms so large in her grandson's organic recollections. Even her voice still follows him, calling, chuckling, sometimes screaming. Some nights as he prepares to plug in, her lullaby sings him off to the dreamless sleep of his own design:

Little Fee, Little Fee, you'll set the world free…

Other nights it is not her song that comes for him, but her scream; the last sound he ever heard her make; a shrill, scarring soundtrack reminding him just how awful the old world could be.

No more memories. Not now. Too much to do.

Felix Hess directs his thoughts forcefully to the tasks at hand. He still feels plagued by the cryptic prophecy, but he can't allow the vague prediction to derail him from the clearly established tasks at hand. First task, maintaining; second task, sustaining.

Maintenance is rote and regulated. The second mission is less regulated, more experimental. Which makes the work more frustrating, more taxing, and far more thrilling. Maintenance is straightforward science. Sustaining still has some art to it.

Sustaining the Syn population is an ongoing mystery to be solved. Syns have the potential to live forever, but only the potential. They can still die, if struck by lightning or light rail. And all immortality is purely theoretical. The whole planet might be struck by meteors or an unforeseen epidemic. Or aliens in spaceships. Nothing's impossible.

The Synt's mission is simple, and insane: identify and plan for anything in the entire universe that might possibly happen.

Maintenance itself plays a role in sustaining the population, since results of the five-year samples are used to ward off any threats. But "sustaining" goes beyond that. It's not reactive management, but proactive planning. Planning for the future. And unbeknownst to almost anyone, these plans include a new spin on an old process: procreation.

This classified project is called Generation Next.

For the sardonic Hess, it's also known as "the mules."

The question of Syn fertility is tricky. Population control and resource allocation led to logical steps taken decades earlier—first limiting procreation, then banning it entirely. Hess had been completely on board with the public ban on procreation, but as a scientist he always knew some Syns needed that ability left intact. There had to be a workaround. If the Syns lost all ability to reproduce, that would be a threat to their society. Procreation had to be controlled, of course, but it also had to be possible.

Cloning was tested, and would be tested again. But Hess isn't a fan of entirely-external models. His views were validated by the fact that when synched, all of his team's laboratory-grown humans had far higher malfunction rates than humans created traditionally. The best way to create more Syns is allowing some Syns to procreate—more to the point, allowing some Syn bodies to produce sperm and eggs. Hess is all for growing fetuses in labs. He just wants to grow them with locally-sourced, all-natural organic seeds.

Trouble is, even though some women were intentionally kept off the standard hormone suppression regimen, eggs are still getting harder and harder to come by. While upgrades and enhancements kept their façades youthful and their overall functionality hale and hearty, their reproductive systems resisted regeneration. Human females have always been born with all the eggs they would ever have; when the female body reaches approximately fifty natural years of life, the egg supply runs out. And once the carton is empty, it's empty.

They could print ovaries with 3-D printers. They could grow new uteruses and transplant them into older bodies. But somehow they couldn't get the manufactured parts to yield consistently viable eggs. If Hess believed in karma, the trouble with Syn women's reproductive capability would seem a no-brainer: the Syns attacked the Original's reproductive rights, and were subsequently robbed of their own reproductive abilities.

Eliminating Original fertility was a decision seen not only as logical but also as merciful. It would avoid bloodshed down the road. No Original babies born meant no new Original soldiers. It was brilliant in its pure simplicity. Originals are designed to die, usually in less than eight or nine decades. Taking that into account, it was swiftly evident that there was no need for more bloodshed. As long as their reproductive abilities were crippled, the Originals' days were numbered. They would quietly age out of existence.

It was history's most compassionate death sentence. The Council agreed unanimously.

The question then became: *how to do it?*

Again, the simple solution presented itself quickly. Water. Everyone needed water. The Originals always set up camp near water. And the Syns controlled all the main water sources. Streams, rivers, tributaries, reservoirs, pipes—all potable water was easy for the Syns to contaminate with the chemicals necessary to achieve their aim.

Different chemicals impact different systems. Prior to infiltrating the water system, the chemicals were tested. Each cocktail consistently impacted the female reproductive system, but none had consistent effects on men. The Council, which consisted primarily of men, found this acceptable. They were more comfortable rendering ovaries useless than messing with other men's sperm counts.

Since infertile women plus fertile men still added up to an infertile population, the goal was achieved. When the Original women learned of this assault on their bodies, there was outrage; some of the fiercest fighting of the final days of the Synthetic War were led by Ruth Fell. The Syns attempted to retake the water processing facilities. They failed.

Syn women gradually becoming as barren as their Original counterparts might seem to some a well-crafted verse of poetic justice. But Hess doesn't believe in poetry, just or otherwise; he believes in science, period.

"Men's reproductive abilities, objectively speaking, are superior to women's," he reminded the fretting Council. "In addition to their diminishing rather than replenishing reproductive material, women can have only one pregnancy at a time. But men can cause countless pregnancies, resulting in thousands of offspring in one generation, given the right set of circumstances. Men have always been better at reproducing."

"Better at fertilizing," Lorraine had sniped, but that was the only real retort. Still, the Council continued muttering their concern that karmic or not, their inability to successfully reproduce might eventually prove problematic. So Hess and his team are still working to solve the infertility issue. Their latest attempt is the Generation Next Project. The Mules.

Mules, the large-toothed and long-faced offspring of a domesticated horse and donkey, are almost always born infertile. In the old world, conventional science theorized that the sterility of mules was chromosomal. A horse has 32 chromosome pairs and a donkey has 31 pairs. When mating animals of different species, the resulting offspring have half the number of pairs. A mule inherits 32 individual chromosomes from the horse, and 31 from the donkey. The result is 63 chromosomes, or 31 and one-half pairs, with one "leftover" chromosome from the horse. When the fertilization takes place, and the chromosomes pair together to share information to build the brand-new baby mule, not all chromosomes can neatly pair off. The theory has been that this chromosomal imbalance is why the mule is sterile.

That small imbalance is the difference between viable and unviable creatures. Male mules produce sperm; females produce ova; however, those sperm cells and eggs are useless. They are the right shape, size, appearance—they just don't work. Mules are a half-step away from being fertile, with bodies still designed for parenthood. In fact, sterile female mules can carry foals, and even produce milk. They make good surrogates.

That's why the idea presented itself to Hess in the braying voice of the barren mule: *Mixed-genetics surrogacy*. But instead of horses and donkeys, the mismatched parents primed to produce controllable, fertility-deprived "mule" offspring were Originals and Syns.

The Generation Next Project, or GNP, has already been in development for some time. The need for mules—embryos created by a combination of Original and Syn parentage—was realized only after several early mistakes were made. Hess would love to claim perfection from the very beginning, but that's not how his beloved science works. It takes trial and error, risk and experimentation to make progress.

Before GNP implemented the mules, Hess' team tried other things. They rounded up Originals, harvested their genetic material, and grew one hundred percent Original-stock fetuses. But this led to something dubbed the Moses Risk: Just as the biblical Moses was born of Hebrew slaves but rescued by Pharaoh's daughter and raised in the palace, when he learned of his origin he sided with the slaves. This unacceptable trait surfaced early. Young stock who learned of their origin and displayed any sympathy for their fellow Originals were destroyed.

One hundred percent Syn stock was an even more miserable failure. There were too few women still producing eggs to yield enough supply, and that scant supply was mostly tainted, or exposed to too much radiation and other elements utilized in synching and upgrades, or simply too old.

The few fetuses produced from Syn stock all displayed deformities—and were therefore all ultimately destroyed.

So it was determined that the combination of Original and Syn genetic stock was the true ideal, because it mitigated the Moses Risk, reduced deformities, and yielded a side benefit: producing completely sterile human mules. Just as with the chromosomal theory of the horse-donkey mules, there were hypotheses as to why this was, but nothing conclusive. No matter, in the short term: Infertility in the resulting "mule" offspring made population control even easier. Since population control remains imperative, this was a tremendous boon to the project.

The mule babies born of Original and Syn parents are born sterile, pristine, primed and ready for synching. Perfect little shells. Ready to be put to use, when their time comes.

The GNP is not a touchy-feely "make babies because the world loves babies" program. It's not an adoption program. It's an insurance policy. Sure, new Syns might be needed now and again. But the mandate is to *sustain* the existing Syns, not to *replace* them. Eventually, if a Syn's organic body eroded so much that it was beyond repair or treatment, with the help of the GNP, the original shell—their old body—can be retired.

And then, if all goes according to plan, the entirety of their consciousness will be transferred to a fresh, waiting body.

That's what the new bodies are for: so that the slowly-aging Syns can rest easy, knowing that when the last of their organic components begin to fail them, their minds can be downloaded directly into their own designated mule. (The organic mind of the mule would then simply be discarded, or dissected for research purposes.) Good as new.

The project is still classified, kept secret from all but the most senior Council members. There are ethical questions that will surely emerge when the program goes public, but Hess is prepared to answer them all. Aging is a common enemy their society must fight. Organic matter ultimately decays, and no matter how they stave off the effects, at some point the clock will run out on their original flesh. Anyone who protests the mule solution will have to come up with something better, or shut the hell up.

Would you rather have your body rot away? Or would you rather step into a fresh new body and continue contributing to the collective knowledge of our world? This is our answer. This is our salvation.

Hess knows all radical change brings resistance. He's seen it time and again. In the seventies, there was a furor over "test tube babies." When Louise Brown, the world's first test-tube baby was born on July 25, 1978, she was a shock to the system. Some posited she would die young; others feared she would be a freak. But she thrived, and within a decade, the first test-tube baby was all but forgotten because she had been joined by so many others as the process became accepted medical practice. In 2010, Robert Edwards, the doctor who brought Louise Brown into the world, was awarded the 2010 Nobel Prize in Physiology or Medicine for the development of in-vitro fertilization.

Progress is often condemned before it is applauded. Hess has no fear of his detractors. He's playing a long game—a very, very long game, if all goes well.

Felix Hess has no time for sentimentality. When it comes to his work, feeling anything other than determination is futile. Even with this project, its risks and its ambiguities. As a young man, he might have given more weight to some of the ethical considerations. He minored in philosophy, after all. But Hess knows now that morality is not the shades-of-gray philosophers might espouse. Nearly all of the time, things are either right or wrong. The only variable is the end goal. Anything furthering the end goal is right; anything detracting from it, wrong.

Standing in the core of Heaven, planning the future, it is very difficult for Dr. Felix Hess to remember that he is not, in fact, God.

At least, not yet.

"ARE YOU FEELING ANY BETTER?"

Ere places another damp rag on his mother's head, trying to bring her some small measure of relief from the fever burning through her. He can feel the heat emanating from her, warming the rag beneath his fingertips.

"Yes, thank you," she murmurs.

They both know she is only saying this to make him feel better. Her coughing has been incessant for days, alleviated only when the fever rendered her completely comatose. Ere and Cal take turns staying up with her, keeping her in cool rags, making sure her hand is never un-held.

The tribe should be on the move. Ere and Cal now know what the elders have known for decades: Ruth Fell is a fugitive. A liability. She is also their hero, and they will never abandon her. So despite the risks, they made camp only a few miles from the fishing village they had abruptly abandoned. The new camp met their two most basic requirements: it had a water source (a river, likely highly contaminated; they boiled this water twice before using it, even for washing); and it was free of Syn cameras or patrols.

Still, the tribe is on edge. Cal informed them all about Ere's tryst with the Syn girl and how she identified Ruth Fell. Ere has tried assuring them that she won't report them, but the elders have no reason to trust this claim. Why would a Syn girl protect them?

And so, while Cal and Ere care for Ruth, the elders keep watch, two or three at a time. None of them are getting enough sleep. An already old and weary tribe has become a collection of half-waking specters, bleary-eyed but stubbornly staying alert.

Cal's head appears through the flap of Ruth and Ere's small tent. Cal has not spoken to Ere since the morning, a week ago now, when he and Ruth found Ere with Ever. Ere knows his cousin is furious. He understands that Cal feels used, manipulated, and betrayed by Ere. But since Ruth's health has taken such a rapid turn for the worse, all attention is on her. And so Cal has been civil to Ere. He will do it for Ruth, until her condition improves or until they lose her. But Cal does not meet Ere's eyes as he leans in, stooping to examine the one he still loves.

"How is she—oh, aunt, you're awake! How are you feeling?"

She opens her mouth to reassure her nephew as she reassured her son, but no sound escapes from the small dry desert of Ruth's cracked, parched lips. Ere looks desperately at his cousin. For the first time in days, Cal met his eyes, but has no help to offer.

"Is there more water boiled?" Ere manages.

"Yes," says Cal quickly.

"Let it cool, then bring us some more, for drinking. Helena says we need to keep her as hydrated as we can. And if you can just get some cold water directly from the stream for the rags for her forehead, too… it might not be sanitary, but we need something cool quickly—"

"I'll bring all of the water. Hot and cold. And I'll bring fresh rags, too."

Any assignment is a welcome relief, something that can momentarily bring some sense of purpose and usefulness. Cal's head disappears from the tent.

"Ere," croaks Ruth.

"Shhh," Ere replies, stroking her cheek, trying to sound brave and reassuring, something his mother was always better at. "Don't try to talk. Just rest. You need to get your strength back."

"Not... getting it back."

"Don't say that." Death might be standing outside the tent, but Ere will not acknowledge him, will not invite him in; he is not welcome here.

She swallows, a dry swallow of nothing. "There are things... you need to know."

"You can tell me when you're feeling better."

"Already... said." She manages to be stern, even in a broken whisper. "Not getting... better. So. Now. You have to know about... your family."

Her eyes close, briefly. He squeezes the last few drops of moisture from the rag across her mouth. Her eyes flutter back open, and she gives him a weak smile, breaking the small corner of his heart that had not yet been completely destroyed.

"Mother..."

"You're a good son."

Not lately, he thinks, hating himself entirely.

"I have a good mother," he says, loving her even more entirely.

"Not... good—" And then she is overtaken by another fit of coughing. Her entire body convulses; Ere has to watch, powerless, with no way to ease her suffering. By the time the coughing fit passes, she is so exhausted she can no longer keep her eyes open.

What was she trying to tell him? Why would she say she's not a good mother? He wants to reassure her over and over again that she is the best mother, the best—but her eyes are closed now, and if she is able to rest comfortably for even a moment, he will not wake her for the world.

"Are you asleep?" He whispers. *Will you ever wake up?* He does not speak this question aloud, not even in a whisper. But Death, patiently hovering nearby, seems to hear him and answer with a cold breeze, freezing Ere to the bone despite the hot southern summer evening.

Cal's head appears again through the tent.

"The boiled water is not yet ready, but I have cold water for rags—"

Ere puts a finger to his lips, then points at his mother. Cal nods, sets down the rags of cold unpurified river water, and leaves them alone, in the dark, the feverish, dying mother and the desperate, guilty son.

For only a moment, as Ere watches his mother's chest slowly rise and fall with each labored breath, he allows himself to wonder what Ever is doing.

CHAPTER 40: EVER

E VER'S HEAD IS THROBBING. It takes her a moment
to orient herself. She looks around, taking in the details
and trying to figure out where in the hell she is now. Tall
white walls. A wide, flat monitor quietly humming beside her.
Her finger, inserted into a bedside port.

She does not remember plugging herself in, and she yanks her
finger out violently. It is hot, uncomfortably hot, indicative of an
extended connection time. She waves her hand to cool it, noting
the IV drip beside her bed and finally concluding that she is in the
Synt's medical wing.

"You're awake." Her mother is seated in a chair across the
room; Ever didn't see her until she spoke. Her tone is as sour as
her expression. "About time."

"How long...?" Ever asks.

"You were picked up a week ago."

"A week? I was out for a week?"

"They induced a coma so you could recover properly. When Jorge found you, you were dangerously overheated. That was truly reckless, Ever. Even for you."

"Duly noted," says Ever flatly. Inside, panic rises like a balloon toward the ceiling, trying to escape without anywhere to go. *Induced a coma? A week? What happened to Ere and his family? What did Heaven upload from me? Please please please let my privacy be protected...*

An orderly enters the room. His face is nondescript, smooth and unlined skin with no defining features. His eyes slide to the side, probably reviewing her chart. He never looks directly at her, never touches her.

"Well," says the orderly. "Vitals look good. Would you like some water, or tea?"

"Tea," Ever snaps, just so the orderly will leave.

"I imagine you'll be discharged, now that you're awake," says Marilyn, snapping her vintage purse shut with a prissy little *click.* "I'll see you at home."

Ever says nothing. She won't give her mother the satisfaction she might derive from Ever asking her to stay or berating her for leaving. Her mother momentarily looks as if she might say something else, or maybe open her purse just so she can snap it shut again, but in the end she does neither thing. She simply *clack-clack-clacks* out of the room in her impractical heels.

Another hospital staffer immediately enters the room and approaches Ever's bedside. This one is a woman, with red hair and a hooked, freckled nose.

"Where's my tea?" Asks Ever.

"I'm sorry?" Says the young woman, carefully examining Ever's monitor.

"My tea," growls Ever.

The woman seems not to hear Ever's question, and continues with the tasks she came to perform. "Stick your finger back into the port, if you would, and open your mouth. Please."

Ever grudgingly opens her mouth. The woman places a thin system analyzer in Ever's mouth. Around the analyzer, Ever asks again: "Where's. My. Tea?"

"I'm just here to get your readings," says the redhead. The analyzer beeps, reading done; She slips the device out of Ever's mouth, and just as quickly slips herself out of the room.

Forgettable Face Man returns with a cup of tea. Right behind him, a third technician enters and wordlessly begins examining Ever, feeling behind her ears, taking her pulse manually. Ever takes the tea, forgetting the man who brought it as soon as he leaves and glaring instead at the latest arrival poking and probing her, a trim Asian woman wearing antique emerald earrings, sparkling green and jarring against her stark white medical uniform.

"What's with this whole work-up here?"

"Standard procedure," comes the curt reply.

"Should I be expecting a fourth tech in here when you leave? There seems to be a whole parade of you coming through here."

The Asian woman with the emerald earrings briefly meets Ever's eyes, then continues examining her. "I'm not a tech. I'm Dr. Chun. I'll be the last to see you for the day."

"What do you mean, 'for the day'?"

Her examination concluded, the doctor heads for the door. "You'll be kept overnight for additional observation. I'm sure you'll be released in the morning, if everything's in order."

"My mother said she thought I'd be released today—"

But the doctor is already gone, and Ever is alone with her tea and her suspicions. Yes, she overheated and passed out, but beyond that, she's fine. She did a quick scan of her own, and the system analysis returned the expected result: normal. No reason for an overnight. Unless...

They can't know. Everything in private mode is safe. It has to be.

Reassuring herself that she can trust in the covenant of privacy settings, she takes a few deep breaths to steady her nerves. Then, sipping her flavorless hospital tea, she closes her eyes and begins quietly downloading from Heaven every available file on Ruth Fell.

CHAPTER 41: RUTH

R UTH SLOWLY OPENS HER EYES, surprised at her ability to lift her heavy lids. For the past week, her nights were tortured with terrible dreams, fever, body aches. But when she drifted off last night, it was to peaceful and dreamless slumber. As she drowsed in that dark and beautiful void, some part of her hoped she had died. It felt right, and easy, and past due. She was ready for nothingness, for sweet restful oblivion. But now her eyes are open once more, and the pain seeps back in quickly, flooding her entire body. With effort, she looks to the left, and sees her son.

Ere. Oh, my Ere.

Ere, the unexpected product of tragedy who became her everything. He is sleeping, still holding her hand, sitting up, eyes closed, breathing softly but steadily. The rhythmic reassurance of her son calms her. There is no sound so soothing to a parent as their child's steady breath.

All her life, Ruth Fell has been a fighter. War came naturally; love was far more difficult to navigate. She has fought far more people than she's loved. Looking at her son, Ruth's scarred old heart dissolves entirely. She feels at once relieved, guilty, and terrified, because as she looks at his rising and falling chest she can feel her own breath slowing. She knows that though last night Death had not claimed her, he cannot be delayed any longer. She is ready—but she knows her son is not. He is unprepared for everything that will come after she leaves him.

She knows with the certainty granted only to those about to die that her son will face exquisite pain. Both his hidden past and his uncertain future promise this fate. Ruth's boy never had a real chance at an easy, normal life. His inheritance is loss, struggle, pain. She'd do anything in this world or the next to bear the pain herself, to bring it with her to hell or heaven or wherever she was bound, to take it on eternally if it meant she could protect him from it.

But her time of shielding him is rapidly approaching its end. She can't keep him safe anymore. She feels a coughing fit threaten; with her waning strength she suppresses it, not wanting to wake Ere.

Damn you. Stop it. Stop, stop, stop.

Miraculously, she wins this final battle of wills with the cough, pushing it away, smothering it. Perhaps the rasp retreats because it knows that even if it concedes this battle, the larger army of cancer has already won the war. It's Ruth's fault; she's the one who lowered the drawbridge to let the damned dragon in, smoking all those two-faced cigarettes.

She was a smoker until tobacco was a luxury no longer accessible to Originals. It's been years since her last cigarette—a parting gift from an old war buddy, savored as the world burned around them—but they did their damage. Even knowing how they turned on her, she misses the little bastards every day. Uncle Howard had scolded her for it when she was a teenager, but by the time the uprisings began, he was lighting them for her. It was the one thing that kept her nerves steady. That, and the whiskey.

God, she loved that troublemaking firewater almost as much as she loved her little cancer sticks. She was a rebel as a child, and another sort of rebel as an adult. Cigarettes and booze were helpful props in her theaters of life and war. She wishes she could say she gave up either habit for her own health, or for her son. Truthfully, she only stopped drinking and smoking because alcohol and cigarettes became nonexistent in the Original world.

What she wouldn't give for a cigarette now, or a sip of whiskey. A final drag, one last toast. Not that there was anything in her life worth toasting.

No, there's one thing: Ere. Cal. My boys.

If there were whiskey to drink, if she had the strength left to swallow, she would lift a glass to her nephew, the one who had her sister's eyes, who was always so protective and dear to her; and to her son, the sole, sweet blessing Ruth herself gave the world.

Watching him in her dwindling moments, she wants to cry. He looks so much like his father. The sandy hair, wiry build, smooth skin, pale shoulders. So much slighter than the men in her family. So much quieter. Always seeking something. All traits from his father.

She wonders what she gave him. Other than the inheritance of pain. Distrust? Paranoia? A predisposition to addiction, if ever he encountered controlled substances? She hopes maybe she gave him something more, something better than all that. A little courage, some loyalty, maybe even the stubbornness that was her own best and worst trait.

Yes. He does have my stubbornness. Bullheaded little bastard boy, heart of my heart…

That was something, at least. She hopes it will help him face all that stretches out ahead of him. She thinks about praying for this, but in the end, she does not. Instead of a psalm or supplication, the words to an old Original resistance song came to her, out of nowhere and everywhere. Everything she has ever done or felt or known seems caught in the web of the old lyrics as they wind their way through her:

> Standing here, I almost see
> The girl I was, the crone I'll be
> The blessing of age, passing of time,
> Teaching us all, profane and sublime
> We will never relent, we will never rely
> Thus we will live. And thus we will die.

She didn't realize she was softly whispering the words, singing the song like a sigh. Not until she sees Ere stir at the subtle sound. It is so quiet, under her breath, barely vocalized, that at first it does not quite wake him. He shifts, stills. Breathing out the last of the words, *and thus we will die*, she knows that her own breath, slowing and slowing and slowing, is coming to a stop. The world around her seems to speed up as her own body slows. As her son begins to rise, she knows her sun is setting.

It'll be his birthday soon, she thinks.

Her boy will be eighteen. God, what a miracle. She wishes she could be there to celebrate with him. Difficult as it is to keep track of days in their nomadic life, Originals never miss an opportunity to celebrate a birthday. Each year of life matters. Each milestone is an excuse for joy. Ruth hates knowing that her son will reject any happiness on his date of birth this year, since it will surely be overshadowed by her date of death.

"Mother?" The boy says, squeezing her bony hand. She wants to reply, but she cannot. Everything is fading, slipping away from her. Darkness creeps into her peripheral vision, steady and non-negotiable.

What to say? If I am given any last words in this last breath. What do I tell my son? Happy birthday? Don't grieve for me too long? Make up with Cal? No, no. Bigger. More important. The truth. Tell him the truth. Or at least a truth...

"Mother?" Ere says again, and there is a tremor in his voice.

"Your father... your grandfather..." she exhales, then stops, holding on to this last swan song, realizing she needs to change her tune. To her surprise, a single tear slips down her cheek, and in her dimming final moments, Ruth relents and allows herself a small and simple supplication.

Please, God, if you exist or if you ever existed, if there is any mercy left, if I can have only one prayer granted, please let him carry these words when I am gone, and forever more, even when he knows the truth...give me the strength to say them, and then let him remember...

The darkness has almost overtaken her eyes, and when she looks up at Ere, she sees only his face, framed in muted dawn light. Her lungs contract, expand, releasing and expelling that last-held note, all of her remaining air. When she speaks her final words, her voice is clear, with no trace of rasp or ruin.

"Love, Ere. That's all. That's everything."

And then the mighty Ruth Fell closes her eyes for the final time.

CHAPTER 42: EVER

THE STEADY ELECTRIC HUM OF THE HOSPITAL monitor combined with the information swirling before her eyes has Ever in an almost trance-like state. Lulled by the research and the repetitive white noise, she knows of nothing and no one but a fierce young Original warrior named Ruth.

Most of Heaven's files on Ruth Fell are heavily, almost laughably redacted. Passages are blocked out and password-protected within the publicly-available files; other files are off-limits entirely to all but those with the highest security clearance. Still, Ever accesses what she can, and fits the bits of information together, re-constructing a story nearly erased. There are gaping plot holes thanks to the redactions, but there's enough of the narrative intact to pull back the curtain on a history very different from the one Ever was taught.

*Ruth Fell was born in Cambridge, Massachusetts to Nathan Moshe Fell and Sarah Proudtree Fell, (**REDACTED**) 2005. Twin sister, Rachel Fell. Both girls attended (**REDACTED**) public school. Mother, Sarah Proudtree Fell, suffered from post-partum psychosis; abandoned family. Killed in automobile accident in 2011. Father, Nathan Fell, relinquished parental rights in 2012.*

*Ruth and Rachel were legally adopted by their paternal uncle and aunt, Howard and Sophie Fell. Howard Fell (**entire page REDACTED**)—continued to lead the anti-transhumanism movement, protesting cyborganics and early Syn testing. Fell formed a group (**REDACTED**)—later radicalized, and nicknamed the Original Way Party.*

*Ruth Fell no longer appeared in public school system records after 2015. She won the regional spelling bee in her final enrolled semester. Howard Fell moved his family, including nieces Ruth and Rachel, deep underground. The Original Way Party was officially designated as a terrorist group. Activities leading up to the designation include (**REDACTED**). Despite her youth Ruth Fell (**REDACTED**).*

*Howard himself was never connected to any crimes, though he was deemed an intellectual threat, particularly because of his direct knowledge of and connection to (**REDACTED**).*

No data exists on Ruth Fell from 2015-2020. The Singularity occurred in 2020.

Here, Ever pauses and zooms in on the word Singularity, causing its definition to momentarily take over the report, a divergence delving into the definition she knew by rote but suddenly sees differently.

Singularity: when man melded with machine. "The Singularity" refers to the initial global event, when synching was no longer considered experimental, no longer a fringe classified theoretical exploration but reality.

The Singularity meant triumph for Ever's people, a death knell for Ruth's. Ever zooms out again, away from the increasingly-problematic definition, back to the redacted but riveting account of Ruth's role in this strange story.

In 2021, on the first anniversary of the Singularity, a bomb went off at the satellite site of the Synt—the original research building in Cambridge, Massachusetts. The bomb was deadly, killing thirty-three staff people and destroying nearly a billion dollars' worth of equipment. Primary suspect identified as sixteen-year-old Ruth Fell. Source of information (**REDACTED**) *was well compensated.*

Reward offered for any information leading to the apprehension of suspected terrorist Ruth Fell. No one came forward with information, despite the reward, of ten million dollars and a coveted spot to join in the next wave of Syn synching, earning any informant a chance to join the evolution.

No data exists on Ruth Fell from 2021-2024.

In the mid-2020s, the organized Original Uprisings began. Ruth Fell was the face of the revolution. She was rarely seen on monitors, but known to still be in the field, wielding weapons, engaging in battle, leading attacks. As one witness described her, Fell was "inspiring, intelligent, beautiful in a wild sort of way."

This detail, too, gives Ever pause. Who had made that observation? Why was it worthy enough to include in this ridiculously-edited official accounting of a wanted war criminal?

*It would have been easier to kill Ruth Fell than to capture her. But due to (**REDACTED**), there were strict orders that Ruth Fell must be brought in alive. More so than that: She must not be harmed in any significant way. Taking alive the most fearless, revered, loyalty-inspiring rebel proved impossible even for the newly-formed Syn tactical forces.*

Ruth Fell was the only survivor in the Drone Station Massacre of 2039. For twenty years, as her comrades died, and the Syns grew in power,, and the world around her changed forever and irreversibly, Ruth Fell fought. By 2043, the Original population had dwindled from nearly seven billion to fewer than one billion. With the fertility-crippling water treatments, the population continued to shrink. It was a losing battle. But Ruth Fell remained unwilling to yield.

In the few blurred images captured by Syn drone cameras of Ruth Fell in her late thirties, observers noted she looked older—scarred, hardened by war, hair almost entirely gray, face haunted and hollow.

At this, Ever rolls her eyes. *What a ridiculously Syn observation of an Original. How could anyone critique Ruth's appearance rather than gush about her tenacity?* (Self-awareness is not Ever's strong suit.) Of course they commented on her being beautiful when young, then aging poorly. The Syn bias to the narrative clanged inescapably.

She had to find one final way to infiltrate Syn society, find
something more devastating than a bomb. The Syn strategic
advisors knew she was probably aiming for some sort of Trojan
horse maneuver. She made her move in 2044, when against all
odds she somehow managed to abduct (**REDACTED**)**.**

And here, the already-patchy data becomes even sparser.
Nearly everything about the 2044 abduction is classified, redacted, and Ever even gets a pop-up alert that the files she is request-
ing will trigger an automatic notification to the Syn Council if
tampered with in any way.

Ruth must have killed whoever she kidnapped, because in
2045, after the dust settled from the final uprising, a new warrant
was issued for the arrest of Ruth Fell as a war criminal, with many
crimes listed against her, including *assassination, 2044.*

But after 2045, there's no additional publicly-available information on Ruth Fell save a series of composite images, updated
every five years to reflect how she might appear, further aged, if
she was somehow still alive. Having recently seen her, Ever notes
that the Syn composite artist was truly unkind in their renderings
of the aging Ruth.

That's not what bothers Ever most, though. What Ever is fix-
ated on is the fact that in all of the documents she was able to review, there's no mention anywhere of a son. Maybe Ere was buried
in one of the long stretches of redacted content, but if so, the information was entirely eliminated, and must have been withheld
from the general public for some very good reasons.

His conception should have been notable for multiple reasons; not only was he an important factor (and liability) in the
war criminal Ruth's life, but also he was an anomaly. Crunching
the numbers in an instant—Ruth born in 2005, Ere almost 18
now—Ever calculates that Ere was born in 2045. When Ruth was
forty. One year after the alleged assassination, and many years after the attacks on Original women's fertility.

Was it possible that Ere was not hers? But no, Ever can so clearly see Ruth in the boy's face—he was slighter and paler, yes, but the curve of his jaw and his deep-set eyes were unmistakably Ruth's. And it wasn't like there were any other Original women who would have been likelier candidates. Original women shouldn't have been having kids twenty years ago; they should all have already lost their fertility.

Ever gets out of the hospital bed and stretches. Her muscles feel atrophied, sore from holding still too long, too much data analysis, not enough movement. She walks to the wall opposite her bed. The entire wall is interactive, currently in a neutral setting and appearing simply as a wall. Ever sends the wall a request—*mirror*—and it becomes reflective.

Ever examines herself carefully. Despite feeling run down, she looks none the worse for the wear. The lightweight white hospital gown barely skims her skin, not showing off her figure, but not completely hiding it, either. She steps closer, her nose nearly touching its own reflection. She looks closely, searching for any wrinkle, any blemish, any flaw at all. As always, nothing.

She tries to imagine what she would look like by now, if she had aged naturally. If she wasn't held in the suspended state of for-ever-seventeen, what would time have done to her? She traces her fingers along her jawline, picturing it soft and wrinkled instead of firm and smooth. If she had not synched, she would be almost at her sixth decade.

Ruth's age.

Realization hits her like a bolt of lightning, sizzling and searing through her. She swears under her breath. How had she missed this? It had been right in front of her stupid ageless face?

Born 2005, Cambridge, Massachusetts.

Sliding her eyes to the left, she blinks and sends a new message to the wall monitor. It goes from reflective to opaque before loading the new content. Ever takes a step back, then another, then another, finally running into the bed sitting down to take in the entire projection filling the wall. Row after row of square images, pictures of smiling kids with missing teeth, oversized glasses, crooked smiles, scratches on their cheeks from recent playground adventures.

A page from a kindergarten yearbook. Cambridge, Massachusetts. 2011. In the middle of the page is a little girl with cinnamon-colored hair in two pigtails. If she had been grinning, Ever imagines she might have been missing a tooth or two. But the little girl is stone-faced, staring down whoever was behind the camera. She is in a red-plaid dress with a white collar. Below the picture, the little girl's name: *Ruthie Fell.*

To the left of Ruthie's picture is another little girl, this one sweet-faced and openly grinning, captioned: *Rachel Fell.*

And there, one row down and over in the right-hand corner, is a picture of another little girl, wearing a green turtleneck, dark hair flowing to her shoulders. She has huge, heavily-lashed eyes and the sort of forced smile a child yields when a grownup tells them to "say cheese."

The caption beneath her photograph: *Ever Hess.*

S HADOWER IS USED TO BAD NEWS. Bad news is twice as regular as the sunrise. Most bad news washes over Shadower like a wave, breaking and just as quickly rolling back out to sea, leaving the surface placid again. This news arrives not as a wave, but as a bullet that lodges itself deep within, there to stay.

Confirmation of whether or not Ruth Fell still lived had evaded the Syn Council for decades. How like that woman, always managing the impossible—hiding from the best seekers on the planet. It was something the clandestine network cheered silently, their heroine still eluding their oppressors. But as of this morning, it's official, and soon the Syns will know: *Ruth Fell is dead.*

Shadower feels nauseous, thinking of how delighted this news will make the Syn Council when they find out. They will probably pop a champagne cork, drink some bubbly and breathe easier, knowing that the last of their fiercest foes are dying off, just as planned. Maybe it will lull them into a false sense of security—a lowering of their guard that will reveal a chink in the armor of the Syn stronghold. Ruth Fell's final gift to her people, perhaps.

Shadower is crafting the official message to Karma, carefully layering encryption upon encryption upon encryption. It will take even someone as skilled as Karma a long time to unravel the content. But damned if Shadower might be the one to leak the information about Ruth.

Just as Shadower is about to send the secured message, a new alert arrives. It catches Shadower's attention first and foremost because it's not from the clandestine network; it's from a Syn, identity anonymized. As Shadower opens it, the message elicits an uncharacteristic gasp:

> To those monitoring the Syns terminating themselves, if anyone actually is: I am a Syn planning self-termination. I'll send a follow-up message, different encryption, letting you know the time and place of my act. I will not give you enough time to stop me, but will provide enough warning to arrive before the Syns can erase all memory of me.

Trembling, Shadower traces the message's point of origin. It came from a public hub. No swift way of pinning down the sender, although determining who composed this message has just gone to the top of Shadower's priority list.

And then, as Shadower still reels from the news of Ruth's death, and the outreach from a Syn planning to die, another alert nearly gives the spy a heart attack.

Comes in threes, Shadower thinks dizzily as the latest message decrypts. *Comes in threes, comes in threes, comes in threes...*

And then the brief but heavily encrypted third message unfurls. Shadower could never have guessed that any message could be more shocking than the first two. But the final missive dwarfs them both in five short words:

Ruth Fell had a son.

CHAPTER 44: ERE

P REPARING FOR HIS OWN MOTHER'S FUNERAL
forever eradicates Ere's love of them, especially since the
awful day coincides with his eighteenth birthday.
Welcome to adulthood; everything is terrible here.

The arrangements were quick and quiet. The elders sent Cal
to find nearby tribes, any within two days' travel, to spread the
word of Ruth's passing. The assignment was dangerous; if Cal's
message were overheard or intercepted by any Syn drone, it would
be devastating. Protecting Ruth from the Syns and allowing her a
peaceful burial was paramount—but her tribe knew she did not
belong to them alone; all Originals deserved to know, and to pay
their respects.

Original funerals traditionally take place no more than a day or two post death. There's no good way to preserve the body, and out of respect for the deceased and their loved ones, a swift burial is the kindest course of action. The individual was returned to the earth, the story-song was sung, and then the healing began for those left behind. That was the typical tradition.

But for Ruth Fell, the elders decided to allow three days for word to spread, and another two to give tribes time to reach them. As if to affirm this decision, the weather took a chilling plunge, autumn swallowing summer and an unseasonable cold settling over the Southern sector, protecting Ruth's small, still body.

The elders took turns sitting with Ruth, wanting to give Ere a reprieve. They came in, one after another, but Ere stubbornly remained as well. He never left her side, save to relieve himself, and then he would immediately return, wordlessly pick up her hand again, and sit beside her, as silent as she was. He even slept there, seated, as he had throughout her final days.

The morning of the funeral, a half-slumbering Ere is awoken by a humming sound he cannot identify. A sudden fear grips his chest: *a Syn drone.* Knowing his mother would want him to protect the tribe, he lurches up from his stiff, seated position, reluctantly releasing her lifeless hand. He kisses her forehead, steadying himself a moment. Then, shielding his eyes in anticipation of the harsh sunlight, he steps out of the tent. He blinks a moment, eyes adjusting—and then, as he gradually takes in the sight before him, he simply stands there, overwhelmed by what he now beholds, for the humming sound is not a Syn drone. It is something else entirely.

It is the sound of a thousand hushed voices, quiet feet, an army of dampened but definite sounds of life. There, outside his tent, filling the remote woods, are more Originals than Ere has ever seen. More than had been at his Uncle Howard's funeral. More than he ever would have guessed there could possibly have been residing within just a few days' walk.

All surviving Originals support one another but have splintered into smaller communities. Tribes consist of extended families, former neighbors, or travelers brought together by circumstance and geography. Small groups are safer and more sustainable. There are no tribal rifts, no territorial battles; their shared enemy is the Syns, and especially with their diminished numbers, that's unification enough to stave off all internal conflict. Still, Ere has never seen more than five or six tribes represented in any single gathering—other than Howard's funeral, which brought together perhaps two dozen tribes. There must be fifty tribes now assembled to pay their respects to the woman who fought for them all, inspired them all, become in her lifetime more than merely a woman. Ruth was an icon. A legend. Their hero.

And then there is a shift in the muted buzzing, a wind passing through the crowd as first one person notices Ere, and then another. They all stare at the boy, and as realization dawns, they all begin bowing their heads, then looking up to meet his eyes. A gesture of honor bestowed upon the unmistakable son of Ruth Fell.

Ere blinks back tears, so grateful and so sorrowful and suddenly so very, very aware of just how much his mother mattered. He bows his head once, then looks up, traveling his gaze across the crowd, locking eyes with person after person after person. Thanking them. Returning the honor. Mourning with them the loss of his mother, his protector, and also the protector and champion of an entire people.

Helena Garrison steps forward, and takes Ere by the arm.

"Come, boy," she says, gently. "Let us remember her."

He allows her to lead him from the tent, escorting him away before Cal quietly enters the tent with two women and two men—the Originals who will carry Ruth to her final resting place.

The funeral is over so quickly, Ere cannot really grasp that it happened. The woman who sang the story song of Ruth Fell's life was a stranger to Ere—but she caught him in a fierce embrace when she saw him before the service. She held him fast, whispering in his ear that she had known Ruth as a little girl, when they were neighbors in the old world, that she fought beside her when they were warriors trying to stave off the new world.

"Learning about you made us rejoice even in our sorrow," she whispered, pulling him close. "You are a miracle, Ere Fell. You are your mother's legacy."

He wanted to thank her, to ask her more about his mother as a little girl, to find out what more she knew of Ere's own history. But he simply let her hug him, and remained silent. Standing upright was all he hoped to manage today. Questions were beyond him; conversation, unthinkable.

When she began the story-song of his mother's life, the stranger's voice was strong and soft, warm and lilting. It seemed appropriate to him that her name was Melody.

The woman called Melody sang of Ruth's brilliance, her curiosity as a child, her bravery as a warrior, her commitment to the Original way. Ere was too gripped by grief to follow it all. Had he been able to pay closer attention, he might have noticed furtively exchanged glances amongst the mourners. Raised eyebrows, nods of confirmation, expressions of surprise at just how many omissions there were in the re-telling of Ruth's story.

When they reached the closing psalm, they all spoke together. Though he knew the words inside and out, Ere kept repeating only a single line, over and over, throughout the recitation.

I shall not want. I shall not want. I shall not want...

And then, hating himself, he thought not of his mother—but of Ever. And he wanted her. He slipped his hand into his pocket, running his fingers across the cold metal of the tiny silver gun she'd pressed into his hand. An odd memoir, but the violent souvenir is all he has.

Ruth was lowered into the ground, and as custom demanded, Ere bent down, filling his hand with earth, and threw the first clump of dirt into his mother's grave. It landed and broke apart across the simple white cloth that covered Ruth's body. As soon as Ere's clump of dirt was thrown, it was followed by another, probably thrown by Cal, though Ere's vision was too blurred to know for certain. And then another. Everyone cast a handful, and within moments, Ruth Fell was returned to the earth. And then the earth was returned to a smooth, level facade, unmarked and almost unnoticeable. As if there had never been the gaping wound in its surface. As if it were not now hiding the greatest of warriors.

Now it is over, and she is simply gone.

Ere feels a soft hand on his shoulder.

Turning around, he sees a girl. She appears to be his age, which makes him immediately suspicious—but she is clearly an Original. Her long, black hair hangs down her back, thick and loose. Her skin is darker than his own, almost as dark as Cal's. Her eyes are ebony, framed with thick black lashes. He hasn't seen her before, but something about her feels familiar.

"You are Ere." She says, her voice strangely accented. "Son of Ruth Fell."

"Do I know you?" He hears his wrecked voice and hopes his eyes aren't too bloodshot.

She shakes her head.

"But... you knew my mother?" Ere presses.

"She was my hero," says the girl.

"And who are you?"

"I am Asavari," she says, her eyes black fire. "And I was sent here by the resistance. We need you, Ere Fell. Your time to fight has come."

CHAPTER 45: EVER

"**E**VER. WAKE UP."

Ever opens her eyes. She's not sure when she fell asleep, but from the warm pulsing of her finger, she realizes that once again, someone plugged her port back into Heaven. She twitches nervously; she'd fallen asleep researching Ruth. She remembers the images filling the screen, especially the brightly colored school photographs of two little girls, one with cinnamon pigtails and the other with flowing dark hair. Ruthie and Ever. Same age. Same school.

Heaven and hell, did I clear the search before I fell asleep?

She resists the urge to look at the full-screen wall where the images so recently displayed. Instead, forcing a neutral expression, she turns her head slowly toward the person addressing her. It's the woman from yesterday, with the antique emerald earrings. Dr. Chun.

"One of your tests came back with… unexpected results. We're sending word to your father, who will be in to see you shortly. Open your mouth."

"Unexpected results? What does that mean?"

Ever tries to sit up, and finds that she cannot. Looking down, she sees that not only is her finger connected to the bedside Heaven outlet, but also that her wrists are restrained. As are her ankles. And her calves.

Cursing, she pulls at the restraints, flailing but achieving little. Her shackles are coded bracelets, locked more tightly than any hands could ever pry apart, though easily unhinged by the right combination of letters, numbers, or perhaps even retinal or five-finger scans.

"Miss Hess, if you don't calm down, I'm afraid we'll have to give you a sedative."

Not wanting anything to alter her consciousness, Ever stills, though her mind races. She doesn't remember falling asleep, or even feeling tired—it must have been something that came on quickly. Her eyes dart to the tea by her bedside. She had only sipped it before beginning her research last night; feeling thirsty hours later, she had hastily finished the rest of it. Was there some sort of sleeping agent in the beverage? What the hell was going on?

Heaven and hell, did he somehow find out about Ere?

No. That would be impossible. She kept her privacy settings locked in place throughout their interactions. She had been so careful when she was down south.

But last night's research. All the searching about Ruth Fell.

She hadn't been in private mode then. She wasn't thinking straight. She'd been medicated, and hasty, and got excited, and now there was a record of her activity looking up Ere's mother.

The Original war criminal.

Stupid, stupid, stupid.

"Open your mouth," Dr. Chun says, holding an old-fashioned thermometer aloft. "We need to finish before your father gets here."

Wanting to spit in this horrible woman's face, wanting to rip the sparkling green earrings from her ears, wanting to scream and smash and tear the world apart until she knew what was happening to her, Ever instead lays back down, and obediently opens her mouth.

CHAPTER 46: HESS

H ESS STRIDES DOWN THE LONG, WIDE hallway, flanked by Jorge and Kennedy. Before today, neither assistant was up to speed on the Generation Next Project. But with the next phase about to begin, Hess needs them on-boarded, and he doesn't trust anyone but himself to orient them.

Halfway down the hall, Hess stops in his tracks, placing a hand to his temple and cursing.

The unexpected halt nearly causes Jorge and Kennedy to run right into him. Growling, Hess raises a hand for them to step back as he processes the emergency message that knocked him off-course. It was delivered with a physical alert, rarely used because it was considered rude outside of apocalypse-level emergencies. It caused a swift pinching sensation to the forehead, which disappeared as quickly as it appeared. The message is from Lorraine Murray:

Meet me in your office immediately. Do not say anything to anyone.

Hess is irritated. Is this about the godawful meeting she made him take with her husband? He hasn't butted heads about anything else with Lorraine recently.

"What is it, Dr. Hess?" Kennedy asks.

"It's nothing—*unggh*," Hess groans, clutching his temple again.

Your office NOW.
CONFIRM RECEIPT.

"Dr. Hess?" Jorge asks.

Wincing, Hess blinks and sends a reply to Lorraine. The physical alert he includes with his message is purely spiteful, since she's obviously on the lookout for his response.

On my way.

"Something has come up," says Hess. "I'll find you later."

His assistants nod and leave him, no questions asked. Hess heads briskly, angrily toward his office to see what the hell the most powerful woman on the Council needs now. When he opens his door and walks into his office, she is already waiting.

Lorraine is a smart, impeccably put together woman. Not a hair out of place, her dark suit flattering without being flashy, complemented by a conservative string of antique pearls around her neck. She exudes the power and influence for which she has long been known. She is not a woman to be messed with, not a woman easily shaken. Thus it is disconcerting, even for Hess, to see that despite her poise, she is pale as a ghost.

"What is it, Lorraine?"

Lorraine Murray never beats around the bush. A self-made billionaire pre-Singularity, she always called the shots. But it takes her a moment to collect herself and answer his question.

"It's Joshua. My husband. Remember him? How you refused to help him?"

"His request was ridiculous, Lorraine—"

She continues, as if Hess had not spoken. "Yesterday, when I woke up, he was gone. No explanation, nothing. But then, this morning, I received... word..."

"Word...?" Hess finds Lorraine's trailed-off sentence to be almost as frustrating as her marked-urgent message. He looks at the grandfather clock, wondering what could possibly be so difficult for Lorraine to say and also so important that he had to drop everything to hear it.

"A message he'd recorded hours earlier, and programmed to have sent only after..."

"After *what*, Lorraine?"

"After he terminated himself."

Heaven and hell.

Hess swears silently, wanting to strike the stupid bitch for speaking these words aloud. He reminds himself that his office is secure, nothing here is recorded, and anything potentially flammable, he has the power to render classified. He has to remind himself of this so he can answer Lorraine with words instead of an assault.

"Don't say things like that out loud. Has a team been deployed?"

"Of course a team was deployed," she hisses back. "But the bodies were already gone."

"That's impossible. What do you mean they were gone?"

"We got the notification as soon as he flat-lined in Heaven, but he was outside the incorporated area—"

"*Bodies*, plural," Hess says, anxiety rising. "Who else?"

"Joshua, and his daughter Shayna. They did it together."

"Were there others?"

"I don't know. And I don't like not knowing, Felix."

Hess puts a hand to his throbbing temple, then jerks the hand back to his side, not wanting to indicate even the slightest hint of strain or weakness. But he's thrown; none of this makes sense. And why was Lorraine alerted before he was?

"We can still erase all records associated with your husband."

"Already done," snaps Lorraine. "As soon as the flat-line registered."

"If someone buried the bodies, we can still trace the tech—"

"That's not the real problem," Lorraine says.

"Oh, no? What's the 'real problem'?"

"The message Joshua sent didn't just go to me. He sent it out over a public channel, and sent it directly to several accounts. Including his coworkers at the communications department."

"No," Hess whispers.

So it's not only Lorraine who knew before he did, thanks to a direct message from the deceased; others know, too. The information is out of Hess' control.

Not. Good.

"Yes," Lorraine says. "We can't just make this one go away. There's no putting Humpty Dumpty together again. Not with all the king's horses, or even his *mules*."

At this, Hess' entire body goes furiously hot. "Lorraine, that is *level seven classified*—"

"And so is this, *Felix*. All of this. Self-termination will no longer be our dirty little secret. There will be inquiries. A publicly declared termination, and by my *husband*. A respected, highly visible Syn citizen. Took his own life, and screamed about it!"

"Keep your voice down," Hess says.

"Why? Your sound-proofed little box is secure, and everyone's going to know about this soon anyway. We can't help that. We can come up with a contingency plan, but we can't stop it. So here's the real question: what the hell are we going to do if the news makes it all the way out to the tribes? They were in an Original camp. It seems quite likely that at least some Originals do, in fact, know that this happened."

"Heaven and Hell," he spits.

"Heaven and Hell indeed," Lorraine growls back. "That's one of our many very real problems. I haven't briefed the rest of the Council yet, obviously. We need to be on the same page before we tell them. Before we make a recommendation regarding what information will be made publicly available regarding this incident. What our statements will be."

For decades, suicide was a disease that the Syns figured they had successfully eradicated. There was widespread depression a decade after the Singularity, as Original friends and family disappeared permanently from their lives, as they questioned their decision. The Syn Council had made the decision to put everyone on mood-moderators, regulating traumatic emotions. This mitigated depression. Problem solved, or so they thought.

A return of self-termination would be bad, particularly as the last of the Originals die off. Psychologists, historians, and The Prophet all predicted that the final extinction of the Originals might trigger an uptick in anxiety. Some Syns might mourn the last of their Original relatives being gone. Others might have survivor's guilt, knowing that they secured themselves a place in the new world at the expense of someone else. Vosts and maybe even some Syns would also be demoralized when they had to take on menial roles—landscaping, cooking, taking out the trash. Class systems would re-emerge. Not exactly the time to also have a resurgence of depression.

"Did he develop an immunity to the anti-depressants?" Hess asks quickly. "We always knew that was a possibility. Too many years of exposure, the effect could decrease over time. Maybe your husband developed an immunity, something we can pinpoint and correct before—"

"No," says Lorraine. "I think he made a very conscious choice."

"And you believe this because—?"

"It's all there, in his message. This was his last resort. He tried everything else. *I can't leave her alone,* he said. *I have to be with her in the end.* The rest—it's private. But trust me, it was a choice."

"A stupid choice."

"An emotional choice."

"Emotional choices are generally stupid."

"She was his *daughter,* Felix."

This statement does not alter Hess' expression, opinion, or reaction. "They did it in an Original camp, you said? You know the location of that, at least?"

"Yes, we've located where—"

"Send it to me, encrypted," he says. "I'll see that the word doesn't spread in the Original world. All Originals in that area will be eliminated. I'll send a unit to locate and take care of your husband's body. We'll deploy a separate unit to deal with the Originals. Is there anything else?"

"Yes," says Lorraine. "You should tell me you're sorry for my loss."

There is a brief pause after Lorraine invokes this archaic phrase of sympathy. Hess has not spoken these words in decades; having been cued to do so, he repeats the phrase in an automated tone. Robotic, even.

"Lorraine, I am sorry for your loss."

"I'm sure you are," Lorraine says under her breath.

She says the words to an empty room because Hess is already striding from his office. His to-do list is rapidly metastasizing. *Clean up this mess. Deal with Ever. Keep the Generation Next project on track. Figure out that damned prophecy.*

At least there was only one dead Syn in this Joshua Murray suicide-pact thing, and the other body or bodies were worthless Original ones. If the news was indeed going public, he was glad this time it was just one body. Not three, like the last time.

His breathing is returning to normal. Cleaning up this mess is doable. He'll have the communications department spin the news item as an unfortunate but isolated incident. The tragic case of Joshua Murray, a suicidal Syn who had also been displaying other glitches and should have sought treatment sooner. An outlier. An anomaly. And an irresponsible citizen to boot. Hess won't have the communications team go so far as to say he deserved it, but that will be the subtext. Containing the information within the Syn world will be clean, simple, easy. It will be a messier process out in the unincorporated territories. There, the rumors will be quelled with necessary force.

Just as he has convinced himself that it can all be managed, he receives a message from Dr. Chun:

Urgent news regarding Ever.

The timing could not be worse. But Hess knows Chun would only contact him if the news was indeed urgent. It's why he chose her to head up the Generation Next medical team. When there was a problem, she handled it. She only called him when it was absolutely unavoidable. Cursing under his breath about raining and pouring, Hess steps into the third floor breakroom for privacy. He waits for the door to slide shut before sending the doctor a terse reply.

Send me the update and I'll decide if I need to see her.

Chun's reply is immediate.

Here's a preview. You'll want to see her.

The doctor's message is accompanied by a large file. It renders quickly, but is hard to make out. It seems to be some sort of image extracted from Ever's internal log. Hess looks at the monitor on the breakroom, blinks a command, and the image fills the massive screen.

It's from Ever's point of view, a snapshot of a moment in time. But unlike most memory logs, it's not synthetically recorded. Memories seized from private mode can only be pulled painstakingly as stills, and this one is borderline corrupted. Maybe due to her recent overheating, combined with private mode—it's grainy, colorless, almost looks like an old-world security tape. But after a moment, Hess can make out what it depicts. Like an optical illusion, piecing itself together slowly and then snapping into clarity. Once he sees it, he can't un-see it.

"No," Hess says. "No."

Hess changes course for the second time that day, aiming now for the medical wing. And for the first time in his adult life, Felix Hess runs.

E RE DOESN'T TRUST THE GIRL WITH THE
black-fire eyes. She's too intense, too young, and too...
something.

After the funeral, the mourners dispersed quickly, knowing
that concentrated masses might draw too much attention from
Syns—an even more dangerous proposition now that their last
great warrior was dead. After Ruth's burial, the temperature began to rise, and the warming weather urged the travelers along.
Soon everyone is gone, save Ere's own tribe and Asavari.

She sits at the edge of the small river running near the tribe's
makeshift camp. Ere sits beside her, kicking off his cracked old
sandals. He dips his dirty toes into the water, the cold a small
shock. He needs new shoes, but it's been a long time since he

found a freebox with anything his size inside. He's in pretty sore need of new underwear, as well.

"You need to tell me your story," he says as soon as they're alone.

"I'm with the resistance," the girl says again, making Ere twitch with frustrated confusion. What resistance? "Planning this trip has taken time, but with new developments—"

"No," says Ere. He wants to know about the resistance, but first he has to know about this girl and whether or not he can trust her. "Back up. I want to hear all about the resistance. But start with you. Who the hell are you?"

Asavari regards him solemnly. "I am inseparable from the resistance."

He glares. "Make some shit up, then. And it better make me trust you."

"Why would 'making shit up' make you trust—oh," Asavari says, her serious brow furrowed. "You're sarcastic."

"Usually," Ere says flatly.

"All right," she sighs. "This is my story—not made up, just what it is. My mother grew up in India, when it was still India. She came to America to study medicine. As the Singularity approached, she secretly returned to India, along with my father. He was an American. They began planning and shaping the resistance there, which was different from the resistance here."

"Different how?"

"It never stopped," Asavari answers, pride in her voice. "We live underground. Off the Syn radar. We chose places so hot that they would overheat. Places they thought were... to use their word... shitholes. When the resistance in America slowed, they thought it was all over. They built their cities. They focused on themselves. And meanwhile, we kept going. With our own water, our own infrastructure. We have no reliance on Syn structure. We are not poisoned by them. We have not fought publicly in my lifetime, but we are still resisting and planning for an Original future. Our numbers are still small, but they are growing, every year. I am one of many children of the resistance."

"Children of the resistance," Ere repeats, tasting the strange words.

"Yes. We are not a dying people, Ere. We are a living people. We are underground, but we are free. That is my story—a story of freedom. A freedom I will help bring to all Originals."

"So you're supposed to be... what, our savior?"

"No," she says sharply. "Your ally. Your comrade in arms. The time to rise up is now, Ere Fell. Before the Syns have completely run Originals out of your part of the world. Before they discover our fortress in mine. We must stand together in the next rebellion."

"It's my birthday," he tells her, not sure why he said it.

"Today?" Her eyes alight, then go dark again. "I'm sorry for it to fall on this sad day. But that is still wonderful. Many more Original years, Ere."

"Yeah, great, thanks." He looks at her. "Your home—India— how far away is it?"

"Very far," she says, and her gaze is very far away as well. "Half the world away."

"How did you get here for the funeral, so quickly?"

"I did not come for the funeral." She says, somber. "I came for... her. There was a rumor Ruth Fell still lived, so I came to find her, the great warrior. My people will be devastated to learn of her death. But to learn of your existence will renew their hope. It is your destiny, Ere Fell, son of Ruth. You must return with me, take your place in the fight to reclaim our world—"

"If it's a warrior you need, you're talking to the wrong guy," a new voice cuts in.

Asavari reaches for her machete; matching her movement, Ere goes for the small knife sheathed at his thigh. But even as he does so, Ere places the voice, and raises a hand to assure Asavari she need not draw. The snide remark came from his cousin.

Cal drops stiffly to squat beside them at the water's edge. He eyes Asavari with suspicion. No, not just Asavari—both of them. It seems to Ere that his lifelong best friend now regards him and the strange girl with equal wariness.

"Who is this?" Asavari asks Ere.

Before Ere can answer, Cal speaks up for himself.

"Cal," he says with a flat smile. "I'm Ere's cousin. But these days, he forgets about me. And he forgets to mention new people to me, especially girls."

"Cal—" Ere warns, but his cousin barrels on.

"Leaves out the details, anyhow. So are you really an Original? Or some Syn whore?"

And then he grabs her by the neck with one hand, by the wrist with another. He pins her to the ground and places his knee on her chest, leaning into it. Hard. Harder. The girl exhales sharply as the breath is pushed from her, but does not cry out.

"Cal! Damnation! What are you doing?" Ere tries to pull his cousin off Asavari, but his fists land ineffectually on Cal's much larger shoulders.

Asavari kicks up sharply with her knee, connecting solidly with Cal's gut. With a grunt of pain, he loosens his hold on her neck, and she twists, lets out a sharp cry—not of pain, but of punishment—and in one practiced snap of her leg, she flips Cal onto his back. Their positions now reversed, Asavari presses her knee to his chest and holds her knife to his throat.

"I gave you enough time to check my neck and finger before removing your hands from me," Asavari glares calmly down at Cal. "So you know I am no Syn. But I warn you, if you ever touch me again, I will remove your hands not only from my body, but also from your own."

"We'll see," he scowls, scrambling to his feet as she releases him.

"For your sake, I hope we will not." She turns to Ere. "This jackass is your cousin?"

"Yes," says Ere.

"Can he be trusted?"

"Ha!" Cal's laugh is humorless. "Good luck asking a liar about who you can trust."

With that, Cal storms off. Ere feels sick as he watches his cousin depart. Cal is angry, and rightfully so, but Ere fears now that he underestimated just how much damage has been done to their relationship.

"What did he mean by 'syn whore'?"

Ere faces Asavari, who is looking at him curiously. "What?"

"He said something about a Syn whore. What did he mean by that?"

"Oh," says Ere, his face flushing hot. He shoves his feet further into the cold river water. "That's, uh, you know. Just an expression."

CHAPTER 48: EVER

E VER'S FATHER BURSTS INTO HER HOSPITAL room, brow glistening with sweat, nostrils flaring.

Everyone freezes. Before his entrance, the room was a hive of activity, orderlies buzzing around Ever's bed while a featureless nurse checked her pulse, a timid Vost medic calibrating the monitor, Dr. Chun overseeing the chaos. But when her father enters, everything stops.

"Get out," he commands, and the room instantly empties.

Ever is wary, but tries to keep her tone neutral; light. "Is this, like, an interrogation?"

"Yes," says her father without mirth or mercy. "Your time in Sector 27. What happened."

"There's really nothing to tell—"

Don't lie to me.

He does not speak the words, but sends them as an urgent missive, the physical alert pinching her skull. While designed to catch one's attention, such messages were usually just abrasive, not painful. In her weakened state, it feels like a sharp sting between her eyes.

"I'm not lying."

"Lying by omission is lying," Felix Hess says. "This is not a game, Ever. Several suspicious files have been retrieved from you. If you were anyone else, this situation would not be so painless, given what we have found."

Heaven and Hell. What had they been able to retrieve?

Working very hard to look wounded and bemused, Ever tries to surmise what her father might know. Surely, they had not been able to access anything from when she was in private mode. Those files were locked, hers alone, inaccessible even to her father.

"Father," she says, her voice low to avoid trembling, "I'm not sure precisely what it is that seemed 'suspicious'. Or why you felt the need to extract my memories against my will—"

"Ever." He says her name softly, almost sweetly. His voice is a thin layer of fresh ice over a vast lake, a veneer that might crack at any moment. Dangerous. He rubs his beard, speaks slowly. "You were in private mode for nearly thirteen hours. You took an early train into District 27. You stole a Chariot. Tell me which of those things doesn't seem suspicious."

He blinks, and the wall beside Ever's bed illuminates. A blurry image fills the wall. Ever recognizes it immediately—her view of Ere, when she woke up in the night and gazed at him. The scene is incriminating—but thank God, the image, yanked from a millisecond of her memory, is almost indiscernible. She knows who it was beside her, but all any other observer could see was a grainy shirtless torso. A problem for her, but, thank Heaven, not for Ere. His face was hidden, body blurred, identity impossible to determine.

"I ..." She needs to think, but thinking fast is not her current strong suit. "It's not what it looks like—"

"Isn't it?" Her father is eerily calm. "You do not have sole custody of your body. The technology belongs to the Synt. Do you want to know exactly why you and your tech matter so much, Ever?"

Her stomach hardens into a thick, cold knot. In a better world, he would tell her she matters because she's his beloved child. Whatever he's actually about to say, she knows in her bones it's something she doesn't want to hear.

"There's an initiative. The Generation Next Project. It's level seven classified."

Level seven? Level *six* meant only senior officials and Synt leaders had access to information. Ever didn't even know there was a level seven. Her father continues.

"We're putting the evolution back in revolution with this project. We're introducing highly selective reproduction for Syns. We'll be making fresh bodies, quality specimens available for neurological transfer when our citizens need full-scale upgrades."

"I don't understand," Ever says, fatigue and sedation further fuzzying information that seems already insanely confusing. And she has no idea what any of this has to do with her.

"The Generation Next project will secure our future. Syn survival, long-term. We'll eventually need new bodies for old Syns. And the best way to do that is through breeding."

"But Syns can't get pregnant—"

"We worked out those obstacles. But now, you've presented me with an unforeseen obstacle. You see, Ever, you are my daughter. Which means you're the best stock. And because of your age, you're one of the only Syn women still able to reproduce. You were critical to the Generation Next program. But now, you have defiled yourself."

"*Defiled* myself?"

"Yes. You were scheduled to be admitted into the in-vitro unit for implantation next month. You've been primed for years, little girl. No hormone suppression for you. And there have been supplements included in your meals and drinks for the past few months. Eating at regular intervals helped ensure the correct dosages of your fertility treatments."

Wait... wait... this is why mother always insisted on six-fifteen? No, this is too much...

Ever's mind lurches from thought to thought, already wobbly and only growing dizzier. Her whole protected life. Her father's strict rules. And her mother was in on it? Or was she just following her husband's directives without really knowing why? In either case, Ever pieces together the meaning of her situation, at least in part.

"You're mad because you think... I had sex?"

She is in shock, but the accusation is clear. Her father thinks she slept *with* Ere, not just beside him. The issue isn't who he is, or anything about Original outlaws, nothing she feared they might discover. A sudden spring of hope wells in her. She won't even have to lie!

"Yes—"

"But I didn't."

His eyes flash angrily. "I told you not to lie to me."

"I'm not lying!"

"Don't. Lie. Even if you kept yourself in private mode, he may not have."

He thinks it was a Syn. Thank Heaven.

She flags this thought as private as soon as it crosses her mind, now more paranoid than ever, but she cannot hide the relief that floods through her. Her father might be furious, thinking she slept with some nobody down South. But he has no clue about Ere, Ruth, any of that.

"I swear," she says honestly. "I didn't sleep with anyone. Run a lie detector. Give me a pregnancy test, for Heaven's sake—I'm sure Chun gave me twelve already! But I promise, I'm not 'defiled,' I'm not even—"

"Lie detectors won't work when you've been in private mode," her father snaps. "You know that. So exactly what were you doing for the thirteen hours you stayed incognito? Unlock the files and upload them to Heaven for the world to see. Prove that you have nothing to hide."

The hope inside her withers away. She has only two choices. She can protect Ere, and have her father abhor her; or expose Ere and clear her name. She thinks of Ere, vulnerable, naïve, gentle. The one who advocated for the importance of choice. She looks at her father, the man planning to use her in a damned *breeding program*, if she heard him right? He's not angry due to any sort of paternal instinct. He's angry because she was one of the variables in his latest scientific experiment, and she messed up his plans.

Her choice is clear. But something in her still wants her father to believe her. Because she is not lying. He should know that. He should believe her.

"No," she says, quietly. "I shouldn't need to reveal my private files. I'm asking you to believe me, because I'm telling you the truth. I misled you about my trip, and yes, I—I met up with a man. But I swear, I didn't—do that. Please, Father. I'm asking you to believe me. Because I'm telling the truth. And I'm not some test subject screwing up your data. I'm your daughter."

The anger drains from his face, the cold fury from his eyes. For a moment, she thinks he believes her. She is still his little girl. Clever Ever. They'll get through this. But when he speaks, his voice is flat, and he turns away from her.

"You'll go home tonight. You'll be supervised and observed while you pack. And then you will check in to the in-vitro unit. You no longer qualify for the alpha group, but you can be in the beta group. You'll still be part of Generation Next. You just won't be the prototype."

A sharp fear knifes through her faster and faster, shredding her lungs so she can hardly catch her breath. "Father—"

"No." He looks disgusted, and worse: disappointed. "You were a perfect specimen."

Ever's whole being is a patchwork of pain, stiched together with confusion and rage and fear. She makes no further sound, but cannot help the hot tears welling unbidden in her eyes. Her broken expression might be enough to reach the last stubborn remnants of Dr. Felix Hess' crumbled ruin of a heart, if he bothered to actually look at his daughter before leaving her hospital room.

He doesn't.

CHAPTER 49: CAL

C AL IS SORE. He's lost a lot in recent months. He rubs his head, which smacked hard against the earth when Asavari flipped him. His neck, his shoulders, his entire back is bruised and strained, thanks to that wretched dark-haired girl. As he works his fingers along his tensed muscles, sore and lonely, he counts his recent losses.

There were homes, of course. Franklin. The fishing village. Cal has lost many homes in his two decades; he's used to that. Home has never been something permanent, it's just a daily goal. Originals lives are not shaped by a sense of place, but by a sense of peoplehood.

That's why it's the human losses that weigh heaviest on him. First there was the loss of Howard. Then he lost the hero he truly idolized—his beloved aunt and surrogate mother, Ruth. And perhaps most painful of all, he lost his best friend. His cousin. Ere.

Ere is still breathing, but as far as Cal's concerned he might as well be in the ground. He betrayed Cal. After Cal defended him, lied for him, protected him, Ere kicked him in the nuts. And for what? A Syn whore. The careless runt endangered their tribe because he was horny.

Furious as this makes Cal, the honest truth is that if their situations were reversed, he might have made the exact same mistake. When he imagines Ere and the Syn girl, the emotion boiling Cal's blood is something far more powerful than betrayal—it's seething jealousy.

If he'd seen Ever first, he can't swear that he would have been able to resist the temptation. Even if he found out she was a Syn. But he never had the opportunity. It was Ere who met the girl in the woods. And now, when another girl turned up, it's Ere again by her side.

What's so attractive about that whiny little kid?

Given the options of mourning his losses or doubling down on his anger, Cal chooses fury. His resentment metastasizes, growing moment by moment, fed by testosterone and anxiety, spreading through him like a cancer. Cal once protected his cousin, loved him more than anyone. But re-playing the image of Ere in the shack with Ever, Cal wants to tear him limb from limb.

He feels differently about Ever.

The Syn girl, the one he calls a whore but wants to ravage. He can't stop thinking about her. As he watches Ere with Asavari, who moves like a fighter and had such strong, lean limbs—all right, fine, Cal does feel some stirrings of desire. But it's nothing compared to what he feels when he lets his mind wander to Ever.

Even though the brown-skinned girl is an Original, she's not as appealing to him as the girl he saw first by the water and later in bed with his cousin. Cal hates it, but can't help it: despite his contempt for Syns, his condemnation of his cousin, how hypocritical it makes him—his body tingles when he thinks of Ever.

The fantasies are constant. He pictures her in his tent. Beneath his blanket. Beneath him. Putting her mouth on him...

For the first time in his life, the protective and moderate Cal is driven by something even stronger than his desire to safe-guard those he loved. He has to have that girl. He will find a way. Whatever it takes.

Taking a breath, he wonders what the strange Original girl and his cousin are discussing. He heard that bit about the resis-tance she claimed to be a part of, half a world away. But now, what snippets of conversation he caught seem to be about Central City. If there is even a chance that their conversation has something to do with Ever, Cal has to know. He moves from the one tree to the next, closer to where they stand, traveling with the silent stealth of a master hunter.

K ENNEDY WISHES HE COULD GET OUT OF this assignment. Usually he's spared the tough-guy stuff. He's the more academic assistant. Not necessarily the brighter one, but the one who defaults to intellect over instinct. He is the light touch, the good cop, the bookish one whose hands are kept clean, right down to the fingernails.

The weenie, basically.

That's why he handles the more analytical tasks, and leaves the dirty work up to Jorge whenever possible. For years, in almost every situation where brute strength or physical risk was necessary, it was Jorge who was assigned to be "the heavy." But this time, Kennedy got the call.

Hess wants him to be the one to oversee an Enforcement Division assignment. They would travel one hundred miles to the west, where a small Original tribe had set up camp. The team had been briefed prior to the mission, and assured that the tribe in question consisted of only a dozen or so individuals, all older, mostly women. These Originals witnessed something they should not have seen. They had to be dealt with, and swiftly.

Kennedy doesn't know why he was selected for this gruesome assignment. If Jorge were any other Vost, it might be a bit more understandable. Vosts tended to be the only ones in their families to have synched, had less social standing themselves in the Syn world, were seen as only a half-step up from Originals. All in all, the average Vost might be more sympathetic when face to face with Originals. But Jorge is a company man, through and through. Kennedy knows beyond the shadow of a doubt that his stoic coworker would feel no pity. Orders were orders, and Jorge is an automaton who does what he's told, no questions asked.

So why aren't they sending the robot? Why me?

To calm himself, Kennedy replays a memory from his life before. Before the Singularity, before his augmentation, before reporting daily to Dr. Felix Hess. Back then, he used to go to parties all the time. He often went with his friend Val. Her father owned a basketball team, and she really knew how to have a good time.

Kennedy and Val loved going to parties, less for the drinking and dancing—although that could be fun, too—and more for the excuse it provided to dress up. Kennedy liked anything shiny and slimming. Val loved dresses with plunging necklines. White ones with gold details were her favorite; they made her dark cleavage pop *like whoa*, she grinned.

There was this one time they were invited to a midnight pool party. It was Los Angeles, late summer, definitely still going to be hot in the middle of the night, but neither Val nor Kennedy would have been satisfied simply showing up in bathing suits. They needed an ensemble. They met in Santa Monica for a day of shopping at the promenade.

Val found her outfit right away—a sheer, clingy, modern riff on the nostalgic muumuu, gauzy white with rhinestone and gold edging. It took Kennedy longer to find something to go atop his red-and-blue flowered swim trunks, but in their fourth and final store of the day he found it: A shaggy white faux fur vest, worn open in the front, ostentatious, over-the-top, and did an amazing job making him look broad-shouldered.

"How do I look?" He asked Val, dropping one shoulder, puffing out his exposed chest and shuffling toward her.

"Like a gay polar bear," she said, snapping a picture on her cell phone.

"Great. Now I'll feel like a homophobe if I don't buy it."

"Nah, just a bear-hater. Which is a kind of homophobe, too, come to think of it..."

Kennedy bought the vest, even though he could only keep it on at the party for about five minutes before it was too hot to bear.

Too hot to *polar* bear, Val drunkenly cracked, and they laughed until their sides hurt.

God. Did that really happen? Was that real life? Or is this?

An alert pops up, slamming him back into the present. The missive is from Hess, with a few additional details about the task at hand. The small amount of additional information makes his stomach lurch. He tries to tell himself what he always tells himself.

It's just another job. It's for the greater Synthetic good. One and done. Right?

Kennedy resolves to make the best out of a bad situation. He composes a short list to organize his thoughts:

First, he and the Enforcement team will depart on their Chariots, heading west, in two hours—just as full-dark night descends.

Second, they will reach the exact location in the geo-positioning report and confirm presence of the tribe.

Third, they will don their masks.

Fourth, they will release the gasses.

Fifth, after seven minutes, they will confirm complete eradication.

Sixth, they will burn down the campsite.

Seventh, they will put out the fire, controlling the damage.

Eighth, they will plant some sapling trees in the ashen forest floor. There was excellent soil west of Central City. Perfect for growing things, if you knew what to plant. Kennedy has always had a green thumb.

Then he'll come back to the city. Maybe he'll go shopping.

Plans made, he begins downloading a few pleasant Heaven files, wandering through virtual gardens and guidelines for the planting of seeds, flipping through fashion articles, filling his mind with blooms and haute couture, anything bright or garish enough to crowd out the carnage ahead.

Y*OU KNOW THINGS ARE BAD WHEN THE BEST part of your week is literally a suicide,* Shadower thinks darkly.

Scratch that: *two suicides.*

Shadower is grateful, though, that the bodies of Joshua and Shayna Murray were laid to rest as planned. Joshua had timed his explosive message to be delivered well after he reached Shayna's tribe and made all preparations for the quiet, independent ending of their lives. By the time the scrambling Syns deployed a team to track Joshua down, he was long gone. He thought his exit through down to the last detail, extracting what he could of his embedded tech and instructing the Originals to pull the rest from him quickly once he was dead, and to scatter the burials across a wide area to throw the Syns off course.

From what Shadower could gather, both the young-looking father and much-older-looking-daughter had been dealt some pretty crappy cards. With any luck, maybe now the poor Murrays could rest in peace. Of course, Shadower doesn't believe in luck; most likely the corpses will be discovered and excavated. Thankfully, even if the Syns interrupt the Murrays' perpetual rest, the network has already ensured it was not in vain. Joshua's death not only allowed him to be with his daughter, but also by trumpeting news of his actions, he'd surely blown the lid right off the Syn's attempts to cover up the growing termination trend.

Change is coming.

Syns, terminating themselves. The network, alight with messages, alive with hope. The fact that Ruth Fell had a son—! (If his existence and potential prove true—then yes, Shadower will have to admit, there's some actually-good news this week.) There's also the curious incidents involving Ever Hess.

What does Hess have planned for his daughter?

Shadower's mind keeps spinning, spinning, trying to piece together seemingly disparate scraps of information, to pull at the stitches and re-sew them until they began taking discernible shape. Nothing exists in a vacuum. Something will tie all the threads together. Unable to see the bigger picture just yet, when tuned in to the all-but-silent hums, Shadower can hear it coming into view.

WHEN ERE FINDS ASAVARI THE NEXT MORNING, he is prepared to pepper her with a thousand more questions. But as he approaches her, opening his mouth form the first query, she turns and nods like she's been expecting him.

"Ere, good. Are you ready?"

"Ready for what?" He asks, confused. (This question is not the one he had been preparing to ask. It was something about—oh, curse of the world, she'd derailed his thoughts.)

"To accept your mission."

Mission.

The word hits him in the chest. It's not the sort of word you just toss around; it has too much power, too much moral clarity, to be used lightly. A mission, like in the old days of the rebellions. Heroes had missions. Heroes like his mother.

"What mission?"

"To come with me to Central City, and make contact with Dr. Felix Hess, and then—"

"Wait," Ere says, already mildly panicked at the specificity of the mission details Asavari launched right into. He was expecting much more of a general *your mission to join the resistance* sort of thing, but apparently his basic involvement was a foregone conclusion in Asavari's mind. But then his panicking brain catches up with everything his ears just heard. The hypnotic, snakelike sound of that name: "Dr. Felix... Hess?"

Hess. Ever's father?

"Yes. You will tell him of your mother's passing. Say how grief-stricken you are. Tell him you want her back by any means necessary—even have her synched, if that is what it takes."

"Have my mother synched?" He's incredulous. Each sentence escaping crazy Asavari's lips is more unbelievable than the last. "Is that possible? Making them a Syn after they've died?"

"It's possible that it's possible."

"It's possible that it's possible." Ere repeats, as if having the words in his own mouth might help them make more sense. It does not. "And they'll let me in because...?"

"Because you're Ere Fell. Son of Ruth Fell. Their greatest enemy."

"Yes, that sounds like a wonderful way to introduce myself," Ere says. He's being sarcastic, but the weird girl nods enthusiastically.

"It is a good start," she says, sincerely. "And then, even better, by asking to make Ruth Fell a Syn—well, that goes against everything she ever fought for. It will paint you as a Syn sympathizer. You will be seen as a great disappointment to your mother."

Ere decides that he hates Asavari. The girl is militant. Insensitive. Compared to his mother, another tough soldier-woman, this girl was a lunatic zealot. Just as Ere is about to write her off entirely and tell her to stuff her mission up her ass, she softens.

"I'm sorry, Ere. I know this must all sound insane. But there is so much at stake. More than you know. But if you trust me, I will show you what we are fighting for. Please, Ere."

He wants to tell her no, but then he thinks: *My mother would do it.*

"All right." Still vowing to be wary of Asavari, Ere nods. Then, feeling sick even asking the question, he demands to know: "So what if they say it's possible? If they agree to… bring my mother back as a Syn?"

"Then they will want you to bring them to her body," she says simply. "But of course, we will never let them discover where Ruth Fell is buried. You and I will have a rendezvous point, and if you are not there to meet me at the given hour, I will assume they are holding you until you can direct them to your mother. And come Heaven or Hell, we will get you out of there."

He thinks about asking her how on earth she planned to do that, but the question is irrelevant. Even if he can't stand her, he also believes that if this girl says she'll do something—come Heaven or Hell, she'll do it.

"Will I have time to bid farewell to my tribe? The elders? Cal?"

"I am sorry, but no. We need to leave immediately."

Swallowing his fear, Ere nods. He has his knife, and nothing else to gather. He will follow Asavari, and carry out the mission, seemingly for the noble reason of helping the Original cause. But he's also going for another, less noble reason. Unbeknownst to Asavari, Ere will have his own mission while in Central City.

Somehow, some way, he will find his way to the other Hess.

Ever awaits.

K ENNEDY CANNOT STOP SHAKING. His knees are weak, and he has already vomited twice.

The first time was mid-assignment.

He zipped his Chariot behind a tree, where the others could not see him. Not that they were looking. They were all too intent on carrying out the job.

Kennedy didn't participate in the assignment, *per se*. His hands are still clean, technically speaking. His job was merely to oversee. He was there as documentarian, so that he could report directly to Hess and assure him that the job had been carried out thoroughly, everything done according to the full extent of the directive.

But he wishes he had not seen what he saw. He had never witnessed anything like it. Never.

Somehow, in putting together his lists and distancing himself from the reality of the assignment, he convinced himself it was something other than what it was. He thought it would be a relatively simple and sanitary set of tasks: Show up, release the gasses, clean up, go home.

But the Enforcement guys had orders upon arrival to get information before eradicating the Original tribe. Locate, interrogate, eradicate, they said.

It was all so much more brutal than Kennedy could have imagined. The agony-twisted faces of the three souls tortured for information, screaming that they had no idea what any of this was about. The screams of pain, the sobbing for mercy. He could never have prepared himself for the sounds. The sounds, or the smells, or the sights. The rivers of deep-dark red blood wetting the famously fertile brown soil of the earth, these acres that had once been farmland.

Kennedy can still hear the shocked screams of protest, echoing like ghosts in the smoke-choked air.

Please! We don't know anything! We don't know! Please, no!

What if it really was the wrong tribe? Kennedy knows everything he just did will haunt him for the rest of his days, as will this horrible question, unless he erases the memories.

He has to erase it. He has to. As soon as he delivers his report directly to Hess, he will erase the massacre from his memories. He's not going to confess to Hess his doubts about whether or not they eradicated the right tribe. He's just going to erase that troublesome thought, too.

Kennedy is too traumatized by this latest incident to stop and wonder how many other massacres, doubts, and other sins he has probably erased after overseeing.

M ARILYN HAS NOT SEEN HER HUSBAND OR her daughter in days. Per Felix's orders, she has also not left the residence. The cabin fever is burning her alive. *Cabin fever. What a silly old-world notion.*

The Hess' penthouse residence at the Synt is a far cry from "a cabin." Marilyn hasn't been in an actual cabin since childhood. But as best she can recall, cabins didn't mean being pent-up; they meant freedom, and youth, and fresh air.

She went to summer camp in the Berkshires when she was a little girl. Those summers were full of mosquito bites, s'mores, ghost stories told around campfires, late nights huddled in bunk beds gossiping about boys. What she wouldn't give for someone to gossip with now; but then again, any juicy dish to which Marilyn was privy was off limits. She wasn't supposed to talk to anyone about her daughter, her husband, his work, anything. Even if she had someone to talk to, there would be little she could say. Small talk really was the highest aspiration.

Marilyn wishes she still lived in a world where people came door-to-door to peddle their vacuum cleaners, their cosmetics, their religions, all with equal fervor. She hated those visitors way back when, but she'd give anything for a drop-in now.

She wonders what other people talk about these days. Best as she can recall, drawing on her faded Original memories, when Marilyn used to meet other women for coffee or cocktails they mostly talked about people they knew, the news (if they were pretentious), and the upcoming milestones they were either looking forward to or dreading: weddings, funerals, new jobs, retirement. But she's not allowed to talk about people she knows. Everyone already collectively shares in the news. And milestones have lost much meaning; how much does a mile marker matter when the freeway stretches out into infinity?

Maybe other people still have milestones, goals, benchmarks to measure the worth of their lives. Her husband does. But Marilyn has nothing, she realizes. She will never become a grandparent, or serve in the military, or pass important legislation, or protest injustice, or do any of the things she watched the generation above her do. Her activities so much smaller, stretching out in front of her forever, as endless and repetitive as they are meaningless: make the coffee, plan the meals, plan the vacation, repeat.

It wasn't always this desolate. At first, synching was exciting; realizing how much information she could take in, the new skills she could learn—language! Karate! French cooking!—were intriguing, and there were the Original uprisings bringing some danger and drama to it all. Even the day-to-day stuff was more interesting a few decades ago—sharing the collective consciousness in Heaven felt like Facebook, only better. Every status update, all at once, people competing for the most interesting uploads and wittiest updates. Now it was just another task to complete. Something to do, not something to enjoy.

And so, although she was never actually tired—*not really, not physically, just emotionally exhausted and isn't that worse?*—she was plugging herself in to Heaven earlier and earlier. Checking out for the day, giving up and going dark, passively absorbing whatever there was to absorb with little interest and zero engagement. She used to value Heaven for the illumination it offered. Now, what she appreciated most was the flip side of that coin: the oblivion that ccomes with pressing her neck port into its outlet—the dreamless suspended state that stilled her mind and stops her life, just for a little while. Leaving the real world to spend a few hours in the blessed void of Heaven is the best part of her day.

An alert from the door interrupts her somber thoughts. She blinks twice, surprised.

Mormons! She thinks hopefully. Then: *Idiot. There haven't been Mormons in forty years.*

Before Marilyn can even call up the security screen display, the door slides down, revealing her husband's assistant Jorge. He gives her an acknowledging nod, even looks slightly abashed about entering without an invitation from her, but Marilyn knows Felix granted him entry.

"Good morning, Mrs. Hess."

"What is it, Jorge?"

"I have some updates for you."

"Will it take long? Shall I have Angela make more coffee?"

"If you like," Jorge says. "Although Ms. Hess will need to take hers to her room."

He steps aside, and behind him stands a sullen, scowling Ever. Marilyn is almost happy to see her miserable daughter, who will surely pick a fight with her later. Things will liven up a bit.

For a day or two, anyway.

E RE AND ASAVARI'S JOURNEY TO CENTRAL CITY begins like any other migration, minus all of the old people—meaning a much, much faster pace. Scrambling to keep up with her, Ere follows Asavari into the woods, through streams, across rocky outcroppings. No matter the terrain, she moves at a good clip. Ere, accustomed to slowly herding trailing elders, realizes he is not quite as robust as he'd thought. Compared to the old folks, he was nimble as a mountain goat. Compared to this Original girl, he feels more like a mountain goat missing three out of its four legs.

Even in the dark, Asavari does not slow down; she insists they keep moving under the cover of night.

"It's safer," she says.

Ere, tripping over a root and tearing open his toe, thinks otherwise. All night, while Asavari strides confidently forward, Ere smacks against every available branch, slips on the small wet pebbles lining creek bottoms, and gets his garments and flesh caught and torn on a variety of bramble. Each time, he catches himself, curses under his breath, and is relieved that at least in the darkness, his clumsiness is somewhat hidden.

After hours of silence broken only by Ere's twig-snapping and hushed cries of *ouch-dammit!*, Asavari stops and looks toward the pink and purpling horizon.

"This way."

Ere wonders why, after leading him through the entire dark night of hazards with no warnings or commentary, with the return of daylight Asavari feels a sudden need to indicate their path. He watches her approach a massive cliff. It seems to have appeared out of nowhere, rising from the misty morning fog—some sort of narrow, steep mountain, absolutely un-scalable.

Asavari grabs a tufting bit of grass protruding from the face of the rock, and begins to scale the mountain.

Ere stares, then looks around, confused. The mountain is not blocking their way; it's tall, but not wide. The path on either side of it is clear. Ere takes stock of the scene in front of him: wide swath of land, narrow stupid sheer-faced mountain, wide swath of land. Why the hell is she climbing this stupid stone slab?

Asavari, now nearly twenty feet up the rock, looks down at Ere.

"Are you coming?"

Curse of the world…

Wordlessly, Ere grabs for the same bit of grass he'd watched her grab, hauls himself up, and immediately loses his grip, He hits the ground. Hard. Gritting his teeth, he gets back to his feet. Grabbing the tuft of dry grass, he strains to lift his own weight. He wraps the grass around his fingers, knuckles tightening, whitening. The grass tears, chafing his hands and giving way, sending him tumbling to the ground again. And now there's no teasing tuft to grasp.

Thirty feet up, Asavari looks back at him again.

"Never mind. Wait there."

He squints up at her, chagrined but not eager to attempt the climb again. He watches her gain another ten impossible feet, straight up the rock, and disappear into some sort of opening.

"Happy birthday, Ere Fell!"

Something comes flying at him from above, catching him on the shoulder and nearly knocking him down. But it isn't heavy, not really. He lifts it up and examines it: a strange fabric. Dark. Durable. It feels unnatural in his hands.

Asavari shimmies down the mountain even faster than she had gone up it. She is wearing different clothing now, garments made of the same dark, durable fabric. They fit her well, and she moves with ease.

"Resistance freebox—Syn clothing, to help us blend in," she explains. "We finish the journey using Syn transportation. We need to look the part."

This does look like what Ever wore. When she wasn't in undergarments...

Shoving the thoughts of an almost-naked Ever aside, Ere protests.

"But just putting on these clothes—I mean, that can't be enough. Won't the Syns be able to tell we're Originals?"

"Yes, of course," says Asavari. "Not at a glance, though. As long as we do not call attention to ourselves, we will be fine. There are Originals living among the Syns, after all. We are just younger than they are. So, when we get there, just try to look old."

"What?"

"Try to look old. Should be easy, you hike through the woods like a drunk blind elder—"

"Curse of—I didn't mean—I meant... there are Originals who live with the Syns?"

"Yes."

"Why?"

"Because it's easier than tribal life. Syn society is full of conveniences. But they come at a cost. Originals living among Syns are almost a slave race. They do laundry, rake yards, devote their lives to making Syn life even easier. Then as they age and get sick, they are denied medical treatment. It is one of the many ugly truths you'll see when—well. Get dressed, we can talk as we walk. We are still several hours from the transportation hub that will take us to the Synt. And we'll want to wash up before we get there."

Asavari turns her back, and Ere slips out of his dirty shirt and soft, worn pants. While she is not looking, he transfers Ever's little gun from his ratty pants pocket to the crisp, clean pocket of his new Syn garb. He tucks his Original garments beneath a bush. They're not in good enough shape to warrant finding a freebox for them, but maybe they'll provide some wild dog or remnant elder with a bit of comfortable bedding.

"How do I look in my Syn costume?" He asks Asavari.

She turns around, and a sound escapes her throat, like a bird squawking. Her expression is one he has not seen before. Nausea? Constipation? No, he realizes. It's amusement.

"The clothing is somewhat large for you, Ere Fell."

He looks down, noticing that the comfortable pant legs are pooled at his ankles, prepared to trip him. The shirt, too, billows around him. Ere squats, tightly rolls the ankles of the pants, strives for dignity as he rises, willing himself not to stumble as he strides past Asavari.

"I think that's just the fashion," he says, puffing out his chest to fill the billowing shirt. A passing breeze becomes a gust of wind, catching the bottom of his shirt, ballooning it at his waist, making him look quite pregnant. Asavari suppresses another squawk.

"Let's go," Ere says, his reddening ears hotter than ever.

H ELENA GARRISON WAKES, PANTING. Her vivid nightmare was filled with screams and the smell of burning. Upon waking, her hot panic is replaced with cold dread. It's the first morning in her entire life that she will be facing a day without Fells.

Howard was there the day she was born. She helped raise Ruth before proudly following her. She views Ere and Cal as grandsons. Now her tribe's founding family is all gone, leaving Helena and a handful of other old people.

A wandering rest home. What a bitter oxymoron we have been handed.

She had been prepared for the death of Howard. Less so, for the loss of Ruth. But losing both boys is more than she can bear. Ere disappeared first. He and the Original girl were both gone, without a word. No one knew where they went. Back to her tribe? Somewhere else? Were they kidnapped? As the elders posed theory after theory, Cal held his tongue. Helena suspected he knew something. Last night, she approached him as he warmed himself near the evening's fire, half-hidden in the shadows, his body guarding his elders while his mind drifted elsewhere.

"Cal. Do you know where your cousin went?"

He remained in shadow, so she could not see his face, but his voice betrayed his rage.

"I will track Ere. I will hunt him down, and I will find him."

"And bring him home?" Helena asked, disquieted by his tone. Cal did not reply.

The next morning, Helena and Cal met with the another tribe to discuss a merger. The tribal leaders assured them that yes, the two dozen elders of their tribe would be welcomed among their people. This tribe's council was helmed by a nut-brown old man called Para. Helena had no reason to doubt Para's promise, no reason to mistrust his people. They were a fellow Original tribe. They had come to honor Ruth at the funeral. But they, too, numbered fewer than thirty individuals, all elderly. To Helena, it felt less like they were connecting with a tribe that would protect them, and more that all of the elders were congregating to face their end together. Elephants marching en masse to their burial ground.

But with the Fells gone, what else was there to do?

The meeting with Para was yesterday. Cal departed mere minutes later.

Helena does not blame either of the boys for leaving. If Ere had an opportunity to connect with a female close to his own age, it was understandable that he would pursue this chance. Helena hopes that he had abandoned them in order to start a new life and family. And Cal—good, solid Cal, who had literally carried so many of them for so long. He did not just up and leave; no stealing away in the night like his younger, flightier cousin. No, Cal did his due diligence. He brokered the tribal merger first. His aunt Ruth would have been proud. His mother would have been prouder still.

Cal's mother, Rachel, was Ruth's twin sister. Both sisters were fiercely loyal, and unwavering in their commitments and beliefs. But where Ruth was strong, stubborn, a fighter—Rachel was frail, accommodating, a peacemaker. Even from a very young age, their personalities were so sharp, so distinct. Helena knew this better than anyone else, because as their next-door neighbor, several years older, she was their babysitter.

From the time they were small, Ruth was independent and driven, and as a young woman she shunned all would-be suitors. Rachel was as soft as her sister was tough, and a hopeless romantic. It surprised no one when she married young. She fell in love with a gentle giant, Geoffrey Harper, who had curly black hair, smooth dark skin, kind brown eyes. It took years for them to have children, but when Cal was finally born, God, how they loved that boy. They were granted so little time with him; the cruel new world robbed Cal of both parents in childhood.

Helena is not related by blood to the Fells. But they are her family. She can trace their family tree, from seeds to roots to branches, all of the apples and acorns. She always lived in the shade of that family tree. She feels exposed now, knowing with a sad certainty that she will never again see any members of her adopted family.

Lost all of the last of them in one Fell swoop, she thinks mirthlessly.

Humor has always seen Helena through. But her humor has gone from light to dark, then to black, and now seems as dead as most of her loved ones. This morning, she cannot lighten her own mood, nor anyone else's. She cannot laugh, but she will force herself to hope. She will hope that her God would be kinder to Cal and Ere than He was to their ancestors. She says a quick prayer for the Fell boys, but does not include any supplications for herself.

Against all odds, Helena Garrison does still believe that there exists a higher power. She still believes in some sort of God. But she gave up the belief that God had any interest in her many, many years ago.

M ARILYN HESS IS ALWAYS THE LAST TO KNOW. But once brought into the loop, she's expected to act in accordance with the new information. No questions asked, no opportunity for debate. Even when it means drugging her daughter. Or, apparently, helping impregnate her.

She knew nothing of the Generation Next Project. Not until her husband's assistant Jorge arrived, delivering the despondent Ever. Ever was sent to her room, and then Jorge succinctly provided a broad-brush overview of the Generation Next project and Ever's intended role in it.

"Do you have any questions?" Jorge asked the question curtly but not unkindly, aware that he had shared more than one shocking bit of information while their coffee grew cold.

"Yes," Marilyn replied flatly, and then told Jorge he could leave.

She had questions, but they were not for him. They were for her husband. And they'd never be answered, so no use asking them. Marilyn just sits. Cursing her compliance, she replays all the instructions she was provided, without explanation, in the months and weeks leading up to this moment.

Make sure Ever eats at the same time every day. Add these supplements to her meals. If she won't eat, slip them in her tea or coffee. Make sure she's plugging in, getting enough rest. Don't let her off the boat when you travel. Don't tell her you're doing any of this. Don't act like anything is different. Don't ask questions.

Staring dully forward, she sits for a long, long time. Finally, after looping through her commands over and over, something snaps in Marilyn Hess. Rising suddenly, she goes to Ever's room. She slides the door down, and gazes into her daughter's room, taking in the details of the space—the old ballet recital photograph, the darkened screen wall, the vanity with the large mirror, an antique, something that had belonged to Felix's grandmother—before finally turning toward her daughter. Ever is curled up on the bed in a tensed fetal position.

"Did they tell you about Generation Next?" Ever asks, her face aimed at a pillow.

"They did."

"Just now, or earlier?"

Marilyn considers lying, loathe to admit she too was kept in the dark. But this time, she tells her daughter the truth: "Just now."

"The whole thing? How my father wants to… breed me?"

"It's a lot to take in," is all Marilyn says.

She stops herself from saying anything more. She looks at her forlorn child, and for the briefest of moments, has the irrational thought that now is the time for mothering. That maybe Ever will cry, and need comforting, and allow Marilyn to hold her and nuzzle her as she had when Ever was an infant, and to tell her it was all going to be all right.

Ever's lip quivers, so slightly that anyone but a mother would have missed it. Marilyn just barely catches it, but it's enough to cue her to lean in—at which point Ever straightens her back, abandoning the fetal position, and sits up, leaning away from her mother, widening the distance between them. She looks at Marilyn, her voice as dry as her eyes:

"So you didn't know, until just now."

"Not... all of it," Marilyn says, implying she knew much more than she actually did, wanting so desperately to seem more looped in than her daughter. As punishment for this lie, Marilyn witnesses her daughter's shocked, shattered reaction to the (fake) news that both parents actively transpired against her.

Ever gets up, brushing her eyes hard with the back of her hand. Pushing past her mother, heading for the kitchen. With nothing else to do, Marilyn follows her. Silly, thinking Ever might want to be comforted. There will be no tears, no embrace, no admission of distress. Emotional distance is the default setting of every Hess. They no longer function in any other capacity.

Marilyn wonders if it bothers anyone else, how fractured this family has become. They had eternity, which was an awfully long time to go without affection. If anyone was going to change the dynamic, it would have to be Marilyn, since no one else seems concerned. But she fears she has forgotten how to cultivate human connection. It has been so damned long.

Beyond that, for too many years, Marilyn has simply accepted that her role in the family is the least relevant. While her husband's intellect and her daughter's beauty set them apart from the crowd, she disappears in their shadows. She realized long ago that in the theater of their lives, Felix and Ever's dramas would always take center stage, and she would be backstage, trying to follow the demanding cues of some unseen director, always afraid of shoving someone out for their entrance at the wrong time, or not having the right props or costumes on hand.

It wasn't always that way. The overlooked Marilyn Hess was once upon a time the prized, privileged Marilyn Kensington. But the curtains went down on that show long, long ago.

Marilyn Kensington's story began like the greatest of soap operas: with dramatic love and tragic loss, big hair and cowboy hats, all set against the oversized backdrop of Dallas.

She was born in the state called Texas, a princess among the royalty of that land. An oil heiress, back when oil still mattered more than technology. Back when old family names still mattered more than new innovations. Back when Marilyn believed in happy endings.

Her father's family had strong connections in Texas, and enviable roots on the East Coast. Edward Adams Kensington IV was one of six children; when the family acquired land out West, he and one of his brothers became the Texas contingent of the Kensington family, moving out there to expand the empire. Politically and socially, their reach was extensive. They were known and welcomed in Boston and Westport, in Dallas and Houston.

Texas was a good fit for Edward Adams Kensington IV—"Four," as he was called. The Lone Star State wasn't for everyone. His sisters and his youngest brother, pale bookish things, were best suited to stay out East. He and Bradley, the brother who ventured out West with him, were Texas naturals, big men with ruddy faces, which eventually became leathery from too much sun and whiskey. They had firm handshakes and booming voices. They inspired confidence.

They were also terrible bigots.

They didn't like the Mexicans, and threw their support to politicians pushing anti-immigrant policies. It wasn't just illegal immigrants that bothered them; they didn't want any immigrants encroaching on Texas, period. This was all despite the fact that Four and Brad only adopted the state as adults themselves, that only four generations earlier, their ancestors were sipping tea in England before setting sail for New England. Never mind all that. Wasn't how the Kensington boys saw it: They'd staked their claim, and they wanted to protect their territory.

They also didn't like the blacks, or the Jews, or the Asians, or the Muslims with all that price-gouging foreign oil. Luckily for them, the company they kept was all fairly homogenous, an old boy's club of powerful and protective WASPs. If an outsider tried to elbow his way in, they drove him out. These were wasps with stingers.

And cattle prods.

And guns.

When Four and Brad moved to Texas, they were single. When they were established enough, their thoughts turned to marriage. Both agreed that they wanted to marry Texas girls (although this was a lie on Brad's part; he had a thing for cowboys, but was business-savvy enough to know that this was a secret best kept very, very quiet in 1960s Texas). From the most ancient days of human civilization, marriages had served as unions not only of individuals but also of families. Empires. Nations. Securing their place in the society where they now lived, and linking their Eastern fortune to Western wealth was a strategic move as calculated as any other the Kensington boys ever made.

Their specifications were exacting: they wanted wives from rich Texas families, well-established, well-connected. They wanted fathers-in-law who could open more doors for them. They had to be prominent, respected, white, church-going, attractive. Brad found someone almost immediately—a reedy young woman from the Matterhorn family, a good solid connection. She was a handsome woman, tall and somewhat masculine (which did not bother Brad). It took Four longer, but he eventually laid eyes on his future wife.

Annabelle Andrews was a hot commodity. Four described her as an A-plus broad with all the perfect Bs: blond, buxom, beautiful, banked. Her father, Frederick Andrews, was a cattleman, but not a rancher. Neither she, nor he, nor anyone in their immediate family had actually set foot on a farm in years. But he owned half the feedlots and most of the breeding stock in the state.

"Our stock is livestock," Frederick Andrews cracked at every single meeting, party, and wedding he ever attended. "And stock's always goin' up!"

Frederick Andrews was more of a garish character than Four would have liked, but the old man had enough wealth and power for all eccentricities to be politely accepted. And despite her clown of a father, Annabelle was perfect. Young, gorgeous, confident enough to flirt and tease back when Four teased her, demure enough to know her place.

So Four threw his hat into the ring, fighting off all her other would-be suitors, cozying up to Annabelle, talking insider-business-talk with her father and laughing at the man's dumbass jokes. Whenever Four laid eyes on Annabelle's mother, Gloria, he would take off his trademark ten-gallon cowboy hat (somehow, his own cowboy-costume never struck him as clownish), kiss her hand and tell her she just kept gettin' prettier.

The Andrews family was impressed by Four. Still, her father made him wait, testing his patience the same way he tested new stock. Of course, Annabelle was only fifteen when Four first met her; when she was eighteen, they were engaged.

It was a beautiful society wedding. Everyone came, even the East Coast Kensingtons. The delicate northerners marveled at the beauty of the massive church and of Four's lovely bride, all while wiping beads of sweat from their faces and whispering amongst themselves, wondering quietly why anyone would want to live in this godforsaken hot-as-hell redneck state.

Annabelle made a beautiful bride, and her sweet-yet-spicy nature seemed a good balance to Four's brash, booming self. They made their home in North Dallas, and became the city's most powerful darlings. The pinnacle of Dallas society. Annabelle Andrews Kensington and Edward Adams Kensington IV were going to take the whole world by storm.

Soon after they wed, Annabelle became pregnant. She lost the baby. This happened three more times, and for awhile, they stopped trying. It was too hard on Annabelle, and anything that was hard on Annabelle was unbearable for her adoring husband. But at last, more than a decade into their marriage, Annabelle carried a child to term.

Though Annabelle had long been told how wonderful her shape was, how perfect her hips were for birthing (*unlike that hipless sister-in-law of hers, poor dear*), pregnancy did not go well for Annabelle. The first four miscarriages had proven that despite the lie her hips told, her body did not welcome the colonization-by-fetus. Even with her successful pregnancy, her body rebelled. She did not glow, she became pallid. She didn't gain weight, she lost it. Her face grew thin, her arms and legs reduced, and even her belly seemed flat for far longer than it should have—to the point that she disbelieved her doctors, couldn't see how she could be pregnant—until the baby started kicking. Then, steadily, her belly rounded and grew, while the rest of her shrank around it.

Annabelle woke up screaming three weeks before she was due. Her water had broken, she was having contractions, and there was blood everywhere—unexpected blood, blood hours before there was a baby, blood that should not have been there. Four rushed her to the hospital.

The labor was long and terrible. Annabelle kept passing out

from the pain, and when she was not unconscious, she was crying out in agony, begging for relief. Four paced the hallways, hearing her scream. For all his bravado, the one thing Edward Andrews Kensington IV could not bear to see was his beautiful wife in pain, sweating, contorted, undone. He could not muster up the courage to be by her side.

Finally, a nurse came for him. A black nurse, which meant Four avoided eye contact. But she had information he needed, so he listened closely as she told him the baby was here. A girl. And Annabelle was awake. Did he want to come see them now?

Four went in to the hospital room. There, drenched in sweat, thin and drawn, with her damp blonde hair plastered to her skull, was Annabelle. In her arms was a tiny, red-faced infant.

When Four reached her side, Annabelle smiled up at him, and for a moment, he could see her. The real her. The stunning, healthy, fleshed-out Annabelle. His beautiful bride, and now the mother of his child. Their whole life stretched out before him in that smile, a big sunny life they'd live out together under a cloudless Texas sky, and he smiled back.

"Let's call her Marilyn," said Annabelle.

"I always wanted a Marilyn," Four said.

"Every girl should have a little Marilyn in her, didn't I tell you that?" Annabelle winked, channeling the flirty fifteen-year-old she had been when Four first laid eyes on her. "And just look at her. She's going to be a star. Biggest star in the Lone Star state, our baby girl—"

Then Annabelle blanched, and her eyes rolled back in her head. She lost her grip on the infant, fingers grasping then going slack; a panicking Four caught their daughter just in time. Machines beeped, a crash team rushed in. Four, clutching their baby, was shoved out of the way, shut out of the room.

He clung to the tiny, red-faced baby, and waited in the hallway while his wife died.

He did not believe the doctor who told him the team was "unable to revive her." She bled out, the lying bastard said. A rupture in her uterus. Nothing they could do. The ugly words all blended together. Four just clung to his baby. Their baby. Marilyn, the last gift given to him by his beloved Annabelle.

In that moment, Marilyn became his world.

In a move that surprised everyone, he ceased being a workaholic. He became the most devoted of fathers. He would let no one else touch the baby—not a hired nanny, not his in-laws, not his own relatives. He changed her diapers, he fed her, he kept her with him at all times.

Annabelle's death was a tragedy that rocked Dallas society; everyone assumed that Four's strange behavior was simply his way of mourning. *This will pass,* everyone said. *His pain at losing Annabelle will ease and he'll let someone else raise the baby. This is all temporary. He'll marry again. He'll do what makes sense.*

But Four did not do "what made sense." He did not remarry. He did not throw himself into the business and allow someone else to raise his daughter for him; instead he threw himself into parenthood, and allowed someone else to run the business for him. He kept a controlling share in the companies, along with his brother Brad, but farmed out the oversight. He knew his vast business interests would continue to thrive day to day without him there. On the days when he did go to the office, he brought Marilyn with him. Unheard of, for a child to be in business meetings and running around the office. But Four was powerful enough that no one protested.

Marilyn grew from a tiny, fussy infant into a lovely and well-behaved little girl who doted on her father as much as he doted on her. At a very young age, she was exposed to things that came later in life for most. Her father took her to the ballet, the opera, the theater, fine restaurants. She traveled to China and Dubai. She ate caviar. She knew what "oil futures" were. Her father exposed her to the world, but kept her from any activity he deemed too dangerous. No horseback riding, despite it being the standard extracurricular for girls her age in Dallas. No sports. No car of her own—he hired a driver for her. And above all, no boys.

Marilyn Kensington did not date in high school, though she was crowned homecoming queen and voted Most Popular. She was as charming as her mother, as gregarious as her father. Despite her father's extravagance with her, Marilyn did not spoil. She missed having a mother, but realized quite young how fortunate she was to have all that she had.

She went out East for college, as was expected, though this was quite hard on her father. She saw his family there frequently, and also saw him quite often. He would fly himself there or fly her back to Texas for every holiday, every school break.

Marilyn mostly did what was expected of her. She joined the right sorority. She made good enough grades. She became queen of the campus. But for the first time in her life, Marilyn also began to move beyond what was expected of her. To step outside the carefully-drawn lines and boundaries. She did not rebel out of anger, or revenge. It was not because she resented her father, or even felt that he had done anything wrong in over-protecting her. She rebelled because she was eighteen. She rebelled because it is what children do as they learn to become adults.

She took up a sport, joining the crew team. She loved getting up early, feeling the cool New England air on her skin, sliding the boat into the water, blending in with the rest of her team, stroking their way across the Charles River. The crew team was her first small act of rebellion, since if her father knew about this activity, the possibility of her drowning in the Charles would send him into a fit, and he'd make her give it up. So that was her first secret.

Her second, and much larger act of rebellion, was dating a young man named Felix Hess.

She knew from the moment she met Felix that her father would not like him. He was slight and pale. He was not charming; he was barely polite. He was not poor, but he was also not rich or connected or important. What he was, was brilliant.

He did not go to her school. He went to M.I.T. And even though he was only twenty, he was a graduate student. In a school packed with brilliant young minds, Felix Hess was the brightest of them all. He had graduated early, from *Stanford*. Now he was putting everyone to shame, *at M.I.T.* It was very impressive, and more than a little bit sexy, especially when paired with his moody dark eyes and trim, tight physique.

They met at a twenty-four-hour coffee shop. It was quarter to five in the morning. Felix was bleary-eyed, having been there since six o'clock the previous evening, fueled by cups of coffee with more shots of espresso than was wise. Marilyn was fresh-faced and alert, having just woken up. She was stopping in for a cup of coffee on her own before meeting her team for their five A.M. practice. It was her little ritual. Having a morning mug, savoring the quiet joy of privacy before the louder joy of rowing with her team. It was her favorite ten minutes of any given day, a precious habit. And this time it led her to Felix.

She didn't notice him when she first walked in to the coffee shop. She walked directly to the counter. The young man behind the counter was named Lenny. He was from South Boston, and Marilyn knew that he nursed a large crush on her. He always tried to give her the coffee for free, and she always insisted and paid the dollar for the coffee, and left a dollar in the tip jar for Lenny. It was all part of the ritual.

"Morning, Lenny."

"Mornin', Marilyn. Good one for rowing."

"Yeah, should be."

"Two creams, no sugar?"

"Like always."

Lenny winked. His face was pockmarked with acne scars, but he had cute, deep dimples and dark blue eyes. In another life, she could see herself falling hard for a sweet, gentle Southie kid like Lenny. Eager to please, tough, ready to protect his girl. He had a certain appeal. In this life, though, they were not meant to be.

"Two creams, no sugar. That's how my grandmother always took her coffee."

Marilyn turned around, locating the source of the voice. Her first impression of Felix Hess was simply that he looked tired. There were deep bags under his eyes. His chin sort of melted into his neck as he slumped blearily against the cheap plastic chair. He had very thick hair, and while his skin was sort of olive in complexion and should have been dark, it had the pallor of someone who spent too many hours staring at screens and pages. But despite the lines around them, his eyes were intense, magnetic; she felt as if he was looking right into her soul.

"Oh, yeah?" She said casually, letting her Texas twang sweeten her words.

"Yes. Coffee was always two creams, no sugar."

Lenny handed the steaming coffee cup to Marilyn, glaring at the other guy.

(*Friggin' scrawny grad student, talking to Marilyn. Who was that guy, anyway? He spent a lot of late nights at the coffee shop, but never talked to Lenny. No personality, never came here with any friends, just books and laptop. A total brain. And now beautiful Marilyn was looking at him. That guy? Jesus Christ, life's unfair.* Lenny turned with resignation back to the espresso machine behind him, which needed cleaning, as Marilyn continued conversing with the brain.)

"Sounds like your grandmother was a woman with excellent taste."

And thus began a conversation that lasted for the next several months. Felix Hess actually took time away from his studies to take Marilyn out on dates. The dates were usually something like a stroll through one of the city's many free museums, or a screening of an indie film at the seedy Cambridge art house cinema, followed by a cheap dinner, followed by coffee that turned cold in their cups as they talked about science, religion, the structure of modern society.

Marilyn began missing crew practice and was eventually kicked off the team, but she didn't care. Felix was addictive. He was brilliant and driven, and entirely self-made. Like her, he was an only child—but unlike her, he had almost no relationship with his parents. He didn't have family money, family support, or family connections; any connections he had, he'd made.

Deliriously infatuated, Marilyn thought her father would adore Felix, too. Her ever-indulgent father would be thrilled that she was with someone so motivated, such a genius! At the end of the term, when Four was flying to retrieve her, Marilyn called and left him a voicemail, so he would hear it when he landed, and be surprised, but not completely blindsided.

When Four deplaned, he didn't turn on his phone, so he never got Marilyn's message about "bringing someone special" with her to meet him at baggage claim. He simply headed directly to the designated meeting point, excited to see Marilyn. It had been months, and he usually preferred to limit their separations to weeks.

When he saw her, she filled his vision. He only barely registered at first that there was a thin young man, some weasely academic type, standing beside his beautiful daughter. He focused instead on his Marilyn, hurrying over to her and lifting her in an exuberant hug.

"Hey, baby doll! Look at you!"

She hugged him back, grinning from ear to ear. Then she pulled back and gestured to the skinny boy, beckoning him to her side. Four wondered if this kid had a car, and if he might be expecting a thank-you for bringing Marilyn to the airport. But then, with a growing sense of dread, Four watched as his baby girl slipped her hand into the boy's hand. Which is when he also noticed the ring on her finger. A small gold band, with a microscopic diamond.

"What's this?" Four barked.

"Papa, this is Felix Hess. Did you listen to your voicemail?"

He hadn't.

They had lunch together that day, an awkward hour of chewing and tension. The usually gregarious Four sat stony-faced while his daughter chatted brightly, trying to cover the awkwardness with a constant stream of endearing tidbits about the two men she loved most. They just sat there, compiling reasons to hate each other.

Later that night, finally free of Felix, Four made his feelings very clear to Marilyn. She was not to marry Hess, under any circumstance. She was too young, and he was all wrong for her. She could do so much better. Marilyn was shocked, appalled.

"Better than Felix Hess? The Einstein of—"

"*Einstein?* Christ—he's a Jew?" Four gaped.

"No, he's not," Marilyn said, quietly. "I don't think. But even if he were—"

"Like hell," Four fumed, not even listening to her. "Like hell!"

She saw for the first time a side of her father that she had never seen. She had always found him protective, but never cruel. As he screamed, condemned, and forbade her love, the rose-colored glasses she had always worn for her father fell off. The lack of diversity in his friends and employees was not a quirk but a flaw, she saw that now.

Marilyn was reeling. Her father had always adored her. She had heard tell of his temper, but laughed it off. When neighbors or cousins referred to "the Old Four," she filed away the comment as just that. *Old.* The way her father was, not the way he ever would be again. That was her father as a boy, before her angelic mother Annabelle, before Marilyn. She believed the legendary bully was long gone, replaced by the kind man whose world revolved around her. But now he stood there, telling her that if she married Felix Hess, she would be cut off forever.

"You'll change your mind," she said. "Please, Papa. You'll change your mind."

"I won't," he said. And he didn't.

Marilyn didn't change hers, either. She married Felix right after graduating. Her father did not even respond to the invitation. Her wedding was as spare as her parents' wedding had been spectacular: A handful of her sorority sisters as witnesses, standing in front of a justice of the peace, the bride and groom wearing thrift-store wedding apparel. Like kids playing dress-up.

Marilyn never spoke with her father again. Two years after her wedding, she received a phone call from his lawyer. Edward Adams Kensington IV had dropped dead of a heart attack. And despite the fact that he had cut her out his life, he had not cut her out of his will. She was suddenly a billionaire, although she would have given up every penny, returned it all for reconciliation, for one more moment of her father's love.

Not everyone felt as ambivalent as Marilyn did about her inheritance. Her father's vast fortune ultimately funded her husband's work. Despite hating Hess, Four wound up helping him in his rise to power. Backwards-focused Four, holding on too hard to the prejudices of the past, posthumously funded his reviled son-in-law's future.

For a few years, Felix Hess felt wonder and gratitude toward his wife, and her money, and everything she brought into his life. He realized, for a time, that she had given up everything to be with him; had chosen him over her father, the man who had given her his full heart and attention. Felix was committed to filling that void, making Marilyn the center of his universe, since that was what she was accustomed to, and that was what she deserved. In the early days of their marriage, he truly tried in earnest. For the first time since summers spent on the Cape with his grandmother, Felix connected and committed to another person.

But as his work became all-consuming, the sparkling Marilyn Kensington he met in Cambridge was filed away, shuffled into a cluttered cabinet somewhere in the recesses of his mind. All that remained was his nagging wife, Marilyn Hess. When they had a child, she finally had someone else to focus on, which should have been a relief. Had Hess paid closer attention, however, he might have noticed that Marilyn did not attach properly to her child. After losing first the adoration of her father, then the adoration of her husband, Marilyn stopped believing in adoration. Postpartum depression pulled her down into the darkness, and she never really saw a good reason to climb back out of that hole.

Nothing good was ever waiting up there on the surface.

Marilyn knows that she needs to tell her daughter the truth. Not the sad stories of Marilyn's own life and losses, no, no point to that. She would never be able to convince Ever that she had once been interesting. The glittering Marilyn Kensington was dead and gone. But Marilyn Hess needs Ever to know the story of the Hess family. How they had come to be who they were, why things fell out the way they did. She's not sure where to begin. She has never known how to talk to her daughter, not even about easy things, let alone hard ones.

Time is not on her side; according to Jorge, things were about to start moving quickly. Marilyn has to deliver Ever to the laboratory in the morning. She feels certain this delivery assignment is a test. Felix is always testing everything, everyone. This test will assure him that Marilyn is still obedient. That even though now she knows about Generation Next and his plans for their daughter, she'll go along with it. Otherwise, why not just keep Ever hospitalized one more night before sending her up to the lab? Why bring her back to Marilyn?

Because he wants to make sure I'll give her back to him.

Delivery is not her only duty. Jorge gave Marilyn two slim, silver-needled syringes, which were waiting expectantly in the leftmost kitchen drawer. The first syringe, with a blue handle, is Ever's final hormone treatment. The other treatments were oral, taken with food, ground into powders. Marilyn kept this medicating a secret even from Angela, slipping in the final chemical ingredients to each meal on her own. But now the pills are a thing of the past. The final dose of pre-program medication is waiting in the blue-handled-needle, which will deliver a carefully calculated cocktail of hormones and antibiotics.

The second syringe, with the red handle, is optional: it's a tranquilizer, to be used if Ever resists the hormone treatment tonight. Or the transport in the morning.

Marilyn considers the needles, blue and red. Blue for new life, wanted or unwanted. Red for stilling, stopping, sedating. Marilyn looks around the kitchen, brushed chrome and stainless steel so highly shined that she can make out shapes and colors, half-reflections of herself and her daughter reflecting oddly toward her.

Ever is fixing a snack.

"Do you know why we named you Ever?"

Ever does not look at her mother, and gives no reply save a shrug.

"We named you that because your father was planning ahead. I think it was your father giving me a hint: 'We'll name our daughter Ever. Because that's what she'll live for.' Your father is not a cheerful man, but your name gave him some happiness. Or something like happiness. Satisfaction. Or something like satisfaction, I don't even know if he can—"

"I'm tired, okay? I'm going to bed."

"I didn't want this," Marilyn says, blocking Ever's exit from the kitchen.

"Didn't want what?"

Marilyn speaks more slowly now, dragging out each word with effort. She leans against the kitchen drawers to support herself. "I didn't want any of this. Not for me, and certainly not for you. After what happened with the first procedure—I said no. I'd stay Original, and so would you."

"You wanted us to stay Original?"

Marilyn nods, dreamy-eyed. She feels something akin to absolution, confessing this much to her daughter.

"Your father walked out. I didn't see him for days, and I was afraid he'd never come back. But he did, and gave me the ultimatum. Not sink or swim, but sink… or synch."

"Mother," Ever says, but Marilyn cannot hear her anymore.

"Well," Marilyn continues, speaking more to herself than her daughter now. "Your father walking out, let me tell you, that terrified me. What would I do if he left? Where would I go? Who would I have? I gave up everything to be with him. I needed us to remain a family. Forever. I'll do whatever it takes to make sure we remain a family."

And with that, Marilyn doesn't even wait to see if Ever will resist or not. She simply sinks the red-handled-needle into her daughter's thigh, catching Ever as she collapses, and briefly holding her. Like a baby, so sweet, pliable, asleep. Then Marilyn lays her gently on the spotless kitchen floor, and reaches for the blue syringe.

D ESPITE ALL OF THE RECENT SETBACKS, Dr. Felix
Hess is dangerously close to feeling pleased. The unfortunate incident with Lorraine's husband was handled.
Hess and Lorraine met with the communications department
and tailored a message painting Joshua Murray's suicide as a single freak incident. With a few skillfully-crafted details, Lorraine
threw her dead husband's credibility into question. Kennedy and
the Enforcement team took out the Original witnesses. The whole
mess was almost cleaned up.

And now, with Ever successfully delivered this morning, things
are back on track. She might have been defiled, but she was still a
viable subject. She arrived primed and right on time, a refreshing-
ly successful task completed by Marilyn. Ever was still sleeping,

but she looked pristine. It even appeared that her hair had been freshly brushed.

As soon as the unconscious Ever was admitted, the GNP team began taking her vitals. Hess asked his wife whether or not Ever had been resistant. He assumed she had rebelled, since Marilyn had used both syringes—sedating her before injecting her with the hormones.

"I didn't give her the chance to resist," said Marilyn simply.

Hess rewarded her with a quick wink. Marilyn flushed red and almost looked pretty. Then she left, telling Hess she expected him for dinner. Angela was making steaks.

Hess didn't stay for Ever's intake exam. He was confident that everything would turn up normal—the last tests had, after all. Including the seven negative pregnancy tests he had insisted on, thank Heaven. He expected to receive word any minute now that she was in her own room, ready, waiting, healthy. Just as the other alpha and beta subjects were in other rooms, ready, waiting, healthy. All was in order. The Council, briefed and brought up to speed, was pleased.

The Council had confirmed yesterday that the general public would be told nothing of the GNP until the first healthy, viable result could be presented along with the description of the project. If the Singularity had taught Syn leadership anything, it was that no information should be shared with the general population other than approved, calming, irrefutable information. Admitting to any mistake showed weakness, and inevitably led to dissent.

Though all scientists know that breakthroughs came only through trial and error, that the next great leap forward came only after many steps forward-and-back, it was best to upload only the successes, and let all failures live and die within the innermost walls of the Synt. Most people aren't scientists. Trusting the masses to understand the intricacies of true progress, well, that's just ridiculous.

For the first time in weeks, Dr. Felix Hess has a few moments to contemplate the one thing still nagging at him. The damned prophecy. The latest algorithm had churned out the same infuriating riddle again this morning.

The outsider inside will end the beginning.

These enigmatic words keep Hess from feeling truly pleased. Just as well. He needs something keeping him alert. Stress is necessary for Hess to function. He has not exhaled deeply in years; doing so would be a real shock to his system.

"Dr. Hess?"

"Yes, Kennedy?" Hess does not bother glancing at his assistants, who now both stand within striking distance.

"There's an issue. With Ever."

"Heaven and hell. What now?"

It is Jorge who takes over then, clearing his throat before speaking. It is this small pause that causes Hess to turn around and actually look at them. Kennedy stutters constantly, but Jorge never hems or haws before delivering information.

"The doctors think she's had a stroke."

S TANDING IN HIS STRANGE SYN CLOTHES, watching the Syn light rail approach, Ere decides Cal was right: Ere knows nothing. He's a total shit-for-brains.

It was bad enough being shown up by Asavari at every turn on their trek toward Syn civilization. Now that they're here, he's even more out of his element than he was when faced with nighttime hikes and scaling sheer rock walls. All he can do is follow Asavari's lead as they wait on the platform, surrounded by Syns.

When they first crossed the border into what Asavari referred to as a "relatively small Southern Syn settlement," Ere had prepared himself to be overwhelmed. He knew "relatively small" for Syns was not the same as in his world. There would be tall buildings. There would be many people—ten times the number in his little tribe. A hundred times, perhaps.

His guesses were woefully inadequate.

The landscape just beyond the border shifted abruptly from swamps and trees to flat, paved pathways, lined with impossibly tall buildings, all with reflective exterior walls. Passing the first building, Ere gasped, spooked by the appearance of a slight boy, with a wild thatch of sand-colored hair, smooth pale skin, giant eyes, wearing dark Syn clothes. It took Ere awhile to realize he was looking at his own reflected image.

He had never seen himself so clearly. It was seeing the girl reflected beside him that caused the realization. It also caused him to flush with embarrassment; did he really look so weak, underfed, and completely out of his element? Meanwhile, Asavari looked solid, strong, confident, rich black hair, straight, strong back. She did not stop to look at herself.

Suddenly, Ere felt a sharp stab of déjà vu. His dream.

The girl with the long dark hair.

He had thought Ever was the girl in his dreams, but could it have been Asavari?

"Hurry!" She whispered.

Hurrying was difficult, because Ere kept looking around, taking it all in. For the first several buildings, his own reflection continued to startle him, but eventually he began taking in other details. The cooling breeze, unnatural but pleasant, rising from small slots in the ground. The patches of green, trees and plants and vibrant green grass—all lush, cultivated, laid out symmetrically, matching the precise layout of the Syn city.

It wasn't until they reached the light rail station that he saw the one thing that had been missing from the breathtaking Syn city. Which was, of course, the Syns themselves.

Asavari had mentioned that this was a "commuter city." Ere was still unsure what that meant when they reached the rail station. It was a large, low building, rounded and almost cylindrical, constructed of the same reflective material as the taller buildings that surround it. Asavari marched them straight up to a wide, clear glass door. She reached into a pocket hidden in the recesses of her shirt, and pulled out a small, glowing card. She held it up to the door and waved it twice. The door hissed, recessing into the ground rapidly, allowing them to pass through, then shot back up again with another quiet hiss.

Ere and Asavari stepped onto a small square of metal, barely large enough for the two of them. It was thin and flat, but sturdy. It emitted the faintest of hums, and twitched beneath them. Ere flinched.

"Hold still," Asavari commanded.

The thin sheet of metal dropped, swiftly descending, carrying them deep underground. Ere's knees nearly buckled, and his arms flew out, grabbing the girl for support—but the entire drop was so fast, they stopped before he had time either to fall or completely steady himself. He jerked his arms away from Asavari, then lurched awkwardly after her as she stepped forward, off the small transport mechanism, which immediately shot back to the entrance level. Ere looked up and saw that they were in the main underground area of the station, at the edge of a platform so long he could not see the end of it, bordering a shining recessed track.

Ere let out a small, startled cry. This earned him a kick in the shin from Asavari. But he could not help it. He was underground, with no way out, staring at an endless electronic pathway, and surrounded by Syns.

Luckily, the noise of thousands of commuting Syns buried Ere's outburst underground. Only the nearest of them glanced his way; seeing nothing particularly interesting, they returned to whatever had held their attention before he distracted them.

He has been standing in their midst for several minutes now, and can't stop staring. Everyone is clad in loose black tops, slim black pants, few accessories or variations of garb. Yet they do not all look alike: their hair color, skin color, the shape of their nose, height and build, all sorts of variation abound. Ere has seen only a few Syns in his life, always government officials, almost always pale and male. He was not expecting them to be so varied in appearance.

"Are all these people... Syns?"

"Well," Asavari says, glancing around. "Syns and Vosts."

"What are Vosts?"

"People who volunteered as test subjects before the Syn process was perfected. So they're sort of like Syns. But they have fewer rights. And they tend to be... more diverse than the moneyed primary Syn population."

"Oh," says Ere, taking this in. He has a thousand more questions, but no time to ask them.

"Here it comes," says Asavari, and even before she finishes her brief statement, the light rail has come to a silent halt at the platform's edge. It too seems to stretch on forever, a white and softly-glowing tube, with glass doors spaced evenly every few feet. As Ere gapes, each door simultaneously opens, just as the entrance to the station had opened, sliding downward and disappearing. The Syns begin boarding the light rail, and Asavari shoves Ere toward the rail, too.

"Hurry," she hisses again.

The girl need not have worried. Ere and Asavari are carried in by the crowd, as every single Syn waiting on the platform presses into the train.

Inside the train are rows and rows of clean, white chairs. Asavari slides into one, and Ere slides into another, right beside her. The smooth-surfaced seats are surprisingly comfortable. As soon as they sit, the seat seems to subtly conform to their bodies. Ere yawns, involuntarily.

"How long will this journey take?" Ere asked.

"If we were to travel by foot? Weeks."

"And this way?"

Asavari smiles at him, a rare flashing of perfect white teeth. "A few hours."

Ere smiles back, thinking that when the girl from India smiled, she was moderately less intimidating. But he'd never ask her to smile. He'd work to earn any acknowledgment he might get from her, which, he knows, is as it should be.

Then he yawns again, realizing that he has not slept at all in two days, and only intermittently in the weeks before that. Still, he will not let himself just doze off into sleep, tempting as that might be. He does not know if sleeping on the rail is safe, or might open them to threats. He vows to stay awake. Ten seconds later, he changes his mind and asks:

"Is it…is it all right if I sleep, for part of the ride?"

"If you can, you should," she says. "We'll be underground for the duration of the trip. There's nothing to see. Rest, if you need it. You'll need your energy to—"

She doesn't bother to complete her sentence, because Ere is already asleep.

C AL PICKED UP ERE AND ASAVARI'S TRAIL WITH ease, thanks to his clumsy cousin still snapping every twig set before him. Moving quickly, he closed the distance between them, hovering only a small way behind by the time they reached the edge of the unincorporated territories.

But Cal doesn't immediately follow Ere and the girl into Syn territory. He has to make a plan. In the woods, tracking and hiding is easy. In Syn territory, he's out of his element. He needs to determine some strategy, procure some camouflage. Cal watched from a distance when the Indian girl had scaled a sheer cliff—he had to admit, her climbing was impressive—and returned with strange Syn garments. Obviously, she had a plan in place. Where had the garments been procured? Who placed them there? Might there be other hidden freeboxes with Syn garb nearby?

He grinds his jaw, working through the problem. The longer he hesitates, the wider the gap will grow between him and his pursuits. He doesn't know their destination. If he loses their trail, he'll have no idea where to try to pick it up again. Beyond the border, he has been told there it's all buildings, no nature. That'll hinder a hunt. He perches in an old tree, yards from the border, the invisible and yet clear line dividing the jungle from the incorporated Syn territory, and realizes he has no idea what to do next.

Whrrrrrrrrrrrr.

Cal cocks his head to the side, pointing his ear upward toward the whining sound. He hears voices. But the whirring is from above, the voices from below. He is surrounded, and knows not by who or how many. His entire body tenses, and he holds perfectly still.

Two Syns walk under the tree. Both are men, and both wear clothing that differs slightly from the all-black garb Asavari and Ere donned. These men have bright silver stripes running up their pant legs and down their shirt sleeves. The same sort of outfit worn by the Syns who had evicted Cal's tribe from home after home. Officials of some sort, Cal decides.

"Beautiful damn day," breathes one of the men, slender and delicate-looking. Cal is confident he could break him within three seconds, flat.

"Whatever," says the broader, rougher one. "We got the last samples. Let's bring 'er in."

"Can't we stay out here for just a little while long—oh, Heaven and Hell."

"What?"

"Just got a message. We have to go back to the Synt. Now."

Just got a message?

Cal is momentarily confused, then reminds himself of the strange mind-connections Syns share. It makes the hair on the back of his neck rise, uncomfortable with that alien power.

"The Synt? Why not just the checkpoint?"

"I don't know. Some admin shit. Go complain to Hess."

Hess.

Cal remembers the conversation in the cabin. That was Ever's family name. And her father was some sort of important Syn leader. It seems likely that they were referring to him, and better still, headed toward him. Hess, at the Synt. Even better than following Ere and Asavari, these Syns might lead him directly to Ever.

"'Pronto,'" mutters the second man, shaking his head. "Well, what Hess wants, Hess gets. So let's head back on board, then."

Board. They must have some sort of vehicle. Cal hopes it is something large. Something with room for a stowaway.

"Right," says the first man. "We'll just take this last one up— old enough specimen, should show good change over time."

He thumps something. The thump reverberates up the tree trunk, all the way up to Cal.

What do they mean, take this up? This tree? The one I'm in? But that might mean—

The whirring sound above Cal grows louder. He looks up, and sees a sharp metal plate, spinning quickly, mere yards away. The whirring, rotating thing is an extension emerging from an even larger metal mountain—the ship, Cal surmises. The ship is all rounded edges, silver and smooth, with recessed lights illuminating its surface. The sharp-whirring-spinning-thing is part of the ship, swooping toward him to collect the tree.

Heaven and hell!

Just as Cal prepares to leap out of harm's way, the whirring whines and fades. The metal plate slows and comes to a stop, revealing the sharp steel teeth of its serrated edges. Cal breathes a sigh of relief, sweat pouring down his back. He presses against the bark, catching his breath and catching the perspiration, not allowing a drop to fall below and give him away.

Cal hears a click, and looks up as a panel reveals itself on the vehicle, slides down, and splits into two metal squares, which land soundlessly on the forest floor. Each of the Syn men steps onto a square. The squares fly back upward, bringing them into the vehicle. Then the panel reappears, slides back into place, disappears. The massive thing is once again impenetrable, and so is incredibly quiet and nimble for something so vast. In spite of himself, Cal admires the workmanship of it.

And then the whirring flares up again, and the cutting plate swoops toward him. Cal looks up and down it wildly for anything to which he might cling, any way to get aboard and hitch a ride to Ever's world, preferably without being sliced and diced en route. As the gleaming steel swings directly toward Cal, he leaps straight up, grabbing another branch higher into the tree, scraping knees and knuckles against bark but avoiding the slicing metal, which slams into the base of the tree. The metal cuts through the solid trunk as if it were soft flesh, severing the tree neatly and instantly. Then the metal flexes and somehow bends around the trunk, catching it in a viselike steel grip. An even larger panel reveals itself on the underside of the vessel.

The tree is hauled aboard the ship through the panel, with Cal still clinging desperately to the tattered topmost branches.

*T*HE ROOM IS WHITE, WITH STRANGE EQUIPMENT *everywhere. There's a hum. Electric energy. I have to go to it. It's there, in the center of the room. Right there. Right in the center. Yes. Here. This box-thing, it's inside there, the thing I need to see. The box thing is glass, but I can't see through the glass. I can and then I can't—this glass is clear when it wants to be, clouding to obscure details when I get too close. I need to see behind the glass, but it won't let me. Is it full of—water? Something? I need to know—*

"Ere."

Mother!

Suddenly standing in front of me, with desperate eyes. She stands between me and the box-thing, between me and whatever is in the box-thing. She pleads with me. This can't be right, this isn't my real mother, she never begs. But she is begging me.

"Don't, Ere. Don't look. Please, don't look. Don't look. Don't look!"

But I have to.

I have to know, I have to see. She cannot keep standing between me and the truth. I take a step forward and she is there, blocking my way again, and now her eyes are not begging but glaring. Anger surges from her. Her nails become claws, her hair becomes snakes. The monster that was once my mother snarls and lunges toward me.

"I said—"

And then there is a flash, a change, and the face is a new one. It is no longer the monster-version of my mother. Now it is Ever, so beautiful, shaking her head and reaching for me—reaching to stop me.

"—don't look," she says, picking up where Mother left off. "Ere, please don't look…"

Another flash. Ever's face becomes my mother's. "Don't look."

Flash. Mother's face becomes Ever's. "Please, don't look."

Before she can change again, whoever she is, I shove her aside. Mother or Ever, I can't care anymore, they're just in the way, I have to get to it, I have to know, anyone trying to stop me will be sorry, I have to know what's in the center of it all—

"Ere, wake up," says Asavari. "We're here."

M Y MOUTH IS MADE OF COTTON.
This is Ever's first non-fragmented thought in far too long, though she does not know exactly how long. The scans she runs on her own systems are fragmented, unreadable. She opens and closes her cotton-mouth a few times, weakly, her jaw resistant to any movement. Her entire body feels leaden, drained of all energy. She recognizes, dimly, that she is sedated.

She slowly begins another internal scan, a more basic search, seeking and reaching for her most recent memory file, hoping to piece together what had happened to her, where she was, what was going on. The information is painfully sluggish to load, and she's having trouble processing anything even as it unfurls before her. It's like something is shorted, somewhere deep in her brain.

Something is wrong, damaged, not functioning properly. She sees images, flashes that leap to the forefront in her mind, flicker, tease her and disappear.

A fight with mother. No, with father. Both? Something about breeding.

That can't be right. Something in my father's laboratory...

It is unclear which thoughts are true and which are misfires. She searches a little farther back. Calls up information about the boy. Ere. These files are still sealed and encrypted, secured thanks to the strength of private mode. She confirms that they were last accessed by her. Yes. Last access: *Hess, Ever.* Whatever had happened these past few days, no one had yet been able to override her protections and get in to these memory files. This brings some relief.

Wondering if she was connected to Heaven while unconscious, Ever attempts to wiggle her fingers. With some effort, she brings movement into them—and, yes, her finger is plugged in to a bedside outlet. She tugs, but cannot muster the strength to disconnect herself. She lets loose a small moan. This loss of autonomy, however temporary, does not sit well with Ever.

"You're awake, then."

Ever looks to her right, moving only her eyes, and sees the doctor with the emerald earrings standing at her bedside. Ever tries to remember her name, but can't. Forming words in her cotton-mouth is no easy task, but Ever manages to choke out a question.

"What ... happened... to me?"

"You had a minor stroke, Ever," says the doctor. "That's extremely rare. But given your recent overheating, medical procedures, memory extraction ... well. There were a number of factors that likely triggered this event. All things considered, it is difficult to pinpoint a single cause. But we'll eventually confirm which particular confluence of events led to your episode. The good news is you appear to have little lasting damage."

"What... now."

"Now? Well, now you're disqualified from Generation Next, alpha, beta, or otherwise, unless your father decides differently. Your official status is 'deficient.' You will be released from the Synt into your mother's custody later today, to return home and recover there. You will be monitored, with a guard assigned to you. For your own protection, of course."

"Of... course. I'm a real flight risk... now."

Her body is weak. Her mind is recovering.

But Ever's sarcasm is still intact.

E RE AND ASAVARI STAND OUTSIDE THE GATES of the Synthetic Neuroscience Institute of Technology. "The Synt." It is a building whose very foundation is intimidation, its sheer mass a menacing display of power.

There are two tremendous sections to the Synt. The big chunks of building are more concerned with size than style: there's the smaller but still massive front section, which stretches skyward higher than any of the other nearby skyscrapers, jutting forward in a long, lean expanse like the lower line of a letter L. This portion of the building gleams, with silver beams and opaque but shining windows.

The adjacent second section of the building is the upper line of the L, and it is both wider and so much taller that its top disappears into the clouds completely. Its darker exterior displays unapologetically tinted windows, revealing nothing. It looms impassively, protected behind the lower structure as well as a gate that encircles the entire campus. There are undoubtedly several more layers of security, cameras, and synthetic safeguards.

"We part ways, for now."

"You're not going in with me?"

Ere gapes at Asavari, then wishes he could retract his asinine question as soon as he asked it. Of course she wasn't going in with him. He's the one with the rebel assassin mother, he's the one with the crazy request. Having her there would raise suspicions. He needed to appear on his own, driven by grief, not united in some unknown cause with a foreign Original girl. The existing resistance movement was still underground and unknown to the Syns. It was dangerous enough that she had risked this much exposure, leading him all the way to the Synt.

"I have my own task, while we are here," Asavari says, not unkindly. "You will meet with Hess. We will find each other tomorrow morning."

"Tomorrow morning," Ere repeats. His breathing feels irregular. His chest tightens. He had seen this happen to an elder once, when they thought she was having a heart attack. It was an attack, all right—not of the heart, but of a deep and wide panic.

"There is a park, behind the light rail station. Meet me there at daybreak. All right?"

"All right." He pauses, hating that he had to ask. "What's a park?"

"It's like a small, manicured forest."

"Right, thought so." His palms are pouring sweat.

"Ere. If you are not in the park at daybreak, I will contact our informant to determine your status. Fear not, Ere Fell. Come Heaven or Hell, I'll get you out of there."

"Come Heaven or Hell, you'll get me out."

She gives a small nod, promising. And then, before he can ask any other questions or delay any further, she turns and leaves him standing alone in front of the Synt's waiting gates.

It is the music in the Synt lobby that catches Ere off guard.

He walked right in, which seemed odd. But as Syns bustled in and out, he followed the crowd through the main gates, which were sealed only at night. After walking through the gates and into the first section of the structure, he approached a large glass door. Just as it did for the other entering and exiting Syns surrounding him, as he approached the door it recessed, sliding down to allow his passage (thank Heaven, it was just like the one back at the station), then slid back up and into place behind him after he crossed the threshold.

The main atrium was a massive room. The building had many floors, but the entranceway was an additional extension, smaller than the first large section of building; it was so low relative to the overarching architecture, he had not even seen it from the other side of the gates.

A lobby, Ere thinks, no idea where the word came to him from, but accepting it as accurate. He realizes there's no serious security yet because this isn't even the real building; it's a holding area.

The lobby's ceiling rises straight up, almost but not quite the entire height of the first-level Synt building, and uninterrupted by floors. It is a vertical corridor extending up thousands of feet, straight into the sky, constructed completely of what appeared to be glass. Ere somehow knows that while the substance is like glass, it is something far less breakable. Clear when it wants to be, clouding to obscure details at other times—recalling his dream, he shivers.

The towering glass lobby is a visual masterpiece, but after all the tall buildings he saw even in the smaller Syn city down south, Ere has quickly come to expect large, impressive architecture.

Which is why it is not the sky-high ceiling that distracts him after he enters this space. It's the music.

Ere has always loved music. But he has known only simple instrumentation. Voices, occasionally accompanied by the flutes carved by his great-uncle Howard, or small drums; once, he'd met a remnant who carried with her a small, stringed instrument which created an sweet lilting sound. A *ukulele,* she told him, stroking its face as if it were a child.

But never has Ere heard music like this. Instrumental, but so many clear, distinct sounds. It is pure, harmonious, transcendent. Ere holds still and listens, never wanting to move. He wants to be lifted and carried away by this beautiful sound. He wishes his mother could hear it.

"May I help you?"

Ere hadn't realized that he had closed his eyes until he opens them, startled by the voice cutting through the music and his reverie, echoing through the massive room. He locates its source: at the very end of the entrance way, against the wall that marked the beginning of the main building, there is a desk. Behind the desk sits a Syn woman, staring at him.

Ere forces his feet to move toward her. As he gets nearer, he can see that she is oddly beautiful. She does not look much older than he, but he knows she is decades beyond his age, and merely preserved as she had appeared when she was a young Original, before becoming an un-aging cyborg. She has dark skin and tightly curled hair, black with bright crimson strands interwoven throughout, like a red-winged blackbird. Her multi-colored hair is gathered on top of her head, pulled so tight that it tilts her eyes up at the ends.

"Yes, I..." Ere's voice gives out on him. He tries again. "I... I wish to see Dr. Hess."

She cocks her head, exaggerating the unnatural tilt of her eyes. "Afraid I misheard you."

He speaks a little louder. "I wish to see Dr. Hess."

"He does not take meetings." She blinks, examining him. "Are you an Original?"

"Oh, um. Yes."

"You're very young for an Original."

"I'm older than I look."

"Aren't we all." She blinks twice, and her eyes slide to the side, there and back, quickly.

"I think Dr. Hess will want to see me," Ere says, more assertively.

"Really?" Her voice drips doubt. "And why's that?"

"It has to do with my mother," says Ere. Just invoking those words, *my mother*, give him a sort of irrational confidence. The music behind him swells and crescendos, and is he buoyed by it.

"Really? And who might your mother be?"

Spurred on by the inspiring instrumentation, and with nothing left to lose, Ere tells her.

E VER'S STROKE WAS A REAL BLOW. In his anger
at her indiscretion, Hess told his daughter that she would
be reduced to a "beta level" participant, but that wasn't exactly true. Like it or not, Ever remains central to the entire GNP
initiative. Her indiscretion had pissed him off, but not rendered
her unviable.

The stroke was another matter entirely.

She might still be salvageable, *maybe*, if the cause of the stroke
can be determined. There was a lot of undue stress on her system
during her jaunts to Sector 27, for her humiliating trysts (Hess is
still working on getting that image cleaned up, so he can take care
of whoever defiled his daughter). If they can ascertain that the

stroke was not organic, but a preventable synthetic malfunction triggered by the heat, they could swap out a few parts, keep her in climate-controlled environments, stave off any future episodes.

That was the best-case scenario. A medical catastrophe of unknown, uncorrectable organic origin would indicate a potential risk factor she could pass along to offspring. A dangerous unpredictability to the genetic tenacity of her organic components; unacceptable.

And so now, the project is delayed. They have other female participants lined up, all of whom had synched in their twenties, all of whom were healthy, all of whom had at least marginally good odds for success. But the entire timeline was designed to begin with Ever.

If he didn't know any better, he would think she somehow did this on purpose.

Hess paces, fumes, the gears in his mind cranking rapidly. He's so focused on the professional ramifications of his daughter's stroke he very nearly forgets to be worried about her—but then, for just a moment, it tugs at him. The flash of her face as a little girl looking adoringly up at him, as a young woman grinning on a Chariot beside him, racing through Greece. Ever isn't just a specimen. She's still his daughter.

But she's fine. It's only the initiative that might suffer lasting damage from this stroke.

The knock at his solid old wooden door makes him jump, and jumping makes him roar with frustration.

"What!"

Jorge enters, and does not react to the yelling. But his mouth twitches and his eyes dart to the side before he steels himself to deliver his message to Dr. Hess. Once again, it is information too sensitive to be sent electronically, and once again, Hess is taken completely by surprise.

"You have a visitor," Jorge says. "A young Original man. A boy, really. And…"

"*And?*" Hess bellows, all patience long gone.

"And," Jorge says, looking uncharacteristically surprised himself, "… he claims to be the son of Ruth Fell."

BEFORE HE KNOWS WHAT IS HAPPENING, Ere is being taken to Hess.

A thin young Syn, summoned by the red-winged blackbird woman (who Ere has decided is probably a Vost), meets him at the desk. He is a thin-faced man, with short, fine blonde hair and piercing blue eyes. He wears a white lab coat, imprinted with the word *Kennedy*. Without looking at Ere, he says to the receptionist:

"This is the Original boy, who says that he's…?"

"Yes," says the woman.

The thin-faced man turns on his heel, and Ere realizes that he is meant to follow him. He quickly legs his way down the long hallway, which ends in a sea of freestanding squares of metal, similar to the ones Ere and Asavari rode down into the light rail station.

"Step on to the levitator," Kennedy instructs, giving Ere the name of the thing.

Ere steps onto a levitator, as does the Syn. Ere is glad they are not sharing one, like he and Asavari had; he would not want to clutch onto this man. Prepared this time, Ere clenches his core, holding himself steady. The levitator immediately rises, moving at a good clip, floor after floor after floor. After thirty-seven, Ere loses count. He is feeling nauseous, unaccustomed to this motion. He closes his eyes as his stomach lurches violently. He wills himself not to vomit. When the levitators cease their movement. Ere's stomach does not, but he swallows back the bile.

"Step off," says the man in the lab coat. Ere does, but the Syn labeled Kennedy remains on his own levitator. Ere stands alone before what appears to be a tall and doorless white wall.

"What now?" Ere asks.

Without replying, the Syn blinks and his levitator drops, carrying him away and leaving Ere alone and unsure of what to do next. But then a series of lights flash silently, here on the wall, there on the wall, and then out of nowhere a door slides down. Ere steps through it, and it slides instantly up, disappearing and leaving only a solid wall behind him.

He looks around. There is not a person in sight, but there are strange objects everywhere, mostly metallic and interconnected: large screens and monitors, flat surfaces, softly humming equipment. Ere does not know the names of most of the items in the room, but he is pretty sure that the word for a room like this is *laboratory*.

Just like in my dream.

Ere walks up to one of the monitors, which is flat and black. As he draws nearer, the screen illuminates. It begins displaying letters and numbers, moving so quickly, Ere cannot keep up. His mother taught him to read, but he has never been a fast reader. Besides, the words on the pages of the Bible and the few other books he'd read had always held their ground; they remained still, never flying past his eyes as the words on this screen insist on doing.

"Slow down," Ere says, as if the screen will respond to him.

It does.

Ere takes a step back, not expecting the screen to obey his command. Now that the letters and numbers have slowed, he can make out a few words here and there, and then three that begin swirling around, repeating, filling the screen:

WELCOME ERE FELL
WELCOME ERE FELL
WELCOME ERE FELL

W HEN HESS ENTERS HEAVEN'S CORE laboratory, he takes care to do so quietly, so the boy will not notice him. Hess wants the opportunity to observe him, to see how he moves, to see what he can ascertain before he begins any formal interrogation.

The first thing Hess notices is how familiar the boy's features are, even at a glance. The slope of his nose, the furrow of his brow. There is no need to draw blood or scan his DNA to know that this boy is a Fell, even if all odds are against it.

The young man stares at the screen, his nose nearly touching the display of his own repeated name. Hess imagines what this all must be like for the youth. Startling and ominous, but wildly intriguing. Something new, to be figured out and understood. Given this boy's ancestry, intense curiosity is surely woven through every fiber of his being. Hess wants to keep watching him, but his own curiosity demands more than observation. He needs to talk to this boy.

"I hear you wanted to see me."

Ere whirls around, one hand flying to what is most likely a home-hewn knife on his thigh. His other hand is digging, searching for the little gun in his pocket. But he fumbles, and Hess knows that the Syn garb the boy wears is not his usual attire. It makes his weapon harder to access. The boy stops fumbling, straightens up, looks right at him with those piercing Fell eyes.

"Dr. Felix Hess?"

Hess smiles—an impersonation of a smile rather than an actual grin. He allows himself one rub of his beard, but then puts his hands behind his back, leaving himself purposefully and obviously exposed. He strolls casually toward the boy.

"I'm surprised your weapons weren't confiscated by my staff before you got up here. Someone's getting fired, trust me! But we saw the knife and gun when you were scanned on the levitator. They're useless here, boy. There are enough nearby guards, monitors, and magnetized equipment in here to make sure you can't hurt me."

Ere does not move his hand from his thigh as he asks again: "Are you Dr. Felix Hess?"

"I am. And you're the one claiming to be the son of Ruth Fell."

"I am her son," says Ere, chin high. Hess has seen this look before, too.

I believe you are, boy.

"And why should I believe you?" Hess asks aloud.

"I have no reason to lie," says Ere. "Why would I come into your territory and lie to you about who my mother is? She's not your favorite person, from what I understand."

"That's true," Hess says mildly. An understatement. That woman's head should have been off her shoulders and on his proverbial wall decades ago.

"I'm telling the truth: Ruth Fell was my mother."

"Was?" Hess says, more sharply, seizing upon the word.

"Yes," says the boy. "Was. My mother died last week."

"I am sorry for your loss," Hess says robotically, recalling his recent exchange with Lorraine Murray and almost wanting to laugh.

"I doubt that," Ere says.

"I was told you liked the music," Hess says, abruptly shifting gears. He knows this is the best way to derail liars, to keep the upper hand in even the most subtle of interrogations. Change subjects. Jump from topic to topic, and watch how they kept up. Or didn't. "In the lobby, when you came in?"

"I—yes." Ere says, recalling the incredible sounds. "It was beautiful."

"You have good taste," says Hess, impersonating another smile. "That was Schubert's Symphony Number 9 in C major, also known as the Great Symphony. Nearly an hour long. A masterpiece of the orchestral world. The version you heard was recorded some years ago by the Syn Symphonic Orchestra. Impressive composition, is it not? And such a performance!"

"I've never heard anything like it," the boy admits.

"Of course you haven't," Hess says, aiming for a note of sympathy in his voice. "If indeed you are Ruth's son. Living with a fugitive Original mother, wandering the unincorporated territories, foraging, always on the run, no time for culture or music—"

"We have music," says Ere, defensive. "We sing. We have flutes. We have our prayers."

"Oh, your prayers! Well, tell me, son-of-Ruth," coos Hess, mocking, enjoying the biblical feel of calling the boy that. He steps closer. "Why are you here, in the core of Heaven?"

"The... what?"

"You're in the core of Heaven, boy. You should feel privileged. No one else has access here. Few others have even seen it."

The boy looks as if he is going to ask more about the place, but then his expression changes. He juts his chin even further forward. *Such a Fell move.*

"I want you to bring my mother back. I want you make her alive again. Even if it means making her a Syn."

Hess can't suppress a sharp bark of laughter. After this unprecedented month of setbacks and surprises, this is the most ridiculous moment of all. This filthy little Original boy shows up, dirt under his fingernails and lines under his eyes, claiming to be Ruth Fell's son, and asks Hess to resurrect the old bitch? Hess almost wonders if someone is trying to revive the practical joke. Hell of a set-up.

"Bring her back?" Hess finally manages. "Heaven and Hell! I almost believed you were her son, but no one who knew Ruth Fell would make that request."

"I knew my mother," Ere whispers, looking nervous.

"Did you?" Hess asks, a new thought occurring to him. "Maybe you knew her, as your mother. But did you know the real Ruth Fell?"

"Yes," the boy says, but less certainly.

"I doubt that," Hess says. "And you definitely know nothing of science. We can't bring back the dead. Not after a week of mortem. And never the *Original* dead."

"You could try," says the boy. "My mother was very strong, and—"

"And very dangerous. And now, very dead." Hess narrows his eyes, genuinely curious, wondering how he might leverage Ruth's mistakes to gain her son's trust. "What did she tell you about her life before you? About your father? Or of her father, your grandfather?"

"My mother did not speak of them often, because it was too painful."

Hess chuckles. The prolonged amusement provided by the Fell boy is a gift that just keeps on giving. *Here's hoping he can wind up providing more than a good laugh.*

"Forgive me, Ere. I shouldn't laugh, it's just—well. Sadly, it seems I know far more about your family than you do."

"Tell me, then," says Ere defiantly. Hess has to admit, the Fell kid's got moxie. "If you know things about my family that I don't, tell me what I should know. I have the right to know."

"Yes," Hess says, considering this statement. Filling the boy in on the reality of his heritage might be the most persuasive argument Hess could possibly make. "I suppose you do. And sometimes it truly is better to show than to tell. If you want, I can do better than tell you. I can show you. The question is, Ere... do you really want to know the truth about the Fells?"

"YOU DELIVERED THE ORIGINAL BOY TO HESS?"
Jorge asks.

Kennedy is surprised that Jorge is initiating conversation. "I did."

"What was—how did the boy seem?"

Kennedy licks his thin lips, pleased to be the one with more information, wanting to savor this moment. Kennedy knows that the entire Synt is already buzzing about this boy, the one who had shown up out of the blue claiming to be Ruth Fell's son.

Was he really her son? What was he like? Why was he here?

The truth is, Kennedy wasn't provided with any more information about the boy than anyone else. He had simply been instructed to collect him from the lobby and bring him to the core—where he was still not allowed to enter, himself. The orders were clear: bring him up, drop him off, and leave, *without speaking to him.* As always, Kennedy followed the instructions to the letter. But Jorge doesn't know that.

This will be fun.

"What do you mean, how did the boy seem?"

Kennedy's coy reply backfires. Jorge's expression goes blank.

"Nothing. Never mind."

"He had huge eyes," Kennedy says quickly, wanting Jorge's interest and attention back on him. "I mean, taking it all in. Like he'd never seen anything like this before, the Synt and levitators and machines. I guess he hasn't. He told me how impressed he was with it all."

Kennedy manages to stop there, much as he would like to build upon the lie and imply that the boy had been impressed with him. Jorge's face is impassive, but he asks another question, continuing the conversation.

"He said nothing to you about... why he came here?"

"No," Kennedy admits, unable to come up with an interesting deception quickly.

The more he thinks about it, the more Kennedy wonders if the arrival of the Original boy truly was out of the blue, or was somehow contrived by Hess. Designed to look random, but all part of a larger plan. After all, no one was allowed in the core of Heaven save Hess himself. Why would he bring the Fell boy there?

Could it have something to do with the Generation Next project they had recently been briefed on? They needed Original stock, didn't they? And then, along comes the Original boy. It was doubtful that he would know anything of the project, particularly if he was indeed Ruth Fell's son. Perhaps Hess had somehow lured him here, to participate in the program—since he, too, was from such strong mental and physical stock.

After decades as his lackey, Kennedy knows to put nothing past his cunning mentor. He assumes that Jorge holds the same point of view, but he cannot be sure since they rarely compare notes on such things. Anyway, Jorge was always so damn discreet.

Kennedy bristles now, resenting Jorge's inquiry about the Original boy, his assumption that Kennedy would be generous with information when Jorge never was.

Why should he share anything with Jorge (even if it was mostly fabricated)? It would be more powerful to hold back. Keep the insights to himself.

"Last week," Jorge says, expression neutral. "Your assignment was... successful?"

At the mention of this, Kennedy's stomach tightens, though his conscious mind is untroubled. He remembers very little from that mission, but he's not an idiot. Even having erased the details from his own mind, he knows the basics of what he participated in. Big picture basics are easier to swallow than gritty, up-close reality. Kennedy had taken special care to relinquish the uglier, grittier bits, but left enough of his memory intact to know what had happened, without recalling the specific unpleasant particulars.

"It was," Kennedy says with no trace of emotion. "Don't need to grill me for the gory details on that one, though. I delivered my report to Hess and then erased it from my own files. No need to retain those memories. Nasty business."

"I see." Jorge's face is marble, his voice stone. "No headaches since the erasure?"

"I'm fine," says Kennedy, then lowers his voice. "Jorge. You know—you know there are rumors. Rumors about that sort of thing happening more often, more than just the Murray guy with the Original daughter. I know the communications department tried to make it seem like it was just this one incident, but rumor is—"

"I have little interest in rumors," says Jorge. "And I thought you were the champion of facts. Are rumors scientific, Kennedy?"

"Rumors are hypotheses," sniffs Kennedy. Jorge's self-righteousness sours Kennedy's expression. Vosts shouldn't be so uppity. *Prick.* "Rumors are theoretical, which makes them valuable. Worth exploring. But if you don't give a shit about Syns terminating themselves and Originals somehow being involved, that's your business."

"I have not heard such rumors."

"It's not in any official reports, or anything, but—there's whispering."

Kennedy used to love trading in gossip, with his friend Val and their whole social scene. Especially as the token science nerd in that group, Kennedy loved the lighter side of information: scandals, rumors, meaningless hypotheses about other people that could be spun to feel more important than actual news or world events. He misses that world so damn much.

He can see Jorge is wearying of the conversation. This shouldn't bother Kennedy, but to finally have exchanged more than terse, perfunctory words is actually adding some rare intrigue to his morning. Along with the arrival of the Original boy, this day is actually interesting, and he's not ready for the momentum to end, not just yet. A guy who erases memories here and there needs some new ones to add into the mix.

"'Whispering'?" Jorge is worse than disinterested now, he's disdainful. "Come on, Kennedy. From what source? If Syns were terminating themselves, it would be in the nightly upload. Preventative measures would be taken. And Original involvement? The last Originals are dying. Not worth worrying about."

"Then how do you explain the boy?" Kennedy fires back, sinking his teeth into the conversation that has become something even better—a debate. A good old fashioned argument. "He looks young and strong. There might be more. More like him. That might mean we need to prepare for, I don't know—some action to be taken."

"Action? What sort of action?"

"The wait-around-for-them-to-die mandate was a stupid idea. I mean, really. Leaving them out in the wilderness without resources, scraping along until they die off? That's cruel and inefficient. Like letting an old dog suffer instead of just putting him to sleep."

"Don't say things like that," Jorge says quietly. Dangerously.

"Why not?"

"Because it makes you sound like a machine, not a man," Jorge says contemptuously.

Robotic Jorge is accusing me of being a machine?

"What the hell are you—" Kennedy begins incredulously, but Jorge cuts him off.

"Weren't you just telling me that you voluntarily erased your own memories of what you did to the Originals last week? Because it was too much, too awful? And now you're suggesting that all of them get the same treatment—"

"I was just following orders."

Kennedy speaks the words as firmly as he can, but nevertheless suppresses a shudder. Even the shadow of the memories he erased is enough to make him queasy.

"The same sort of orders you would give, if you had the power."

"I was just being theoretical," Kennedy backpedals. "Just saying it's a possibility the Council should consider. Logically speaking. Straight-up elimination should be on the table."

"Until you have more than rumors," snaps Jorge, "I think you should stop those sorts of theories. Until and unless Originals show up on our doorstep with knives, I'm not on board with talking about exterminating helpless old people."

"One showed up this morning. He's not old. And he had a knife. And a gun."

For a moment, Jorge is silent, and Kennedy gloats, certain he has won. They debated, and he bested his colleague. What a good day to be Kennedy. Then, Jorge does something entirely unexpected. He cracks the smallest of smiles.

"Well, then," Jorge says. "I guess you're right. We should just kill them all."

D R. FELIX HESS' QUESTION HANGS IN THE AIR: *Do you really want to know about the Fells?*

Ere does want to know. But he's also terrified. He doesn't trust Hess, and he doesn't want to get tricked into anything. He chooses his next words carefully, wanting not only to ask the right question but also to sound intelligent. Capable. Not like the clueless moron he really is.

"I want to know, but if it involves any sort of connection to your machines—"

"Oh, no," Hess chuckles, dismissing Ere's stupid statement with a wave. "I can do an external simulation. Tell me—what do you know of Heaven?"

"Uh," Ere stalls, still committed to sounding smart. "There are many theories regarding heaven. Whether it's where God lives, or where we go after we die, or both, or—"

He stops when Hess lets out a sharp staccato laugh.

"For Christ's sake! I don't mean some made-up harps-and-angels heaven. I mean *Heaven*. *My* Heaven. The non-hypothetical Heaven—our central server?"

Ere remains silent, preferring now to keep his mouth closed and be thought an idiot rather than open it and prove himself one. He remembers Ever saying something about Heaven. But he does not know what it really is, so he keeps quiet.

"I'll spare you the logistics," Hess says dryly. "All you need to know is that Heaven is where Syns share information. Think of it as a giant shared brain. I can run a simulation with projections—share your family's history with you, in great detail, without making you 'one of us.' You will be just as Original as ever you were, just a little less ignorant. All right?"

Ere can tell that Hess enjoys feeling superior, revels in knowing Ere does not understand most of what he's saying. Anger spreads through him like a fever, heating his body, but he got the important bit from what Hess had just said: he's not about to make Ere a Syn.

"Okay," Ere says. He wants to know.

"Good," says Hess. "No sense waiting, then."

And the world goes black.

As quickly as the world goes black, it illuminates again. But it is not the same world. Ere recalls something his mother told him, a week ago; a lifetime ago:

You will be surprised to find how quickly the world can change.

He is standing in the middle of a street, lined with boxy architecture. There are buildings with slanted tops, wide bottoms. They are various colors, soft creams, grays, yellows. They have glass windows, like at his Franklin commune. Each has a small garden in front of it, with the shortest, greenest grass Ere has ever seen. Some have flowers, some shrubs, others small trees. They remind him of the small patches of land that the Elders of his tribe had so loved to tend when they were at Franklin, and of the place Asavari had told him about: parks. But each is connected to a single structure. Structures like the fishing village cabins, but larger and sturdier.

Houses. Not abandoned half-houses like in the old fishing village, but real, lived-in homes. And then he thinks of an even more specific word, from somewhere deep in his memory, a fairy tale he was once told: A *neighborhood*.

Families lived here. No sooner does he realize this than his thoughts are interrupted by a burst of laughter. Two little boys come tumbling into the street from behind one of the houses, one boy chasing the other. There is a round object they are trying to keep from one another, a black and white patchwork of plastic.

"Give me the ball or I'm telling!"

"You don't even like playing soccer!"

"But it's *my ball!*"

The boys are fighting in that way that makes Ere know they're family. Cousins, brothers, something. One boy is slightly older, with sandy-brown hair and a sneaky smile. He is holding the ball just out of reach of the younger boy, who is glaring up at him with unusually intense slate-gray eyes. The smaller boy seems to be limping slightly as he pursues the older boy, refusing to jump for the ball, but steadily stalking him.

"You want it?" The taller boy asks.

"It's. Mine."

"Then come and get it, Nathan."

Ere watches them, fascinated. They are completely oblivious to his presence; the boys continue the game of keep-away and pursuit, running around him, close enough that if Ere reached out, he could touch them. Ere had forgotten what this was like, play. He and Cal had played so little, when they were boys. Play was a luxury. When they did find such moments of abandon, he recalls now the unbridled joy he felt as they would chase each other or climb trees, until the first adult to see them scolded them and made them stop, reminding them of the danger of losing oneself in fun rather than maintaining constant vigilance.

Ere takes a step closer to the boys, who still seem not to notice him. A bee alights on a blossom hanging from a tree branch just in front of Ere's eyes, then buzzes its way lazily toward Ere. It lands on his left arm, and promptly stings him. Ere flinches and lets out a sharp "Hey!" of pain; the boys still do not look at him. Ere swats at the bee, but the little stinger easily hums out of reach, and then it's gone. Rubbing his arm, Ere continues tracking the children.

"I mean it," growls the limping little gray-eyed boy. "Give it to me now, Howie."

"Boys!"

All three boys—Howie, Nathan, and Ere—turn immediately to look at the woman calling out. She is lovely; she has Nathan's gray eyes and Howie's mischievous grin, though her smile seems somehow sad. She reminds Ere of his own mother. He wonders if all mother have that same strong, tired, protective look.

"Stop fighting and come on in, now," the boys' mother calls. "It's almost dinner time. Wash your paws. And Howie, you be nice to your little brother."

"I am nice to him," Howie argues.

"Don't say 'wash your paws,'" Nathan says to his mother. "It sounds ridiculous."

"Really?" The mother says. "You know what sounds ridiculous to me? A little boy telling his mother what she should and shouldn't say! Howie, teach your little brother some manners."

The taller boy rolls his eyes. "Yeah, right."

"You could try," the mother sad-smiles. "Teach him some patience, give him a hug—"

"Mooooooooom!" Both boys moan.

But after moaning and eye rolling, they obediently trot inside, poking and pinching each other when their mother turns her back. Neither cries out when pinched; both are committed to the brotherly torture. Ere follows them into the house.

When he opens the door, the scene shifts. The world contracts, turns and twists and then rights itself again. Ere is inside the house, but the boys have changed. Howie and Nathan still wear the faces of their childhood, but they're older now. Ere's age. They are arguing, not the bickering banter of children, but a darker, angrier, adult disagreement.

Ere somehow intuits that their mother is in the next room, which is why the boys kept their terse tones hushed.

"Be reasonable, Nathan," says Howie. "You can't really think—"

"You're the one who's not thinking," Nathan says, shriller than Howie. "'Be reasonable'? I am being reasonable, you're being emotional. Emotion is not reasonable! I want to move the world forward, you want to keep it in the past."

"You don't want to move the world forward, you want to break it apart and re-make it in your own image," Howie volleys back. "You're not God."

"There is no God," returns Nathan angrily, rage darkening his slate-grey eyes. "Do you get that? There's no God, so it's up to us to make things a little bit better if we can. And we can. If you'd accept that little bit of reason, maybe you'd listen to what I'm trying to tell you."

As if unable to stop himself, Nathan grabs the pretty glass plate in front of him and slams it onto the table, shattering it.

The mother enters the room just then, carrying a roast bird on a giant platter. She is wearing an apron, and her hair is streaked with gray, but she is still lovely. She looks from Nathan, to Howie, to the shattered plate, and finally back to Howie, the heartbreak plainly written across her face.

"You can't even be civil on Thanksgiving? We haven't even sat down, and I hoped—"

Nathan limps from the room, scowling, not saying a word. Their mother shakes her head.

"Howie. You're still the big brother, you know. You should take the lead here, be the bigger person." She sets down the roast bird, which makes Ere's mouth water. Removing her apron and letting it fall to the floor, she hurries after her younger son. "Nathan? Come back in here, darling, let's try again—"

Howie lowers his head and sighs. Ere waves a hand in front of his face, testing. No reaction. Ere is a ghost. He places his hand on Howie's shoulder, a gesture of comfort, but his hand passes through it as if through the air. He begins to understand what Dr. Hess had meant by the word, *simulation*. Ere is not actually in this house with them, not really in this time or place. He feels certain that he is witnessing real events, things that happened, long ago.

But can he trust Hess that these things were true? That they actually happened, like this?

Why was this family so important?

Howie abruptly rises, a decision made, and goes after his disappointed mother and disenfranchised brother.

"Mom, I'm sorry. Nathan—"

Howie is out the door, and Ere is hot on his heels. Once again, when he passes through the door, he enters not only another room but also another time, another place, another situation.

Everything seems clearer now, a much sharper memory. There is a man sitting behind a desk, with a long black graphite wall behind him, covered in scrawling white letters and numbers. There are rows of chairs in front of him, each with their own built-in table. Ere saw something like this in a tattered old photograph still framed at Franklin: A classroom.

It takes Ere a moment to place the man, because he's even older now than he was at the dinner. But when he looks up, directly at Ere (not at: through), Ere can see that it's Nathan. Middle-aged, and wearing a scowl, he begins pacing. There it is: the tell-tale limp. There is no one else in the room, and Ere detects no sound, but Nathan seems to be expecting someone.

Ere looks behind him just as someone else enters the class-room, a man with dark features and a nervous energy. Having recently seen him, appearing not so very much older, Ere recognizes him quickly. The man is Felix Hess.

"Right on time, Hess," says Nathan, almost approvingly. "Papers are all graded?"

"Yes, the papers are graded," Hess assures him. The oily slick to his voice makes Ere's skin crawl. He looks around, and Ere presses himself against the wall, then curses under his breath, reminding himself that Hess can't see him. But then, Hess winks at him.

Creepy bastard.

"Good," says Nathan, reacting neither to Ere nor Hess' acknowledgment of Ere.

"Well, I wouldn't say good," Hess snickers. "Half of them failed, even with the curve. These students are mentally deficient."

"Not all," says Nathan. "Derek Abelson. How was his paper?"

"Solid," Hess admits. "He even caught the implications of the outlier we threw in there. He pays attention, I'll give him that."

"I want to read his paper. We should think about offering him an internship."

"Fine, fine," Hess rolls his sallow eyes. "Did the grant come through?"

Nathan smiles. It seems he's enjoying toying with Hess.

"I wanted to mention, Hess. I liked your suggestion for the post-procedure testing. Your whole multi-pronged, cognitive, physical, emotional assessment structure—I have some revisions we'll work in, but it's the right base, I think."

"Professor!" Hess says, almost whining now. "The grant! Did we get it, or didn't we?"

Nathan pauses, then limps back to his desk and slowly sits, making his assistant wait a few more tortured seconds. "No. We didn't."

"Government assholes! Small minded, partisan *pricks!*" Hess cries, visibly deflated. Ere likes seeing Hess disappointed. "Dammit. I mean—*shit hell dammit*. We were counting on that. We'll stall out. We needed that funding!"

"We did," Nathan says, nonplussed. "But now we don't. Our funders have increased the ceiling on our budget. The new facility is ready for us. What I'm saying is screw the grant. I know you worked hard on it, but trust me, this is better. Our funders will give us a lot of leeway. We won't owe anyone quarterly reports. We're good to go."

"YES!" Hess whoops, then quickly claps a hand over his mouth. Nathan chuckles at his young protégé's enthusiasm, obviously just as pleased about this turn of events.

"We'll need to find more funders, but for now we have enough to get started with—"

"Nathan."

Nathan, Hess, and the mostly-invisible Ere all look to see a tall, bearded man, with a little girl in his arms. Ere gasps aloud. He can't believe he didn't recognize him earlier. *Howie*. How dumb was Ere, to have missed it until now?

"Yo, Nathan," Howie says, and Ere almost weeps.

Howie was none other than Ere's great uncle, Howard Fell. And that meant—

"Daddy!" The little girl cries, scrambling down from Howard Fell's arms and running toward Nathan. She runs behind his desk, tries to crawl up into his lap, but Nathan stands, thwarting her attempted embrace.

"Not now, Ruth," he says sternly. The little girl's face falls, and Ere trembles.

"But Daddy, I made you a picture…"

Nathan ignores her, turning to Hess.

"We need to meet with the funders immediately. That's why I asked you to have an overnight bag—there's a car picking us up right after class, and straight from here we're heading to the airport. We need to scout out a few more of the options in Manhattan—"

"Hey, whoa," Howard says, stepping forward. "Nathan—you're moving to New York?"

"Yes," Nathan says simply. "That was always the plan."

"The plan before you had kids," Howie says hotly. "When things change, plans change."

"My plans don't change."

"Maybe they should."

"Maybe they shouldn't," Nathan retorts. "Maybe if you were a little less willing to make compromises, you would have more of a career. But we each made our own choices."

The little girl is watching the whole exchange, eyes huge and shining, at first with hope and excitement. But as the conversation continues, the shine shifts almost imperceptibly to the sheen of tears just barely kept at bay. A vein appears in Howard's forehead, but he keeps his voice calm, eyes darting from Ruth back to Nathan.

"You know we love having Ruthie and Rachel with us, but are you sure you can't take some time out for your own daughters, at least spend a little time with them before you move—"

"It will be easier when I move now; it would be harder on them if we were attached."

"Do you really think this is what Sarah wanted?"

"Sarah?" Nathan's voice is ice. "She wanted you to have them. If she wanted something more than that, or to have any continued say, she should have thought twice before leaving."

With an expression more sad than angry, Howie picks up the little girl, whose lip trembles. Ere can see the pain in the little girl's face. His mother's face. But she doesn't cry.

"Come here, Ruthie," says Howard Fell gently.

Ere wants to stay with Howard and Ruth, to comfort them, to be with them and hold onto them. But he feels compelled to follow Nathan and Hess, and he knows Howard and Ruth cannot see him anyway. So, casting a long and regretful look back at his beloved mother and uncle, he takes off after Nathan and Hess, through the classroom door, and into the next leap forward.

They stand now in a laboratory, not as well-appointed as the one at the Synt (where Ere still actually is, he reminds himself; the rest is illusion) but similar in layout. Nathan, Hess, and another man are staring at a screen. Each holds a clipboard, and they keep glancing back and forth, clipboard to screen, screen to clipboard, all fascinated by something, too excited to speak.

Nathan finally breaks the silence: "It seems pretty conclusive."

Hess glances at Nathan, at the clipboard, at the screen, back at Nathan: "You're sure?"

"Absolutely," says Nathan. "Unless you disagree, Derek?"

"With the—this is about the—the report?" The one called Derek sounds nervous. He is younger and slighter than the other men. His hair is sandy and thick. He wears wire-rimmed glasses. Something about him catches Ere's attention, but he cannot put his finger exactly on why or what it might be. There's already too much to absorb here.

"Yes," Nathan Fell is saying. "Looks conclusive enough to take the next leap. Don't you think?"

"The next step, meaning...?"

"Don't play dumb, Abelson," snaps Felix Hess. "It doesn't look good on you."

"I have a subject in mind, of course," Nathan says, almost absently.

In mind for what?

The world goes black again.

The return of light makes Ere see stars. He leans forward, hands on his knees, head down, willing himself for what feels like the hundredth time that day not to be sick.

"You'll be fine," says Hess. "It's to be expected, the mental motion sickness."

Ere straightens, breath almost back to normal, stomach still rebelling. He is in the lab, standing in front of Hess. His head is throbbing, and there is a ringing in his ears, and he really does want to throw up. He blinks, the bright light still feeling violent on his eyes. As his vision adjusts, Ere notices something behind Hess. It is a large container, half-hidden in shadow and blocked by Hess' body. Something begins tingling in the back of Ere's mind. He has to know what is in the container, but dreads approaching it. He recalls the voices, warning in his dream.

Ere, don't look.

Ere tries to speak, but finds no words. He has too much information and not enough insight. Everything he has seen in the last few minutes rattles around his head, marbles rolling wildly, flashing bits of information in shiny orbs, scattering and disappearing into dark corners, falling into cracks in the floor. He focuses on one thing. The box-thing.

"I'll be happy to answer any additional questions after you view the exhibit." Hess says.

He steps aside, fully revealing the container, although Ere cannot yet tell quite what he's looking at. The container is large, white, cylindrical, with a glass panel in the front. It is filled with water or some sort of clear liquid. And there's something inside.

Almost against his own will, Ere walks forward, toward the container. Bile rises in his throat. The glass clears, revealing what it has hidden, beckoning Ere to look.

Ere, don't look... please, don't look.

He pushes past the voices, the warnings, the fear.

He looks.

Suspended in the container is a man with a clean-shaven face and slate-gray eyes, eyes that gaze vacantly ahead. Ere's own eyes lock with the empty ones, and after a moment, the dead eyes blink, and Ere stifles a scream.

He knows this man. His frame, always wiry, is now emaciated, sharp, bones pronounced. Wires connect him to various smaller machines nestled within the container, and run from the container to other machines and outlets throughout the lab. The man in the container is the same age that he had been when last Ere saw him, moments ago, in the simulation. The same age, but battered and wasted away; an awful parody of alive, profoundly ruined, barely human.

Ere whispers the question, knowing part of the answer already. "What is... who is he?"

"Both such good questions," Hess says, a professor patting an apt pupil on the head. "*What is he?* He is the organic component to our most intricate Heaven algorithms, including the one called the Prophet. He is the mind behind and within all Syn technology. He's the real brain behind this whole operation, you could say. As to who he is, don't tell me you don't recognize him by now, Ere."

Don't look, Ere. Don't look.

But Ere has already looked. He can't stop looking.

"This is Nathan Fell. Your grandfather," Hess says, savoring every word. "The original Syn."

A SAVARI IS ON HER WAY TO MEET THE informant. She told Ere she had a meeting, but stopped short of telling him it was with an informant. She doesn't have a good read on Ere Fell. Not yet. He bears little resemblance to the legends of his mother, the legendary warrior Ruth Fell.

Asavari's own middle name is Ruth, in honor of the greatest fighter of the first Original resistance. Someday, she might tell Ere that. She wonders what he'll think, knowing children half a world away are not only being born, but also being named for his family. Howard is as common a name as Ruth, and some children are even given the name Fell.

She hopes she is living up to the promise of her namesake. From the time she began to understand history, what the world was like then and now and how it all came to be, her life has been devoted to the movement. To restoring a future for her people, a future where they can all be out in the sunlight, as she is today.

Not that she can enjoy this sunlight, shining obnoxiously on the leering, gleaming Central City.

She moves quickly through the busy Syn streets, keeping her head low, avoiding eye contact. She hopes no one notices her, or if they glance at her they will think her a Vost, a menial, employed at someone else's house, on her way to an acceptable job of clearing tables or scrubbing toilets. If anyone notices that she is a young Original, she might be in trouble. She steps up her pace.

Getting to meet the informant, find out the latest updates directly instead of through heavily encrypted, often-enigmatic messages, is an exhilarating prospect. Asavari rarely gets to do field work. She is hungry for action, eager to prove her salt in a new and more visible way.

"Where are you off to in such a hurry there, little lady?"

A bony hand lands sharply on her shoulder.

Asavari jerks away, shielding her face with her arm as she turns to see a spindly Syn man. He sways as he lurches to grab her again; his breath reeks of alcohol.

"Lemme see that face," he slurs. "I bet you're a pretty girl. Don't know if I've seen you before, you seem pretty famil—framil—I've seen before. D'you work at the—the Synt?"

"No," says Asavari, wrenching out of his grasp, and continues walking.

"Hey," he calls after her. "I said hey!"

She ignores him and continues walking. She cannot be late; it is a limited window of time to meet the informant. This drunk is unsteady on his feet. She knows she can outpace him.

"D'you think you're too good for me, y'Original slut?" He bellows from behind her.

Asavari stops in her tracks. She is not offended by his state-ment; his words mean nothing to her. But if he continues scream-ing, he might call even more unwanted attention her way. And somehow the drunken idiot had noticed she was an Original. She must deal with him, as quickly and quietly as possible. She turns in his direction, but keeps her head down, hiding her face.

"I have to get to work, sir. Please let me be."

"You thought I didn't know you were an Original," he grins, the alcohol assuring him of his wit. He lurches toward her, wag-ging a crooked, slender finger. He forms his words slowly, trying to sound less inebriated and instead sounding all the more so. "But I always know. I can ... smell it on you. You have that ... Original stink."

The closer he gets, the more she can smell the stink on him. One hundred proof.

"Sir..." Asavari begins.

"Come on, Original-girl. Lemme get a good whiff. I like your stink. S'natural."

Asavari nods, then inclines her head toward an alley. She slips into the narrow space between two buildings. The drunk man fol-lows her, a lecherous grin on his face. When he sees Asavari get down on her knees, his grin grows wider and he hurries her way. Asavari puts up a hand, stopping him.

"Go into private mode first."

She keeps her face down, glancing up just barely enough to see the blink and know he has gone into private mode, as requested. She needn't have bothered to request it. Even as drunk as he is, he wouldn't take a girl in an alley without going into private mode.

"Let's get this started, girl, 'fore a monitor drone lights up back here."

"Indeed," says Asavari, and slams her fists upward, hard, into his crotch.

"Heaven and Hell," he wheezes. "What the f—"

Asavari is back on her feet, and the second blow is to the man's skull. He drops hard, face connecting heavily with the ground. He does not even moan, and does not try to get up.

"Asshole," she growls. Then she leans down and whispers right into ear: "Your authorities do not take kindly to drunks in the daylight. I know who you are and where you live, and if you ever tell anyone about this, I will report your drunkenness and destroy your reputation. And then I will *kill you*, fully all-the-way dead."

She does not actually know who he is or where he lives, but he is drunk and in pain and this was all probably enough to make him believe every word. He winces, squeezing his eyes closed and staying put.

Asavari knows they are not all like this, that some Syns are even allies. But this pathetic excuse for a person makes her hate Syns all the more. They have everything—technology, medicine, education, shelter, food, freedom, everything—and here he was, leering at teenage girls, drunk before noon, reeking of desperation. Asavari hurries away from the battered Syn. She has already wasted too much time on the bastard.

And she can't afford to be late.

CHAPTER 70: ERE

"THAT... THING... IS NOT MY GRANDFATHER," Ere
chokes, shaking.

"Well, he is and he isn't," Hess allows. "He's so much
more, now. But once upon a time, this is the man who fathered
Ruth Fell. Your mother. So he is, in fact, your grandfather.
Nathan Fell was also a brilliant research scientist. He was called
the Synthetic Moses. The Cyborganics Cowboy. And later, the
Original Syn. Didn't your mother ever tell you?"

"No..."

Hess shakes his head, chiding the boy's dead mother.

"Pity. That is your real history, Ere. That is the Fell family legacy. Your mother kept you in the dark because she was angry at her
father, angry that he gave more time to his work than to her. But
he was the one with real vision. You should be proud."

Against his own will, Ere's eyes slide again toward the container. "Is he dead?"

"No," Hess says, almost reverently. "He is not dead, although he is not 'alive' in the way that, say, you are. Or I am. He was the first to attempt a full synch; in hindsight, him going first was foolish, but he was so sure the technology was ready to go, and wanted to be the pioneer. But it didn't work. There was a missing piece; we needed something to help more deeply connect the mechanical and organic components. In terms of the individual fate of your grandfather, his procedure could be seen as 'a failure'—but we learned so much from his sacrifice that we were able to make incredible adjustments. And his contributions did not stop there."

Ere stares harder at the floating man. His grandfather. He already knows more about him than he ever wanted to know. Too much. But Hess is still talking. Each word assaults Ere's ears.

"Stop..."

"I knew that a mind this powerful couldn't be discarded," Hess continues, relishing this history, ignoring Ere's plea. "We needed to utilize it. Although the synch left him 'inhuman,' it also gave us the opportunity to connect him at the deepest level to the world for which he laid the foundation. He became that missing piece. Your grandfather's mind powers our entire world. Heaven needed an organic component, and your grandfather is that component. It's his legacy. And now as his only living descendent, it's yours."

"No," whispers Ere.

His mind is still swirling, chasing all the haphazardly rolling mental marbles. He catches one, then another. *These are not marbles*, he thinks. *These are puzzle pieces*. He begins piecing together the puzzle, connecting the disparate parts, realizing something still doesn't fit, tearing it all apart, re-placing the pieces, trying to see the bigger picture.

His grandfather created the technology that led to the Singularity. His mother and her uncle cut ties with him, clinging to the Original way. They became leaders of the rebellion. On both sides of the bloody war... Ere's own family. One side paving the way for the new, the other protecting the old. Now his mother was dead, his uncle was dead, and his grandfather was this creature suspended in a laboratory container, staring at him with unseeing eyes.

Ere feels a sour sickness rising in his throat. Everything Hess is telling him is too much, and not nearly enough. There is an abundance of assaulting information and a dearth of details. Ere struggles to grasp for something solid, one detail to dig in on more deeply.

"My father," Ere says. "If you wanted to show me my history, what about my father?"

"So even that, your mother kept from you?" Hess *tsk, tsk, tsks.* "Well. I guess that's not surprising. But Ere, I don't think you'll like that part of the story very much."

"Tell me," growls Ere. "You've already told me plenty. How much more damage can one more truth do?"

"Have you ever heard of the proverbial camel? The miserable creature's already over-burdened back, finally broken by the addition of one last piece of straw? No—I imagine not. Well, this truth is not a single straw, it's a thousand straws. It'll snap your back."

"Tell me."

"Since you asked," Hess smiles wanly. "Your father's name was Derek Abelson. You saw him in the simulation. Very promising young man. Worked directly with your grandfather, and with me. And a few months before you were born, he was assassinated."

"Assassinated?"

"Yes," says Hess, and fires the final bullet. "By your mother."

A SAVARI IS WAITING FOR THE INFORMANT like the parched earth awaits rain. She has never met him. Or her? She does not even know that much. Not a name, a title, a synched status, nothing. She does not know what their position in the Syn world might be, or, if she is being honest, whether or not they can truly be trusted...

Trust is such a tricky thing.

She thinks guiltily of Ere, hoping he will forgive her. Hoping he is unharmed. Delivering him to the Synt was a necessary evil. When Ere emerges—*if* he emerges—

No. She cannot think like that. She reminds herself what her mother would say.

Always focus on the mission, Asavari. Nothing matters more.

So she forces her mind back to the mission, taking in her surroundings, back on high alert. She is in a park, a manicured little forest called Wren Wood. It is within the city limits of Central City, a dangerous meeting place. But the informant was adamant that since they worked in the Synt, meeting outside of the city limits would raise more suspicion.

Sometimes the safest place is in the mouth of the wolf; the teeth can't get you if you're already behind them.

So they are meeting in public, in the heart of the Syn world. They will speak only in code, until it is firmly established that they could trust one another, that he was in private mode, that he had not been followed and they were not being observed. They would not use real names. They would keep the exchange to under five minutes. They would—

"You're here on Wednesdays?"

The voice, hushed, comes from behind her.

Asavari whirls around and sees a man, wearing dark nondescript clothing, a hood pulled low, covering his face. Asavari has seen other Syns in similar garb; the hood is popular for fashion and function, protecting skin from sun exposure. Just common enough to blend in, while adding a bit more protection, obscuring the details of his face.

"Most Wednesdays," Asavari says, responding to his coded phrase with her own.

The man gestures for Asavari to follow him, and leads her a little deeper into the thicket of Wren Woods. Looking quickly about to make sure no one is near, the man focuses on Asavari.

"We're offline," he says, assuring her of his shift to private mode.

"The package I brought was successfully delivered?"

"As planned." Confirms the informant.

"Where do you think he will land? Which side?"

"You're the one who spent time with the package."

Asavari bites her tongue; she should have more insight into Ere, but finds that she has little. She shakes her head, frustrated, and moves on.

"What else do you have for me?"

"We moved quickly when we learned the daughter was part of a breeding program," the informant says quickly. "Found a way to neutralize her. I had the opportunity to replace one of her scheduled fertility treatments with something else. This resulted in a medical episode, which presented as a stroke. She is no longer considered a strong candidate for the fertility program, and as the youngest Syn, she was their best bet."

"A fertility program? Syns want to reproduce?"

Asavari must have missed this update while traveling. That was the risk of clandestine journeys; being out of touch in a world where things changed fast.

"Not to make new people. Just to make new bodies."

What is the difference between people and bodies?

"New bodies?"

"Yes. For when an aging Syn wants a full upgrade into a brand-new body."

"No," Asavari whispers, horrified.

The informant goes on: "They can transfer the consciousness—mind, memory, everything, just upload the whole thing into the new model. They tested alternate options, but had the most success when starting with 'naturally made' infant bodies, kept in induced comas, nourished and exercised by staff as they mature. There's no rush; eighteen to twenty years is the blink of an eye for the Syns. 'Mules,' the director calls the new bodies."

Asavari shivers, the soullessness of this too much for her to comprehend.

"They have not successfully implemented this program yet?"

"Only a matter of time," stresses the informant, and the subtext is clear.

Hurry. Don't delay the rebels' next moves. Soon the Syns will grow in strength and their longevity, vitality and dominance be all the more assured. It is only a matter of time.

"I understand," she says. "Any more bodies?"

"Not since Murray. His wife issued a statement claiming he was mentally unstable, seeking publicity," says the informant. "In some reports, she said he never actually intended to end his life, that it was an accident—a publicity stunt gone wrong. And the word never got out that they failed to recover the body. They had a funeral and everything. It wasn't the major news item in the Syn world we hoped it would be. But it got a few people talking."

"Anything else?"

"We're almost out of time," says the informant. "I need to shift back to regular mode soon, to ensure there's nothing suspicious in my log. My goal is to make it seem like I just took a nice long shit."

Asavari nods, as if this is a perfectly normal thing to say.

"But there is one more thing," the informant says, speaking even faster now. "There's a prophecy making the director uneasy."

"A prophecy... from his Heaven? What is it about?"

"Don't know," the hooded figure says, shaking his head.

"Is it about the breeding program, or Originals, or—?"

"Don't know," the informant says, tersely. "I'll find out more, as I can. Will you be able to come, or send another representative, within two weeks' time?"

"I will find a way."

He nods, turns to leave, then stops and faces her again. Before Asavari can stop him, gesture in some way that it is too danger-ous, he slips the hood from his head. She can, for the first time, see his full face. Brown skin, almost as dark as her own. Light golden eyes, a strong chin. A smooth, bald head. Unlike most Syns, his skin is not perfect, but bears the faint scars and pock-marks of once-severe acne. In another swift move, he pulls up the edge of his sleeve, revealing a short set of numbers across the back of his hand. She just has time to memorize the numbers before he lowers his sleeve again, hiding them from view.

5/333.

He is not a Syn, but a Vost. She now has an idea as to why this man sympathized with the plight of her people. But why would he take the risk of revealing his identity to her?

He answers her unspoken question, perhaps seeing it in her eyes.

"I need someone to know who I am. If I die tomorrow, I want my true allegiances known. Who better than you to deliver my truth, Karma?"

Her stomach churns. Even her mother does not know that she is the one called Karma, that in addition to her missions for the resistance she is part of the elite band within the clandestine network, the ones who have learned to manipulate some Syn technology in order to share the most important information as quickly as possible.

How did he know? Unless...

"Are you... Shadower?" Asavari asks, her heart leaping up into her throat.

"No. You'll never see Shadower."

"But have you? Do you know him?"

"Karma," chides the golden-eyed Vost. "Why do you assume Shadower is a he?"

And he gives her a slightly longer smile, which Asavari cannot help but return. The informant pulls the hood back over his face, obscuring himself once again.

"What is your name?" She asks, knowing she has already asked too much. But now that she has seen his face, his Vost number, his eyes—there is no going back. Besides, if she might need to reveal his alliance someday, will she not need to know his name?

The informant hesitates.

"I'll tell you my name right before shifting back into public mode. Don't tell me your real name, Karma. And turn your back before I tell you, so there's no chance I'll see your face as I shift my settings. Even with every precaution, I fear anything I know may someday be mined from my 'enhanced' brain. But your Original mind is yours alone, and so I will tell you my name. Keep it safe for me."

"I will," she swears, turning her back to him as requested.

He whispers his name softly, gently, as if handing her a precious gift.

"Jorge."

CHAPTER 72: HESS

HESS KNOWS THAT THE FELL BOY IS ON THE verge of meltdown. He's processing too much information at once (an overwhelming amount of data for an Original brain, with its limited storage capacity). Hess knows it is almost more than a mind can take, though it does not occur to him what damage it might also be doing to Ere's heart and soul.

He might have thought more about the emotional toll, at one time. But that time has long since passed. Instead, Hess is enjoying this cat-and-mouse game more than he should, and draws it out a little longer. It's better stress relief than he ever could have imagined.

"It's a sad story, your father's death. I'd tell you all about it, but I have some very pressing matters to attend to now. If you would like to wait in my office—"

"I thought you had all the time in the world," Ere interrupts, looking not at Felix Hess but at the living corpse once called Nathan Fell. "If you can't tell me the details of how my mother killed my father, you must not know. Or you're lying about the whole thing."

"I have no reason to lie to you," says Hess. "Given enough time, you will come to realize my reliability. And I hope that time is something I might be able to interest you in, Ere. I want us to be allies. So let's not waste time on the wrong questions. Let's get to the right ones."

Even as he speaks these words, Hess is busy calculating just what he means by them. And then a notion strikes him, sparking a fire in his mind that instantly blazes with power.

"The outsider inside will end the beginning."

Ere was from the outside, and now stood inside the very inner sanctum, the beginning of the entire Syn world. Hess had not known that this boy existed before today, but now that he is aware, it's so blindingly obvious that the prophecy has always been about him.

Ere's heritage is both fiercely Original and pioneering Syn. This boy is the dividing line. Hess feels a gleeful rush of anticipation. The boy's birthright enables him to inherit either legacy. The question is which legacy he will choose, and what "end the beginning" means. Hess feared it was a death knell—the closing of a door. But perhaps it means leveling up. Ending the beginning, the early era of Syn civilization—and ushering in a shining next stage of progress.

It could go either way; it had to be malleable. Wasn't everything? As much as he believes in algorithms, calculations, data sets—Hess believes even more firmly in manipulating data to yield a desired result.

Ere knows nothing of his own true birthright, and thus it is up to Felix Hess to convince him that his Syn legacy is nobler than his Original upbringing. The prophecy did not specify which line would end, and which would continue. Standing at the helm, Hess feels certain that he is the one with the power to determine the ultimate outcome.

"Ere. Have you given enough thought to your destiny?"

"My destiny?"

"Your grandfather and your father were two of the most brilliant men who ever lived. They saw the flaws in the Original world—the hunger, the war, the rapidly depleting resources. They dreamed of something better."

"They played God," Ere argues, regurgitating a typical Original talking point.

"Did they? If they went against God, why didn't He stop them? Why have we flourished, while the Originals fade away?"

"Because you set it up that way! You exiled us! You sentenced us to die."

"Ere," Hess says, as gently as he can manage, "I know this side of the story is new to you. But think about it: Wasn't the Syn approach more logical—more humane? If you believe the ancient stories, God started the whole world with two Originals, Adam and Eve, who were given free will—and did bad things. Generations kept messing up. God sent a flood to give them a clean slate. And time after time, Originals kept on sinning. We overran the world. We poisoned the seas, the sky, the earth, animals, everything. And then someone had a better idea. *Your grandfather's* idea. What if, instead of all the suffering generations, we limited our numbers and lengthened our days? Lived within our means, healed the planet, all while broadening opportunities to learn and grow? You never knew the old, fully-Original world, Ere. You cling to the 'Original way,' but do you really know what that means?"

"It means… everything was natural," Ere says, but his voice wavers. "And everyone had the same chance for a good life."

Hess shakes his head, genuinely somber. "It never meant that."

"But—"

"No," Hess says. "No. You weren't there. You don't remember the bad things, only the pretty stories your mother told you. There was so much suffering, Ere. Death, disease, hunger, unspeakable cruelty. Here—see for yourself."

CHAPTER 73: ERE

THE ROOM VANISHES, plunging them into blackness for the briefest of moments, and then Heaven begins assaulting Ere with new simulations. Horrific visions surround him, so vivid and lifelike that he begins to shake as they assail him in quick succession:

Children with distended bellies—

A man with a gunshot wound, lying in a dark alley, bleeding and alone, convulsing in pain—

An old woman in a hospital bed, some sort of liquid dripping into her veins, her eyes shut as she prayed for her own end—

Gaunt prisoners in tattered striped uniforms, prodded at gunpoint by soldiers to march into ovens—

A man approaching a little girl, terrible intent in his eyes, and what he is going to do to her, it will not be for the first time, oh God, oh God, not for the first time and not for the last time—

"Make it stop!" Ere screams.

"WE DID," HESS REPLIES, QUIETLY.

The simulations disappear, and they are standing again in the middle of his laboratory.

"We made a better world," Hess continues, telling a truth he has not articulated in quite some time. "That was your grandfather's dream. Your ancestors set this change in motion. I'm the sole surviving pioneer, honored to continue fulfilling the dreams of your grandfather. Yes, someday all of the Originals will die out, and I understand how painful that might seem to you. But in the old world, thousands of people died every day. Often in terrible, unspeakable ways. When the last of the Originals die, an era will end. But a new era, a more peaceful, prosperous, more painless era has already begun."

"I didn't know it was like that," Ere whispers.

"I know you didn't," Hess says. "And look, our world isn't perfect. Not yet. But that's the goal, Ere. No more pain. No more aging and forgetting—" Hess stops, then starts again. "I want to offer you something. It's something we rarely extend these days, but you're an exception in every way. So I hope you'll fulfill your destiny, and follow in your ancestors' footsteps."

"Which ancestors?" The boy asks dully, probably already guessing at what Hess means.

But Hess doesn't want to blow it, so he smiles wanly. Then, having baited the hook slowly, skewering the worm, angling for the biggest fish of all, he casts the line and begins to reel it in, *steady, steady, steady.*

"You know what I am offering you, Ere. You can become the first Fell to successfully join the world your grandfather designed for you. You can live as an eternal Syn."

E VER IS THINKING, which is still no easy task. Her mind keeps blinking itself on and off like a lamppost flickering on a dark street.

She is in her bed, still weary, but gaining strength. She has been researching strokes, and based on what she's learned, she doubts that she had one. Regardless, she's recovering well from whatever it was, physically speaking; other than a slight headache and some lingering vertigo, she feels all right. She has no paralysis. Her speech has returned to normal. Her vision is clear.

She has been taking steps to reclaim a sense of herself, small as the steps might be. Her hair, for example, is freshly colored. She selected a deep, lustrous black, almost blue. Midnight Express #17. She is wearing a silken robe, which she usually loves for the alluring way it hugs her curves, but tonight she appreciates it for its soft, almost weightless feel, gentle and cool on her battered body. Her mother will be in to check on her soon, to make sure she's eaten her dinner and taken her medication. She doesn't know why those meds still matter. Dr. Chun made it quite clear that she was no longer a suitable candidate for motherhood.

Fine by Ever.

Pushing aside her anger at her father's abuse, she wrestles her thoughts back to the task of keeping Ere safe. She might have come up with the perfect solution. At the very least, her plan will protect him against any danger that might befall them if her memories are mined by her father. It's a drastic measure, but the more she thinks about it, the more certain she is that it's the only way.

She lays there, counting the seconds, because there are so few left of these seconds. These precious, Ere-saturated seconds, where she can be in her bed and wrap herself in the memory of him. Knowing what she needs to do, she knows she has to take action soon.

But oh, Heaven and Hell. She wants more time, more nights spent with Ere teasing her, touching her—

No. Stop dreaming. Just do what has to be done.

But she can't bring herself to do it. Not yet. Because once she takes this irreversible step, he will no longer exist for her, and she is not ready to part with him yet. She wishes she could see him again. Just one more time, she wishes she could see Ere before he is forever erased.

There is a knock at her door. Her mother, undoubtedly, with another meal in tow. Ever sighs and does not move from the bed.

"Come in."

But the door remains closed, and after a moment, it occurs to Ever that her mother would not knock. Nor would Angela. No one would, because these aren't the sort of doors you knock on. Outside of her father's office, she can't think of any doors designed to be knocked on, nor any people who would opt for knocking—not any Syns, anyway.

Her curiosity piqued, Ever rises, wincing a little. Her fatigued body is still sore. She is unaccustomed to this feeling, and hates every moment of weakness. She walks stiffly to the door, unsure what she will see when she slides her finger across the panel and the door drops down to reveal whatever is behind it. As soon as the door is opened, she lets out a small cry.

She must be hallucinating again. She can't be seeing what she's seeing.

For there, on the other side of the door, is Ere.

He gives her a small shake of his head, indicating: *do not speak.* The look she gives him in return is confused, but she follows his instructions and does not acknowledge that she knows him. She says nothing. She waits for him.

"My name is Ere," he says. "You must be Ever."

"Yes. I'm Ever."

"Your father sent me here."

"What?"

"It's a long story. I also just finished speaking with your mother."

This is even more unexpected than his statement about her father—to the point that it almost causes Ever to burst out with inappropriate laughter, in pure shock.

"And how was that?"

"Awkward," Ere says, unable to suppress a bemused grin. "She touched my knee a lot and called me darling. She kept leaning in... I think she wanted me to look down her shirt."

"Gross," says Ever, giggling. And then, trying to maintain their façade of being strangers but desperate to know how he made it to her door, and when she can get her hands on him, she clears her throat: "So how—I mean, why are you here? And, um, what was your name again?"

"It's Ere Fell," he says. "My mother was Ruth Fell. And I recently learned that her father was Nathan Fell. So your father has offered to make me a Syn, to join your people."

"*What—!?*"

"—and before I give him my decision, he granted my request to talk with you about what that might be like."

"I don't understand—" Ever begins.

"And he has granted that our conversation can take place in private mode."

Clever boy.

She shifts into private mode, pulls him into her room, and slides her bedroom door shut. She looks into the eyes of the boy she loves, and falls against him. She doesn't even have the energy to kiss him, she is so tired, but just the feeling of his arms around her is enough. He kisses her face, gently, aware that she is weak. He is so tender. The tenderness makes her want to cry. He holds her tighter, and she cannot help but wince. Ere immediately pulls back, concerned.

"Are you all right?"

"It's nothing," she says quickly. "I've been—I've had a few ups and downs since they hauled me back in from Sector 27. But you! You met my father? He wants to make you a Syn?"

"Yes."

"But you're not really considering it."

His gaze is achingly sincere.

"If it's the only way to be with you, why wouldn't I consider it?"

"Ere, no—"

"And it turns out… the Original way is not what I was always told—"

"Ere, listen. My father can be very manipulative. He'll only tell you what he wants you to hear, and twist things to sound as if—"

"Not just things he told me. Things he showed me. Things my mother kept from me. I had to at least consider—and Ever, don't you want me to? Don't you want me, here, forever…?"

"Of course I do," she says, kissing him, softly.

"And I want you," he breathes.

"I know," she says, fighting every physical urge to wrap herself around him and forsake her own better intentions. "I know. But there's so much—about this world, this life, all of it. Ere. It's not what you're thinking, either. You told my father you wanted to hear about this life, from me? I can't believe he'd send you up here to get that point of view, because... oh."

"What?"

"Since he doesn't know I know you, he's probably hoping..."

She shakes her head, trying to catch up with whatever her father must be thinking. That she'd be so intrigued by Ere, she would talk him into synching? The sick truth is, she would probably do it to selfishly, temporarily relieve her own boredom. If she didn't already know him. If she wasn't already halfway certain she was in love with him.

"Listen to me, Ere," Ever whispers fiercely. "I don't know how much time we have, so listen. If I were given the choice, *I would not choose this life*. I would choose independence. I would choose experience. I would choose the weight of time, a limited number of days to give meaning and urgency to life. I have none of that."

"But you have time, and health, and—"

"No, no," Ever says, frustrated. She's losing her train of thought, another headache chipping away at her. "I mean yes, I have time, but for what? Endless time is meaningless. Some say transhumanism saved us, the machines freed us. But freed us from what, and to do what? In this life, we have so few choices. As Originals, we could make choices, including the wrong ones. And yes, people made a lot of wrong choices. Over and over. But at least they were free to make them. You are free to make them."

"So let me make this one. I choose you, Ever."

"No, Ere. Don't. Choose the Original way. Choose your mother, your people—"

"My mother was a liar."

"So is my father," Ever says, then pauses. "Wait—you said your mother *was...*?"

"She died," Ere says, and Ever hears the catch in his throat.

"Oh, God," she whispers. "I'm so sorry..."

"It doesn't matter now," he says, quickly, swallowing his evident sorrow. "And if they're both liars, why does it matter which lie I decide to accept? This world is unfair, the last world was unfair, I don't even know what I believe anymore... but I do know that I want to be with you, Ever. And my people are dying. There's no life for me out there. That's the truth."

Ever almost relents. Having Ere in her endless life might make it bearable. Here he was, impossibly, standing in her bedroom, telling her he was willing to synch. For her. Forever. But then she recalls her father coldly informing her of her role in a breeding program. She flashes on her mother's unending dissatisfaction. Tempting as bringing him into her world might be, Ever cannot imagine Ere being subjected to the whims of her father and the Syn Council.

He cannot see it now, but she can—this life would kill him; increasing frustration would ultimately lead him to resent the choice to synch, the life sentence of too much life. He would eventually resent her. Resolution restored, she trusts anew that her earlier decision is the right one. Fighting every physical instinct, she moves away from him. She knows what she has to do; the only thing she does not know is how to tell Ere.

Unable to think of a better option, she decides simply to tell him, plainly, clearly, and with as little emotion as possible. Channeling her parents, she straightens her back, tightens her jaw, and speaks in a tight, controlled voice.

"Don't synch. If you love me, remain as you are. That's how I love you. As you are."

"But—"

"No," she says. "You have to remain as you are. And I have to erase you, Ere."

It is both the most logical and most emotional statement of her life.

She looks at Ere, knowing he will not understand right away, but someday he will. Ere's face suggests that while he doesn't get exactly what she means, he already doesn't like it.

"Erase me?"

"Erase you from my memory. From the files that document my experiences with you. All of them. If you're not in my memories at all, then no matter what happens to me, you're safe."

"I don't understand," he says.

"They haven't been able to extract much from me about you," Ever says. "Not yet. But they will. Eventually, they will. And now that your face is recognizable to my father—I have to make sure there's nothing in my head for him to find. If my father learned the truth about us, I don't know what he would do."

"Ever—" He reaches for her, but she intercepts both his words and his caress.

"I have to erase you," she repeats. "You, your mother, and everything connected to—"

"Don't!" Ere is desperate, wild-eyed. "Don't do it. If I have to leave, okay, I'll leave. But you can come with me."

"Don't be an idiot! I'm easily traceable. I'm trapped. Remember what I told you about choices? It's simple. I don't have them, you do. It's too dangerous for me to go with you. It's too dangerous for me to know where you're going. Or even to know you exist."

"No. I can't let you forget me."

She blinks, trying hard to hold on to her resolve, which remains in danger of slipping away, dissolving into nothing.

"I could never forget you. That's impossible. That's not what erasing will mean. It will mean something else entirely. It will be more like... I never knew you at all. As far I'll know, you will never have been. And that will be safer, for you. And less painful. For me."

With this statement, everything slows for Ever. She has a painful bout of clarity, staring into Ere's wide eyes, disbelieving, protesting. She feels the cold condemning metal weighing down her port finger, and her blood, pumping, pulsing, thudding her resolve. She feels the weight of what her actions will mean. Worse than nothingness, her choice will leave her with the whole wide world, minus the one thing she loves.

Erasing Ere will not lead Ever to something as simple as hell. It will leave her instead in purgatory: deletion after deletion, removing love from her life until she is left with an eternity of solitude.

But she has to do it. What she loves about Ere is his individuality. His naiveté. The way he has to figure things out, rather than simply download an update to increase his knowledge. She needs Ere to stay Ere, even if she will no longer know him. The alternative is worse.

"No," Ere tries again. "No. There has to be another way. You'll come with me, and stay in private mode, and then when we're far from any synched sector, then we can find a way to—"

"It won't work, Ere. I'd be located swiftly, taken in. This is the only option. You can't change my mind. If anything happened to you, I'd..." Ever's face sinks into a gallows smile. "...well, if I were allowed to, I'd die."

"This is crazy. There's never just one option. I'll figure out the way to disconnect a Syn, and make them Original again. If I can't be in your world, we'll find a way for you to join mine."

"That's impossible."

"Nothing is impossible," says the naïve boy. "I'll find the way, and then I'll find you, and then we'll be together. And if that doesn't work, I'll come back here, beg for mercy, synch, and that will be my choice. Okay? Listen to me. *This is not how we end.*"

She can no longer maintain the rigid spine, the clenched jaw, the authority. She loves this idiot boy and all his absolute absurdity. It occurs to her that although they appear the same age, she has been around for four decades longer. She feels suddenly old, recalling yet another thing she would never tell him, and would soon forget herself: she is the exact same age as his mother. They were little girls who lived parallel lives, two little girls with distant fathers who landed in different worlds. She is overcome with a desperate need to be gentle with this boy.

"Ere... this is our end. After we do this, I won't know you."

"Then when I come back here for you, I'll just have to introduce myself. I'll say 'Hello. My name is Ere.' And then you'll probably tell me that that's a stupid name."

He kisses her. She kisses him back, losing herself in his mouth, his smell, everything that will soon be gone. She absorbs it all, creating a hundred more sensory files which will live in her mind for only moments before she destroys them. And then she forces herself to stop, to pull back. Meeting his eyes, she takes a deep breath.

"How will it work?" He asks quietly.

"I'll run an internal search for all my memory files on you, sort them in chronological order, each day's file containing every individual moment. Then, in batches as large as possible, I'll delete them."

"And when you delete them, then they're just ... gone?"

"Nothing is ever really gone. But they will be erased. Unsearchable, and lost from my storage, and kept out of the archives of Heaven. They will exist somewhere, I guess. I just don't know where. And neither does anyone else, so we'll be safe."

"Will it take long?"

She shakes her head. No.

He hesitates. "Can I stay with you? While you... erase..."

She had already decided on her answer to the question she knew he would ask.

"Yes. You can stay with me until I get to the final two files. Then you have to leave. You can't be here after I delete the final two. Promise me."

"I promise."

"All right."

She sits down, back against the wall, steadying herself. Ere sits beside her, holding her hand. Ever closes her eyes, selecting the files, lining them up by day. She allows herself to open the first one, to re-live the moment when she first met Ere, one final time.

A snapped twig. Catching her breath.

Irrationally thinking: an alligator!

Then seeing eyes—not evil, but warm.

A boy.

ESS RARELY SECOND-GUESSES HIMSELF. But he's feeling a little hesitant now. He received the message from his wife, an hour ago, that all had gone well in her conversation with the boy. She had followed his directions, been flirtatious but appropriate, painted out the virtues and potential of life everlasting. She then directed him to Ever's door.

And he's been in there for an hour, with Ever in private mode for most of that time.

Ever's room is small, with no screens or microphones for him to remotely access. There is a camera just outside her door, but once the door is shut, no eyes on the inside. It is a sparse abode, with no technology save her Heaven outlet, bed, dresser, and reading screen.

Plenty of access points in other rooms, she had argued. *Don't I deserve some privacy?*

So Hess has no way of knowing what is transpiring in the room. Hence his growing anxiety. The boy had wanted a private conversation—fine. Ever would surely say things Hess would disagree with, but she would also be intrigued by the boy. She would relish the idea of a Syn her own age, especially one who was good-looking, and—

Oh, Heaven and Hell!

For a brilliant man, Hess suddenly realizes he has been colossally stupid.

He sent a teenage boy who had very likely never even seen a girl his own age right into his hormone-infused daughter's bedroom, and let them shut the door.

Even if he ultimately wanted them to pair together, rushing into it right at this moment, before running compatibility tests and keeping it all under his own watchful eye—this was a potential disaster. Unregulated desire often led to undesirable results. Hess curses himself for being too focused on the big picture to remember the basic banal realities of human bodies.

"Jorge!" Hess bellows.

In an instant, his trusted assistant is at his side. "Yessir."

"Go to Ever's room immediately. Whatever is going on, you get in that door, grab the Original boy, and bring him to me. Go. Now."

CHAPTER 77: ERE

ERE WATCHES EVER'S FACE. HER EYES CLOSED, every feature so perfect. He does not know which moment is on her mind right now, or what it feels like to let it go. For a brief instant, a small smile plays on her lips. In spite of everything else, this makes him smile, too.

But then the sides of her mouth straighten, and turn down. Eyes still closed, her expression shifts from tranquil to troubled.

He squeezes her hand more tightly.

I hate this.

"ERE."

"Air? That's a weird name. Like 'the air we breathe'?"

"No, Ere, as in—the way things were."

"Huh. I don't know if that's weirdly nostalgic or just stupid."

Ever has to make herself do it before she changes her mind. Without another moment's pause, she deletes the file. A searing pain blazes through her, making her cry out. She was not expecting pain; she had erased memories before, small or embarrassing moments that she simply did not want preserved in Heaven, and never once had it hurt.

This is different.

This is terrible.

She selects the next file, and without opening it, deletes it. It hurt a little less.

Then she feels a gentle hand on her cheek. His hand. Ere's hand. Trying to comfort her. She raises her own hand, grabbing him by the wrist, pulling his hand away from her, as if untangling herself from a net. She stares at him, desperate.

"Ere, don't. Please. Don't touch me. Don't give me any more moments I have to erase."

Oh God, she shouldn't have looked at him.

His wide brown eyes are full of pain—not only his, but also a raw reflection of her own torment, and to feel it and see it at the same time is more than she can bear. She shuts her eyes again, and clicks through file after file, crying out now and again. She writhes, miserable, because she keeps glimpsing files as she prepares to delete them, small moments filling her senses and overwhelming her, then disappearing from her memory and leaving an aching void.

Her woe becomes an angrier and more confusing pain as she became less and less certain of why exactly she is doing this.

Suddenly: quiet.

Calmly, and without opening her eyes, she reads the script she had written for herself before beginning the process.

"Just two files to go. You have to leave now. Don't touch me. Don't say anything. You promised. Now go."

She finds that she herself cannot recall what this promise might be. She only has the faintest notion of what she is doing, of who this boy beside her is, but at her words, he gives her hand a final squeeze, and then she hears the sound of footsteps, the door sliding open, then sliding shut. She tries to block out the sound.

She knows she has to focus on the task at hand, though she cannot quite identify what this task represents, or why it is so important. She can see only the next step. She can only read the message she generated for herself, and act accordingly. She's the only one she trusts, right?

Ever deletes the first of the two files in her queue—the script she had just read. And now, with no time in between, essentially on autopilot, she begins to erase the final file. A folder containing today's memories, a confusing, painful, haunting collection of sensory and emotional files filled with the name of someone she loves, without knowing why.

She knows she must delete this file so that "Ere will be safe." She doesn't know what that means, but if she told herself to do it, she should probably do it.

She erases the file.

Blinking, she wonders what the search term swimming before her eyes means. E-R-E. The search results appear to be an empty folder.

No sense holding on to an empty folder. So she erases the empty folder as well, sending whatever E-R-E once was spinning out into oblivion.

CHAPTER 79: JORGE

THOUGH HE TOOK CARE TO SHOW NO PANIC as he left the Synt, Jorge is panicked.

He made it back from his meeting with Karma just in time to receive Hess' summons, showing up immediately, as required, but he'd cut it pretty close. Learning that the Fell boy had been sent to Hess' daughter was disorienting.

Of all places… why would Hess send the boy there? We're missing some critical intel…

Hurrying to the Hess residence, on Hess' orders but with the fate of the resistance in mind, Jorge has no idea what he will find when he gets there. He also doesn't know what he'll do upon arrival. He knows he can't just hand the boy over to Hess, not when

Hess seems so furious. Not when Jorge would then have to tell Karma that the package was lost, on his watch.

He doesn't know what to do, but now he's here, and he needs to figure out something, and fast. He overrides the security system upon arrival, letting himself in, sending a message to Marilyn informing her that is there on Hess' orders. As an afterthought, he adds:

Fell boy might be dangerous.
Lock yourself in the kitchen, Mrs. Hess.

Hurrying down the hallway to Ever's room, Jorge shifts into private mode. He'll figure out a cover for that later, but in case he has to act instantly, he needs to be sure what he witnesses or does is protected content. He is startled when the door to Ever's room drops open just as he reaches it, and Ere Fell rushes from the room and slams right into Jorge.

Exhaling sharply, Jorge grabs him.

"Do as I say, and don't make a sound." He leans in close to the terrified boy, knowing how he must look—a hooded Synt official—and whispers: "Long live the resistance."

Jorge then touches a small panel on the wall. It illuminates briefly, widens, slides open.

"What—where—" Ere Fell stutters.

"It'll drop you a mile west of the park where you'll meet your companion. GO."

And with that, he shoves the Original boy through the waste chute.

Ere is gone. Now it's time for damage control, always a harder task when you don't know what the hell kind of damage was done.

Jorge decides to deal first with the cameras, then with the girl. One thing at a time. He looks around; there is a camera just in front of Ever's bedroom door, and another at the end of the hall.

Approaching the bedroom-door one from behind, he swiftly dismantles it, erases the past two minutes of content to be safe, and then replaces it. Loping down to the end of the hallway, he does the same thing with the second camera.

Racing back to Ever's room, he reverts back to public setting, knowing he's already been off the grid for too long. He has to talk to the girl on the record, establish his alibi, see what she knows but also make it appear that he knows nothing. When her bedroom door slides down again and Jorge enters the room, he sees the Hess girl crumpled on the floor, leaning against the wall.

What the hell…?

Had the boy attacked her? Was he fleeing the scene of a crime when he crashed into Jorge? The Vost runs up to Ever, keeping his private thoughts hidden but tracking every visual memory as it forms in his synched mind. He grabs Ever by the shoulders, shaking her.

She opens her eyes and looks at him, disoriented.

"Jorge? What's going on?"

"The Original boy," says Jorge. "You saw him?"

Ever blinks her beautiful eyes, long-lashed and vivid. Her eyes, though still lovely, are wet, and rimmed with red. Finding her like this, on the floor, in tears, not quite coherent, Jorge tenses. He has no love for the girl, but bears no ill will either. He fiercely hopes she has not been violated. He feels immediately protective, the way he used to feel about his sisters. But surely the Fell boy would not have done anything terrible to Hess' daughter.

"What Original boy?" She asks, confused.

"You—you didn't see him?"

"I think I'd remember that," Ever says, almost cranky. She pulls from his grasp, rises, stretches, yawns. She displays no sense of trauma, no injuries beyond her recent medical issues. She seems completely oblivious to her own tearstained face.

"You'll forgive me, Miss Hess, but… it looks like you've been crying?"

She reaches up, touches the edge of her eye, seems genuinely surprised to find it damp.

"Huh. That's weird. I wonder if it's a side effect of one of my new medications."

None of this makes sense...

Jorge wonders what actually happened. And then he thinks of the medication switch he had so recently maneuvered, swapping Ever's hormone treatment for the cocktail that caused her stroke-like episode. Had it done permanent damage to her brain? Was it why her memory seems to be malfunctioning? A sharp stab of guilt slices through the other ricocheting questions in his mind. But now is not the time for guilt or wonder, now is the time for damage control.

"Well, he's gone now. You're all right?"

"Fine," she says. "I'm fine. I think."

Glancing around the room again, Jorge had no idea what he is going to tell his boss. He helps Ever to her feet. And then a message lands in his mind, flashing before him with urgency.

It's from Kennedy.

Hess requests update. What in Heaven and Hell is going on?

Jorge is not sure how to respond to that inquiry just yet, since standing right there in the middle of the confusing mess, he finds that despite being an insider in both of the worlds that just collided, he has absolutely no idea what in Heaven and Hell is going on.

S HADOWER COULD USE A SHOT OF WHISKEY. The spotty, intermittent messages coming through are maddening and terrifying. Hess had inexplicably sent the boy, alone, to his own residence at the Synt, to meet with his daughter.

The boy arrived.

Talked with a flirtatious Marilyn Hess.

Entered the girl's room.

An hour later, Hess sent Jorge to retrieve the boy.

No messages yet from Jorge reporting on what happened when he reached the residence.

Shadower would like to do more, to be part of the on-the-ground action. Being the veiled demigod is not all it's cracked up to be, especially when Shadower's lack of actual omniscience is exacerbated by an inability to actually do something to make a difference

You make a difference by staying in the shadows. Keep them safe by making small suggestions, revealing what you can, hiding what you can.

Cold comfort when someone's life was on the line—but millions of lives are always on the line. Shadower clings to the certainty of the ultimate mission, knowing that while staying put is the only option in this very moment, tonight there is more work to do.

No matter what happens with the Fell boy, the next steps toward an Original uprising must still be planned. Tonight, Shadower will venture out to siphon more information, searching specifically for any mentions of the prophecy from Heaven that Karma and Jorge discussed. Shadower needs to find something more concrete on that prophecy. Unfortunately, the deepest well of information usually tapped by Shadower has run dry this week, though it will fill again.

And new corners will be found, new pathways carved out, new wells discovered.

But it'd all go down a lot easier with a whiskey chaser.

W*HERE IS ERE? HE SHOULD BE HERE BY NOW...*

    The sun is climbing steadily in the sky while Asavari waits. There is no sign of Ere. Was he apprehended, locked up by Hess in some Synt cell? Or had he chosen to stay among the Syns, once he learned of his own lineage and connections within this world?

    Suddenly, she recalls a stray comment his angry cousin Cal had made. Something about a "Syn whore." Ere had brushed it off, but was he lying? Did Ere have contact with a Syn girl? Might that tempt him into joining their ranks?

If Ere allied with the Syns, after Asavari had shared with him as much as she had, she might well have doomed her tribe and the entire resistance by trusting him.

Even if he had no prior Syn connection, if he found out how she had manipulated him into meeting with Hess, would Ere decide to pay Asavari back by betraying her and her people?

No. Stop. Calm yourself.

She is being paranoid. The boy will come. He will come, and then go to India with her, and he will join the ranks of the rebels and march alongside them when the uprising begins—

"Asavari?"

She breathes a sigh of relief. "Ere."

He is behind her. She turns to see him in the dawn light, alive and intact. She places a hand on his shoulder. He flinches, but does not react further. Then a scent assaults her nostrils, and Asavari's hand moves from his shoulder to her nose. The boy reeks.

"Ere, are you—"

"No questions from you until I get some answers." His voice is hard. "You didn't bring me to the Synt to have me find out if the Syns have the ability to resurrect the dead, did you?"

"No," she confesses, lowering her head. She had always known that at some point she would be held accountable for her manipulation of him. But it was all for the mission.

"So you sent me in because…?"

"Because you had to know," she says, lifting her gaze and reminding herself again, too. "You had to know your entire history, and choose for yourself. Demonstrate your commitment to the Original way, not because it was your mother's choice, but because it is your own. You had to know the whole truth not from me, but from the other side."

"If you ever lie to me again—"

"I swear on my life, I swear on the mission, I will never lie to you again."

"Fine." Ere says. "Let's go."

She wants to ask him more, to tell him more, to make things better between them before they begin their next perilous journey. But the soldier in her takes command. They are already behind schedule. The rebels await them. The Syns are likely on the hunt for Ere. And, Asavari reminds herself, this journey is about more than one boy, one girl; it is not the mission of a person.

It is the mission of a people.

CHAPTER 82: JORGE

FORTUNATELY FOR JORGE, Hess is too angry to pick up on the vagueness of some of Jorge's answers. As soon as Hess sputters out a question, he subsequently offers his own possible explanation, never giving Jorge a chance to respond. All Jorge has to do is nod and occasionally offer a word or two of agreement to demonstrate his shared frustration and confusion.

Kennedy stands beside Jorge, taking it all in. The whiny little prick seems to be getting a kick out of this whole scene. Despite the fact that a livid Hess usually terrifies him, Kennedy seems damn near close to giggling. Apparently, from the outside, this conversation is amusing.

Hess: "You said that the boy was gone and Ever was on the floor. But what happened?"

Jorge: "I—"

Hess: "You think he tried to have his way with her? He probably tried to have his way with her. Why didn't she scream? Maybe she hit him. Would she have hit him? And then the boy ran. But how would he have gotten out? You checked at every door? No one saw him leave?"

Jorge: "No—"

Hess: "BUT THAT DOESN'T MAKE SENSE. No one? Not Ever, not Marilyn, not you, not Angela, not the damn cameras? ORIGINALS DON'T JUST DISAPPEAR, JORGE."

Jorge: "Yes, sir. I know that, sir."

"Heaven and Hell," mutters Hess, finally winding down a bit.

"Yes, sir," agrees Jorge.

"Heaven and Hell and SHIT," Hess adds, to demonstrate that he is not done being furious. He pounds emphatically on the screen in front of him, which flickers and opens a command portal, which goes dark again at Hess' angry glance.

"Sir?" Kennedy ventures, his voice unnaturally high. "Should we deploy a search team?"

"YOU HAVEN'T ALREADY?" Hess screams, veins popping out like corded ribbons from his beet-red neck.

"Request sent, sir," Kennedy squeaks.

"I'll join the team, sir," Jorge says quickly.

"We'll find him," says Hess, to himself more than anyone. "I won't tolerate any further delays on Generation Next, either, but finding the Fell boy is top priority. Understood?"

Kennedy nods, no longer looking amused. Jorge also nods, adding a silent prayer that in reviewing every inch of what had transpired today, Dr. Felix Hess will somehow miss the thirteen seconds that his assistant had shifted into private mode, and later erased. It would be hard to notice such a tiny gap in a memory log, but Hess just might.

And if Hess ever found out that those thirteen seconds were spent grabbing the Fell boy, whispering something to him, and shoving him down a waste chute—it would not go well for Jorge.

MARILYN HESS IS FIXING HERSELF A CUP of coffee. She dismissed Angela yesterday after all the drama with Ever and the Fell boy. Angela was there when the boy arrived, preparing food in the kitchen. Marilyn told her to just stay in the kitchen and mind her business.

Following her husband's directives, Marilyn talked with the boy—an attractive young thing, if somewhat small and horribly filthy—doing her best to charm him and up-sell the glories of Syn life before sending him to Ever's bedroom. (Sending the boy to the bedroom seemed an odd judgment call to her, even then— but Felix was already planning to breed their daughter in his next evolutionary experiment, so what was there to worry about, really?)

She was curious, though. It had taken all of her resolve not to press herself against the wall of Ever's bedroom to listen in to their conversation. She had instead lingered in the hallway, wishing that her hearing were augmented or that Ever hadn't insisted on a camera-free bedroom. Angela had popped her head out of the kitchen once, to ask if Marilyn wanted another coffee.

"No, no," Marilyn said, shooing her away like a pigeon.

The minutes ticked by. The suspense was killing her. She was about to open the door and insert herself into whatever situation the boy and her daughter was in (only in hindsight does she realize how inappropriate that sounds)—and that's when Marilyn heard their front door slide open. An immediate message arrived, from Jorge.

Here on your husband's orders. Retrieving the Fell boy immediately.

Before she could reply, Jorge sent another message.

Fell boy might be dangerous. Lock yourself in the kitchen, Mrs. Hess.

What on earth?

She bristled at the command from her husband's subordinate. But nevertheless, Marilyn automatically followed the order, hurrying into the kitchen, keying in the lock-code and securing the door behind her. Angela was holding an eggplant.

"What's going on?"

"Jorge's here for the Fell boy," Marilyn whispers. "Says he's dangerous. Hand me the steak knife."

"Are you sure that's a good—"

"Hand me the goddamn knife."

Angela wordlessly slid open a drawer, pulled out a glinting steak knife, and handed it to Marilyn. Both women then stood there, unsure what to do next. Marilyn leaned toward the door, listening intently. There was nothing; complete silence. Then they heard what sounded like a punch to the gut—a thump, a sharp exhalation.

Angela and Marilyn stared at each other.

A moment later, there was a quiet clatter.

And then, silence again.

After several long seconds passed, Marilyn flexed her pale fingers around the knife.

"I'm going out there."

"Don't," Angela said, stepping forward, and then stepping back again when Marilyn waved the knife to emphasize her words.

"This is my home and I'm going out there."

Every Texas hold-your-ground-old-homeowner gene lit up within her, propelling Marilyn Kensington Hess forward as she unlocked the kitchen door and barreled into the dining room. There was nothing and no one there, so she continued toward the hallway. There, she saw something odd—Jorge, alone in the hallway, re-attaching a security camera. Something was up, and Marilyn didn't know what, and she didn't like it. She watched as Jorge ran down the hallway, into Ever's bedroom, the door sliding shut behind him.

What the hell is going on around here?

"Marilyn."

Marilyn startled, almost dropping the knife before whirling around to face Angela.

"Get back in the kitchen. I've got this."

"You said Felix sent Jorge to handle it. Let's let him handle it."

Marilyn opened her mouth to protest, but what could she say? Angela was right. Jorge could handle it. And what was Marilyn going to do? Stab the kid without knowing what was going on? Felix wouldn't be pleased about her doing something that drastic without his say-so.

"Fine," she muttered, fight seeping from her, already missing the momentary adrenaline rush and the fleeting feeling of being her old self. She strode past Angela into the kitchen and waited for whatever would come next.

Not much did come next. The boy disappeared. Ever had no recollection of meeting him. And he never appeared on their security footage. Not after he entered Ever's bedroom. He went in, and then just—disappeared.

According to Felix, who provided Marilyn the most cursory of updates this morning, Jorge noticed that the light was blinking on one of the cameras, signaling a possible malfunction. He had tried to retrieve the data but had been unable to do so; hence some time missing from the monitor (less than fifteen seconds). But Marilyn has her doubts, seeing as Jorge's quick adjustment of the camera was *before* he raced into Ever's room to make sure she was okay— before he would have known the boy had disappeared.

What are you hiding, Jorge?

Felix trusts that Vost implicitly, but Marilyn doesn't trust anyone. Still, without more evidence, Marilyn isn't outing Jorge just yet. Trusting no one means her husband is also on the long list of those whose intentions she doubts.

Marilyn sent Angela home and told her not to come back for a week. Although it's only been a day, she's already contemplating asking Angela to stay away next week, too. Maybe to not come back at all, ever again. She doesn't want anyone to witness her family's brokenness, or her own misery. Not even Angela. Besides, having some extra chores will be good for Marilyn. She's not a great cook nor a great housekeeper, but tasks might be therapeutic. Temporarily.

She wishes Felix would confide in her. He had seemed almost grateful when she delivered Ever to him last week, even winking at her. But after giving her the brief glimpse of the man she fell for all those years ago, he has cast no warm glance her way since.

So at home, once again it's just Marilyn and Ever. And Ever is being uncharacteristically neutral, showing up for dinner without complaint, responding to questions but making few unsolicited remarks. She claims to have no memories of the Original visitor, despite the camera footage clearly showing her in her doorway when the boy entered. But she voluntarily submitted to a memory scan, and nothing on the boy was discovered—nothing at all.

Marilyn wonders if Ever is malfunctioning. She hasn't been the same, not since Marilyn slammed the needle into her thigh.

This thought makes Marilyn's cheek twitches involuntarily. She quickly moves that memory, again, to a more remote file, hoping that will slow it from dominating her thoughts. She feels no small amount of guilt over that action. She wonders for the thousandth time which role matters more: Wife, or mother? Honoring a mutually agreed upon commitment, or protecting something—someone—she herself had created?

Marilyn has always chosen Felix. But what if she has always chosen wrong?

When she doesn't know what to do, Marilyn goes through the motions of something she knows well. She finds rituals soothing. She has no spiritual rituals left, not the Southern Baptist religion she was raised with, nothing from her collegiate explorations of Buddhism and New Age and whatever else. But repetitive, secular, trivial things can calm her. Ordered tasks and rote activities that provide satisfaction once completed. Easy steps, predictable conclusions.

Step, step, step, complete.

Until and unless she can figure out whether or not to tell Felix about Jorge, until and unless she can figure out how to interact with her daughter, she'll need plenty of mindless satisfying tasks to keep her going. *Step, step, complete.* She needs simple things to do.

Like brewing a pot of coffee. Watching it drip through her antique coffeemaker. Pouring it into a simple silver mug. Preparing it how she likes it. Entirely within her understanding and control. Two creams. No sugar. Like always.

CHAPTER 84: EVER

E VER IS IN HER BED. UNDER THE COVERS.
She feels like she's spent way too damn much time in beds
lately. She doesn't feel weak, but she does feel out of it;
more than anything, she feels something she can only describe as
the gap, a new and yawning emptiness within her. It's something
like hunger, but not for food; she doesn't know what she wants,
only that it's missing.

She remembers next to nothing about yesterday. Nothing until Jorge showed up.

*Jorge. Why was he here, in my bedroom? Something about an
Original boy, but what?*

Everyone kept asking her about an Original boy, but she has
no memory of one. It seems like sort of a big thing to just forget.

She allowed her father's team to scan her memories, which backed up her claim, yielding no data on an Original boy. The whole episode was just so weird.

She sits up quickly—too quickly. A searing white light cuts through her brain. She stills, recovering, before beginning a gentle scan of her memories. Searching the files, she finds almost nothing from last night. Or yesterday. Everything is just snippets, partial snapshots of mundane things like eating breakfast, up until Jorge came in and asked her about the boy she didn't see.

Going even further back, her past month's memories are all patchy at best. Shadows here and there of showering, or her mother plunging a needle into her, or Ever doing research on... something, but she can't remember what. Her mind holds almost nothing of any substance. She blinks, trying to focus. Was this some sort of system error? Was it the stroke?

Shaking at the idea that she might continue losing her own thoughts, Ever eases herself back, leaning gently into her pillow. She forces herself to regulate her breathing, and tries to let all of the tension go from her body. Release and relax, like her virtual yoga coach reminds her.

She feels like she's been trampled, inside and out. Slowly, she reaches her finger toward her bedside outlet. She tries to slip her finger portal into the outlet, but something is blocking it. Something small, flimsy. A piece of paper.

Who leaves notes instead of sending messages?

She can barely make out the scratchy writing:

I have left, but I will return.

With Love For Ever,

Ere

"What an odd message," she thinks, or says aloud—she can't even tell, she's so out of it. And then, though she does not know who wrote it or what the note means, her heart swells, and breaks. For the first time in her Synthetic life, or the first time she can remember, at least, a tear rolls its way down Ever's perfect cheek. Wiping away the tear, she carefully smooths the note, reads it once more, then folds it into a tiny, neat square. Without any awareness that she is doing so, her mind creates a new folder: "*Ere.*"

For reasons she cannot explain, she marks "Ere" as *private,* and within the protected category, she files away a virtual copy of this strange little note. She reaches into a drawer and pulls out a little locket she used to wear as a child. Opening the clasp of the locket, she finds that when folded, the neat square of the original note fits perfectly within the small silver heart.

Snapping the heart closed, she fastens the necklace around her neck, and curls up on her bed. Her foot throbs slightly, and she absently flexes it as she plugs her finger into her bedside outlet. Almost immediately, her eyes begin to close. Hopeful that maybe the next time she wakes up, everything will be clearer, she looks forward to sleep. To once again be able to simply lose herself, dreamless and secure in the cloud called Heaven.

But before she fully shuts down, Ever hears a tap on her window.

Her first thought is that she imagined it—but once plugged into Heaven, imagination recedes. It must have been something real. And then it comes again—a soft but distinct rapping. Somehow, someone was at her bedroom window, several stories high.

She pulls her finger from the outlet. As the daughter of the Synt director, she is always seen as something of a target, despite the extremely limited threats in their world today. But it's why she was allowed to carry her own small gun, a freedom not afforded to the average Syn citizen. She reaches quietly beneath her bed to pull out the gun. She always keeps it there, just in case. Her fingers feel around the floor—and come up empty. No familiar feel of polished steel.

What in Heaven? Where's my gun?

She slips out of the bed, onto the floor, and, illuminating her hand to see beneath the bed, she looks for her weapon—but it's not there.

Father must have confiscated it after my stroke. Or after I ran away. Wait. Did I run away? What happened when I ran away?

She's so distracted by her own misfiring mind that she almost forgets the tapping, until it aggressively asserts itself for a third time.

Ever should feel nervous, but she doesn't. She rises and walks toward the window. No gun, no fear. She doubts anyone with malicious intent would have been able to make it to her quarters, anyway. They would have to be remarkably stealthy. The Synt was a fortress. And her room in their penthouse residence is almost a mile high; the rapping must be a bird or something. She goes to the window, pulling her thin silken robe a little more tightly around herself.

At the window, impossibly clinging to the edges of its frame and the sheer face of the Synt exterior wall, is a boy—no, a man. He is young, but grown, with a full beard and intense eyes. His dark complexion is clear and healthy, and beneath his ratty clothing, she can see a taut, muscular physique. She feels a rush of fear and excitement as he stares at her. Although he is a stranger, and much larger than she, he is unthreatening; his expression looks almost... affectionate?

"Identify yourself," she says, more curious than commanding.

"You may not remember me, Ever," he says slowly. His voice is muted by the thick pane of glass. "We met only briefly, when you and Ere—"

She gasps. *The name on the note!* This man must know something about it.

"Who's Ere?" Ever demands.

"What?" The man clinging to her window looks at her with confusion. Then his expression changes. She sees the change, but cannot interpret it.

"He doesn't matter. He's just—nobody. He's not why I'm here."

"Why are you here?"

"I'm here for you, Ever," he says, with such conviction that she instantly believes him.

She notices again how attractive he is. She goes to the window, presses a button, and it slides fully open. The stranger climbs carefully through the opening.

"Who are you?" She asks.

He steps closer to her, and she can smell his rich, earthy scent. "My name is Cal."

"Cal," she says, tasting the name. Liking it. She shrugs her shoulder, encouraging her robe to slip, just a little, exposing some neck. She likes the dangerous feeling of having this stranger in her room. "Why don't you tell me a little about yourself?"

Cal lets out a shaking breath, and goes to Ever.

ACKNOWLEDGMENTS

The whole spiel about how "this book couldn't have been written without the support of so many people" feels unbelievably cliché… but as with a good number of clichés, it also has the distinction of being accurate. So I'm about to thank a whole slew of people without whom this book would not have been written—or at the very least, wouldn't have been worth reading.

Thank you, Scott Stinson, for reading an embarrassingly early version of this story and believing in these characters before I even did. I will never forget that.

Playing with my siblings and making up stories from a very young age taught me how to build whole worlds and complex storylines and pick threads up from where we left off. Thanks to my brothers and sister for playing our way into life and stories. I'm inspired by the lives you are living, and holy moly the next generation is cute. Excellent character development, you guys.

Thank you to my paternal grandparents for coming to this country, seeking something better for your children and their children. I wish I could have known you, Zayde Jake; I miss you and wish you could see these words, Bubbe Lill. Your memories and legacy are a blessing in my life.

Thank you to my maternal grandparents and extended family on both sides for loving me even when I made unexpected choices, like bouncing around the country or wearing a bridesmaid dress for a week or writing books about strange new worlds.

Thank you to my MFA classmates and teachers at Mississippi University for Women. Our workshops, residencies, and friendships have made me a better writer. And thanks for the baby shower, too.

Gratitude and congratulations to the Electric Eighteens, my debut author group. Your advice, insights, shared triumphs and struggles, and author-helping-author kindnesses were invaluable. #FMLFridays forever.

Thank you, L.M. Browning, for believing in stories and working to ensure that the mainstream isn't the only stream.

To my Original Synners— Adrian Allen, Amanda Jane Long, Amy Horning, Amy Smith, Andrew Slack, Angela Woods, Anne Malina, Brandi Pannell Pillow, Daniel Remington Todd, Danny Dauphin, Debra Kassoff, Denise Halbach, Exodus Brownlow, Gina Brent, Isabel Dieppa, Jackie Giardina Dauphin, Jessica De Young Kander, John Hardaway, Katie Del Ciello Burda, Kyla Hanington, Leah Walsh Alvarez, Lisa Kander, Monique Tracy Stuart Troth, Neill Kelly, Olga Lynette Henderson Hanson, Ray Dailey, Richard Lawrence, Robin Taylor Murphy, Ryan Foy, Sally Cassady Lyon, Sara Treinen Baker, Scott Stinson, Talamieka Brice, and Tammie Ward Rice. Your generosity in jumping on board, helping with early readings, ongoing encouragement, power-proofreading, publicity help, and general cheerleading keeps me going; thanks for being the inner circle on this endeavor.

Thank you to the teams at Mad Genius, Stage Rights, and the Goldring/Woldenberg Institute of Southern Jewish Life. Writing like a woman possessed while maintaining "day jobs" is a tall order, but luckily over the past half-dozen years of writing these books I've had the privilege of working alongside the world's nicest people.

To my parents, Ken and Lisa, you instilled an early love of people and stories and justice that took root and continues to bloom. I am the luckiest for getting to claim the parents so many other children adopted as "Mom and Dad." You are heroes.

To my daughter, I will never be able to thank you enough for cracking my heart open ever-wider… but at least in this round of acknowledgments, thanks for being a pretty good sleeper so Mama could get her edits in on time.

And finally, thank you, Danny, for being my biggest cheerleader, most honest critic (you brave soul, you), and my everything. I love you the most. All.

(PS Things you might not know, Part 7,234,567: You don't do the acknowledgments of a book until after all the advanced reader stuff/proofing is done, because of course you wind up with more people to thank over the course of that process, and you wind up cramming in the thank-yous last minute right before everything is due for The Real Main Printing Of The First Edition Of Your Book. So someone obvious and critically important probably gets left out of the acknowledgments. BUT LUCKILY THERE'S ANOTHER BOOK COMING OUT SOON, AND ONE AFTER THAT, so please politely let me know to whom I must grovel and I'll shower copious praise on you next time. Xoxo.)

BORN IN SYN

BOOK TWO

COMING AUTUMN 2019

CPSIA information can be obtained
at www.ICGtesting.com
Printed in the USA
LVHW03s2227241018
594724LV00003B/4/P